Destiny's Crossing

Destiny's Crossing
By Carrie Carr

Lynn,
Thanks for reading!

Carrie Carr

Destiny's Crossing

Carrie Carr

Yellow Rose Press
a Division of
RENAISSANCE ALLIANCE PUBLISHING, INC.
Austin, Texas

ISBN 0-9674196-2-X

First Printing 2000

9 8 7 6 5 4 3 2 1

Cover art by Barbara Maclay
Cover design by Tammy Poulsen and Mary Draganis

Published by:

Renaissance Alliance Publishing, Inc.
PMB 167, 3421 W. William Cannon Dr. # 131
Austin, Texas 78745

Find us on the World Wide Web at
http://www.rapbooks.com

Printed in the United States of America

This is dedicated to my family,
who always believed in me;
and to AJ – always and forever.

Destiny's Bridge

Chapter
1

As she fought the urge to cry, Amanda Cauble stomped angrily towards her car. The potholed asphalt had begun to resemble a lake, due to the constant rain that had fallen for the past several days. A few steps before she reached the Mustang, her left foot sank into a small hole, soaking it all the way up over her ankle. The young woman staggered sideways, dropping her briefcase into another puddle before she was able to get her balance. Amanda grimaced and gingerly shook her foot, relieved to be pain-free. *At least I didn't sprain my ankle... that's all I need,* she thought. She shook the excess water off the mud-spattered briefcase as she opened the car door. Sitting behind the steering wheel, Amanda gently laid the briefcase in the passenger's seat floorboard. She then proceeded to dig through her purse for her car keys. *Good thing about small towns, you never need to worry about locking your car!* Amanda smiled as she leaned back in the bucket seat with relief. With a heavy sigh, the young woman gently closed the car door, happy to be out of the rain. The classic Mustang was a graduation present from her beloved grandfather over five years ago...

"Oooooh!!! Grandpa Jake... you've got to be kidding!" the young blonde girl squealed in delight when her blindfold was removed. Directly in front of Amanda sat her grandfather's pride

and joy... a 1967 powder blue Mustang, fully restored, with a very large red ribbon and bow adorning it.

Jacob Cauble laughed. "What's the matter, Peanut? Would you rather have one of those new fancier sports cars?" he asked with a grin. "Is this car too old for Neiman High's valedictorian?"

Amanda turned suddenly serious. "No, Grandpa, that's not it at all...it's just that..." she stammered, trying to find the words to express what her heart was aching to say.

The older man put up a hand to forestall her argument. "Shhh... we worked together on this old clunker for almost three summers... and nothing would make me happier than for you to enjoy the end product," he smiled. "Besides, what's an old coot like me going to do with a car like this?"

Amanda wrapped her arms around him in an exuberant hug. "You are NOT an old coot, Grandpa. I think you're quite debonair!" she contended with a saucy wink.

Jacob Cauble was still a very handsome man, even in his early sixties. Tall, with thick salt-and-pepper hair, he still turned quite a few heads. Unfortunately for the ladies, he was completely devoted to his wife. He returned his granddaughter's hug. "If you say so, Peanut." He handed her a set of keys. "I hope you have as much fun driving her as I had rebuilding her with you!"

Amanda gently took the keys from his hand. "Well, what are we waiting for?" She used her other hand to capture his. "Let's go try this baby out! Ice cream's on me, handsome!" she laughed, as her grandfather followed in her footsteps.

Amanda wiped a tear from her eye, saddened at the turn her thoughts had suddenly taken. *We almost lost him.* Jacob Cauble had been severely injured in a horrible automobile accident six months ago. Amanda had immediately moved from her parents' home in Los Angeles to her grandparents' house here in Somerville, to keep her grandmother company while Jacob was in the hospital. She also wanted to help take care of him once he was released. Now the only outward signs of the accident that had nearly taken his life were a jagged scar on his forehead near his hairline, and a pronounced limp that Jacob himself swore would not be permanent. With a deep breath, Amanda pulled the rear view mirror towards herself to check her reflection. *I look like a drowned rat,* she sighed to the vibrant green eyes looking back at her. Running her fingers through her strawberry blonde shoulder-length hair, Amanda turned her attention to the task at hand. "Sitting here feeling sorry for yourself isn't gonna get the job done," she mumbled out loud. "Now get a move on and take care of business," she scolded herself, starting the car and backing out of the parking space.

****

In a large ranch house nestled in the foothills a few miles away, someone else was cursing the continuing rain. Lexington Walters' long frame was sprawled comfortably on the porch swing, her muddy boots propped up on the rail that outlined the large wraparound porch. While they always needed rain, she knew that storms such as this one tended to cause problems with the fence that surrounded the ranch.

At twenty-eight, Lexington Walters had been running the Rocking W Ranch for ten years, since her father had left for a rodeo and never returned. Oh, they still received the occasional postcard from Rawson Walters, and once in a great while he would actually use a telephone, usually asking for a "loan" until his next ride. Lex felt she owed the man something, since in her mind she was the reason he continued to travel. She knew he had trouble looking at his daughter, since Lexington was the spitting image of Victoria, Rawson's beloved late wife – from her electric blue eyes to her long midnight-kissed hair. The only features she had of her father were his temper and his propensity to get into trouble. Every time Rawson saw his only daughter, he was reminded of the woman that he lost when Lex was only four.

Victoria had died while giving birth to their third child, Louis. The pain wasn't as noticeable when Lex was a youngster, but by the time she was a teenager, Rawson's heart ached each time he was near his daughter. On her eighteenth birthday,

unable to stand the hurt any longer, Rawson Walters did the only
thing he could think of – he turned over control of the Rocking W
to Lex, and left to rejoin the rodeo circuit.

With a heavy sigh, the dark-haired woman stood up. She
stretched her arms over her head and grasped one of the supports
above her, gratified to hear the gentle popping as her spine slid
back into place. A quick twist of her head, first one way and then
the other, then Lex released the support beam and stomped into
the house. She grabbed her long brown duster from its hook in
the hallway, and snatched a bedraggled black cowboy hat from
the hook beside it.

"Martha!" she yelled down the hallway, "I'm gonna go and
check the fence down by the creek." She crammed the dusty hat
onto her head. Lex was almost back to the door when a heavyset
woman in her mid-fifties came scurrying out of the kitchen.

"Lexington Marie Walters! Don't you be bellowing in this
house... I raised you better than that!" she snapped, wiping her
hands on a dishtowel.

Lex hastily removed her hat, looking properly chastised.
"I'm sorry, Martha," she deferred to the housekeeper, "I just
didn't know exactly where you were, that's why I yelled." She
smiled charmingly into the older woman's kindly brown eyes. "It
won't happen again, I promise," she finished, placing the disrep-
utable hat back on her head.

Martha just shook her head and smiled. She'd been the
housekeeper here at the Rocking W for almost twenty-five years,
hiring on when Mrs. Walters became pregnant with little Louis.
After the death of Victoria, Martha took over the care of the
young child. She treated Lex as she would her own daughter,
since Rawson had no idea how to raise a little girl. As Lex grew
up, her father spent less and less time with her, letting the rowdy
ranch hands become her surrogate family. Although Martha had
tried to show little Lexington more ladylike ways, the older she
got, the more like the hired hands she became. Martha's heart
had nearly broken in two when Rawson left behind the short note
giving Lex complete control over the ranch, not even having the
decency to ask the girl if that was what she wanted. Only Martha

knew what young Lexington had wanted to do with her life: go to college and become a veterinarian. But her father's desertion had nipped that dream in the bud, the housekeeper remembered. Lex only ran the ranch out of some misplaced sense of duty. Now ten years had passed, and the ranch was thriving under her leadership. The men respected her, and her only problem seemed to be her obstinate older brother, Hubert, who questioned her at every turn.

Martha reached out and began buttoning the duster closed. "Try not to get too wet, Lexie," she said, smiling at the consternation that crossed the younger woman's face. "You know how long it took you to get over that last bout of the flu." She stepped back with a stern look. "And don't you dare be late for dinner... I'm cooking a big batch of chili, and I'm even making your favorite cornbread to go with it." With this, Martha turned around and headed back towards the kitchen. "And don't you be clompin' back in here with muddy boots... you're not too big for me to take my spoon to!" She bustled back through the kitchen doorway.

Lex looked after her with a fond smile. "Yes, ma'am," she muttered, then turned back around and headed through the front door.

****

Amanda squinted hard against the heavy rain pounding her windshield. Her thoughts were going back over the reason she was out in this horrible weather. "I don't know why I continue to let that jerk get to me," she grumbled out loud, once again using her hand to wipe the condensation from the inside of the window. "And I can't believe I'm actually out in this mess!" The jerk was her boss, Rick Thompson at Sunflower Realty. Rick had been the office manager since her grandmother, Anna Leigh Cauble, retired two years ago. She still retained ownership of the prosperous real estate office, but decided to relegate the day-to-day activities to the manager so she and her husband could enjoy their retirement. When Amanda moved in with her grandparents last year, the older woman had wanted her to take over the family business. The younger woman declined because she thought that she really didn't have enough experience yet to run the office. *Now that decision is biting me on the butt,* Amanda grimaced to herself.

Without taking her eyes off the road, Amanda searched her purse for the directions that Rick had handed her. Having not actually lived in Somerville, Amanda was not really familiar with the area. She had spent a lot of summers at her grandparents' house, but her time was spent with them, not running around with kids her own age. So here she was, driving in the pouring rain on her way to an appointment that she herself didn't make. The young woman was understandably nervous. Rick had looked too smug when he'd handed her the appointment sheet.

"Look, it's a huge ranch. Just go and meet with the owner." *He glanced at the appointment sheet, as if to verify the name.* *"The ranch is owned by L. Walters. Guess they're getting tired of the ranching business."*

Back at the office, Rick was also thinking about that moment. He smiled to himself. *This was gonna be one sweet payback. Two for one, too!*

He had been the captain of the football team, and considered the best catch by the girls at Somerville High School. It had been a dare by some of his buddies. "Ya think you're such hot shit, Ricky," Tom had said, elbowing him in the ribs as they watched another cute girl smile their way. "You've had nearly every girl in school."

"Yeah," Amos agreed, leaning back against the lockers, "but I bet there's one girl who you couldn't get to first base with."

Rick smirked. "There ain't a girl in this school that I couldn't have."

Amos smiled back. "Wanna make a small wager on it?" He got right up into the bigger boy's face. "I'll pick the girl, and all you have to do is get her to go out with you on a date."

Rick laughed. "No problem, only a date? What are the stakes?"

Amos looked thoughtful. "If you win, I'll keep your car washed and waxed for the entire summer. If you lose, you have to do the same for me."

Rick put out his hand. *"It's a deal...shake."* After they shook hands, Rick leaned back. *"Okay, genius, who's the lucky girl?"*

Amos smiled an evil grin and waved his outstretched arm down the hallway. *"Her,"* he said, his finger aimed at a tall, dark-haired lanky girl in faded jeans and a denim shirt.

"Kentucky? She's just a sophomore – she'd probably jump at the chance to go out with a senior." Rick laughed. *"This is gonna be way too easy!"*

Amos shrugged. *"I dunno. Rumor is she doesn't even like guys – spends all her time in the livestock barn with all the animals."*

Rick ran his hands through his dark wavy hair. *"Stand back, boys, and watch an expert show you the finer art of picking up girls,"* he said as he made his way towards his next 'victim'.

Not only did the quiet girl turn him down, she humiliated him, too. *"No, thank you,"* she said to his offer of dinner and a movie, then she just turned around to walk away.

Rick was furious! *"Now just wait one damn minute, Kentucky,"* he growled, grabbing her arm and spinning her back around to face him. *"Nobody turns me down!"*

She looked down coolly at the hand gripping her arm. *"I suggest you remove that hand before it gets broken,"* she stated in a quiet, menacing voice.

Rick laughed. *"By who? You, little girl?"* He yanked hard on her captured arm. *"I don't think so,"* Rick snarled, his six-foot-four frame shaking with rage.

The girl grabbed the offending hand and twisted the wrist until he howled. *"Hey! Cut it out!"* He released his grip on her arm. The girl smiled, and quietly turned to walk away again. *"Hold it, bitch!"* he barked, reaching for the back of her hair. Before he could blink, the girl spun around and threw her elbow into his chin; then as he was starting to fall, she slammed a well-aimed knee into his crotch. Rick fell to the ground clutching himself, whimpering.

"I said, NO!" she stated loudly as she looked down on his trembling form. *"And my name is Lexington, you ass!"* she finished, amid the catcalls and cheers from the large group that had

gathered around them

After that, no one bothered the quiet girl. Sure, several of
the girls who had previously been 'conquests' of Rick's stopped
her and thanked Lex for 'putting that arrogant beast in his
place', but she never joined in any of the after-school activities
or clubs, and seemed content to study in the school library for
hours instead. Even her brothers left her alone. Rick had been
surprised when he ran into the Ice Bitch a few years later in the
local supermarket and she had no recollection of humiliating
him in high school. When he had walked up to her and asked,
"Do you remember me?" She gave him a slight frown and
replied, "No, should I?" He had been livid!

Well, what better way to get back at her than to send Miss
Goody Two Shoes to try and place that dusty old ranch of hers on
the market? The last time he tried that a few years ago, the menacing beauty nearly handed him his head on a platter. "Oh, yeah,
this is gonna be great!!" With a devious chuckle, Rick stopped
daydreaming of his revenge, and got back to work.

If this was such a great deal why was he giving it to her?
Amanda thought. The office manager had been short to the point
of rudeness since she'd turned down his last dinner offer. She
couldn't quite say why, but anytime Rick came near her,
Amanda's skin began to crawl.

*Okay, so I should be coming up to a small road on the left
anytime now,* mused Amanda, reading her directions. Seeing the
road, she slowly steered the car towards it. Amanda grimaced at
the mud that spattered along the side of the car. Up ahead, she
could barely make out the shape of a large covered wooden
bridge. "Oooh... how pretty! I'd love to see this when the sun is
shining," she exclaimed as the car began inching across the
bridge.

Chapter
2

Lex began filling up the hole around a post, thankful this was the last one. As she had suspected, a portion of the fence had been knocked down when a tree near the now raging creek had toppled. After clearing away the tree with an axe because it was raining too hard to use a chainsaw, Lex had spent the past hour rebuilding this last section of fence. Now all she had to do was finish stringing the wire, and she could go back to the ranch house for a much-needed cup of coffee. As she attached the last strand of wire to the post, a bright flash of lightning illuminated the creek, followed far too closely by a huge clap of thunder. *That's it! Waaay too close that time!* She picked up the remaining tools and began making her way back to the jeep, when another type of light caught her eye. "What the..." Narrowing her eyes under her increasingly soggy hat, she wondered, "Who in the hell would be fool enough to come out on a day like today? I know we're not expecting anyone." When the car got about half-way across the bridge, a huge tree that had made its way downstream crashed heavily into the structure. A large section from the center of the old bridge crumbled. Lex watched in horror as the small car fell into the creek and was shoved downstream by the tree.

Cursing, Lex ran to the nearby jeep and tossed her hat and coat inside, trading them for a long length of rope. The cold rain quickly soaked through her thin tee shirt, causing the rancher to shiver a little in response. She ran towards the creek and saw that the car had already been pushed about twenty yards downstream. Without another thought, Lex tied one end of the rope around a nearby oak tree, and the other end around her waist. Taking a running start, the tall woman jumped feet first into the creek, letting the violent current take her to the half-submerged vehicle. The car was being held in place by the same tree that had knocked it into the raging creek, and Lex wasn't certain how long it would stay in one place. The nose of the automobile was already under water, but she made her way up onto the trunk anyway, oblivious to any danger. Squinting through the rain and the debris littering the car, Lex peered through the rear window and saw a young woman slumped over the steering wheel, apparently unconscious. Thankful that she still had her boots on, Lex viciously kicked in the rear window, which popped inward in one piece.

As Lex slowly crawled through the open window, another tree, albeit smaller, slammed into the car. The action tossed the would-be rescuer over the back seat and into the floorboard face first. Grimacing, she pulled herself up slowly, hoping that the car would stay in place for just a few more minutes. Not feeling any more movement from the outside, Lex moved towards the still figure in the front seat. She reached over the seat and gently shook the woman's shoulder. "Hey." No response. The car lurched sideways again. "HEY!" she insisted. Still no response. Lex knew that time was running out. *I know you shouldn't move accident victims, but I don't think there's much of a choice here.* She put a hand on each shoulder and gently pulled the woman back from the steering wheel. The only injuries Lex could spot were a small lump and a sluggishly bleeding gash on the young woman's left temple. Lex moved to unfasten the woman's seat belt and noticed the water level was already up to the young lady's knees, and still rising. With the seat belt unbuckled, Lex gently placed her hands under the woman's arms and pulled her between the seats. Lex propped the unconscious woman upright in the backseat, then scooted out feet first through the rear window.

As she tried to keep her balance on the slippery trunk, Lex reached back into the car and pulled the still form through the open window. She placed her charge onto the trunk just as the nose of the vehicle began to slip deeper into the water. Lex tried once again to awaken the young woman, to no avail. She quickly pulled off one leather glove and checked the girl's pulse. *Nice and strong; think she'll be okay.* The rancher replaced her glove and wiped the wet hair out of her eyes. Untying the rope from around her waist, Lex pulled the slight form up onto her own back, draping the loose arms around her neck. With the rope tied around them both, Lex positioned the girl's head beside her own, then slowly dropped into the racing water. She used her gloved hands to pull them across the churning creek. They'd made it over halfway across before Lex felt her instincts rise sharply. Upstream she saw a large object rumbling right towards them. With no time to think, Lex turned her body so that she was able to get between what appeared to be part of a barn and her unconscious cargo. The object hit her chest with such force that she nearly passed out from the pain. She managed somehow to hang onto the rope, only to feel frantic arms wrapping tightly around her neck. Loosening one hand from the rope that had become their lifeline, Lex gently tried to pry the convulsive limbs from her throat before she was choked to death. Apparently the young woman realized what she had almost done, and she quickly released her death grip on her savior.

Several minutes later, an exhausted Lex dragged herself and her passenger up the muddy creek bank as she untied the rope from around them with shaking fingers. Her strength almost gone, the taller woman felt her erstwhile passenger slowly slide off. With a groan, Lex rolled over onto her back. She turned towards the young woman, who was on her knees trembling, rocking back and forth crying softly.

"Oh, God...wha.... who..."

"Damn..." Lex gasped in pain as she attempted to sit up. She looked over at the smaller woman. "Hey—you okay?" Grimacing, she struggled to a sitting position. *Ugh...it feels like someone pounded a spike in my chest...no time for that now.* She gently laid a muddy, gloved hand upon the distraught woman's shoulder. "Shhh... everything's all right now. C'mon. Let's get out of this damn rain, okay?" Holding one arm across her chest, Lex slowly rose to her feet and offered her other hand to the still-seated woman.

Amanda glanced up and made eye contact with her rescuer. *Wow...what an incredible blue.* "Uhmm...sure." Lex grasped her upraised hand and pulled her gently to her feet. Amanda felt her head spin and she began to fall forward dizzily.

Lex caught her automatically. "Hey, take it easy there." The movement caused another sharp pain to her chest. *Not good,* she thought, fighting back the pain, *not good at all.* She quickly wrapped an arm around the smaller woman, ostensibly to assist her, but more to keep her own balance. The two of them slowly trudged up the muddy creek bank, as Lex directed her young charge to the waiting jeep.

Once they had settled in the jeep, Lex handed her brown duster to the now trembling woman. "Here. This should help ward off the chill 'til we get back to the house."

Amanda took the coat shyly. "Thanks. But what about you?" she asked, as she snuggled under the oversized coat, sighing in relief. "Aaah... much better."

"Don't worry about me," Lex stated, impatiently wiping the wet hair out of her eyes again. "It's not that far." She buried her hand in one of the pockets of the coat and pulled out a dark blue bandanna. "Here," she said, gently applying pressure with the bandanna to the still-bleeding gash on the girl's temple, "I promise it's clean."

Amanda smiled, moving her left hand to replace the one the beautiful stranger...*Whoa! Where did that come from? ...* had pressed against the wound. "Uhmm... okay." Then she smiled a little bigger. "Well, anyway...Thank you for saving my life." Tears welled up in her deep green eyes. "I don't..." she stammered with a frown, " I just..." she took a deep breath, "I'm sorry. Reaction, I guess." Another deep breath. "I don't even know your name." Her smile returned. "My name's Amanda."

The dark woman pinned her with a direct gaze. "Lex... and you're welcome," she finished, with a smile of her own. Lex turned the key in the ignition, and the jeep thankfully sputtered to life. The continuing rain pounded a loud beat upon the hard top of the jeep. The grumbling of the engine made normal conversation difficult, at best. Lex reached for the gearshift and felt a sharp stabbing pain to her chest, causing her to hastily bite off a groan.

This action did not go unnoticed by the smaller woman in the jeep. "What is it? What's the matter?" She used her right hand to hold the bloody bandanna in check and placed her left hand gently on Lex's wrist, concern etching her lovely features. Amanda temporarily forgot her headache as she studied the quiet form across from her.

"Nothing...just a little sore," Lex answered, throwing the jeep into gear and starting towards what was left of the road.

Amanda turned slightly in her seat, so that she could gaze fully at the quiet woman beside her. "Uh-huh... if you say so."

Lex gave her a raised eyebrow in response. To get the subject away from herself, the older woman posed the question that had been bothering her since she'd first spotted Amanda's car. "So...what in the hell were you doing driving around deserted country roads on a nasty day like this?" She grimaced as the jeep hit a particularly deep rut in the road. "And why were you driving across my bridge?" she finished, straining to see the road through the windshield.

"YOUR BRIDGE????" Amanda squeaked, incredulous. Then she began to giggle.

"Whaat?" Lex asked, drawing out the word.

Amanda giggled harder. "Sorry...but I just got this picture in my head." She continued her mirth at the other woman's expense.

Lex just glowered at her. "C'mon, let's hear it."

"No, really, it's not important."

Another glare from the driver of the jeep.

"Okay." The younger woman wiped errant tears from her eyes. "I just had this mental picture of you as a troll, waiting for the Three Billy Goats Gruff," she wheezed, trying unsuccessfully to contain her glee.

The dark-haired woman couldn't help it. She smiled. "Cute, real cute." But part of her was relieved. The head injury couldn't be too bad if the girl was making jokes. Maybe everything *would* be all right, after all.

They continued along towards the ranch house in silence. Amanda had worn herself down with the giggling fit and was now quietly curled up in the passenger's seat, thankful for the warmth of the large coat. The thunderstorm was still raging, making it look more like late evening instead of late afternoon. The small blonde took the opportunity to study her erstwhile rescuer. The glow of the dash lights flickered across Lex's still face, caressing her features with an eerie glow. Amanda could clearly see the pain and exhaustion on the face across from her. Her own head was still aching, and she was feeling a little bit sick to her stomach. As she took a breath to speak, Lex turned the steering wheel sharply to the right.

"Hang on!!!!" she ordered, her voice strong and assured. The jeep slid sideways in the mud as she valiantly tried to avoid a tree that had fallen into the middle of the road. The front left tire hit what used to be the top of the tree, causing the jeep to tilt dangerously to the right.

THUNK!!!

The muddy vehicle slammed to an unexpected stop. "Dammit!" Lex growled, grinding the jeep into a lower gear. A high pitched whine answered her, as the tires spun helplessly in the mixture of mud and leaves. Lex laid her head against the steering wheel and closed her eyes. "Some days it just doesn't pay to get out of bed," she sighed. She turned her head and looked over at Amanda. The young woman had one hand braced on the dash, the other gripping the handle on the door. "Sorry... guess I'm not real good at this 'rescue' business, huh?" She gave a small smile. "Look... the house isn't that much farther, maybe a mile or two at the most." She looked out through the windshield at the continuing rain. "Hard to tell how long it will take in this weather, though... feel up to a little walk?"

Amanda returned her smile with one of her own. "Sure..." she said, looking down at her feet. "Don't think my shoes could get any wetter, anyway." Silently, Amanda thanked her grandmother.

"Why on earth are you wearing high heels and a dress on a nasty day like today?" Anna Leigh had asked her granddaughter after she came downstairs for breakfast. *"All you are going to accomplish is catching a cold when your feet get soaked,"* she admonished. *"Why don't you go back upstairs and put on those new black jeans? They'll go great with your black sneakers...don't you agree, dear?"* she asked her husband, who reached across the table and squeezed her hand.

"You're absolutely right, my love." He looked at Amanda. *"No sense in being miserable, Peanut."* He winked at her. *"Besides, young cuties like you look great in jeans!"*

Anna Leigh removed her hand from his and playfully slapped his arm. *"You lecherous old goat!"* But she smiled, then looked over at her granddaughter. *"Well?"*

Amanda laughed, *"You're right, as usual, Gramma. I really don't feel like wearing a dress today, anyway."* She hurried back up the stairs to change, her grandparent's laughter right behind her.

Lex blew out a tired breath. "We'll cut through the woods... It'll shave some distance off the trip. Besides," she said with a wry grin, "this road is obviously too muddy." She cautiously reached into the back seat to grab a large flashlight and her battered cowboy hat. Lex crammed the hat on her head and reached for the door. "Hold on...let me go around and make sure your door is clear." Pocketing the keys, she opened the door and gingerly stepped out.

Thunder still rumbled ominously, punctuated by the occasional flash of lightning. Lex slipped in the mud several times on her way around the rear of the jeep. Every step brought renewed agony to her chest. *I hope nothing's too badly broken in there.* Once she reached the passenger side of the jeep, Lex was gratified to see it relatively clear of debris. Opening the door she cautioned, "Careful. Kinda slippery out here." She offered her hand to the smaller woman.

Amanda accepted the proffered hand as she eased her way out of the jeep. "Thanks," she said quietly. Trying to hand the coat to Lex, she said, "Here... You're only wearing a tee shirt, at least I've got on a long-sleeved shirt."

Lex looked at the way the younger woman was dressed – she did have on a long-sleeved shirt, but the green satin didn't look very warm. The tall woman shook her head and pushed the coat back into Amanda's hands. "No, you wear it. I'm fairly hot-natured anyway." She noticed that the head wound had stopped bleeding. "How's your head?" she asked, as she led the younger woman off the road and into a stand of trees. Amanda slipped the coat on, feeling like a small child wearing her father's clothes.

She considered the question seriously. "Not too bad," she said, "aches a little." Amanda peered through the rain and gloom. "Is this safe?" she asked, gripping Lex's hand. "Walking through all these trees during a thunderstorm?"

Lex looked down at her. "Safer than the road, actually. There's probably a lot of washed out places there, and with all the mud it would be nearly impossible to walk on." Another flash of lightning and rumble of thunder interrupted her. She felt the grip on her hand tighten. "Hey, it's okay. We should be back to the house before long. It's just a little rain."

Amanda sheepishly loosened her deathgrip on the other woman's hand. "Sorry," she apologized, but made no move to release the hand. "I've never really liked storms." She felt the hand holding hers tighten.

"No problem. I think the worst is over for now. That last blast sounded pretty far away," Lex tried to reassure her.

They reached the top of a slight rise. Amanda could see where the trees gave way to open fields. "Is your home much farther?" she asked, looking up at the woman beside her.

Lex shook her head. "Not too much... 'bout another hour or so and we'll be in front of a nice warm fire." She met the slightly foggy green eyes looking at her. "Unless you'd rather sit for a few minutes and rest. You're not looking too good," she said with a worried frown.

Amanda thought about waving off her new friend's concern, but then realized that the older woman was becoming increasingly pale and drawn herself. *She looks worse than I feel, and she's been keeping that one arm really still across her chest.* Amanda smiled inwardly. *Maybe SHE needs a short rest.* Out loud she said, "The thought of getting out of this rain is tempting, but I'm afraid if I don't rest for a few minutes I'll fall flat on my face." She didn't miss the fleeting look of relief that passed over the other woman's features.

"Yeah, you're probably right. We might as well take advantage of these trees for a short break. The rest of our walk will be out in the open, and the rain doesn't look like it'll be slowing down any time soon." Lex slowly dropped to the ground then leaned her back up against a large oak tree.

Amanda released her hand and sank down beside her. "Ahhh..." she exhaled, "I never realized how wonderful sitting in the mud could be," she joked, leaning up against the same tree. "I know this stuff is supposed to be good for your complexion," she flicked a blob of mud off her knee, "but I think I'll just take my chances without it." The small blonde wrapped the huge overcoat tightly around herself. "Are you sure you're warm enough? I feel really bad that I'm hogging your coat."

Lex waved off her concern. "No, really. I'm fine. I only had it with me because Martha threatened to whip me with a wooden spoon," she smiled. *Besides, my chest hurts too much to try and put my arms in a coat.*

Amanda was about to continue this line of questioning when she realized what Lex had said. "A spoon?!?" She grinned widely. "Who's Martha?" She hazarded a guess: "Your mother?"

Lex chuckled. "Nah...more like my nanny." She looked pensive for a moment. "She's actually our housekeeper... but she's just about the only mother I've ever known." She smiled again. "And believe me, she can sure swing a mean spoon!!!"

Amanda laughed. "Remind me to be on my best behavior, then." She dropped her hand onto the older woman's knee. "Maybe I should give you this coat back... I'd hate to get you in trouble."

The dark-haired woman smiled at her again. "Nah... I'd probably get into more trouble if I brought you home without it...'sides, I think she'll be okay. Just be prepared to be clucked over, big time."

The younger woman took a deep breath and slowly released it. The longer they sat there, the worse Lex looked.

"Hey…maybe we should get started again." She strained her eyes through the oncoming darkness. "I think the temperature is beginning to drop… it's starting to feel colder, anyway." She had noticed the taller woman trying to repress a shudder. "I think I'm rested enough to go on." Amanda climbed to her feet and offered her rescuer a hand.

****

The duo slogged through the mud in silence, each lost in her own thoughts. Lex was moving slower and slower, in deference to the sharp, stabbing pain in her chest. *Definitely something broken in there,* she worried to herself, as she found it harder and harder to breathe normally. She spared a glance at her companion. Amanda was moving fairly well, although she kept tripping over the heavy coat she had wrapped around her body.

The taller woman didn't realize it, but Amanda was keeping a close eye on her as well. The young woman noticed her companion was finding it more difficult to breathe with every step she took. Lex's pace continued to slow by the minute. *This is ridiculous! We both know she'll never make it much farther this way, but she's too stubborn to ask for help. I gotta do something!* Amanda purposely stumbled and then stopped.

Lex stopped as well, looking at her with concern. "What's the matter? Is your head getting worse?" she managed to ask, drawing a shallow breath.

Amanda grinned inwardly. *Gotcha!* "Look. I hate to bother you, but do you think I could kinda hold onto you? It seems like I'm having a little bit of a balance problem." She looked up at the older woman innocently.

Lex frowned slightly. She had a feeling that the little blonde was not being completely honest, but she was too tired and hurting too badly to call her on it. "Sure," she agreed, gingerly raising one arm and draping it around Amanda's shoulders.

The younger woman eased her body under Lex's arm and wrapped one arm gently around the tall woman's waist. Amanda couldn't help herself, she giggled.

"What?" Lex asked, not seeing anything particularly funny

about their situation.

Amanda peeked up from her position under Lex's arm. "You are really tall," she laughed. "I feel like a little kid next to you."

Lex smiled down at her. "Well," she drawled, "in that coat, you kinda look like one, too." Without realizing it, Lex began to lean more on the smaller woman.

Amanda felt the pressure, and smiled inwardly. *There's more than one way to skin a cat.* With her head so close to the older woman, she could hear Lex struggling for every breath. *That doesn't sound good at all... hope we have some way to get her to a doctor once we're back to her house.*

Amanda noticed with great appreciation that the open field was carpeted with some sort of grass. It was too dark for her to see much, but it was still more pleasant than the nasty mud they had waded through on the main road. Amanda estimated that over two hours had passed since she had fallen into the raging creek. If the sun *had* been shining, it would be close to dusk by now. Her head still ached, although it was more like a dull throb. She frequently cast her gaze at the tall woman whose weight she continued to support. Through the infrequent flashes of lightning, she was able to see just how exhausted her companion had become. *It's amazing that she hasn't completely collapsed by now.* Something was nagging at the back of her mind, though. *What was* she *doing out in this weather? And just how did she get hurt? Guess I could just ask.* Amanda cleared her throat. "Lex?" She felt the older woman flinch slightly.

Damn. Almost dozed off there, Lex chastised herself. "Yeah?" she asked, bringing her attention back to the conversation at hand.

Amanda tightened her grip somewhat, trying to comfort the dark woman. "You haven't told me why *you* were out in this nasty weather – or do you usually hang around raging creeks, waiting to rescue women who happen to float by?" She felt Lex stifle a laugh.

"No, not usually." Lex was thankful for the distraction. "I was repairing a break in the fence when I saw that tree smash into the bridge. Then, when I saw your car fall in, I really didn't even think..." She looked down at the young woman snuggled close to her side and shrugged. "Right place, right time, I guess."

Amanda looked up in surprise. "You jumped into a creek feeling the way you do?" Her voice rose incredulously.

Lex shook her head. "No. I was okay then. A little tired from chopping up a tree and digging a few post holes, but okay." She glanced away from the younger woman's gaze.

"Okay... then what happened? And don't try and tell me you're okay..." She tightened her grip. "You're about to fall over, I can tell." Amanda wasn't real sure where this sudden protective streak for a virtual stranger came from, but at this point, she really didn't give a damn.

Lex looked down at the grass they were walking through. "Ah, well..." another squeeze from her companion. "When I was pulling us back across the creek, right before you came to, I kinda got hit by some sort of debris." She suddenly stopped, because the arm that was wrapped around her pulled her back.

"Debris? What kind of debris? Where did it hit you?" Lightning flashed, giving Lex a clear view of the deep concern etched on the face across from her.

Trying to change the subject, Lex turned to start walking again. She must have twisted wrong, because she collapsed to her knees in pain. " Damn..." she exhaled, trying to get past the black spots swimming in her vision.

Amanda had followed her to the ground. "Lex!!" she exclaimed in a shaky voice. "What's wrong?"

The older woman was leaning forward with her left arm wrapped tightly around her chest. The dark hat hid her features from the younger woman's view. "Just give me a minute," she gasped, trying to remain conscious.

Amanda gently eased Lex onto her back. "Here... just lie back for a few minutes and catch your breath." She pulled the battered hat off the dark woman's head.

Lex tried in vain to get back up. "No, I'm all right. We're almost to the house." But she couldn't seem to gather the energy needed to defy the small blonde.

Amanda tried another tactic. "Well, if we're that close, then a short break can't hurt now, can it?" She looked up and tried to see the house in the distance. Due to the oncoming darkness and

the driving rain, she could barely see a few feet in front of them.
"Look, if you'll just point me in the right direction, I'll go and
get some help." She glanced back down at Lex, whose eyes were
now closed. "Lex?" She gently touched the older woman's face.
"Hey." She was gratified to see the woman's eyes open slowly.

"Sorry," Lex whispered. "Guess I musta moved the wrong
way." She took a cautious breath.

"Please – let me go and get some help," Amanda entreated.

"Can't," Lex whispered. "Only person at the house is Martha. My brother doesn't live there anymore, and the ranch hands
are in town for the big rodeo and livestock show this weekend."
She attempted a smile. "Thought I could handle things until they
got back on Sunday."

Amanda smiled back at her. "I'm sure you could have, if you
weren't playing hero for me."

Lex choked back a laugh. "Yeah, right. I should have been
paying closer attention." She reached up with her right hand.
"Wanna give me a hand up? I'm really getting tired of this damn
rain."

Twenty minutes later, the lights from the big ranch house
came into view.

"Wow," Amanda breathed. "It's huge!" Even in the rain and
darkness, Amanda could tell that the home was impressive. The
two-story house had a lovely wraparound porch and a balcony on
the second floor. Amanda felt that the stucco structure would be
equally at home in the more expensive subdivisions of Somerville.

Lex pulled her around to a side entrance. "We'll go in
through the mud room," she said, opening a plain looking door.
"No sense tracking in half the ranch through the house." She
motioned the small blonde inside. "Martha would probably break
her best spoon on my rear end." She closed the door behind them
and flipped a light switch.

The soft light was almost blinding after being in the rain and
darkness, and it took Amanda a moment to adjust. The room was
small, with a bench along one wall and hooks for hanging items
by the door. It was plain, yet clean.

Lex collapsed wearily on the bench, with Amanda right next

to her. "Whew...it sure feels great to finally be out of the rain."
The young blonde brushed her dripping hair out of her eyes. Her
companion was leaning back against the wall with her eyes
closed.

"Oh, yeah. Gimme a second and I'll get you something dry
to change into."

Now, with decent light, Amanda took the opportunity to
study the quiet woman sitting next to her. Tall. *Gotta be at least
six foot.* Long, dark hair still gathered in a loose ponytail; she
had broad shoulders and a very muscular build. *That tee shirt
can't disguise a body like that.* Then Amanda noticed something
else – the light blue tee shirt had a dark stain that started just
below her breasts, and spread down her right side.

"Lex?" She placed her hand on the silent woman's arm.

Lex slowly opened her incredibly blue eyes and turned her
head towards the other woman. "What's the matter?" she mumbled, trying to focus her eyesight on the young woman.

"I...I... th... think you're bleeding," Amanda stuttered, at a
loss for words. "Why didn't you tell me?" she asked, wanting to
help but not quite sure how.

Lex groggily looked down at her chest. "Didn't know –
besides, I don't think it's that bad," she said, trying to reassure
the stammering woman. "C'mon. Let's get the mud off our feet
and go find Martha. She'll get you something dry to wear." She
was about to reach down and remove her boots, when Amanda
slid off the bench to kneel on the floor below her.

"Here, let me." She gently tugged the muddy boots and
socks from the taller woman's feet, then pulled off her own mud-
encrusted shoes and drenched socks as well. "Yuck." She stood
up and removed the heavy coat. "That thing must weigh fifty
pounds!" she joked, as she hung it up on a hook next to the door.
"You were saying something about dry clothes?" She slowly
pulled Lex to her feet. "Think I can sweet talk Martha into something to eat? All this exercise has made me hungry," she finished
with an impish grin.

Lex allowed Amanda to help her to the door. "Oh, I think
that can be arranged. She'll probably stuff ya like a prize hog."

They walked through the door to find themselves standing in

the kitchen. Amanda spotted a short, heavyset woman talking on the phone, obviously very upset.

"No, Mr. Hubert, she's not back yet, and I'm really beginning to get worried. It's been almost four hours since she left..." She turned around and stifled a gasp. "Oh, my lord! Lexie, what have you done to yourself, child?" She hung up the phone without another word, and rushed over to the two women who were dripping puddles in her kitchen.

"Hey, Martha... picked up a friend today... think you could find her some dry clothes?" Lex smirked, still leaning heavily against the smaller woman.

Amanda gave the woman a large smile. "Hi, I'm Amanda. Lex rescued me out of the creek today when my car got tossed in."

Martha laughed in relief. "My goodness Lexie, you always did have a habit of bringing in strays." She quickly closed the distance between them. "You both look like you could use a warm bath and a cup of hot coffee." She gently placed her hand on the taller woman's face. "Honey, think you could take your friend upstairs, while I fix you something warm to drink?"

Lex smiled. "Sure, Martha." She pulled the younger woman through the kitchen and into the hallway. "C'mon.... let's go upstairs and I'll find you something to change into after you've had a hot shower." She gently guided the younger woman through the hall and up the oak staircase.

Halfway up the stairwell, Lex stumbled. She would have fallen except for the tight grip Amanda was keeping on her waist.

"Okay, that's it." The young blonde gently guided Lex to a sitting position on one of the steps. "Now you sit right here and don't move! I'm going to go get Martha, so she can help me get you settled."

The older woman was about to protest, but was stopped by a soft hand covering her mouth.

"No," Amanda said, shaking her still damp head. "Please don't try to argue with me." She removed her hand and patted the sitting woman on the head. "I'll be right back." She quickly turned and hurried back down the stairs, disappearing into the kitchen.

Lex leaned back against the banister, her eyes following the lithe body. *Quite a little spitfire, eh? Lexington, ol' girl – you may have just met your match,* she sighed softly and closed her eyes.

Amanda burst back into the kitchen, a little breathless. Martha spun around from where she was stirring something on the stove. "What's the matter, dear? Did you get lost?" She could see the twinkle in the housekeeper's smiling brown eyes.

The young woman shook her head. "No, nothing like that. I need your help." She reached for the older woman's arm and pulled her out of the kitchen. "Lex is hurt, and I need some help getting her upstairs. She won't tell me what's wrong, but she practically collapsed on me!"

The two women reached the foot of the staircase and promptly looked up.

"Oh, my!" Martha exclaimed, lifting her skirt and practically running up the stairs. She stopped at the slumped form. "Lexie, honey? Can you hear me?" She gently turned the quiet face towards her.

Blue eyes slowly opened at her appeal. "Hmm?" They blinked. "Sorry," Lex reached up with one hand and rubbed her eyes, "guess I am a little tired." She tried to sit up, but the pain in her chest pushed her back down. "I suppose a little help would be good." She smiled weakly up at Amanda, who was standing in front of her with a worried look on her face. "And I bet you could use some aspirin, right?"

The young woman returned her smile. "Yeah, for some reason I seem to have the darndest headache."

Lex chuckled, as Martha pulled her slowly to her feet. The housekeeper gently wrapped an arm around her charge, and Amanda moved to support her from the other side. The three of them then moved slowly up the remaining stairs in silence

Martha led them down the hallway and into the master bedroom. Amanda couldn't help but glance around in awe. The room was huge – a large rock fireplace took up one entire corner; a cheerful fire already blazing, with two comfortable stuffed chairs in front of it. On the side wall opposite the door stood a huge bay window, complete with a padded window seat. The front of the room had beautiful French doors, which opened on to what looked like a balcony. But the thing that caught Amanda's attention most was the enormous king-sized bed that almost took up a quarter of the room on its own. It was a four-poster oak with a massive carved headboard. Amanda thought that an entire family could sleep on it.

Lex noticed where the younger woman's attention was. "It was my mother's," she explained softly. "Dad had it made for her as a wedding present." She bit back a groan when her two 'nurses' gently placed her on the object in question. The exhausted rancher laid back and closed her eyes.

Martha noticed the stains on Lex's shirt for the first time. "What happened here?" she asked Amanda, who had sat down on the edge of the bed by Lex's feet.

"I'm not real sure," she started, her eyes taking in the exhausted woman. "I was driving across this beautiful wooden bridge, when all of a sudden, something hit it, and sent my car crashing into the creek. I must have hit my head, because the next thing I remember is that she had me tied to her back, and was using a rope to pull us both out." Her hand touched the damp denim leg next to her. "She told me she had been hit by 'some debris', but I never did find out exactly what that was."

The housekeeper rolled her eyes. "Some things never change." She looked down at Lex, who was obviously asleep. "Let's get you some dry clothes, and then you can help me with her." She walked over to a large oak dresser, which must have been designed by the same person who made the bed. Opening the bottom drawer, the older woman pulled out a pair of maroon sweat pants and a matching sweatshirt with a Texas A & M University logo on each. "Here... go hop in the shower and then put these on. Lexie hasn't worn these since high school, but she never could seem to get rid of them. Just leave your wet clothes on the floor by the shower, and I'll get 'em washed up for you." Amanda was about to protest when the housekeeper shook her finger at her. "Now, don't you be giving me any lip – that's my job around here." She gently shoved the blonde towards the bathroom with a wink and a smile. "Hurry up... I'll probably need all the help I can get with little Lexie. She hates when I fuss over her."

Amanda returned the smile as she walked into the bathroom. "I'll be right back." She closed the door and then turned around. *Good grief! It's almost as big as my bedroom at home!* The young woman walked past the large dressing area, complete with a huge gray marble counter with two separate sinks, one at each end. Opening another door, she found the bathing area: a huge Jacuzzi tub in one corner, and a very large freestanding clear glass shower. Another door showed her a comfortably sized lavatory. She opened the shower door, noticing a built-in bench and two different nozzles, one on either side of the shower. *A whole team could shower in here,* she mused. Amanda turned on the water, removed her still-dripping clothing and piled them as neatly as possible by the door.

Stepping into the steaming water, Amanda couldn't help but moan. *Aaah, bliss! Never thought standing under more water would feel so good!* She quickly finished her shower, hoping to get another chance to use this wonderful contraption again. *Having the sprays hitting from two directions feels great! I gotta get one of these at home.* She dried off hurriedly, then slipped into the sweats – the sleeves fell several inches from her fingertips, and the pants promptly fell to her knees. The young woman chuckled as she pulled the pants back up to her waist and tied the drawstring into a bow. Amanda rolled the shirt sleeves up a few turns until she could see her hands. *Wow, she was a pretty good size even in high school!* She ran a comb through her hair without bothering to dry it. Walking back into the bedroom, Amanda spotted the housekeeper trying to pull Lex's jeans off.

"Oh, honey. Am I ever glad to see you." The older woman wiped her brow with the back of her hand. "I'm having the darndest time with these blasted jeans. They normally fit like a second skin, and now that they're wet, well..." She shook her graying head. "Lexie was trying to help, but it got to hurtin' her so bad that she passed out."

Amanda stepped towards the bed. "Well, between the two of us, we should be able to handle it." She grabbed the bottom of the jeans. "I'll pull from here, and you try to work them from her hips." Martha nodded.

It took the two of them almost ten minutes to rid the unconscious woman of her jeans. During that time, the rancher never
stirred. Martha was brushing the drying hair off Lex's forehead
while she and Amanda caught their breath. "Well, that was fun,"
she muttered, taking another deep breath. "Now, I guess we go
for what's left of this shirt!" She gently began peeling the shirt
up and stopped. It was stuck to Lex's skin. The housekeeper was
afraid of the damage she would find. "Amanda, honey, could you
go and bring me a few warm washcloths from the bathroom?"
She had noticed that the younger woman was looking frighteningly pale, and was worried that she was about to faint.

Amanda looked up gratefully. "Sure." She rushed out of the
bedroom to do the older woman's bidding.

A few moments later, Amanda returned to the bedroom with
a couple of damp washcloths. What she saw made her gasp, and
she nearly dropped her cargo. Martha had removed Lex's shirt
and was looking at the damage with a clinical air. She had pulled
a quilt over the unconscious woman's legs, keeping the shirt
draped across her breasts. The only other thing covering Lex's
chest was a soft, white lace bra. She looked up as Amanda came
over and handed her a washcloth.

"Thanks, honey. It looks a lot worse than it actually is, I
believe." The large gash started just below her breast on her right
side, and edged down her ribcage as well. "Just scraped up a little, but I think she's got a couple of busted ribs too," Martha
reported while cleaning the injury. She pointed to the other
washcloth that Amanda was still holding. "Why don't you wash
her face and arms while I go get something to put on this?" She
stood up and left the room. "I'll be right back," she called out as
she went downstairs.

Amanda sat for a moment looking down at her rescuer.
"Why do I feel such a strong connection to you? Have we ever
met?" she smiled gently. "No... I don't think I'd forget meeting
you, although I feel as if I've known you forever." She patiently
washed the dirt from the older woman's face, not realizing she
was speaking aloud.

The housekeeper crept back into the room, smiling as she

noticed the tender care the young woman was giving Lex. *Ah, she's a sweet one, that girl. I wonder what business she had that brought her to us.* Out loud she said, "I told you I wouldn't be long," as she stepped over to the bed. Martha had a jar of something as well as some strips of cloth in her hands. "I didn't have enough gauze, so I cut up an old sheet instead." She traded the stained shirt for a towel, then began to gently dab the cream onto the still-bleeding scrape. Once all the injury had been covered to her satisfaction, she motioned Amanda forward. "Could you climb up on her other side, and help me sit her up?" She waited until the younger woman complied. "Now, let's lift her forward...slowly now." The dark-haired woman moaned softly, but didn't waken. Amanda sat behind her, holding her upright while the housekeeper wrapped the strips of sheet around her. "This should keep things in place a little better, anyway," she said, using safety pins to finish the job. They slowly laid Lex back against the pillows, Martha covering her completely with the quilt from her legs, making certain she wasn't lying flat, in case she had internal bleeding.

Amanda eased herself off the bed and walked over to the housekeeper. "You act like you've done this before," she commented, awed at how calm the woman stayed.

Martha laughed. "Oh, goodness, yes. That little mite was always coming home with some sort of scrape or bruise." She eyed the small blonde carefully, and then grasped her arm. "Now, you come on into the bathroom, and I'll check out that bump on your head." She led the younger woman out of the bedroom.

"Oh," Amanda reached up to touch the spot. "I'd forgotten all about it." She followed dutifully. "It hardly hurts at all, now," she said, as Martha motioned for her to sit on the dressing table. Amanda complied, feeling like a small child.

Martha looked her in the eye and smiled. "Don't worry, honey," she assured her, "This won't hurt."

Amanda smiled back. "I know, I trust you."

The housekeeper gently used a cleanser on the small gash then put some of the same cream on it that she had used for Lex. Covering it with a large Band-Aid, she added, "That should keep it from getting infected." Martha reached behind her and grabbed a bottle and glass. She poured out two white tablets from the bottle, then filled the glass up with water. "Here." She handed the girl the tablets and water. "These should help with your headache."

Amanda snickered, but took the offered pills and glass. After she drank the water, she jumped down from the counter and laughed. "I feel like a little kid playing dress-up in these clothes." She pulled the material away from herself, showing how baggy they were.

Martha chuckled. "Don't feel too bad, dear. You look just fine." She went into the bathing area and returned with the wet clothes. "Now I'll just go take care of these and Lexie's wet things."

Amanda put out a hand. "Really, I can take care of those; just point me towards the laundry room."

Martha moved around her. "No, honey. I'll take care of this. You just go lie down and rest." When the young woman began to argue again, Martha placed a hand on her shoulder. "You could help me by keeping an eye on Lexie. Watch to see if she develops a fever. I'll just get these started and bring you both something to eat."

Amanda acquiesced. "Okay, I'll do that. But shouldn't we get her to a doctor?"

Martha shook her head. "That bridge that you came over on is the only way on or off this ranch. And until this weather lets up, they can't even bring a helicopter in."

Amanda froze. "Are you saying we're trapped here? What if she's hurt worse than you think? What can we do? What..." Her babbling was stopped by a gentle squeeze of her shoulder.

"It's going to be okay. Yes, it's true it's just the three of us here for now, but we've got more than enough supplies, and we do have a telephone. So we can always call a doctor for advice if we need it. Now don't you worry." Martha gathered up the rest of the wet clothes and headed for the door. "It would be easier to keep an eye on her if you lay down beside her. It's a big bed." She walked out the door, with a confused Amanda staring after her.

She watched the housekeeper leave, then switched her attention to the bed. *She's right, that thing's huge. And I am worn out – maybe I'll just lie down for a few minutes.* She walked over to the other side of the bed and lay down. *Oooh... I could be in serious trouble here – this is waay too comfortable.* Amanda rolled over onto her side and gazed at the still form next to her. *She seems to be looking better already,* she mused, noticing that the color was returning to the sleeping woman's face. Moments later, Amanda joined Lex in sleep.

Chapter
3

Lex was somewhat disoriented when she first opened her eyes. Glancing up, she realized that she was at home and in her own bed. *Yeah, now I remember. The stairs...* Her mind was still a little fuzzy after that. She heard soft breathing next to her, so she slowly turned her head towards the sound; Amanda was deeply asleep on the pillow next to hers, with her right hand tucked under her cheek, and her left hand... *holding my arm?* Sure enough, the small blonde had a gentle grip on Lex's forearm, as if she were afraid Lex would leave. Before Lex could disengage her arm, Martha walked in carrying a large silver tray laden with food.

"Well, hello there!" she said brightly. "How are you feeling, honey?" She set the tray on a nearby table and walked over to the bed. Sitting gently next to her 'patient', Martha casually used her hand to brush the hair off Lex's forehead, also using the motion to check for fever.

"I'm fine, Martha. Don't worry so much," the younger woman said, slowly pulling herself into a sitting position.

"Oh, sure. You were so 'fine' that *we* had to undress you, and you probably don't even remember it!" the housekeeper exclaimed with a frown.

Lex sighed. "I think I was more tired than actually hurt," she smiled. "Honestly, I feel much better now." She tried to peek around the heavier woman. "Is that food I smell?"

Martha laughed. "Oh, Lexie... you're gonna be the death of me yet."

Amanda was awakened by the sound of voices. The sight before her made her smile. "Hey..." She sat up and rubbed her eyes. "Sorry...I didn't mean to drop off like that." She sent a timid smile to the housekeeper. "How long was I asleep?" She looked outside, but it was still dark and raining.

The short heavyset woman got up to set the tray on the middle of the bed. "Only a couple of hours."

"A COUPLE OF HOURS?? Oh, no!" Amanda moved to get off the bed, but Lex grabbed her arm.

"What's the matter?" she asked, as the younger woman looked horrified.

"My grandparents – I really need to let them know I'm okay." She was almost in tears. "They'll be worried sick..." *Especially with this weather...We're all a little paranoid about car accidents, now...*

Martha halted her babbling with a wave of her hand. "Now hold on there, honey." She picked up the cordless phone that was stationed on Lex's bedside table. "Here... last time I checked, the lines were just fine."

Amanda took the phone with a grateful smile. "Thanks – I'm sorry, I don't usually fall apart this easily." She dialed her grandparents' number, and after three rings it was picked up.

"Hello?" an older woman's voice answered.

Amanda smiled into the phone. Just hearing her grandmother's voice was soothing. "Gramma? It's me, Amanda."

"Mandy, sweetheart, are you okay? We were getting a little worried. You're usually home before now." Concern colored the older woman's voice. In the background, she could hear her grandfather's deep voice asking his wife a question. Anna Leigh covered the mouthpiece with her hand and spoke to him. "Yes, Jacob, it's Mandy. I will, sweetheart." Then to Amanda, "Where are you, dear?"

The little blonde grimaced. *What to tell her without lying, or causing her needless worry.* "Well, it's like this. I went out for an appointment today."

Anna Leigh interrupted her. "You went out in this awful weather?"

"Yes, Gramma. Rick gave me the appointment sheet..."

The older woman was livid. "That pompous ass! I'd fire him if I could find a replacement for his worthless hide," she hinted. "So where are you now? You're not still out somewhere in the rain, are you, dear?"

Amanda laughed. "Gramma! I've told you I'm not qualified to be an office manager just yet. And no, I'm not out in the rain. I'm...uh... kinda stuck at a friend's house." She looked over at Lex and Martha with an apologetic grin.

"Where? Are you okay? You didn't get the car stuck, did you?" her grandmother questioned.

Amanda blanched. Between being worried about Lex and the bump on her head, she had forgotten completely about the car. "Oh... um... well, yes, Gramma, the car is stuck," *in a creek,* she mused to herself.

Anna Leigh sighed in relief. "Well, dear, don't you worry. Jacob will be the first to say that you're much more important than some old car. Besides, we'll just wait until it dries up some and have Randy down at the garage take care of it," she said calmly, hearing the upset in her granddaughter's voice.

Tears began to fill Amanda's eyes. *It'll probably take a lot of drying out.* "I know, Gramma. I guess I'm just a little tired."

"That's perfectly okay, sweetheart. When will you be home? Do we need to send a cab for you?" Jacob's leg cast had been recently removed but he had not been cleared to drive, which frustrated him to no end. Anna Leigh refused to leave him at home alone, afraid that he would need something and try to get out anyway. And she certainly didn't want to get him out in this weather. The older woman could tell that their granddaughter wasn't telling the entire truth. Amanda sounded far too upset for the car to be "just" stuck in the mud.

"Well, Gramma, that's kinda hard to say...I guess I'm stranded." Her voice began to tremble.

"Stranded? What exactly do you mean by that? Are you sure

you're okay?" Anna Leigh was beginning to get upset as well.

"Uh, well..." Amanda looked frantic. She covered the mouthpiece with her hand and whispered to the women looking on. "Help! I don't know what to say, and I don't want them to worry!" Her hands began to shake.

Lex pulled the phone out of her nerveless fingers. "Hello? This is Lexington Walters." She paused to listen to the woman on the other end of the line.

"Lexington? What a surprise...is my granddaughter with you?" Anna Leigh's delighted voice questioned.

"Yes ma'am, she's here, Mrs. Cauble. How are things with the Historical Committee? I'm sorry that I've missed the last few meetings." *Well, more like avoided,* Lex mused, *but no sense in going over that now.*

Amanda's jaw dropped. *Lexington? Historical Committee? MY grandmother? She knows MY grandmother?*

Anna Leigh sighed. "Dull as dirt without you, dear. Is Amanda at the ranch?"

Lex smiled. "Yes, ma'am...she's here with me, but I'm afraid she'll be stuck out here for a while."

"Did she go and get herself lost? I'm afraid that she still doesn't know the area very well." The older woman was concerned.

The rancher chuckled. "No, nothing like that. Seems our old bridge was washed out, and your lovely granddaughter got stuck on our side of the creek." She mischievously raised an eyebrow at Amanda.

She thinks I'm lovely? Oh, this is getting more bizarre by the moment. Amanda closed her eyes shyly when Lex smirked at her.

"Is that going to cause a problem for you, Lexington? Having someone there at the ranch?" Anna Leigh wondered. *I know how she values her privacy.*

"No ma'am, it'll be just fine. It's just Martha and me out here right now, so she'll be good company. The boys are staying at our house in town, so if y'all need anything, just give them a call. You still have both numbers, right?" Lex saw the incredulous look that crossed Amanda's face.

Anna Leigh breathed a sigh of relief. "Yes, dear, I do. But

you let me know if she becomes too much of a bother, okay?"

Lex continued to smile. "Yes ma'am, I will. Oh...I think Amanda has calmed down now."

"That's grand. You take care, all right? It was wonderful speaking to you again, Lexington. Don't be a stranger, dear." Anna Leigh left the unspoken invitation in the air.

"Yes ma'am...it was good to hear from you too...goodbye." She handed the phone over to a very curious Amanda, who gave her a look that said, *You'd better tell me all about this later!*

"Hi, again, Gramma. I'm sorry I fell apart like that. Guess being stuck out in the rain today wore me out."

Anna Leigh laughed. "Don't apologize – I'd probably be the same way." Now she became serious. "At least we won't worry about you any... Lexington is one of the sweetest people I have ever met. She helped me get the old Taylor house declared a historical landmark last year. She's a good person, no matter what others might say." Fearing that she'd said too much, Anna Leigh stopped. Rumors abounded about the Walters girl – some said she was unnatural, running the ranch when she had an older brother perfectly capable of it. Plus the fact that she never dated in high school and wasn't married now... all this added up to fuel for the town's gossips. *Not to mention that unfortunate wild streak she had a few years ago.*

Amanda paused. *What others might say? Well, if her grandmother said she was a good person, that's all that mattered to her.* "I know, Gramma... she practically took me in today." She grinned at the dark-haired woman, who smiled back. "I'll give you a call in the morning to see how you're both doing, okay?"

"Why don't you make it tomorrow evening? Your grandfather and I have a few errands to run tomorrow – he has his physical therapy, then we thought we'd take in an early movie." Anna Leigh didn't want her granddaughter to think she had to be with them every minute of every day. *The girl is so sweet, but she really needs to get out more and meet people her own age. Maybe this is the perfect opportunity.* "And you try and get some rest... you sound tired, sweetie."

Amanda grinned. "I will. Don't go out if it's still raining too hard, please?" She paused. "I love you, Gramma. Please give

Grandpa Jake a big hug and kiss from me."

Anna Leigh chuckled. *She treats me more like a child, than a capable woman. She's too sweet.* "I promise we'll stay home if it's too bad...we love you too, dearest." She hung up the phone and sighed. *I hope you and Lexington get along well...she is so much like her mother – so lonely, but refusing to admit it.* Standing up and walking over to Jacob, she embraced him tightly. "Let's go to bed, love." Arm in arm they started upstairs. "And I'll tell you what our darling granddaughter is up to."

Amanda turned off the phone and handed it back to Lex. "Thanks. I feel much better now." She gently slapped the older woman's arm.

"Ow! What was that for?" Lex questioned, as Martha looked on and laughed.

"You didn't tell me you knew my grandmother!" Amanda accused indignantly.

Lex smiled. "I didn't know either, until I recognized her voice on the telephone." She looked at the small blonde. "*You* didn't tell me you were Jacob and Anna Leigh Cauble's granddaughter."

Amanda laughed. "Okay, you got me there. It's sooo weird that you know my grandparents, and yet we've never met." She reached for the tray and grabbed a bowl of chili. "Mmm..." she mumbled with a mouthful, "This is fantastic!"

Lex grabbed her own bowl and nodded. "Oh, yeah. Martha makes the best chili I've ever eaten." She looked over at the housekeeper who was bringing over a large, button-down cotton nightshirt.

"Put that down and put this on – I don't want you to catch cold," Martha grumbled, somewhat embarrassed by the high praise.

"Why? Isn't quilt-wearing fashionable this year?" Lex teased, putting down her bowl and allowing the older woman to help her remove her bra, and slip the nightshirt over her head. "Well, I must say this will be easier to eat in, that's for sure." She picked up her bowl and began to eat again, ignoring the snort of laughter from the small woman on the bed beside her.

Martha shook her head. "Sometimes..." she sighed. "I'll

remember that when you whine to me that you have nothing to wear... I'll just drag out your quilt." She turned to leave. "After you girls finish that tray, give me a buzz, and I'll come back to clean it up. I've got some laundry to finish in the meantime." She walked out, still shaking her head and smiling.

Amanda looked over at Lex. "Do you think she would be too awfully mad if I took the tray downstairs? I don't want her to be waiting on me hand and foot. I'm not an invalid," she said between mouthfuls of chili and still-warm cornbread. "Although if I stay here too long, I'll weigh too much to get down the stairs."

Lex laughed, then stopped and wrapped one arm around her chest. "Ouch! Don't make me laugh so much..." she smiled at the young girl. "Nah. She'll fuss about it, but she never gets mad." She finished her bowl and set it down. "I've been trying for years to stop her from fussing about me, and nothing has worked yet. I even offered her the chance to retire, and travel." A mock horrified look. "I thought she was gonna break every spoon she had on my backside, I've never heard so much yelling in my life. So now, I let her fuss, it seems to make her happy..."

Amanda finished up her bowl and placed it on the tray as well. "Let me take this downstairs before she makes another trip." She got up off the bed and reached for the tray. A loud snort of laughter stopped her. "What?" she asked, perplexed by the older woman's mirth.

"Heh... sorry..." Lex was trying, without much success, to control her laughter. "It's just you...you..." She wrapped both arms gingerly around her aching chest.

"Me, me...What?" Amanda was beginning to get a little angry.

"You look so cute in my old sweats!" She lay back on the bed, tears beginning to run from her eyes. "Ow!"

Amanda rolled her eyes. "Serves you right, making fun of me...I don't look that bad, do I?" She sat the tray down and walked into the bathroom where a full-length mirror stood.

"Oh, jeez!" Amanda exclaimed as she looked into the mirror. *These clothes have to be at least three sizes too big,* she grinned. Then she giggled. Lex had finally calmed down, but when Amanda walked in giggling, she lost her composure again.

"Bwahahahaha!! Ouch!" She laughed out loud, holding her chest in pain. "Ow!" she continued to laugh.

Amanda was laughing as well, and she staggered over to the bed and sat down next to Lex. "Hahahahaha... shhhhhh... you're just gonna hurt yourself worse." She placed her hand on the older woman's shoulder, trying to calm her down. "Shhhh..." she finally stopped laughing, and Lex wore down as well.

Gasping for breath, Lex closed her eyes. "Damn...that hurt, but felt really good." She took a semi-deep breath and opened her eyes. "Thanks."

"For what?" the blonde asked in confusion.

"For being such a good sport and not smacking me when I started laughing... I wasn't really making fun of you, you know."

Amanda smiled. "I know. And besides, I do look like a little kid in these things, but they're really comfortable." She walked around to the other side of the bed and grabbed the tray. "Now I'm going to try to take this tray downstairs, again." She started to walk away, then turned back towards Lex. "You didn't hurt yourself laughing, did you? Should I ask Martha to come up and check your bandage?"

Lex waved her hand. "Nah, just a little sore. Really, I'm fine."

Amanda was skeptical, but kept quiet. "Okay, then I'll run this downstairs. Why don't you try to get some more rest? I'll be back in a little bit." She picked up the tray and started out the door before Lex could say another word.

****

Amanda had just made it to the bottom of the stairs when Martha's voice boomed, "All right, young lady, just what do you think you're doing?" The housekeeper had stepped out of a doorway at the end of the hall, and she walked over to meet the young blonde at the kitchen door. Martha had a neat stack of clothes in one hand. "Well?"

Amanda motioned with the tray. "Umm...I thought I'd save you a trip upstairs?" she said with an innocent look on her face.

The heavyset woman laughed and motioned her towards the sink. "Okay dear, I'll let it slide this time." She placed the stack of clothes on a nearby stool, then began removing the dishes from the tray. "How are you feeling, hon?" Martha asked as she put the dirty dishes in the sink and wiped down the tray with a dishcloth.

Amanda sat down on the other stool. The younger woman grabbed her now-clean socks and put them on her feet. "My head is barely hurting, so I'm feeling much better. How did you find my socks?" She looked up and smiled. "Thank you for washing my things...you didn't have to, but I do appreciate it."

Martha turned to face her, wiping her soapy hands on a dry dishtowel. "You're welcome. I found your socks when I was cleaning up the mudroom. I was washing Lexie's things anyway and thought you might need something clean to wear." She smiled at the small woman. "Although you look like you're mighty comfortable right now."

Amanda blushed. "Well actually, I am. These," she plucked at the shirt, "may be big, but I think I'm addicted to them already."

The housekeeper patted her on the leg. "Well, I don't think Lexie will mind...she hasn't worn them herself in years."

The blonde looked at her curiously. "She doesn't seem like the type to keep things that aren't useful. Why would she keep these?" She looked down at the Texas A&M logo on the shirt. "Did she go to school there or something?"

Martha looked as if she were weighing a heavy decision. *Well, better she asked me than Lexie.* She picked up the clothes on the spare stool and sat down opposite of Amanda. "No, dear, she didn't go to college. Oh sure, she certainly planned to, even got a full scholarship. But the spring before her high school graduation changed all of that." She sighed, the pain from long ago still showing in her eyes.

"About two months before graduation, Lexie's dad decided he wanted to go back on the rodeo circuit. After he took the next bus out of town, we found papers he'd had drawn up that gave her complete control of the ranch." She shook her graying head. "And Lexie, being the responsible type that she is, stepped right in." The housekeeper released a heavy sigh. "So, she gave up her dream of college and ran this ranch full time and never spoke one word of complaint."

Amanda was stunned. "She said she has a brother...why didn't she let him run the ranch while she went to school?"

Martha lowered her voice, anger in her tone. "Now this is my opinion, mind you, but that man would have run this ranch right into the ground within a year... he's a smart enough pencil pusher, but Hubert doesn't know enough about ranching to fill a thimble. Besides, Lexie is a natural. I don't think there's anything that girl can't do." She took a deep cleansing breath. "Anyway, I wanted to tell you, 'cause I think it still hurts Lexie that she wasn't able to go to college."

Amanda had tears in her eyes. "Don't worry, Martha. I would never intentionally hurt her." *She means too much to me, and I don't even know her that well...strange.* "Do you know what she was planning on studying?"

The housekeeper smiled a sad little smile. "Oh yes...she told me right at the beginning of her senior year...she was so excited when she got the letter that told her of the scholarship." She paused, lost in her memories. "Oh, sorry dear. She wanted to be a veterinarian. That girl has always had a way with animals. I think that if she didn't feel so responsible for all the hired hands, and me, she would have sold this ranch years ago and gone to school anyway." She shook her head again. "But no, Lexie will stick with this place until the end of time." She looked over at Amanda, who had a strange look on her face. "What's the matter, dear?"

"That sorry, son of a..." Amanda trailed off, anger beginning to flare in her bright green eyes. "He probably knew that she'd never sell, and just wanted me to make a fool out of myself."

Martha grasped the angry woman's hand. "Honey, what's the matter?" Concern etched her weathered features.

Amanda shook her head and smiled apologetically. "I'm sorry, Martha. I just realized that someone was trying to make me look like an idiot, and probably trying to hurt Lex as well." *Rick most likely knew all of this, and realized how it would make*

Lex feel to talk about selling the ranch. "You see, I work for my grandmother's real estate agency."

Martha placed a hand over her mouth in dismay. "Oh, no..."

Amanda nodded. "Oh, yes. The manager, Rick, gave me an appointment sheet and a map to find my way out here earlier today."

The shocked housekeeper interrupted her. "Rick? That wouldn't be Ricky Thompson, would it?" Small towns had their bad points too...everybody knew everyone else, and there were few secrets.

Amanda exhaled. "Yeah...he's had it out for me ever since I turned him down for a date." She shivered. "I can't help it, the man makes my skin crawl!" she stopped, thinking. "Why? Do you know him too?"

Martha laughed. "I guess you could say that you and Lexie have something in common with him. When they were in high school together, Rick was a senior when Lexie was a sophomore...she turned him down for a date. Well, he wouldn't take no for an answer, so she basically flattened him in the main hall," she smiled. "I probably would have never known anything about it, but she got suspended from school for three days. Her father just laughed." She paused, trying to gather her thoughts. "I was pretty upset at first, until the school counselor called me and explained. They had to suspend her for fighting, since that was the rule, but they made sure that she didn't miss anything important in class. I think they appreciated that someone had finally stood up to Ricky... he was such a bully in those days." She closed her eyes for a moment. "Poor Lexie...he's always looking for an excuse to get back at her. Without being caught, anyway."

Amanda nodded. "That would explain why he sent me out here today. I was supposed to meet with 'L. Walters' to discuss putting the ranch up for sale – he said that they were tired of ranching." She clenched her fists. "That rat...I ought to..."

Martha stood up next to the angry young woman. "Now, now dear." She rubbed her hand lightly on the girl's back. "Everything turned out okay, didn't it?" *Other than the poor child nearly dying in a flooded creek.*

Amanda took a deep steadying breath. "You're right. I

would have probably never met you or Lex. Maybe I should call
him up and thank him." She smiled an almost evil grin.
"Wouldn't that just twist his shorts?"

The housekeeper hugged her. "Oh, it certainly would! I'd
love to see his face!" She sobered. "Unfortunately, we're all
three stuck here until the weather clears up enough to start
rebuilding that bridge, or the creek goes down enough to walk
across in one of the shallower areas...and I don't see that happening any time soon."

The young woman returned Martha's embrace. "Well, at
least we're dry and safe." She stood up and took the folded
clothes. "I'll just go put these away for now, since I'm pretty
comfortable in my present outfit." Amanda started towards the
doorway. "But please, let me know if there is anything I can do
to help around here. I feel bad that you're doing all the work."

Martha walked back over to the sink. "If you can keep Lexie
occupied without her driving me crazy, I'll consider it a fair
trade." She put her hands back in the water, then turned and
looked over her shoulder. "Try to keep her still for as long as
possible – I'd really like those ribs to get at least a little time to
mend properly."

Amanda sighed and rolled her mist-green eyes. "I'll try. But
she seems like the type that doesn't like to stay still."

The housekeeper laughed. "Mercy! Have you got her number! Now shoo! Go get some rest yourself, okay?"

The blonde nodded and started for the staircase. "I will. See
you later."

Amanda tiptoed towards the bedroom, in case Lex was still
sleeping. She decided to check on the injured woman and then
ask Martha if there was a guestroom or couch she could use. She
peeked around the door and looked towards the empty bed.
Empty bed?!? She stepped the rest of the way inside. *Now where
could she be?*

The bathroom door opened, and a slightly damp Lex walked
slowly into the bedroom.

"What do you think you are doing?" Amanda asked, striding
over to the tall woman. Lex had a towel around her neck, drying
the ends of her hair. She was wearing flannel boxer shorts with a

faded blue nightshirt that was similar to the one she had been wearing earlier.

"Huh?" Lex eased her way over to one of the chairs in front of the fire and sat down gingerly. "Oh...well, I felt kinda grimy after that swim in the creek and the mud bath, so I thought I'd take a real bath." Seeing the flash in Amanda's vibrant green eyes, she hurried to explain. "Don't worry – I was real careful...didn't even get my bandage wet." *Whoa, those eyes sure do sparkle when she's angry.* Lex blinked, *Wait a minute! Don't you be going there, Lex ol' girl.*

Amanda sat in the chair opposite of Lex. "I'm sorry...but Martha asked me to keep an eye on you, and I didn't want anything to happen on 'my watch'," she smiled. "You do look a lot better than you did earlier." *Oh, yeah...does she! Whoa, where did THAT thought come from?*

Lex leaned back in the chair with a quiet sigh. "Yeah, amazing what warm water and soap can do for a person." She looked at the clock on the mantel. "It's getting kinda late and you're looking a little tired yourself." She stood up slowly and took a deep breath. "C'mon, let's go get you tucked in." She smiled and offered her hand to the young blonde, who blushed at her choice of words.

Stop that Amanda – she doesn't mean anything by it! She didn't take Lex's hand, but she stood up next to her and smiled. "Okay, point me to the couch." Amanda followed the tall woman out of the bedroom and to the room across the hallway.

Lex smiled and flipped the light switch. "Here's the guestroom. We just finished remodeling it, so you're our first..." she smirked, "guest."

Amanda walked behind her in awe. The room almost matched Lex's room in size; about the only thing missing was the fireplace. A large brass bed sat against one wall. The side walls had two large picture windows with colorful windowseats and pillows that matched the brightly flowered bedspread. One corner had a sitting area and a small bookshelf covered with books.

Lex laughed at Amanda's expression. "What? It's not *that* bad, is it?"

The younger woman slapped her on the arm. "Not that bad? Are you kidding? It's incredible!" She shook her head. "Did you do the decorating?"

This got another laugh from the tall woman. "Oh yeah, right... Not." She led Amanda to a door on the other side of the bed. "You've seen my room. This was all Martha's doing." She opened the door to a more modest bathroom, but it had the same type of shower as hers. "You should find everything you might need here...Martha's always real thorough."

Amanda turned around and looked up into Lex's clear blue eyes. "Thank you... I don't think I'll ever be able to say it enough. You saved my life, took me into your home, and have taken care of me. I don't know how I'll ever repay you." She grasped Lex's hands and squeezed them gently.

Lex looked down and got lost in that verdant gaze. "You don't owe me anything. I'm just glad I was there." She bent down and placed a gentle kiss on the young woman's forehead. "Now try to get some sleep. I'll see you in the morning." She turned and walked out of the room, closing the door quietly behind her.

Amanda opened her eyes. *Wow!* She drew a shaky hand through her hair. *And I'm supposed to be able to sleep after that?* She sighed, then walked into the bathroom. After brushing her teeth with the new toothbrush she found in the cabinet, Amanda walked through the bedroom and to the door. Opening it, she looked across the hall. *Light's already out. Guess one of us will get some sleep tonight.* She walked back over to the bed and crawled under the clean sheets. Moments later, in spite of her racing thoughts, Amanda fell deeply asleep.

Chapter
4

It was dark and very cold. She could hear a roaring sound coming nearer, but for some reason, her legs were paralyzed. As it got closer and closer, she could feel something holding her down... Noooo!!! *Water lapping at her feet... the roaring getting louder and louder.* Help!! Can't break free!! *The strap holding her in place getting tighter... the water now up over her thighs and still rising.* Please help me!! *The cold, dirty water up to her chin now... the band tightening around her chest...*Can't breathe...NOOOOO!!

Amanda jerked upright, screaming, and found herself wrapped in strong arms. "Shhh...you're okay," a low voice murmured in her ear. Warm hands rubbed her back soothingly.

"Wha...?" She blinked her eyes open, startled to see Lex sitting on her bed.

"S'okay... you were crying out." The older woman pulled back. "Must have been one doozy of a nightmare." Her dark hair was in disarray, and she had a gentle smile on her lips.

Amanda took a shaky breath. "S..s...sorry." Quiet tears began to fall from her misty-green eyes. "It was dark...I couldn't get loose...the water..." she began to sob.

"Hey, it's all right." Lex gathered her back in her arms,

rocking slowly. "Shhh... you're safe now."

The young woman clung to Lex as if she were a lifeline, strangled sobs now wracking her body. Lex began to feel the pain in her ribs, but refused to let the distraught woman go. *This feels so right...* She began to hum softly, still gently rocking Amanda.

After a short while, Amanda's sobs quieted. She was halfway asleep, enjoying the gentle touch of the older woman. She suddenly realized how tightly she was attached, and slowly loosened her stranglehold. "Thanks," she sniffed, taking a deep breath. "I...I don't know what came over me. I haven't had a nightmare since I was a little kid." She pulled away from Lex, feeling an extreme sense of loss from the act. To compensate, she grasped both of the dark woman's hands and held them loosely.

Blue eyes locked with hers, almost startling in their intensity. "You've had a pretty rough experience today – any normal person would be having nightmares. Add to that the bump on your head and that you're sleeping in a strange bed – this can't be easy for you." She gently squeezed the small hands held in her own.

Amanda managed a smile at that. "Hearing it put that way, I don't feel so bad now." She took comfort in the strength of the callused hands that she held. "I'm sorry that I woke you." Looking closely, Amanda could see a flicker of pain in those incredible eyes. "Are you okay?"

Lex smiled. "Fine...are you doing better now?" She couldn't seem to look away from those trusting eyes. *I could look at her forever.* She blinked. *Huh?*

Amanda noticed the glazed look in the older woman's eyes. "Hey." Blue eyes focused back on her. "Let me help you back to bed." She stood up and pulled Lex up with her. "Besides," she touched the Band-Aid on her temple, "I could use a few more aspirin." On impulse, she pulled the tall woman into a soft hug. "Thank you, again. You seem to always be pulling me out of scary places."

Lex returned the hug. *Oh, I could get addicted to this real easy.* She pulled out of the embrace slowly. "Glad I could be of service, ma'am." She tipped an imaginary hat and winked.

The small blonde laughed. "You nut." She wrapped an arm around Lex's waist and started towards the door. "Let's get *you* tucked in..."

They maneuvered their way through the doorway and across the hall easily. Amanda led her companion to the bed. Placing her hands on the broad shoulders, she gently pushed until Lex sat back on the bed. "Down you go."

"This isn't really necessary, you know." But even as she said this, Lex allowed Amanda to lift her legs and then cover her body with the sheet and comforter. "You gonna tell me a story, too?" A grin crept across her face.

Amanda slapped her arm. "Only if you want me to." She sat down on the edge of the bed next to Lex. "Any requests?"

Several requests ran through the dark-haired woman's mind, none of which could be voiced without embarrassing her 'nurse'. She cleared her throat. "Yeah...go get your aspirin."

Amanda laughed then stood up. "Good idea." She patted a nearby leg. "Be right back." She stepped into the bathroom and Lex could hear the sound of water filling a glass. A short pause, then more water running. Amanda stepped out of the bathroom with a glass of water in one hand. "I've had mine," she opened the other hand and gave Lex two white tablets, "and here's yours."

Lex raised an eyebrow, but took the offering without complaint. She patted the bed on the other side of her. "If you're gonna tell me a story, might as well get comfortable." She had a feeling the younger woman was still shaky from her nightmare, and was determined to help her.

Amanda blushed. She walked around and gently climbed into the bed, rolling over onto her side. Propping her head up on an upraised hand, she asked, "Okay, what story do you want me to tell?"

Lex turned her head and looked at the amused face across from her. "Oh, I dunno..." She appeared to be thinking hard. "How about a happy childhood memory? You know, something to take your mind off what happened today?"

The blonde smiled, touched that her new friend was trying to help her get over her bad dream. She turned over onto her

back. "I can do that. Close your eyes, now… what good is a bed-
time story if your eyes aren't closed?"

The other woman chuckled, then reached up and turned off
the lamp beside the bed. "Okay, I'm ready." She closed her eyes
and smiled.

Amanda took a deep breath, then slowly released it.

*The summer before Amanda turned sixteen was one of the
best she could ever remember. It started like every other summer,
with her parents traveling to Europe. Her older sister, Jeannie,
decided to go on a church camp retreat and she went to Somerville to stay with her father's parents. She was always given the
choice of traveling with her parents or even going to camp, but
she really enjoyed the summers spent with Jacob and Anna
Leigh.*

*The day after she arrived, the three of them packed up a pic-
nic lunch and piled into Jacob's Suburban. Amanda and Anna
Leigh questioned Jacob about the details of the trip. He good-
naturedly refused to give out their destination. Curiosity about
the extended flatbed trailer behind the large red vehicle nearly
drove the two women to distraction. Two hours later, they pulled
off the main road. Ten minutes after that, they pulled up to a
rusty looking gate.*

*"Peanut, would you mind getting out and opening the gate,
please?" Jacob smiled at his granddaughter.*

*Amanda quickly jumped from the vehicle to do his bidding.
"Sure thing, Grandpa!"*

*She swung the gate open, and he motioned for her to climb
back into the vehicle. "C'mon! We'll close it up when we leave."*

*She ran back to the truck and hopped in. Buckling up,
"Ready to go, captain!" she saluted.*

*Jacob laughed and drove on through the gate. The road
wove through a small thicket of trees, which soon opened up to
an old abandoned farmhouse.*

*Weeds and wild bushes had grown up around the old house,
causing it to look as if it had been deserted for ages. The dilapidated building was two and a half stories tall. Most of the shut-
ters were lying on the ground since all the windows had been*

boarded up some time ago. Amanda loved it.

"Oooh, Grandpa Jake...whose house is this?" she cried, with her face pressed against the window for a better view.

Anna Leigh spoke up. "Yes, darling. Please. Why are we here?" She reached over and clasped his hand.

Jacob pulled his wife's delicate hand to his lips and kissed it softly. "Soon, my love." He waggled his eyebrows at her teasingly.

She smiled and returned his look with one of her own, filled with love. "Okay, you rascal. You know I could never resist that look." She leaned over and kissed him on the lips. "But you'd better spill the beans soon!"

He grinned and turned to Amanda in the back seat. "Well, whaddya say, Peanut? Wanna go exploring?"

The young girl giggled with excitement. "Can we really, Grandpa?" She reached for the door handle. "Do you think the owners would mind?" She was out of the truck before he could answer.

Jacob got out of the truck and walked over to the passenger's side, opening the door for his wife. He extended a hand to the gentle woman to lovingly pull her from the truck. "I don't know. Do you want to ask them?" With his left hand he grasped his wife's fingers, and extended his right hand to his granddaughter who immediately latched onto it tightly.

Amanda looked up at him seriously. "I think we should, don't you, Gramma?" She looked over at Anna Leigh, who smiled.

Her gray-streaked auburn hair shone in the summer sunshine. Jacob looked at his wife, feeling a lump in his throat. Medium height and shining pale green eyes, she looked the same as when he married her over forty years ago. And I've never loved her more. Then he turned his mind back to the conversation.

"That would be the responsible thing to do, Mandy." Anna Leigh looked at Jacob, who was looking at her with undisguised love written all over his strong face. The years had been good to her husband. His tall frame was still lean, and his wavy dark hair was only lightly sprinkled with gray. His carpenter's hands

were rough with calluses and strong, but oh so gentle with her. And his smile can still melt my heart.

Jacob looked over at Amanda, seeing how much she resembled her grandmother. *She's gonna break some hearts soon,* he sighed to himself. "Okay, then. Why don't you ask permission?"

Amanda studied him with a confused frown. "Sure, Grandpa. Where's the owner?"

Jacob stopped walking and turned to Amanda, releasing Anna Leigh's hand. He bowed deeply to the young teenager. "At your service, M'lady."

Amanda giggled, and his wife gasped. "You own this, Jacob?" Anna Leigh shook her head. "Since when?"

Jacob captured her hand again and pulled them both towards the dilapidated house. "Oh, 'bout a month ago. Do you remember Alistair Tucker?" he asked her as they walked on.

Anna Leigh thought for a moment. "Wasn't he the gentleman you made those cabinets and matching desk for years ago? I remember that he never could stop raving about your work — didn't he pass away recently?"

Her husband nodded. "Yes, he did. Anyway, when I made those cabinets, he didn't have enough money for them at the time, but he needed them for his business. I told him not to worry about it, that he could pay when he was able."

Anna Leigh stopped him. "But he paid that off some time ago, didn't he?"

Jacob squeezed her hand. "Yes, beloved, he did. But since he had no surviving family, his lawyer said he wanted to leave everything to someone he knew. He didn't want it to go to the state. So," he led them up the steps to the old porch, " You're looking at the proud owner of 'Tucker Estates'."

Amanda, who had been silently absorbing these facts, finally spoke up. "That is so cool, Grandpa!" She looked around the porch as Jacob released his grip on both their hands and pulled a key out of his pocket. "I bet this place was really beautiful at one time," she said, her imagination restoring the old house to its former glory.

"I'm sure it was, Peanut," he agreed, unlocking the door and opening it wide. Jacob leaned inside the door and pulled out *three battery-operated lanterns. "Well, well... now how do you suppose these got here?" He turned all three lanterns on, giving Anna Leigh and Amanda each one. "Can't explore very well in the dark now, can we?" He laughed at the twin looks of surprise on his companions' faces.*

"You are such a sneak, Jacob Wilson Cauble!" Anna Leigh playfully slapped his arm.

Amanda poked his other arm. "I gotta agree with Gramma on this one," she laughed. "Do you think it's safe to look around upstairs?" she asked him.

"Sure, Peanut. I've already walked through this whole house, and there's nothing here that could hurt you. Have fun!" he said, ruffling her hair. She took off up the stairs, laughing.

After the three of them had explored the old house from top to bottom, Anna Leigh grabbed the picnic basket and a large blanket out of the Suburban. They all sat under a huge oak tree in the backyard to enjoy the picnic.

Amanda had finished with her lunch and was lying on her stomach, her hands holding up her head and her legs kicking gently back and forth. She was absently gazing off into the distance when something caught her eye. "Hey, Grandpa Jake, what's that building over there?"

Jacob looked in the direction her finger was pointing. "I'm not sure, Peanut...looks like some sort of barn."

The young girl jumped up excitedly. "You mean you haven't 'explored' it yet?"

Her grandfather laughed, and stood up. "Nope...it's undiscovered territory." He offered a hand to his still seated wife. "Care to join us on our search of the uncharted waters, my dear?"

Anna Leigh graciously accepted his offer with a curtsy. "But of course, kind sir. Lead on, Lady Amanda!" They linked their hands together laughing and walked towards the structure.

The key that unlocked the house also worked for the barn, so Jacob had no problem opening the huge double doors. Amanda stood behind him with her hands resting softly on his back. "What's the matter, Peanut? Are you scared?" he chuckled.

She patted his back. "Hey, I may be adventurous, but I'm

not stupid!" she proclaimed, looking over at her grandmother for support.

The gentle beauty's smile widened. "That's telling him, Mandy!"

"Great! Now I'm outnumbered," her husband grumbled good-naturedly. He pulled the heavy doors open slowly. The inside consisted of one massive room with a dirt floor – shelves covered in junk lined the three walls, and more paraphernalia hung from the ceiling. In the center of the room was a large object covered with a dusty tarp. The three 'adventurers' crept in slowly, each staring at the huge lump.

Amanda tiptoed up to the tarp as if it were a large creature merely sleeping, one that she was afraid to disturb. As she was reaching over to lift the edge of the tarp and peek under it, Jacob sneaked up behind her and poked her in the ribs.

"Watch out!!" he yelled, as she jumped backwards and screamed.

"Aaaaaaahhh!!!!" She almost leapt into his arms as he and Anna Leigh nearly collapsed with laughter. "Ooooh, I'm gonna get you for that!" Amanda growled, then began laughing herself.

"I'm sorry, Peanut...you just looked so intense while you were sneaking up on that thing." Jacob had to wipe the tears from his eyes.

"That really wasn't nice, Jacob," Anna Leigh chastised. "But it was quite funny!" She was holding her stomach from laughing so hard.

He wrapped Amanda up in a big hug. "C'mon, sweetheart, let's unwrap this 'monster'."

His granddaughter returned his hug. Amanda moved to the other side and grabbed the front corner of the tarp. They slowly pulled the covering back. Once the dust had settled, the 'beast' was unveiled.

Jacob whistled. It was a 1967 Mustang hard top, in a partial state of restoration He could see where someone had begun sanding and smoothing the surface to paint. The body was sitting up on blocks and looked to be free of rust and dents. The four tires were placed on top of the car to keep them from rotting.

Amanda looked through the driver's window. "Hey,

Grandpa Jake...there're no seats in here!" She carefully opened the door, halfway afraid it would fall off in her hands. "Look! I think that's the key, hanging from the rear view mirror!"

Jacob opened the passenger door so he and Anna Leigh could look inside. "Well..." he smiled at the excited face of his granddaughter, "I was going to use the trailer to haul some of the old furniture to my shop and refurbish it." He gently patted the top of the car. "But why don't we put the tires on this baby and cart her home? Maybe we could work on her together this summer. What do you say, Peanut?"

Amanda rushed around the car and nearly tackled him with her hug. "Do you mean it, Grandpa? Could we work on it together?"

He ruffled her hair and laughed. "Of course, sweetheart. I think it would be a fun project for the next couple of summers." He turned to his wife. "Well? You get a vote in this too... we'd be using your garage!" he winked at her.

Amanda looked at her with soulful eyes. "Can we, Gramma? Use your garage, I mean? I promise to keep it clean, honest!" She chewed on her bottom lip, waiting for the verdict.

Anna Leigh crossed her arms across her chest, appearing to give the matter great thought. "Hmmm...does this mean you don't want to help me at my office this summer, Mandy?" She couldn't help it. She had to tease the girl a little bit.

Amanda cocked her head thoughtfully. "No, not at all. I could still help you during the week, and then maybe Grandpa and I could work on the car on the weekends?" She peered hopefully at her grandfather.

Both adults burst out laughing. "Oh, honey..." Anna Leigh gasped, "You are so precious! Of course we'll take the car home!" She barely got the words out when Jacob picked her up and spun her around the room. "Jacob! Stop that this instant! You're going to hurt yourself!" But she was laughing all the while.

Amanda looked on with a huge smile. Her grandparents were the greatest. They were always acting like this... And it made her heart ache with sadness, that her own parents didn't have this kind of love. Oh, they cared for each other, in a way;

they just weren't as demonstrative as the wonderful couple in front of her. This was the definition of love. Maybe someday she would find someone who would make her feel like that...she hoped...

Amanda looked over at Lex, who had just drifted off to sleep at the end of her story. *Yeah, maybe I will find that person...* Then she closed her own eyes and dreamed of her grandparents, dusty old cars, and cool summer days.

Chapter
5

Lex woke up at her usual time. *Just once, I wish my internal
alarm had a snooze button.* It was still dark outside, and the
thunderstorm from the previous night had settled down to a more
peaceful rain this morning. She cautiously took a deep breath,
pleased when she only felt an ache and not the sharp stabbing
pains of last night. Lex turned her head and saw Amanda still
peacefully asleep beside her. *Glad she got over the nightmares
and was able to get a good night's sleep.* She took the opportunity to study this sweet young woman. Amanda's face was even
more youthful in sleep. *She looks barely old enough to drive,* she
smiled. Once again the small blonde had reached over during the
night and grasped Lex's arm. She gently pried the hand loose and
then got out of bed. Lex padded quietly into the bathroom, shut-
ting the door behind her. *Might as well let her sleep as long as
possible.* She washed her face and brushed her teeth, then
sneaked downstairs.

Martha was already up puttering around the large kitchen.
Humming to herself, the heavyset housekeeper pulled several
items from the refrigerator and carried them over to the kitchen
counter.

Lex waited until she was directly behind the older woman

before speaking. "Morning, Martha."

"Blast it, Lexie!" The housekeeper whirled around, one hand covering her heart. "You're gonna be the death of me one of these days!" But she was smiling as she raised her hand and cupped the cheek of the tall woman. "How are you feeling this morning, sweetheart?" Truth be known, she had been a little worried last night. The way Lex had looked, she was half-afraid of internal bleeding. But the young rancher looked fine this morning. *In fact, she looks better than she has in a long time,* she mused.

Lex covered the hand on her face with one of her own. Martha was so dear to her. *I wonder if she realizes that? Maybe I should tell her...*

Martha Rollins had been the only maternal figure that Lex could really remember. She did have a brief memory of a beautiful dark-haired woman sitting at the piano in the drawing room, singing to her as she sat next to her on the piano bench. But this woman... this woman raised her. Cleaned her scraped knees, spanked her with a wooden spoon when she misbehaved, and listened to her hopes and dreams as a kid growing up.

When Lex was about eight or nine, the housekeeper had just held her as she cried over the cruel teasing that she had gotten in school. Martha had gently wiped the tears away when the young girl innocently asked, "Why don't I have a momma like the other kids? Am I too bad?"

The plump woman nearly cried herself. "Oh no, sweet child, you had nothing to do with your dear mother passing on. God just needed her, that's all."

Those big blue eyes looked into hers and asked, "Why can't you be my momma?"

Martha hugged the child tight. "Baby, I wish I was." She kissed the child on her dark head. "I love you as if you were my own, and I always will...that's a promise!"

This seemed to make the girl happy, and she leaned up and kissed an ample cheek. "I love you too, Martha." Then she climbed off the now teary-eyed housekeeper's lap and scampered back outside to play.

Lex snaked her long arms around the shocked housekeeper. "You know, Martha, I don't think I've told you lately that I love you..." She felt the older woman take a deep breath, and then return the hug. "Thanks for being here for me. I do love you, you know." She leaned down and kissed the graying head. Lex pulled back and saw tears springing up in Martha's deep brown eyes. "So... is that fresh coffee I smell?"

The older woman patted her gently on the stomach and bustled over to the stove to begin breakfast. "Of course it is...help yourself, sweetie."

****

Amanda woke a short time later, feeling completely rested. *Oh wow...I can't believe I fell asleep in here last night. I hope Lex didn't mind.* She looked around the room to see that the older woman was conspicuously absent. *Now where has she wandered off to?* Then the aroma of coffee and sausage assailed her senses. *Ah ha! I think I know where she might be!* She climbed out of bed and wandered back to the guestroom bathroom to wash her face, brush her teeth, and comb her hair. Feeling more human now, she jogged down the staircase, following the enticing smells of breakfast.

In the kitchen, Lex was sitting at a small round table talking with Martha, who was busy at the stove. "Good morning!" Amanda warbled, walking over to the counter where the coffeepot sat.

Martha turned around and smiled. "Good morning to you too, dear. Cups are in the cabinet above the coffeepot," she added, correctly guessing the young blonde's quest. "Are you ready for breakfast? Hope you like scrambled eggs, sausage, biscuits and gravy." She grinned at the blonde's surprised look. "I was just about to send Lexie up to fetch you." She turned around and resumed her cooking.

Amanda filled her cup and leaned over it with a sigh. "Mmmm... that smells great. Is there anything I can do to help?"

Lex raised an eyebrow, waiting for the older woman to attack. *Uh-oh...should have warned her about how territorial*

Martha is in her kitchen.

But to her complete amazement, the housekeeper smiled. "Well, you can get the plates and silverware that are on the counter and take them to the table for me, if you want." She turned back to the stove, purposely ignoring the sputtering noises coming from the table.

"Whaaat??? You never let me help you!" Lex cried indignantly.

Amanda carried the dishes to the table and casually set three places. "Maybe you just never asked the right way," she teased with an innocent look on her face.

Martha laughed as she started placing platters and bowls of food on the table. "Now calm down, Lexie...you've got enough to do around here without helping me out in the kitchen." A mischievous grin split her face. "Besides, don't you remember what happened the last time you tried to cook?" Lex blushed, and looked down silently at the plate in front of her.

Amanda looked on; charmed by this new facet to a woman she was quickly becoming attached to. "Oh?"

Lex mumbled something, but didn't look up.

Martha patted her shoulder, then sat down in the chair next to her. "Oh my... that had to be what? Twelve or thirteen years ago?" She looked at the rancher for confirmation.

Lex nodded, wanting to be anywhere else but this kitchen at this time.

Amanda looked at Martha with a curious gaze. "Oh please...share." She smiled at Lex, who rolled her eyes in disbelief.

They all began filling their plates as Martha began her story. "I guess little Lexie was fifteen or sixteen, then." Lex nodded in resigned agreement. "She wanted to do something special for me...I believe it was Mother's Day, wasn't it honey?"

Lex took a deep breath and sighed. "Yeah..."

Martha smiled, and continued, "Why she decided on cooking, when she *hated* working in the kitchen, was beyond me..."

The subject of the story quietly interrupted, "I just thought that since you had to cook for everyone else all the time, someone should cook for you for a change."

The housekeeper nodded. "Ah, so that's it... anyway, she must have spent half the night in here, trying to make pancakes," she chuckled. "The little imp couldn't find a recipe for pancakes, so she used a cake recipe instead."

"Well...they're called pan-cakes, aren't they?" Lex defended herself.

Amanda covered her mouth to keep from laughing, her eyes twinkling. "Oh, no..."

Martha nodded, smiling. "Oh yes... she must have used ten different pans, and flour was everywhere."

Lex tried to explain. "They never said how hard it was to mix all those different things together..." she shrugged. "I thought you had to use an egg per pancake."

Martha laughed out loud. "By the time I got up to fix breakfast, Hurricane Lexie had completely demolished the kitchen. I opened the door, and sitting on the countertop trying to wipe dough off the cabinets, was this powdered apparition... she looked so sad..."

"I was trying to get the mess cleaned up before you got up..." Lex smiled, remembering. "But it took me most of the morning – I just knew Dad was gonna whip me for sure over that mess." She looked to Martha for confirmation. "You talked him out of it, didn't you?"

Martha smiled fondly, her eyes misty. "Yes, I did. Your daddy never did understand why you did it...It was just about the nicest thing anyone ever did for me."

A pained look crossed the rancher's face. *Oh yeah, he understood.* She remembered the conversation with her father the week before Mother's Day.

"I want to do something special for Martha for Mother's Day, Dad," an eager Lex told her father as they were cleaning out stalls.

"What?" He dropped the shovel he was using and walked over to her. *"Why?"*

"Because I want to," she answered, confused. *"What's wrong with that?"*

He grabbed her shoulders. "She's not your mother!" he

yelled, getting right up in her face.

"She is as far as I'm concerned," the defiant teenager growled back.

Rawson looked at his daughter closely. He was not a tall man, only five-foot-nine, and his girl was already taller than he was. Must have gotten that from Victoria's side of the family. The dark good looks and magnetic blue eyes all came from Victoria. Pity she got my temperament.   "She's the damn housekeeper!" He put his hands on her shoulders and shook her.

Lex angrily brushed off his hands. "Don't talk about her that way!"

He pulled his arm back and slapped her face, hard. "Don't take that tone with me, girl."

They both froze. Rawson had NEVER raised a hand to his daughter. Sure, when she was younger, a spanking once in a blue moon, but he had never struck any of his children in anger.

She held her hand to her cheek, a bruise already forming. "Don't you...ever...do that again," she whispered, her cobalt eyes flashing. "And," she stood in his face, "never...speak about Martha that way again, or so help me..." she paused, her entire body trembling, "I WILL make you regret it!" She spun around and walked out of the barn.

After that, Rawson avoided his daughter. She never knew if it was out of shame for his actions, or out of fear of what his headstrong daughter might do. All she knew was a little over a year later Rawson Walters left the Rocking W, and never looked back.

Lex felt a warm hand on her wrist. "Hey...what's wrong?" Amanda could see a flash of pain in those azure eyes. Lex blinked and the look was gone.

"Huh?" *Snap out of it...that's old history...* "Sorry...guess I'm just not completely awake yet." She gave the young woman a small smile.

Amanda decided to let it go. "Hmmm...maybe you should go back to bed, then."

Lex shook her head and stood up. "Can't. Gotta go down to the barn and feed the horses, take some hay to the cattle in the far field, then do a quick fence check." She carried her plate over to the sink, her look challenging Martha to say something.

Martha watched Lex's act of defiance. *I know that she's just trying to get a rise out of me. Brat! I should ...* Then she noticed Amanda's face. *Hmmm... or maybe I'll just let this little one take care of her. Heh.*

"Whaat?" The small blonde leapt out of her chair. "You should be resting, not out gallivanting around in the rain!" She picked up her plate and deposited it in the sink.

Lex looked at her with a fond smile. "I'm fine this morning. Besides, I'm the only person here that can do all of that. You don't want the stock to go hungry, do you?"

Amanda chewed on her lower lip. "Well..." she started, then she shook her head. "Of course not. But I'll go with you to help...no arguments, okay?"

The tall woman laughed. "Okay...but I think we'd both better get dressed first. It's kinda cool out this morning." She looked Amanda over critically. "I think I can find some clothes to fit you, if you don't mind wearing boys' clothes."

"Hey, if they're warm, I don't care." The younger woman put her hands on her hips. "Just as long as you don't laugh at me anymore...I don't think your ribs could handle it!"

Lex shook her head. "Nah, I won't laugh...think I was just overtired last night." She started towards the doorway and stopped. "You coming?"

Amanda smiled at Martha, who was still seated at the table. "Thanks for breakfast. Are you sure I can't help with the dishes or something?"

The older woman made a shooing motion with her hands. "No, get out of here and try to make Lexie behave herself this morning. I've got this all under control."

Once they were upstairs, Lex steered Amanda to a door down at the end of the hall. The rancher took a deep breath and opened the door. Flipping on the light switch, she moved into the room, with Amanda a few steps behind her.

It looked like an adolescent boy's room. There was a twin bed against one wall, and a built-in bookcase with model cars and airplanes decorating it. There was also a small desk with a reading lamp sitting on top. The walls were adorned with posters of airplanes and horses, and a ragged baseball cap hung silently on a hook by the bed. Amanda looked at Lex. She was staring at the cap, a faraway look in her eyes. Lex shook her head and walked over to the closet door. Pulling out some faded jeans and a flannel shirt, she turned to Amanda and smiled slightly.

"These should fit you just fine. You're about the same size." She took a deep breath. "Don't think I can find you any shoes, though...you'll probably have to make do with yours."

Amanda ached at the pain lurking in those blue eyes. "That's okay. Are you sure it's all right that I wear this?" She had to stop herself from reaching out and giving the tall woman a hug. *She looks so sad...I wonder why?* "Whose clothes are these?"

Lex took a couple more pairs of jeans out of the closet, along with several shirts. She opened the top drawer of a small dresser and mechanically got out several pairs of socks. The dark-haired woman took in a shaky breath and sank down heavily on the bed. "This was my younger brother Louis' room. He...he died nine years ago."

Amanda rushed over to the bed and sat down next to Lex, gently grasping her hand. "I'm sorry..."

The older woman shook her head. "Martha still cleans his room...I know I should pack this stuff up, but..." she closed her eyes. "I've completely remodeled the entire second floor of this house, but I can't bring myself to destroy..." her voice faded to a whisper, "the only thing I have left of Lou..." Silent tears tracked down her face.

They both sat quietly for a few minutes, Amanda just lending her support to Lex, who wiped at her face with her hand. "Sorry...must still be tired from yesterday. I don't normally..."

Amanda squeezed her hand, placing her other arm around Lex and giving her a small hug. "Don't apologize...are you sure you want me to wear these clothes? Martha has cleaned my shirt and jeans..."

Lex shook her head. "No. You'll be more comfortable in these...Besides, I think he would have loved to have shared with you." She stood, pulling Amanda up with their still-linked hands. "C'mon... I'm gonna show you how to run a ranch."

****

"So…" Amanda asked, trying to keep up with Lex's long legs, "Just how big is this ranch of yours, anyway?" She adjusted the hood on the raincoat she was wearing, another 'hand-me down', this time from Lex.

The rancher adjusted the black hat on her head. "It's a little over six thousand acres. I've been slowly building it up over the past few years." She turned to talk to the other woman. Lex stopped when she realized Amanda was quite a few steps behind, puffing to catch up. "Why didn't you ask me to slow down?" she asked as Amanda caught up to her.

The little blonde smiled sheepishly. "I didn't want to bother you. I just kinda forced myself on you this morning." She tried to look down at her shoes, but a strong hand gently tilted her chin up.

"You are not a bother, and with my ribs like this, you will most definitely be a big help to me." She wrapped a companionable arm around Amanda's shoulders. "C'mon. I'll introduce you to my friends."

Lex led them down a clean concrete breezeway that divided the large barn. About half of the twenty stalls were vacant, which seemed odd to Amanda. Lex noticed the question in the young blonde's eyes. "I've been trying to gradually phase out the cattle and make this a 'horses only' ranch," she explained, as she opened the door where the feed was kept.

Amanda followed her in, fascinated by all the sights and sounds around her. "Are these all the horses you have?" she asked, as the other woman opened a large barrel and pulled out a bucket of grain. "Well, these are the *working* horses." She handed the container to Amanda and filled another one from the barrel. "The rest of the horses are in one of the far pastures. We bring in a few at a time, break them, then take them to the auction to sell." She led the small blonde back into the main part of the barn. Lex dumped her bucket into a trough in front of one of the stalls. Amanda pointed to the next occupied one, received a nod, and followed suit. They repeated this procedure until all ten horses were fed.

"Okay, boss," Amanda brushed her hands off, "what's next on the agenda?"

Lex laughed and pulled her gloves out of the pocket of the duster. She walked to the back of the barn to a door which led outside. "Next," she held the door open for her companion, "we go to the hay barn and take the cattle and the other horses their breakfast." She pointed to another building about twenty yards away.

The rain had slowed down to a slight drizzle by the time they reached the large structure. Lex opened the large double doors and waited for Amanda to precede her.

"Wow! This place is huge!" There were stacks of hay bales that almost reached the ceiling in some places. A large battered blue pickup truck sat alone in the middle of the room. Amanda flipped the hood off her head and looked towards the tall woman. "Now what?" She followed the rancher to the far side of the truck.

Lex got in on the driver's side. "Just let me back this up to the hay, and we'll get started loading." The truck rumbled to life, and Lex quickly put it in reverse and slowly rolled it back towards the hay. She parked the old vehicle in position. The tall woman grabbed another pair of gloves, slipped out from behind the wheel, and moved to the rear of the truck. Dropping the tailgate down, Lex climbed into the back and grinned. "Well? You gonna stand there all morning, or are you gonna help?" she teased as she tossed the extra gloves to the smiling blonde.

Amanda slipped the gloves on and jumped up into the rear of the truck beside Lex. "I'm here...what do you want me to do?"

Lex pulled off her duster and laid it over the side of the truck, leaving her in a dark blue tee shirt. Amanda couldn't help but notice the play of muscles along her back before she straightened up and turned around. "We need to load up the truck with bales of hay, then take it over to the next pasture."

She was about to grab one of the bales when a gentle hand grasped her arm. "Do you think it's wise for you to be hefting these things around?"

Lex shrugged. "Not much choice, Amanda. With all this

rain, we gotta make sure that the cattle have enough to eat. Otherwise, they have a tendency to knock down the fence looking for something to munch on." She quirked an eyebrow at the young woman. "And I've already had my quota of fence building this week."

Amanda smiled and removed her hand. "At least let me help you." She grabbed the other side of the bale Lex had her hands on, and together they pulled it into the truck. "See? That wasn't so hard, was it?"

Lex shook her head and grinned. She hated to admit it, but the young woman really *was* a big help. *I don't think my ribs would appreciate me tossing these around like I usually do, anyway.* "No, but you may be singing a different song by the time we get finished today."

Amanda gave a slight frown. "I'm a lot stronger than I look, you know." She reached for another bundle of hay.

Lex stopped her with a hand on her shoulder. "I'm sorry, I didn't mean anything by it...I just don't want you to hurt yourself." She looked a little lost. "I really do appreciate all the help...I don't think that I could have done it by myself today."

Amanda reached up and wrapped her hand around Lex's arm. "I'm sorry, too. I guess I've spent so long trying to prove myself that getting defensive about my size is second nature to me now. You're the only person besides my grandparents who has actually believed in me." She reached for the bale. "So...are we going to stand here chatting all day, or are we going to get those animals fed?"

Lex smiled and helped her drag the bale down to the bed of the truck.

The rain started up again in earnest after they unloaded the last of the hay. Both women hurried back into the truck, heaving a great sigh of relief to finally be out of the weather. Lex leaned back in the seat and closed her eyes. "How much longer is this damned rain gonna last?" she sighed, taking a moment to catch her breath. She wasn't going to tell Amanda, but her ribs were really beginning to bother her again.

Amanda pushed the hood off her head. "I know what you mean. I keep expecting to see the animals begin pairing up."

The dark woman stifled a small laugh. "Yeah...and at this rate, we may want to book passage for ourselves, as well." She turned her head and opened her eyes. "Thanks again for all the help. I'd probably still be piling hay in the truck if you weren't here."

The blonde blushed. "Well, I thought I'd better begin to earn my keep somehow," she smiled. "What's next on the program?" *Hopefully lunch figures in pretty soon...I'm starving!* Her stomach agreed and took the opportunity to announce itself.

Lex raised an eyebrow at her. "Well..." she drawled, enjoying the blush on her companion's face, "I was going to suggest lunch, but I didn't know if you were hungry or not." She smirked, as Amanda's blush deepened. "Besides, Martha gets kinda upset if I'm late – and I don't want her to break any more spoons." She sat up and started the truck.

Chapter
6

Lex and Amanda came in through the mudroom again and hung up their soggy raingear. They had rinsed their feet off outside, trying to stay on Martha's good side. As they stepped into the kitchen, the housekeeper turned around and put her hands on her hips. "I'm so glad you're back, Lexie...your brother called, and he's in some sort of tizzy...wants you to give him a call as soon as possible." She shook her head. "Didn't even ask how you were, just demanded that you call."

Lex's jaw clenched. "Was he rude to you again, Martha?" She remembered the last time she saw Hubert here at the house.

He had come out to the ranch about some minor thing. Hubert had sat down in Lex's office and demanded that the housekeeper 'fetch' him some coffee. After she had brought it, he took a sip and yelled. "Where's the cream and sugar? Can't you do anything right, old woman?" Unfortunately for him, Lex happened to walk in at just that moment. She stalked over to the desk and pulled him over it by his neck. "You sonofabitch! Apologize before I snap your worthless head off!!" Martha had to forcibly pull her away, or she would have surely done just that.

Martha shook her graying head. "No, honey, he wasn't. I

think you scared him out of all good sense the last time." She looked over at Amanda, who seemed a little confused. "C'mon, dear. You can help me set the table for lunch."

Amanda gave her a grateful smile. "Sure. Just let me go upstairs and clean up a little." She looked back at Lex, who smiled and nodded.

"Go on. I'll go into the office and get that phone call out of the way." She shook her head as the small blonde left. "Did Hubert give you any clue as to why he called?"

The older woman sat down on a nearby stool. "Yes. I just didn't want to get into it while Amanda was here...she's such a sweet thing." She paused, gathering her thoughts. "He said his old friend Rick called him -" she wrinkled her brow in distaste "- and told him Amanda would be staying out here for a while." She paused, seeing the rancher suddenly go pale. "Apparently Mrs. Cauble had called him to let him know that Amanda wouldn't be at work for a week or so." She could see Lex visibly trembling now as she fought to control her anger.

"Amanda works for Rick?" Lex questioned quietly.

Martha nodded. "Yes. Didn't she..." Here she paused. "Oh, that's right. You were asleep when we talked about that last night. Seems that Ricky thought it would be fun to send Amanda out here on a wild goose chase."

That explains a lot of things. "Okay, that makes sense. I'll deal with him later." *She could have been killed because of his pettiness — Bastard!* "So, what's Hubert's problem?" She took a deep breath to calm down.

Martha was almost afraid to say what Hubert had 'related' to her. But she had never lied to Lex, and wasn't about to begin now. "He said he didn't want a repeat of the 'Linda fiasco'." She held her breath as she waited for the eruption. But it didn't happen. Martha looked into Lex's eyes and saw quiet defeat there. *Oh, no...please don't give up, Lexie...that's what he wants.*

Lex sighed. "Okay. Thanks Martha. I'll just go give him a call and get it over with." She left the room without another word.

Amanda met her in the hallway. "Hey, 'bout ready for some lunch?"

The older woman stopped and turned. She looked pale and drawn. "I'm really not all that hungry right now. You and Martha go ahead, I've got to call my brother back." She turned and continued down the hall.

The small blonde looked after her quizzically. "Okay." She continued into the kitchen, where Martha was busy at the stove. "Martha? Is Lex all right?" She walked over to the counter and picked up three plates and some silverware. "I just saw her in the hall, and she wasn't looking very good."

Martha shook her head. "No dear, she's not. That older brother of hers has always been a thorn in her side...he's always resented the fact that Rawson put her in charge of the ranch instead of him – after all, he's seven years older than she is. And he has always used that guilt to get her to do whatever he wants."

****

Lex closed the office door behind her and let out a deep breath. *Might as well get this over with.* She sat behind the heavy oak desk and dialed the number for the house in town.

She had signed the house in town over to Hubert several years ago and made him move out of the ranch completely. He really didn't mind since all he really liked about the ranch was the money it gave him. He was much happier in town with all his 'friends' – men like himself that usually spent the majority of their time harassing women and jumping into one 'get-rich' scheme after another.

Using the trust fund that her mother had set up for her, Lex began remodeling the ranch house. She combined Hubert's old room with hers to make a large guestroom, and another spare bedroom had been annexed to the master bedroom to almost double its size. She tried to move Martha into the renovated guestroom, but soon realized she was fighting a losing battle. "It's not my place, Lexie...I just can't," Martha had argued. Instead, Lex had a cottage built just away from the main house. She deeded it and twenty acres to the completely surprised housekeeper.

Hubert was furious that Lex had given the housekeeper the land just east of the main house. He had never liked the older woman whom he felt was supposed to be a replacement for his mother. Hubert had been eleven when Martha came to work for them. She had to assume the household duties for Victoria, who had been bedridden five months into her pregnancy. He resented the heavyset woman for taking his beloved mother's place in the home, and also because young Lexington immediately adored her. After Victoria died in childbirth, the young girl tied herself to Martha's apron strings. Lex's treatment of Martha as a surrogate mother caused even more bad feelings between the already volatile siblings. Little Louis had worshipped the housekeeper and called her Mada. The smiling woman treated both of the younger children as if they were her own.

Lex sighed as she waited for Hubert to pick up the phone. On the fourth ring, he finally answered.

"Hubert Walters..." his somewhat nasal voice intoned.

"Yeah, Hubert...this is Lex. You wanted to talk to me?" She picked up the letter opener on the desk and casually began to clean her fingernails.

"'Bout damn time you called..." he complained. "Or did your 'maid' forget to give you my message?" he asked, trying to anger her.

"Yeah, Martha gave me the message some time ago," she lied, "but I was busy." *Two can play this game, Hube ol' boy.*

"Busy? Doing what? Playing with your new little 'friend'?" he sneered. "That's what I was calling about...I don't want you dragging our family name through the mud again."

Lex clutched the phone with an iron grip. She swore she could almost hear it moan under the pressure. "You bastard..." she growled.

Hubert laughed humorlessly. "What was the little trollop's name? Lulu?...no...Loretta?... nah... oh, yeah, Linda! That was her name, wasn't it?"

"You know what her name was, Hubert...she dumped *you*, didn't she?" Lex couldn't help the jibe.

"Oh, yeah...but that's okay, 'cause she played for the other team. Was she good in the sack, Lex?"

Creak. Lex looked at the stainless steel letter opener she had just bent in half with one hand. "I never heard her complain, but you wouldn't know anything about that, would you Hube?"

The older man realized that he had pushed his sister just about as far as he dared. "Okay, okay. Look... I just don't want your libido to get you into trouble again."

"What the hell are you talking about, Hubert?" Lex stood up and searched around for something to throw.

"Aw, c'mon, Lex. Rick told me she's a cutie. She must be *one* like you, 'cause she wouldn't even go out with him."

Lex laughed. "All that proves is she has good taste! Why is it if a woman isn't interested, men automatically think she has to be gay?"

Her brother wasn't so easily dissuaded. "C'mon, Lex – the little tart won't socialize with anyone from the office...just spends all her time with those two old farts."

Lex saw red. "Now you listen to me, Hubert – you will *not* speak of her *or* the Caubles that way...they're good folks. A lot better than that riff-raff you run around with." She paused to let her words sink in. "*And,*" in a very low voice, "if I hear of you even *thinking* badly of any of them, I *will* make you regret the day you were born...*Ya got that?*" She slammed down the phone before he could reply. The walls began to close in on her. *Gotta get out of here for a while...* the angry rancher stomped down the hallway and out through the door.

****

They sat together at the table in silence and ate their lunch. Lex was conspicuously absent, although they could hear her raised voice boom through the house from time to time. They heard bootsteps thud down the hallway and then the back door slammed shut. Both jumped up from the table and hurried over to the window in time to see a tall figure walking quickly through the yard. Lex went into the barn, and a few moments later left again with her tall form riding astride a beautiful black stallion. Horse and rider quickly disappeared into the falling rain.

"Oh dear. He must have really upset her. She never rides Thunder unless she's going to ride really hard." Martha shook her head and stepped away from the window. "C'mon honey. Let's get these dishes cleaned up, and then we'll sit and visit for a spell. She's probably gone to check the fence by the creek again."

Amanda allowed the older woman to lead her away from the window. *Please be careful...* she sent her thoughts after the angry rancher.

Lex and Thunder rode hard for about thirty minutes, until she could feel the great beast begin to tire. *Old boy, I'm gonna have to get you out more often.* She also felt the need to slow down due to the complaints she was getting from her own body. *Not the smartest thing you could have done, Lexington.* They had ridden across the winter rye fields, and then through the stand of trees she and Amanda had walked through last night. She pulled the horse to a stop before they got to the road. *No sense in getting either one of us hurt in this damned mud.*

As she looked at the fallen tree and halfway flipped jeep, Lex was surprised that they weren't both seriously injured. The jeep itself was leaning precariously on three wheels with the top of the tree sitting almost on top of it. *Whoa...that was a close one!* She reined the horse back towards the creek. *Might as well see that in the daylight, too.*

The old bridge was not in as bad of shape as Lex as previously feared. Only the middle section was gone, so it probably would not take that long to repair. She looked downstream and saw the tail of the little Mustang sticking up out of the water. *Hmm...* An idea began to form in her mind. Lex turned Thunder around and headed back towards the house. *Got some planning to do...*

****

"....And then she hands me this piece of paper and says, 'Happy Birthday, Martha.' I tell you, I was never so surprised in my life. She even had me pick out everything to decorate it with. It sure was a big change from that little room in the back." The older woman wiped her eyes. She had just told Amanda how Lex had surprised her with the deed to her little cottage, where they were now drinking coffee. Martha thought it was the best place to wait for the rancher. They could sit in her living room and look out through the huge picture window towards the main house and barn.

Amanda and Martha had spent the afternoon getting to know each other better. Amanda had told the older woman about her grandparents. She also shared some of her favorite memories from her childhood, including the story about the summer they found her car. That sparked a small burst of tears when she realized that it was probably miles downstream by now. Martha had related several humorous stories about Lex, and how hard it was to raise a girl on a ranch full of men. She also told of the sad young girl who never fit in at home or at school, and how she slowly closed herself off from the pain of being different, and the loneliness of running a ranch.

"My grandmother said that Lex was about the sweetest person she had ever met. How did she get involved in the historical society?" Amanda had been wondering about this since her talk with Anna Leigh last night.

Martha laughed. "Actually, Lex did it mostly out of spite, at least at first." At Amanda's confused look, she continued, "Hubert had been really nasty towards all of us here at the ranch. He had decided to become a big real estate developer. So, he had picked out the old Taylor house, and he was going to buy it and level it ...wanted to turn it into a shopping center or some such nonsense. Anyway, Lex had gone into town to get the cast taken off her arm..."

"What??" Amanda gasped.

"Oh, she broke it instead of one of the horses..." She chuckled at the memory, and pushed her hair out of her eyes. "Where was I? Ah, yes. She was coming out of the doctor's office and nearly tripped over your grandmother, who was hanging up a sign in the window. She was chairing a meeting of the historical society that evening to discuss the historical significance of Loren Taylor's old house. Lex read the sign and asked Mrs. Cauble about the meeting. Then after she had gone to the meeting, she decided that it was important from a historical standpoint, not just as an excuse to get back at her brother. And now she tries to help out whenever they need her. I think Mrs. Cauble uses her as 'muscle' to keep some of the more vindictive dissenters from harassing the ladies of the society, but I think Lex actually enjoys it," she smiled. "You should see her in her boots and jeans at one of their little tea parties. I don't know who has more fun, Lexie or the ladies. It's really a sight to behold. She's even hosted a couple out here, trying to get me interested."

Amanda giggled at the mental picture of Lex's dark good looks in a dainty tea party setting. She could just see the ladies with their fancy dresses and pearls, and Lex with her denim jeans and flannel shirt. "Oh, I bet that's a riot!" she laughed. "My grandmother had invited me to their meetings before, but I was afraid I'd be the only one there under sixty!" she laughed again. "Wish I would have taken her up on the invite... maybe I would have met you and Lex sooner."

The older woman smiled. "I don't know. Sometimes things are just meant to happen a certain way." She looked through the window. "And I think we should get back to the main house. Lexie just took Thunder back into the barn...she'll be awhile brushing him down." She stood and took her coffee cup into the kitchen with Amanda hot on her heels.

****

Lex walked out of the barn and looked at the house. *I've got a load of explaining to do when I walk through that door...* It had been over two hours since she stormed out of the house. The tall rancher was...nervous. *What do I say to her?* Lex continued walking as she silently berated herself for her childish actions. *Running out of the house like my tail was on fire... real adult, Lexington.* Martha would probably swat her with a spoon, and Amanda...*Oh, boy... I can't believe I just took off like that...*She slowly opened the back door and stepped inside. Hearing voices coming from the kitchen, Lex took a deep breath and slinked in.

Martha and Amanda were sitting at the table drinking coffee, and looked up when they heard bootsteps in the hall. "Did you have a good ride, dear?" Martha asked as she bustled over to the stove to get Lex's lunch. "I kept your plate warm, just in case." She turned and looked at Lex, who had the most confused look on her face. *I do so love keeping her off balance.* "Now you go upstairs and get some dry clothes on, and I'll have your lunch ready." When the younger woman opened her mouth to argue, Martha put her foot down. "Don't argue with me, Lexington Marie...you've spent way too much time out in the elements the past couple of days, and I don't want you adding pneumonia to your other ills." She shook a chubby finger in her direction. "Now git!"

Lex looked over at Amanda. The blonde had her hand over her mouth to stifle a giggle. She quirked a sardonic brow the young woman's way, then turned and left the kitchen.

"Oh, Martha...you are absolutely vicious!" the small blonde laughed, unable to hold back her mirth. "The look on her face..."

Martha smiled and resumed her seat at the table. "She really is like an overgrown child, sometimes. I know she was expecting to get yelled at, so..." she shook her head. "She's already whipped herself about storming off, and I know her brother can be such an ass..." She picked up the carafe from the center of the table and refilled their mugs. "She was always tougher on herself than I ever had to be."

Minutes later they heard Lex's footsteps on the stairs. Martha set a plate piled high with food at the empty space at the table just as the tall woman walked in. "Sit down and eat...don't let your lunch get cold." As the rancher silently took her place, Martha stopped and placed a gentle kiss on the top of her head. "Now I expect you to eat every bite of that, young lady!" She patted her shoulder and moved towards the doorway. "I've got some chores to do, so I'll see the two of you later." She left the room humming to herself.

Lex pushed the food around on her plate. "I'm sorry for running out like that earlier." She glanced up at the young woman beside her. "I just needed to get out for a while, and I wanted to check the fence down by the creek to see if my patch job held up."

Amanda smiled. *Martha was right. She is like an overgrown kid. Cute.* "That's okay. Martha and I had a good chat...she really is a wonderful person." She looked at Lex's plate. "But she might come back and throw a fit if you don't eat your lunch..." Amanda smiled. "So how's the fence?"

Lex took a bite of food and nodded. "The fence is fine. And the bridge looks like only the middle is gone, so it shouldn't be too hard to fix. 'Course I'll have to check the supports and make sure they weren't knocked loose." She continued to eat. *I hope she doesn't ask about her car. I've got to get Martha to help keep her occupied while...*

"How are your ribs? All that riding couldn't have made them feel any better," Amanda questioned, knowing that the rancher had probably pushed herself to the limit today.

"Hmm?" Lex was knocked out of her musings when the young blonde laid a gentle hand on her arm. "Ribs?" She swallowed another bite. "Oh. Ribs. Right," she smiled. "A little sore, but not too bad."

Amanda gave Lex a light squeeze on her arm. "So, what do you have planned for the rest of the afternoon?" She took a sip of her coffee. "Is there something I can help with?"

Lex finished her lunch, not even realizing she had been hungry until she had begun to eat. "Well," she leaned back in her chair, "I thought we'd take it easy for the rest of the day." She interlocked her hands and laid them on her stomach. "It's too muddy to do anything outside, and there's not much else to do. Besides, we've got a large collection of movies in the den...and I just recently finished wiring the surround sound system. Been wanting to try it out." She stood up and carried her dishes to the sink.

"Sounds like a plan to me." Amanda took her cup and sat it in the sink as well.

Lex looked around, then ran hot water in the sink. She looked to the younger woman and grinned. "Shhh..." she placed a finger to her lips, "I just gotta tweak Martha somehow." She stuck her hands in the now soapy water.

Amanda bumped her with a hip. "Scoot over...I'll rinse and dry. No sense in you having all the fun!"

They made quick work of the dishes, and had just put them away when Martha came into the room. "What are you two up to?" she asked, as both younger women spun around and looked extremely guilty.

Amanda hid the dishtowel on the counter behind her back. "Who? Us?"

Lex smirked. "Nothing, Martha. We were just going to go into the den and watch movies...you interested?" She walked towards the housekeeper to block the view of the sink.

Martha reached up and checked her forehead. "What's the matter? Are you not feeling well?" *She never takes the day off. I wonder why?*

The tall woman grabbed Martha's hand and held it in her own. "I'm fine. It's just too nasty to do any work outside, and I thought Amanda would enjoy the break." She pulled the older woman into a surprise hug. "You care to join us?"

Martha returned the hug. *She sure is touchy-feely lately... Not that I'm complaining.* "No thank you, honey. If you're going to relax today, I think I'll go over to my place and get some things done, if it's all right with you."

Lex stepped back. "Martha, you don't have to ask me if you want to do something – you know that."

The heavier woman smiled. "I know you say that, dear...but you run this ranch, and I respect that."

Lex thought about that. "Not exactly."

The graying head snapped up. "What do you mean by that?"

Lex motioned for Amanda to follow her out of the kitchen. "You're the one that runs this house, Martha...I just work the ranch." She stepped out behind the small blonde before Martha could say another word. Just as they reached the entry to the den they heard, "Lexington Marie Walters!!! I'm gonna take my spoon to your backside!!!"

They looked at each other and smiled. Lex led Amanda into the den. One corner was filled with a massive fireplace. *What is it with these folks and fireplaces?* A huge entertainment center with a big screen TV took up an entire wall. There was a large comfortable looking leather sofa with a heavy oak coffee table in front of it, and leather plush chairs on either side of the sofa. Lex pointed Amanda to another wall where a bookcase full of video-tapes and CDs awaited her perusal. "Go on...pick us out something to watch. I'll go beg Martha's forgiveness, and nab some sodas and popcorn."

Amanda wandered to the bookcase, in awe at the selection of videos. *Comedy or drama?* She smiled when she saw that the movies were grouped alphabetically, except some that were grouped by series. *Mel Brooks? She has the entire collection of Mel Brooks??* she laughed. *Indiana Jones, Die Hard, Star Trek...someone's an action junkie...* She continued to browse through the titles, looking for something lighthearted. *Sleepless in Seattle? While You Were Sleeping? Hmmm..... Ah! A Fish Called Wanda... I love that movie!!* She pulled the tape from its allocated spot, and set it on the coffee table.

Lex walked into the room with a tray loaded with goodies. "Hope you like butter on your popcorn." She sat the tray on the coffee table. "Did you find something to your liking?" She noticed the tape on the table and picked it up. "Ah...that's one of my favorites." Lex took the tape and crossed the room to the entertainment center, placing the tape into the VCR. She grabbed the remote control from atop the TV and sat down on the sofa next to Amanda. "I figured we could just set the bowl between us and share." She looked at the younger woman uncertainly. "I brought some extra bowls if you'd rather..."

Amanda scooted closer to her and grinned. "There's no sense in dirtying up more dishes. Unless you think we can get away with washing these too?"

Lex shook her head. "Uh-uh...I'm lucky to have escaped the kitchen with my rear intact as it is!" She mock shivered.

Amanda barely bit back a giggle. "Was she really angry?"

The older woman leaned back and propped her sock covered feet on the coffee table. "Nah...but she did threaten." Lex turned on the TV and surround speakers with the remote control and looked over at Amanda. "Might as well take your shoes off and get comfortable." The smaller woman grinned and complied. She put her feet up next to Lex's and settled back to enjoy the movie.

Martha went in search of the two a couple of hours later. There was no sound coming from the den, and the only light was that of the fireplace. She peeked inside the door and saw Lex slumped back against the sofa sound asleep with her feet propped on the coffee table. *Well, at least she wasn't wearing boots this time,* the housekeeper sighed to herself. But the biggest surprise was her companion. Amanda was curled up against the rancher asleep. Her head was pillowed on a broad shoulder and her arm was wrapped tightly around the dark woman's waist. Lex had her arm gently over Amanda's shoulders with her head leaning up against the blonde's. Martha smiled, then tiptoed back to the kitchen to begin dinner.

Amanda woke a little later, somewhat disoriented. She was warm and quite comfortable until she realized where she was. Amanda thought about getting up, but when she glanced at the woman still sleeping next to her, she didn't have the heart to disturb her. *She looks so tired.* The young woman was still studying her companion when she felt the arm around her tighten.

Blue eyes blinked open, looking for a moment as confused as Amanda had upon wakening. Lex quickly removed her arm. "Ummm...I'm sorry about that..." She struggled to sit up. "I didn't mean..." Lex looked a little panicky.

Amanda smiled, and gently patted her stomach. "Don't worry about it – I kinda climbed all over you like you were my own personal mattress." She sat up and stretched. "That was a good nap, though."

Lex cautiously stretched as well. "Yeah, it was. Guess I was still pretty tired from last night."

Amanda looked at the clock on the wall. "Me too. It's early evening, don'tcha think?"

Lex gave her a puzzled look. "Yeah, I guess so. Why?"

"Well, if it's okay with you, I'd like to call my grandparents and see how they're doing."

The older woman stood up and smiled. "You don't have to ask permission to use the phone." She held out a hand. "C'mon. I'll let you use the one in the office so you'll have some privacy."

Amanda accepted the hand and allowed herself to be pulled up. "Thanks."

Lex escorted the younger woman into the office and around the desk. "Siddown. Just push a button for an outgoing line. We have three lines coming in, but the computer is hooked up to the third." She turned to leave. "Take all the time you need. I'll be in the kitchen harassing Martha." She winked and walked out the door.

Amanda's eyes followed the tall woman out through the doorway as she picked up the phone to call out.

It rang twice before her grandfather answered. "Hello?"

"Grandpa Jake? How are you feeling?"

Jacob released a deep chuckle. "Great, Peanut. We just got back from the movies about twenty minutes ago." He noticed the happy lilt in her voice. "How are *you* doing, sweetheart?"

Amanda let out a happy breath. "I'm doing much better today, Grandpa. I helped Lex feed the horses, and then we took hay to the cattle." She paused, thinking about earlier today. "After lunch we sat down and watched a movie."

He laughed. "Sounds like you've had a busy day."

"Well, not really. I'm trying to keep Lex from overdoing it because of her broken ribs." *Oops! Now how do I explain that?*

Jacob cursed. "Broken ribs?"

Anna Leigh came into the room. "What's the matter, sweetheart? Is that Mandy?" She grabbed another phone. "Mandy? Is everything okay?"

Amanda hid her face in her hand. *Time to bite the bullet, I guess.* "I'm fine. Lex broke a couple of ribs yesterday."

Anna Leigh sighed. "Is she all right?"

"She's sore today, but I think she'll be okay."

"Peanut, how did her ribs get broken? Was she in an accident?" her grandfather asked.

Amanda rubbed her eyes. "Umm...I'll tell you, but you've got to promise to stay calm, okay?"

Both Jacob and Anna Leigh complied. "Okay, sweetheart, go ahead and tell us," Anna Leigh said, taking the cordless phone and perching on the arm of the chair Jacob was sitting in. She took a firm grasp of her husband's hand.

"You remember when I told you I was on my way to Lex's yesterday because of an appointment sheet Rick gave me?" she asked them.

"Yes... And I'm still pretty hacked off at the little turd,"

Anna Leigh grumbled.

Amanda stifled a giggle. "Okay... well, anyway, I followed his directions, and finally found the road to Lex's place. I was crossing the old wooden bridge, when a tree came out of nowhere and crashed right into it!" She paused, unsure if she wanted to go on.

"Go ahead, Peanut... I know it's hard," her grandfather encouraged.

"Umm... the bridge kinda collapsed, and my car fell into the creek." Silence. "I must have hit my head, because the next thing I remember is being tied on Lex's back, and being towed across the creek." She only heard breathing from the other end of the phone, so she continued. "From what I understand, when we were about halfway across the creek Lex was hit by some debris. It slammed into her chest and gave her a nasty gash."

Jacob finally spoke up. "Are you okay? Why didn't you tell us this last night, Peanut?"

"I'm fine...I didn't want you to worry...and I have to admit, I was kinda woozy last night."

Anna Leigh sighed. "Mandy, please don't feel that you have to cushion us from things...I'm just very glad you're all right." She paused. "And Lexington really means a lot to me as well...I'm happy that she's okay, too."

"Thanks, Gramma...she means a lot to me too..." Amanda felt tears tickling her eyes. "She's very special to me..." She had to tell someone how she was feeling. Her grandparents knew she was gay, and had always been very supportive of her. "I only met her yesterday, yet I feel like we've been together forever...do you think it's just misplaced hero worship? She did save me...maybe I'm just crazy."

Jacob chuckled. "Honey, I felt the same way the first time I saw your grandmother. She became my whole world the first time our eyes met..." He kissed the hand he was holding.

Anna Leigh joined in. "That's true, sweetheart. I felt as if we were destined to meet. My mother once said, 'Two old souls meeting again for the first time...' Is this what you felt when you met Lexington?"

Amanda had to tell the truth. "I feel more complete around

her, Gramma."

Anna Leigh laughed. "I know exactly what you mean, dear. Does she know how you feel?"

"Oh, good Lord, no! I'd probably scare her out of ten years!" Amanda gasped.

"I don't think so, sweetheart," Anna Leigh answered.

Amanda was at a loss. "What do you mean by that?"

Jacob, who had been silent so far, chuckled. "Oh, Peanut... I keep forgetting you haven't lived here...Lexington certainly shook up the town gossips a couple of years ago... But I think you should ask her about it." He gave her a minute to think about that. "Let me put it this way...I don't think anything you could say would shock her."

Anna Leigh took over. "True...the poor girl has been through a lot in the past few years... Do you care for her, honey?"

Amanda choked back a sob. "More than I thought possible, Gramma. She's become such a deep part of me in such a short amount of time..."

Her grandmother clucked. "Now you listen to me...I think she's a wonderful person, but she has a tendency not to think that way..."

Jacob spoke up. "Is there anything we can bring to you, Peanut? I'm sure we could find a way to get it across that damn creek."

Amanda laughed out loud. "No, Grandpa Jake...Lex and Martha have made sure I have everything I need. But thanks for asking. I guess I'll let you go now..."

Both grandparents laughed. "Okay, sweetheart, but let us know if you need anything, okay?" Anna Leigh asked. "Give us a call again tomorrow. We'll just be goofing off around the house."

Amanda smiled. "Okay... I love you both... I'll talk to you tomorrow...Goodnight." She hung up the phone, somewhat relieved that she had told them the truth about her accident. *They took that well. Guess since I'm still alive and kicking it didn't sound so bad.*

****

Lex wandered back into the kitchen, a smile still gracing her dark features. Martha turned from the pantry, her eyes twinkling. "Did you enjoy your movie, dear?" She began to carry an armful of items across the kitchen. Lex crossed the room and took them out of her hands.

"What do you mean by that?" Lex followed the housekeeper like a lost puppy. "Where do you want this stuff?" She was continually amazed at how Martha could take such an array of foodstuffs and turn them into wonderful meals. *I would have starved to death a long time ago if it weren't for her.*

"Just set it on the counter there." She patted Lex on the back. "And I didn't mean anything by what I said... I just asked a simple question. Why are you getting so defensive, honey?" Martha turned and studied the young woman.

"I'm not defensive!" Lex snapped, then sighed. "Yeah, I guess I am. Sorry Martha. You didn't deserve that." She leaned on the sink and stared out the window, vaguely noticing the rain had finally stopped. "This can't be happening..."

Martha walked up and wrapped an arm around her. "What's that, sweetheart?"

Lex turned and looked down at the slightly wrinkled features. "I'm not sure...but this feels so...so different."

The housekeeper nodded knowingly. "And you're scared?"

The rancher blinked, then swallowed hard. "Terrified," she whispered, "I don't think I could go through that again." She paused, "I don't know if I *want* to go though that again." Lex shook her head. "Moot point, anyway." She took a deep breath and audibly blew it out. "Hey, I came to ask a favor of you. I need you to keep Amanda occupied for a couple of hours tomorrow. I'm working on a little surprise for her."

Martha accepted the change in topics. "Okay, I'm sure I can come up with something, but you have to tell me what you're up to first." She stood back and placed her hands on her ample hips, trying to assume a threatening manner.

Lex almost laughed at the older woman's attempt at toughness. She cleared her throat. "Did she tell you about the car she was driving yesterday?"

Martha nodded. "My heart nearly broke in two when she realized that it was probably gone forever." She noticed the gleam in the rancher's eyes. "What?"

Lex smiled. "I don't know how, but her car is still in the same place it was when I pulled her out of it last night. By tomorrow the creek should be down enough for me to tie it to the jeep and pull it back to the house."

Martha gaped. "You're not..."

The dark-headed woman nodded. "Yep. Figure I can hide it in the maintenance shed until I get it cleaned up enough to run. Then we can take it into town and have the seats and carpets cleaned."

The housekeeper chuckled. "You are devious, aren't you? She'll be thrilled. But how long do you think you can keep this a secret? That young lady is pretty darn sharp."

"I know. That's why I'm going to need you. She really wants to help out around the house, maybe..."

Martha waved her arm. "Okay, I'll try to keep her busy. But are you sure it's a good idea to try and pull that car out alone? Broken ribs do not heal overnight, even for you." She had always been amazed at the girl's recuperative powers. *Must be a high metabolism.* "And that reminds me. You are going to go upstairs right now and let me re-bandage those ribs and put some more cream on that scrape, aren't you?"

She knew when she'd been beaten. Lex sighed. "Yes ma'am. Right behind you, ma'am. Whatever you say, ma'am."

Martha lightly backhanded her in the stomach. "Enough of your lip, young lady! You're not too big for me to use my spoon on, you know." They both laughed as they went upstairs.

Amanda hung up the phone and stared at it. Both her grand-parents seemed very fond of the young rancher, and it appeared that they had known her for quite some time. She turned her attention to the desk. It was clear of clutter, and the only object that looked out of place was a u-shaped piece of metal. Amanda picked up the item and studied it. *Looks like...a letter opener?* She tried to straighten it out, but even with both hands the steel would not budge. *I have a pretty good idea when this happened.* The thought of that kind of strength mixed with anger should have frightened her, but for some reason Amanda felt strangely comforted. She heard footsteps above her and smiled. *I wonder what those two are up to now.* Then she heard a scream. *What the...* The small blonde was out of the office and running up the stairs in a flash. She skidded to a halt at the master bathroom door.

Lex was standing in the bathroom shirtless, her back against the wall. "Dammit, Martha! Have you been storing that mess in the freezer or something? It's ice cold!" she whined, trying to fend off the determined housekeeper. Martha continued to spread the cream on her injured chest.

"Stop your complaining Lexie...I'm almost finished."

They both turned to see a breathless Amanda standing at the door. "I heard a scream," she puffed, "is everything all right?" She leaned against the doorframe, trying to catch her breath.

Martha laughed. "Lexie was just being a big baby."

"Hey, you'd scream too if she was trying to turn *you* into a human popsicle!" the tall woman complained.

Amanda laughed and shook her head. "I thought something horrible had happened." She couldn't help but notice the strong body still leaning against the wall. *Down, Mandy...you'd just give her another reason to scream.* But then something her grandparents had hinted about drifted into her mind. *Hmmm...Maybe...?* She realized belatedly that someone was speaking to her. "Sorry, what?" Amanda turned her attention back to Martha, who had directed a question to her.

"I was just wondering if you were still interested in helping me around the house. We were going to rearrange the cabinets and pantry. But I don't want Lexie putting any strain on those ribs."

The person in question snorted, then gasped as Martha pulled the bandage tightly against her chest. "Ouch! You trying to kill me?" she grumbled.

The housekeeper gently slapped her on her good side. "Hush! I'd be finished a lot faster if you didn't squirm so darn much." She pulled the material tight again, getting a groan.

"There. Amanda, could you hand me the safety pins on the counter, please?" She held out a hand.

The young blonde stepped further into the room to pick up the requested items. She handed them to the heavyset woman, and picked up the flannel shirt that had been lying next to them.

"Stay still, or I'll end up poking you, Lexie," Martha admonished her patient. "I swear you're worse now than when you were a child!" She finally completed pinning the bandage and stepped back.

Amanda moved forward and held out the shirt to Lex. She was trying very hard not to smile, but by the look on the tall woman's face she had failed miserably. "Here, put this back on, it'll help warm you up." *Although it feels pretty warm in here right now, to me anyway.*

"Thanks." Lex took the shirt with trembling hands. *I gotta get a grip, here...* She slowly pulled the shirt on, but her hands were shaking so bad she couldn't seem to get it buttoned. *What's going on with me? This is ridiculous!*

Amanda noticed the difficulty Lex was having, but assumed it was due to pain or the aftereffects of the cold cream. "Here," she stepped closer, "Let me give you a hand." She took over the buttoning duties, finishing the job quickly.

Martha smiled to herself and left. *Moot point, eh Lexie? I don't think so.* Neither woman noticed as she slipped quietly out the door.

Lex looked down into Amanda's face. Being this close, she could see golden flecks sparkling in those bright green eyes. She almost stopped breathing when the young woman edged closer.

BrrrrRing!

Both women jumped. Amanda stepped back, startled by what she had almost done. *Stupid, stupid, stupid! Where's your head, Mandy?*

The tall woman was berating herself as well. *Great! Probably scared her to death. Just look at her face!* She moved past the little blonde, heading towards the bedside table. "Excuse me...I'd better see who that is." The phone had only rung once, and she was reasonably certain that Martha had picked it up. *Saved by the bell. If I'd stayed in there much longer, I would have scooped her up and tossed her on the bed.* She ran a shaky hand through her hair as she picked up the phone.

Martha was speaking calmly to...*Hubert. Figures. He's always had impeccable timing.* "Hello, Hubert. What do you want now?" Lex could hear the housekeeper release a soft sigh. "It's okay Martha, I've got it." The other phone clicked quietly. "Well? Did you call for a reason, or are you just trying to piss me off?" she growled, her nerves on edge.

"Nice to talk to you too, sis. Do I have to have a reason to call?" His nasal tones oozed insincerity.

"You always have. Now what have you called to complain about today?" She could feel her body clench up, causing her newly wrapped ribs to ache.

Her brother laughed. "You are such a hardass, dear little sister. Okay, as a matter of fact, I do have a reason for calling."

"Are you going to tell me sometime tonight?" Lex felt her teeth grind together.

"Chill, sweetie...I just came across some property on the county books, and I think we could pick it up for a song. I just need a little extra capital to get the ball rolling."

Lex was about to let him have it, when she felt a gentle hand on her arm. She took a steadying breath. "Why would I give you money for another one of your real estate schemes? I told you months ago that I wasn't going to lend you any more money. What makes you think I'd change my mind now?"

Amanda pulled her slowly to the bed and sat her down. She slid her hand down the tense arm, gently prying Lex's fisted hand open and placing her own hand in it.

"I just thought you would help me out, since I was willing to help you out," he wheedled.

Lex's voice trembled with suppressed rage. "And just *how* are you supposedly helping me out?"

"Well, since you've got a *houseguest* out there, I'm offering to try to keep it quiet for you. No sense in your little *friend's* reputation getting damaged, right?"

Lex shot off the bed. "You sonofabitch!!!" she exploded. "If you cause any trouble for Amanda or her family, I will personally take care of any aspirations you may have about fatherhood, brother or not!" She paced back and forth across the room, her face flushed with anger. "So don't you *dare* try to blackmail me for your idiotic little schemes, you little shit!" She turned off the phone and slammed it onto its base, then looked over at Amanda. "Sorry about that."

The small woman was sitting on the bed, eyes wide. "What was that all about?" She was about halfway afraid of the answer.

Lex walked over and sat down in one of the chairs by the fireplace, defeat in her posture. "Why don't you come over here and sit down – it's kind of a long story."

Chapter
7

There was a cheerful fire burning in the fireplace. *Martha must be some sort of magical sprite. When does she find the time to do stuff like this?* Amanda shook off her musings and sat down in the chair opposite Lex. *Whatever it is she has to say, it can't be good. She looks like she's expecting the worst.*

Weary and resigned, Lex wiped a hand over her face. "I'm not sure where to start," she muttered, looking into the flames of the fire. She intentionally avoided the sweet face across from her. *Well, it was fun while it lasted.*

Amanda cleared her throat. "You really don't have to tell me anything, if you don't want to. I mean, it's really none of my business."

The older woman took a deep breath and finally met the intense green gaze directed at her. "Yes, I do. It does pertain to you in a roundabout way."

Amanda's fair brow wrinkled. "But I just met you yesterday. And I don't even know your brother. What could he do that would have an effect on me or my family?"

Lex looked down at her own hands, clenched together in her lap. "He threatened to spread the word around town that you were staying out here with me."

"So?!? What's the big deal? For God's sake, Lex...you saved my life!!!" Amanda was beginning to realize where this conversation was heading, and she could almost feel the fear and pain radiating from the older woman.

"He would probably...forget...to mention that you are stranded out here." Lex paused for a moment. "I've got the supplies. I can start first thing in the morning, and probably get at least a walkway built across the bridge by the late afternoon. You can call your grandmother to come and pick you up."

Amanda slipped out of her chair and knelt at Lex's feet. "Tired of me already?" She gave the rancher a timid smile.

Lex looked down, and became lost in those twin pools of green. "No, of course not!" The denial came out sharply. "I just don't want your name dragged through the mud. My brother is quite good at that," she reflected. Without her conscious permission, Lex's hand found its way to Amanda's cheek.

The young blonde placed her hands on Lex's thigh. "I really don't think you should start to work on the bridge until your ribs have had more time to heal. I'm perfectly happy here."

Lex removed her hand from the soft cheek. "Your reputation might be tarnished. Hell, if my brother has anything to do with it, it would be ruined!" She looked away, unwilling to show the young blonde too much.

"Why?"

"It's kind of a long story."

"So? I don't see us in any hurry to go anywhere. Unless you don't want to talk about it."

The older woman sighed. *I might as well get this over with.* "A couple of years ago, when Hubert was still living here at the ranch, he had gone to Las Vegas on an alleged 'business trip.' A week later, he came home with a young woman he had met at the blackjack tables, who had given him some hard luck story about being dumped by her fiancé." A small smile crossed her lips. "They hit it off immediately, and Hubert invited her to come home with him to 'his' ranch." Here she laughed. "He must have really played it up. The ranch was only about half the size it is now, and we hadn't begun remodeling yet. Needless to say, it was a little...rustic." Lex slipped out of the chair and onto the floor next to Amanda. "I guess Linda felt a little betrayed by Hubert's exaggerations, because she started coming on to me." She looked over at Amanda, expecting shock or disgust, not the gentle smile she was receiving.

"Hmmm...go on."

"Well, she told me that she and Hubert had decided to break off their relationship, and were going to just be friends. I was young, I believed her. Shame she forgot to tell Hubert." She gave the younger woman a sad smile. "So, she stayed here at the ranch with me for about six months." Mentally bracing herself, Lex quietly added, "as my lover."

Total silence. Lex thought she could hear her heart pounding throughout the room.

"So, what happened? Why isn't she still here?" Amanda gave the strong leg under her hand a slight squeeze.

Lex blew out a breath. "Hubert had moved to the house in town, and Linda began asking me to take her on trips. I tried explaining to her that this was a working ranch, but she always cried about being bored, and tired of living out in the middle of nowhere." She shook her head sadly. "Later on, I realized that she was just a little gold-digger, and the luster wore off when she found out I really didn't have the kind of money that Hubert had hinted at." She ran her hand through her hair. "I came in from tagging the cattle one evening and found all of her stuff gone." She laughed bitterly. "The note said, 'Been a great ride, going to Atlantic City for a change of pace.'" It still hurt, all these years later. *I thought it was love...what a joke I must have been to her.* "Hubert was pretty vocal in town about what 'went on' here at the ranch. And now he's telling me that if you stay here, people may think the same of you." She looked down as Amanda's hand gently grasped hers, then Lex searched the depths of Amanda's eyes. "I don't want your grandparents to hear nasty rumors about you...I'm sure they've already heard all the stories about me."

Green eyes sparkled with unshed tears. "I am so sorry you had to go through something like that." She squeezed Lex's hand. "I really don't care what anyone says about me. And my grandparents have never cared much for gossip." She longed to take Lex in her arms and hug the hurt away. "So, if you don't mind, I think I'd like to hang around here for a while...you need help with the chores, don't you?" She paused to let her words sink in. "And I don't walk out on my friends just because someone *may* say something derogatory about me."

Lex returned the squeeze. "Are you sure? My brother can get pretty nasty."

"Puleez! He's the very least of my worries." Her stomach growled. "See?"

Lex laughed and stood up, pulling the younger woman up with her. "So I hear. Let's go invade the kitchen...Martha probably has dinner cooked by now."

Amanda allowed Lex to help her to her feet. On impulse, she wrapped her arms around the tall woman and squeezed. She felt warm arms surround her as Lex returned the action.

"Thanks...friend." A whisper so quiet, Amanda thought she might have imagined it. Then she was released and led towards the door.

"C'mon. Let's go get underfoot...Martha just *loves* when I do that!!!"

****

Dinner was quite an animated affair. Amanda and Martha traded humorous stories back and forth, while Lex sat back and absorbed it all quietly. *I can't believe she's still here.* Lex had been afraid that the younger woman was going to run off screaming into the night after hearing her story. She watched as the two women interacted. *Should have known. Martha adores her...she was always a good judge of character.* The heavyset housekeeper had disliked Linda immensely, although the young woman always made sure to be sickeningly polite to Martha whenever Lex was around.

"Lexie?" The housekeeper tapped her arm. "You with us, honey?"

The rancher smiled. "Uh, yeah. Just thinking." She turned her attention to Amanda. "You gonna help Martha here in the kitchen tomorrow?"

"Uh-huh...after we feed in the morning, why? Do you have something planned that you need my help with?"

"No, not really..." Lex hedged. "I was going to ride one of the horses down and get the jeep."

Martha, knowing what else she was going to do, piped up. "You're not going to overdo it, are you? Those ribs aren't healed, you know."

Lex raised a dark eyebrow. "Of course not. I'm just going to take a leisurely ride down the road, attach the jeep's winch to a tree and then let it do all the work. If it hadn't been raining so damn hard last night, I would have done it then." She smiled at the housekeeper. "The road should be in good enough shape tomorrow to bring it back to the house."

Martha looked less than convinced. "Promise me you will not put any undue stress on yourself, sweetheart. I have no desire to try and find a way to get you to the hospital."

Amanda spoke up. "Are you sure you don't need my help?"

"Nah...I was going to check part of the fence first... won't be back until late afternoon, at the earliest. You'd be bored to tears." Lex tried to appear nonchalant.

The housekeeper stepped in. "She's right, honey. When Lexie goes out on her horse, time has a tendency to slip away from her." Looking at the rancher, she sighed. "Take your cell phone, just in case you happen to get into trouble, please? You should have taken it with you last night." When Lex rolled her eyes, Martha slapped her arm. "Watch it! Or we'll *both* go with you!"

The dark woman put her hands up in surrender. "Okay, you win...I remember the last time I got you up on a horse."

The gray-haired woman chuckled. "That wasn't a horse, it was a four-legged messenger from Hades!! I like transportation that doesn't bite, thank you very much!"

Lex started laughing. "She didn't bite you, she nuzzled your pocket looking for treats!"

Martha joined in. "If you didn't spoil those horses so bad, that would have never happened!" She got up and began clearing the table.

Amanda giggled. "Don't feel bad, Martha...I don't ride much either...horses are way too tall! It's a long way to the ground!"

Lex continued to laugh. "Maybe I'll find you a pony with a seatbelt!" Tears of mirth began to streak down her cheeks. She could just imagine the small blonde on a shaggy Shetland pony, buckled into a saddle resembling a child's car seat. She clutched her ribs. "Ow..."

"Serves you right, making fun of me!" But Amanda was smiling also.

"I wasn't making fun of you...I was...uh...simply making a helpful suggestion!" Lex snorted, trying to curb her laughter.

"Oh, you!" Amanda threw her napkin into the laughing woman's face.

Lex stood up and carried her dishes to the sink, Amanda following right behind her. The taller woman gently bumped Martha with her hip. "Since we've goofed off all day, let us at least do the dishes." Seeing the housekeeper's resolve weakening, she added, "Please?" giving Martha her best pleading look.

Martha sighed, but backed away from the sink. "Okay, you win. You know I can't resist that look."

Amanda took up her position next to the triumphantly grinning rancher. "Yeah...we'll take care of everything. Why don't you go relax?"

The housekeeper gave in gracefully. "Not a bad idea. I think I'll go home and take a long soak in a hot bubble bath." She pulled off her apron and slung it over her shoulder. Martha sashayed out of the room, swinging her hips with an exaggerated motion.

Lex and Amanda looked at each other and burst out laughing. They made quick work of the dishes, Lex washing while Amanda rinsed and dried.

The smaller woman placed her hands on her back and leaned back into the counter with a groan. "I think Martha may have had the right idea. I think I've found some muscles that didn't exist before today."

Lex finished putting the dishes away. "No problem. You can use my tub. It even has little Jacuzzi jets in it." She draped a casual arm around the small shoulders. "I've got some book work that will keep me busy for a while, so feel free to soak." She led Amanda up the stairs. Once inside the master bedroom,

Lex released the younger woman and made her way to the large oak dresser. She pulled several sleep shirts and tee shirts from one of the drawers. "These should be more comfortable than those sweats." She handed the items to Amanda.

"Thanks. But I have no complaints with my other wardrobe." Amanda took the clothes with a smile.

Lex raised an eyebrow at her then turned her attention to digging through the massive walk-in closet. "Ah-ha! I knew it was in here somewhere." She pulled out a bright flowery terry cloth robe, which looked about two sizes too small for her. Handing it to Amanda with a flourish, she said, "My great Aunt Loretta sent this to me for Christmas last year and I couldn't bring myself to throw it out." She eyed the smaller woman. "Now I'm glad I didn't...it looks more like you, anyway."

That much was certainly true. Amanda looked at Lex, and then at the robe. "Mmm...I don't know..." she giggled. "Thanks. I appreciate the loan."

Lex shook her head. "No problem...you keep it. That way when I write to Aunt Loretta telling her it's useful, I won't be lying," she smirked. "As it was, I told her on the phone after Christmas that I was enjoying it." She steered Amanda towards the bathroom. "And I was...every time I pictured myself in it, I had a good laugh." Pulling a towel from a cabinet, Lex tossed it to the young woman then headed for the door. "There should be some bubble stuff by the tub." She shrugged her broad shoulders when the blonde looked at her questioningly. "I enjoy a good soak every now and then myself," she smiled and closed the door behind her.

****

Steam quickly filled the bathroom as Amanda lounged gratefully in the huge tub. She leaned back and closed her eyes, letting the water cover her aching body up to her neck. *Poor Lex...how could anyone treat her that way? At least that explained what my grandparents were trying to tell me.* Amanda vowed to bring that exact subject up the next time she spoke to them on the phone. Letting her mind wander, she thought back to when she was in high school, and finally figured out she wasn't 'like the other girls'.

Amanda was sitting in the back row of the science lab, listening to her friends giggle and carry on about the Junior Class dance. It was going to be patterned after an old-fashioned sock-hop, and the girls had been actively planning their wardrobes, and placing bets on who would go with whom.

"I'll just die if Charlie doesn't ask me!" Francine whispered melodramatically. She had a crush on the lanky basketball player, and had been shamelessly flirting with him for months.

Karen, the sturdily built brunette sitting next to her, grinned. "Bobby already asked me." She poked Francine in the ribs. "And I didn't have to practically fall on top of him in study hall to get his attention. Like some people I could name, but won't."

Francine returned the poke. "I couldn't help it...my books were falling out of my hands, and I lost my balance," she whined, flipping her dark blonde hair over her shoulder. She was taller than Karen and Amanda, and her coordination was still trying to catch up with her body. Francine looked over at Amanda, who was just staring at the front of the class with a slightly dazed look on her face. "What about you, Mandy? Have you gotten anyone lined up for the dance?" She waved her hand in front of the smaller blonde's face. "Hellllooo? Earth to Amanda Cauble..."

Amanda jumped. "Sorry, guys... What were you talking about?" She loved her friends, but sometimes they could be so... immature.

Karen nudged her with an elbow. "WE were talking about the dance...you know, that thing where everyone gets together and then moves around to music? Where were you just now?" She leaned in closer. "Who are you going with? Has Ronnie talked to you yet?"

Amanda sighed. "No, he hasn't. But I don't know if I even want to go..." She caught herself staring back towards the front of the class, where Judith Patterson was sitting. She was fairly new to the school, and Amanda had taken it upon herself to show the new girl around. They were quickly becoming friends, although Judith didn't care much for Karen and Francine. They usually would just meet after school to study, or go to the local mall. Last night, Judith had held Amanda's hand, and told her she was gay, and that she'd understand if Amanda wanted to break off their friendship.

That had certainly opened Amanda's eyes. It made her sit back and think about her own feelings. She'd never really been interested in boys like her friends were. Amanda thought that maybe she just wasn't as mature as they were, and that she'd grow into it after a while. She thought about asking her mother, but a discussion like that would probably send Elizabeth Cauble straight to the emergency room. Her mother had a problem discussing sensitive matters – and if her younger daughter were to ask about sexuality, she'd most certainly have a stroke.

"Mandy! You have to go...everyone's going to be there!" Francine saw where Amanda's eyes were pointed. "Is it because Judith can't get a date?" She lowered her voice, "She's weird, Mandy...I don't know why you're friends with someone like her."

"Don't say that!" Amanda snapped, turning her head and glaring at Francine. "She's not weird, she just doesn't like to sit around all day and giggle about guys." The bell rang, and the girls picked up their books and followed a large group into the hallway. "Look. I'll call you later, okay?" She quickly made her way through the crowd and caught up with Judith.

"Hey, Judith!" She pulled on the back of the girl's sweater. "Want to come over tonight and help me study for the chemistry exam? Mom and Dad have a banquet to go to, so the house will be quiet."

The redhead stopped and turned around. "Are you sure you want to be alone with me, Amanda?" She had a sad look on her face. "I don't want you to be uncomfortable."

The little blonde smiled. "How can I be uncomfortable around you? We're friends, aren't we?" She leaned in closer and whispered, "And you'd be surprised at how much I think we may have in common." Amanda stepped back again. "So...you coming over, or what?"

Judith smiled. "I'd love to. Somebody's got to get you past this semester of chemistry."

After that, the two girls developed a deep friendship. But it wasn't until the end of their junior year that they got more serious about their relationship. Hours were spent in each other's rooms, snuggling and kissing. But they had both agreed early on that they didn't want to just jump into bed.

"Just because we're both girls doesn't mean it won't count," Judith said, when Amanda asked her why they had never taken that final step. "You may find someone later on that you want to share that special moment with, and I care too much for you to ruin that."

"But Judith, I really care about you!" Amanda looked into the dark hazel eyes below her. She was sitting on Judith's lap in her bedroom, where they had just finished Judith's term paper. "Have you ever...umm...been with someone?" She was embarrassed to ask, but was curious as well.

"Yes, I have. Last year, at my other school." Judith traced a light pattern over Amanda's face with her finger.

"Did," she faltered, "did you love her?"

Judith wrapped her arms tightly around the smaller girl. "I thought I did. But now, I don't think so. I really cared for her, and she cared for me...but there were no 'fireworks', if you know what I mean."

Amanda snuggled into Judith's neck. "Yeah." Then she sat up, alarmed. "Summer's almost here!" She looked panicked.

"So? What's the big deal about the summer? We'll have more time to spend together." Judith was confused at the look on the blonde's face. "What's the matter?"

Large tears welled up in Amanda's mist-green eyes. "I spend every summer with my grandparents in Texas." Several tears fell. "We'll be separated all summer..."

Judith gently brushed the tears from Amanda's face. "Okay...we'll just have to write back and forth like crazy, and maybe call each other once a week." She hated to see Amanda in pain. "It'll be okay, really."

Amanda wrapped her arms tightly around Judith, not wanting to let go. "We only have about a month before I leave..." She kissed the other girl's neck. "Please Judith, make love to me tonight. I want to be loved by you as much as possible before I have to leave."

Judith hesitated. "*Amanda, there's nothing in the world I would rather do, but do you think it's wise?*" *She brushed the fair hair away from the bright green eyes.* "*I do care about you a lot, but this is a major step.*"

Amanda could only nod. "*Yes...please.*" *She kissed Judith tenderly.* "*Let's go to bed. I already told Mom and Dad you are spending the night – they think we're watching movies.*" *She stood up and pulled the other girl to her feet.* "*C'mon...I've got some serious studying to do.*" *Amanda led Judith to the bed then pulled her into an embrace.* "*And I intend to work at it all night.*"

Amanda smiled to herself. *That was one heck of a study session.* Looking back at that time in her life, she was so glad she had met someone like Judith. The young woman had given her what she had so desperately been missing. They never called it love – *but it sure was fun!* Her grandparents were so cool about it, too.

Amanda had been at their house for over a week, and every day she seemed sadder and sadder. Anna Leigh figured it had to do with someone back in Los Angeles, because the young woman would spend hours every night writing letters, then mailing them off the next morning.

Anna Leigh took Jacob aside one morning before Amanda had come downstairs. "*Sweetheart, I'm terribly worried about Mandy. Something is definitely bothering her. Has she said anything to you?*"

Her handsome husband scooped her into a hug. "*No love, she hasn't. I think she's missing someone back home.*" *He knew the signs of lovesickness. He was nearly incapacitated with it when Anna Leigh had gone overseas with her parents, back when they were just dating. He leaned down and gave his wife a sweet kiss.* "*Do you want me to talk to her?*"

Anna Leigh returned his kiss, wrapping her arms around his neck. "*No. I think this should be one of those 'woman-to-woman' chats...I'm sure that it would be easier.*" *She pulled his head down for one more kiss. "And if we keep this up, she'll get quite a show...I hear her coming down the stairs." But she didn't release him, just turned around in his arms. "Good morning, sweetheart," she directed her greeting towards the doorway, where a sleepy-eyed young woman appeared.*

Amanda rubbed her eyes and smiled. "Good morning." Seeing her grandparents all snuggled together reminded her of Judith, and she felt a wave of sadness wash over her.

Jacob noticed the change and squeezed Anna Leigh a little tighter. "Well, ladies...I'm off to the shop. Got to finish that table for Mrs. Wilcox." He released his wife, and kissed his granddaughter on the head, as he walked through the kitchen.

Anna Leigh opened her arms, and Amanda stumbled into her embrace. "What's the matter, Mandy? You seem so sad. Is there something Jacob or I can do?" She kissed the blonde head.

"Oh, Gramma..." she cried, her head tucked under her grandmother's chin. "There's nothing you can do...it's something I have to handle myself." She backed up and wiped her face.

"Oh, honey...we love you. If there's something we can do to help, even if it's just to listen, we're here for you." She gently led the sniffling young woman to the kitchen table. "Would you like some breakfast? We had donuts...Jacob had a yen for apple fritters."

"No thank you, Gramma. I'm really not very hungry." She sat down at the table and sighed.

Now Anna Leigh KNEW something was wrong. Her granddaughter could out-eat the football team on a good day... "Okay, that's it." She sat down at the table next to the young woman, taking one of her hands and squeezing it. "You can't go on like this any longer...please talk to me..."

Amanda began crying again. "I really don't think you want to hear this."

Anna Leigh lifted Amanda's chin with her hand. "Honey, there is nothing you can say that I don't want to hear. Nothing will change the fact that we both love you dearly."

Amanda looked into her grandmother's eyes, and saw nothing but truth and love. Maybe it was time to tell someone. "I've met someone, Gramma." She felt the older woman squeeze her hand. "And I care for this person very much... we've only been together for a little more than a month...and I miss her so..." Not exactly the best way to tell someone, but she already felt like a huge weight had been lifted from her chest.

Anna Leigh was not too surprised. She knew that love had no boundaries... Look at her and Jacob. He was from a poor, but loving home. She was raised by nannies in mansions all over the world. Poor child...I know she could never speak of this with her own parents. She and Jacob raised their son Michael with all the love and support they could, but somehow it wasn't enough. He was so unlike the both of them. Business came first, family second. His wife, lovely woman that she was, would rather be shopping in Paris than raising a family. How this dear girl turned out so well, I'll never know. But part of her did know... she and Jacob practically raised Amanda... they tried with her older sister Jeannie, but she was more her mother's child. "Would you like to tell me about her, sweetheart? If she has your heart, then I'm sure she's a wonderful person." Amanda took a deep cleansing breath and smiled. "She is wonderful, Gramma... and I know she would love both of you."

They continued their letter writing throughout the summer... during that time, they had become much better friends, and decided that while the affection they had for each other was deep, it certainly wasn't love. When school started again in the fall, they still spent most of their free time together. Judith then met a girl at the local college, and fell deeply in love, but she still maintained her close friendship with Amanda. They still went places together, determined to keep their deep bond.

Wasn't that long ago that I got her last letter, either...Judith and Emily had two children, with another one on the way...and Amanda had been present at each christening. She looked back on her first love fondly, and with a great deal of appreciation.

****

Lex stared at the computer screen and then rubbed her reddened eyes. *I've got to be missing something somewhere.* She had been searching her accounting program for over an hour, trying to find missing funds. Almost ten thousand dollars worth of missing funds. She flipped over to her Internet account and sent an email to her bank, requesting that they send her the bank statements for the last several months, since Hubert usually handled the paperwork end of the ranch. It appeared they were losing more than normal, so she also vowed to do a personal head count of the stock. And she was not about to confront her older sibling until she had something to go on. *Maybe I'm just tired.* She looked at the clock and blinked. "Amanda's probably upstairs bored to death by now," Lex mumbled, as she shut down the computer and left the office.

After navigating the stairs, Lex stopped at Amanda's room. *Empty.* She shrugged her shoulders and went into her own room. *Strange...she's not in here either.* Confused, Lex knocked gently on the bathroom door. "Amanda?" No answer. Now becoming concerned, Lex slowly opened the door. *Total silence.* She walked towards the tub area, where she spied a damp blonde head poking out of the bubbles. She could see that the young woman was sound asleep; the only sound in the room was the gurgling of the Jacuzzi. "Amanda?" Lex whispered, trying not to scare the poor woman to death.

No response. "Amanda."

The young blonde's eyes popped open, as she sank under the water, startled. She whooshed up out of the water immediately, gasping and sputtering. "Wha...???"

Lex hurried over to the tub and knelt down. "Hey, careful there." She grasped Amanda's shoulders without a second thought. "Didn't mean to startle you like that." The dark-haired woman eased Amanda into a sitting position.

Amanda coughed a couple of more times, then stilled. "Sorry about that. Didn't realize I had dozed off." She enjoyed the closeness of the other woman. "How long have I been in here?"

Suddenly realizing where her hands were, Lex pulled back and stood up. "Umm...almost two hours." She put her hands in her back pockets, trying to calm her pounding heart. "I'll just let you get dried off then...you're probably feeling pretty waterlogged." She began backing towards the door.

Amanda smiled and brushed bubbles off her own forehead. "Thanks...I'll be out in a minute." She watched with some amusement as the usually sure-footed and composed rancher backed directly into the doorframe, a slight flush to her dark features.

"Yeah..." Lex beat a hasty retreat into the bedroom, slamming the door behind her.

Amanda giggled slightly as she let the water run out of the tub. *So...I guess I'm not the only one who can feel this...electricity...between us.* She quickly dried off and then looked at her sleepwear options. *Hmmm...do I go modest, or do I tease her a little more?* She picked an oversized nightshirt that would hang a little past her knees. *Modest. She's looking a little too shook up...maybe tomorrow night.* With a smile, she pulled the shirt over her head.

Stepping out into the bedroom, the small blonde saw Lex sitting in the light of the fireplace, slouched down in one of the overstuffed chairs.

"All yours." She moved to the other chair and sat down, toweling her hair dry. "Thanks for the loan of the tub...I'm most definitely relaxed now."

"I'm glad. You're welcome to use it anytime you want." Lex shifted slightly in her chair. "I'm sorry I barged in like that, but when you didn't answer me, I got a little concerned." *A little concerned? Try scared to death!*

Amanda looked over at the older woman. Her face was bathed in shadow, and the firelight turned her usually bright eyes almost black. "You look pretty worn out yourself."

Lex sighed, and ran a hand through her hair. "Yeah. Been a long day." She twisted her head to one side, and her neck popped. "Think I'll take a quick shower and then jump into bed." She stood up slowly.

Amanda stood up with her. "Do you need any help?" At Lex's raised eyebrow, she blushed. "Ummm... I mean, with taking off your bandage?" Lex's other eyebrow shot up into her bangs. "Oh, damn! You know what I mean!" The young woman didn't think she could get any more embarrassed.

Lex took pity on her. "Nah...I can get it off okay, and I'll probably just leave it off for the night."

"I don't think that's a very good idea. What if you roll around in your sleep?" Martha's horror stories about punctured lungs and internal bleeding had scared her. Because she was concerned for her hostess while she was out riding, Amanda had quizzed the housekeeper about Lex's health. "I really don't think you should go to bed unprotected."

Lex chuckled. "I don't think that I am in any danger that would require *protection* in bed, am I?"

Amanda covered her face with her hands. "Ah, probably not..." She looked at her bare wrist. "Would you look at the time?" She gave a fake yawn and a stretch. "Mmmm.... guess I'll let you get your shower. I'll be across the hall if you need me to help you wrap your ribs." She started for the door. "Goodnight." Amanda hurried out of the room, still red as a beet.

Lex watched her go with an amused look on her face. *I really should be ashamed of myself, teasing the poor woman like that.* But somehow, the camaraderie they shared seemed right, like they had done it for years. *Strange.* She shook her head and walked into the bathroom, shedding clothes as she went.

Amanda had just finished brushing her teeth, and was brushing her hair when she heard a knock on the door. "Come in!" she yelled, sticking her head out of the bathroom.

A sheepish looking Lex walked in, wearing a robe and carrying a large elastic bandage. "Hey, your offer still open?" She smiled slightly, looking like a lost child. "I can't seem to get this damn thing on straight."

Amanda set the hairbrush down and moved into the bedroom. "What's the matter? A torn sheet not good enough for you?" she teased, trying to get the older woman to relax.

"No, it's not that. I just remembered that I had this from the last time I broke a rib. But don't tell Martha. I've kinda kept that little accident a secret from her."

"Really?" Amanda asked. "I'll help you, but only if you tell me what happened." She hitched an eyebrow at the dark woman.

Lex shrugged. "Nothing, much. It happened last year. She told me not to try and ride a certain horse, but I didn't listen. He threw me into the fence, and I broke a rib. No big deal." She looked a little worried. "Promise not to tell?"

Amanda laughed at the look on the rancher's face. "Oh, Lex. You look like a little kid who got caught stealing from the cookie jar." She moved toward the tall woman and took the bandage from her hands. "Okay, I promise. Now get over here and I'll get you fixed up."

Lex turned her back slowly to the younger woman. She silently removed her robe and laid it on the bed, leaving her in just a pair of flannel pajama bottoms. She took a deep.breath and then released it slowly.

*She's beautiful...*Amanda heard her mind whisper. She willed her shaking hands to steady, as she began to wrap the bandage around Lex's body. *Such broad shoulders and her skin is so soft.* She had to lean into the strong back to wind the bandage around Lex's ribs. The younger woman bit her lower lip, trying to control her feelings. Once she finished the wrapping, she gently draped the robe back over Lex's shoulders. "All done," she said, hoping her voice didn't betray her.

Lex was having control problems of her own. She could almost feel the heat coming off the smaller woman from her nearness. "Thanks." She turned around, barely missing the longing in Amanda's eyes. "Guess I'll let you get to bed now." As she made her way to the door, Lex turned to look at her guest. "See you in the morning." She walked out and closed the door behind her.

Amanda stood at the bed and stared at the closed door. *Oh, boy...Lex, my friend, I think we're gonna have to have a little talk, REAL soon.*

Chapter
8

The next morning, Lex and Amanda finished feeding the horses and made their way into the hay barn. Lex backed the truck up to a tall stack of baled hay then looked around for Amanda. There was no sign of the small blonde anywhere. *Now where in the hell did she go?* She was about to put the tailgate down on the truck when she felt something dropping on her hat and shoulders. "Hey!" Lex looked up and brushed the straw from her body.

A slight giggle was the response. "Yep! It's hay," Amanda cheerfully admitted and readied herself for another throw. She had climbed up to the top bale and couldn't resist dropping hay onto the unsuspecting rancher.

"I thought you didn't like heights." Lex took off her hat and shook the hay free. "Now climb down from there before you get hurt." She put her hands on her hips and mock glowered at the young woman.

"No, I don't like *moving* heights. I get motion sickness." Amanda plopped down on the bale and started swinging her legs back and forth. "Besides, this isn't that high – maybe twelve to fifteen feet, at the most." The young woman was about to make her way down when the bale suddenly shifted and she began to fall.

Lex saw the movement and dropped her hat. She rushed to position herself under the falling woman. "Ooof!" She grunted as she caught Amanda and cradled her in her arms as if she were a child. "Are you okay?"

Amanda felt the woman holding her tremble and looked up into Lex's frightened eyes. "Yeah." Then she realized where she was, and how she got there. "Oh, God...are *you* okay??"

Lex looked into Amanda's eyes, barely breathing. "Uh-huh." She couldn't seem to take her gaze away from the younger woman's face. Words failed her, as she felt Amanda's arms wrap around her neck.

Amanda didn't think. She gave into her instincts and wrapped her arms around the taller woman's neck and pulled Lex's head down to meet hers. When their lips met, the blonde was amazed at how soft the rancher's lips were. As she deepened the kiss, Amanda's heart raced at the feeling of belonging.

Lex was having strong feelings of her own. When their lips met, she felt a gentle tickle in the pit of her stomach. When the smaller woman deepened the kiss, a jolt of electricity shot throughout her body and caused her legs to give out. Lex collapsed back into a soft pile of hay, never releasing the woman in her arms.They spent a few moments just enjoying the kiss, until Lex pulled away slightly to breathe. "Wow," she gasped, still trying to catch her breath.

Amanda laid her head on Lex's chest and took a deep breath. "Sorry...I'm not sure what came over me." She looked into sparkling blue eyes. "I can't believe I did that."

"Are you sorry that you did?" Lex held her breath, afraid of the answer.

"God, no!!" Amanda reached up to caress a tan cheek as she tried to calm the erratic beating of the older woman's heart. "It's just that I don't usually make it a habit to throw myself, this time quite literally, at someone I've only known a couple of days." She could feel the rancher struggling to pull air into her lungs. "Are you sure you're all right? What about your ribs?"

A relieved Lex turned her head slightly and kissed the small palm cupping her face. "Never been better." Seeing several emotions cross Amanda's face, Lex kissed her forehead and gave her a gentle hug. "If that's how you're going to react after falling from a stack of hay, remind me to bring you in here more often."

"Works for me...I've always wanted to roll around in the hay." Amanda gave her an embarrassed smile. "Ummm...I mean..."

Lex understood. "Relax. Let's just take things slow and easy, okay? No need to rush."

Amanda's answering smile lit up her entire face. "Yeah...I guess we'd better finish up the chores, huh?" She felt Lex's breathing return to normal. "And Martha is expecting me pretty soon."

She's right...got to be responsible. "True. But first..." Lex leaned down and captured Amanda's lips again and felt small hands tangle themselves into her hair. *This feels waaay too good...better stop now while I still can.* She ended the kiss slowly and tried, without much success, to back off. "Whew...I, ummm...."

Amanda brushed the dark hair out of Lex's eyes. "Yeah, that goes for me, double." She climbed off the rancher's lap and offered her hand to the still seated woman. "Here, since I got you down there, might as well be the one to help you back up."

Lex smiled and allowed the younger woman to pull her to her feet.

Not releasing the large hand that enveloped hers, Amanda pulled the older woman into a very gentle hug. "Thanks." She stood on her tiptoes and kissed the strong chin.

"For what?" Lex returned the hug and enjoyed the feeling of the smaller woman in her arms.

Amanda pulled back a little so she could see the rancher's face, partially bathed in shadow. "For working on your fence in a thunderstorm, for pulling a complete stranger out of a raging creek, and for catching me when I fell."

Lex kissed the top of her head. "Anytime." Her voice broke on the word. She released the younger woman, but kept one arm draped casually over her shoulders. "C'mon. I imagine the cows are about to mutiny."

****

Sometime later, Amanda was standing in the stable, watching as Lex saddled up the powerfully built Thunder. "Are you sure you don't need any help? I mean, Martha would probably understand if I was a little late today." She reached up and rubbed the large horse's head, as he butted her gently in the chest.

"Nah. Not that I wouldn't enjoy the company, but I really don't want Martha to try and reach some of those higher cabinets by herself." She tightened the cinch and looked over at the younger woman. "She and stepladders don't always get along." She finished with the saddle and patted the horse on his flank. "Last time, she fell and twisted her ankle...I thought she had broken it, and it scared the hell out of me," she smiled. "And she's a worse patient than I am." Lex led the huge horse out of the stall. "I'd really appreciate it if you could kinda keep an eye on her, if you don't mind." She turned and reached for the saddlehorn, but a hand on her arm stopped her.

"I don't mind at all...but you have to do me a favor in return." Amanda grasped her coat with both hands, pulling the taller woman close.

"Yeah?"

"Try to stay out of trouble, and please be careful." She saw Lex open her mouth to argue and covered it with her hand. "Please? Don't hurt yourself trying to get that old jeep out of the mud – it's not like we can go very far anyway."

Lex pulled her into a quick hug. "You're starting to sound a lot like Martha." She stepped back and gently chucked the blonde under the chin. "I promise, I'll behave." She climbed into the saddle, causing Thunder to dance sideways. "I'll also be checking some of the fence line by the creek, so I may not be back until dark." *It all depends on how easy it is to get her car out of the creek and into the maintenance shed.*

Amanda patted her leg. "Okay. Just give us a call on your cell phone if you have any problems." She walked beside the huge horse as Lex moved him out of the stable.

"Yes ma'am." Lex tipped her hat with a smirk. "Do you

want a ride to the house?"

Amanda looked up at Lex and then to the house, which was only about twenty yards away. An unexpected thrill raced down her spine as Lex held an arm out to her. "Sure." She allowed the dark-haired woman to pull her up behind her. Wrapping her arms around the tapered waist, Amanda leaned into the strong back with a small sigh. "Now *this* is the way to ride horses."

Lex chuckled and kneed the stallion forward. "Really? Are you sure you don't want a seatbelt?" She felt the small arms around her waist tighten slightly.

"Nope…this is perfect."

They rode the rest of the way to the house in companionable silence. The only sounds were Thunder's heavy hooves falling to the ground.

Lex pulled the massive horse to a stop by the back porch and gently gave Amanda a hand down. "There ya go, ma'am. Door-to-door service, as promised," she joked and felt a light slap against her leg.

"Thanks," Amanda curtsied. "That terribly long walk would have worn me out!"

Lex laughed as she backed Thunder away from the porch. "Anytime." She tipped her hat again and gave the younger woman a wink before turning the big horse away.

"Be careful!" Amanda called after her. She winced as Lex sent Thunder into a strong gallop.

****

Lex charged Thunder through the fields and leaned over his neck with a smile. Feeling only a slight ache in her ribs due to the activity, she laughed out loud to the wind blowing into her face. "It's a great day, isn't it boy?" The racing horse snorted in disagreement. Low dark clouds had begun to cover the sky. They threatened to erupt at any moment, and the cool breeze blowing through the surrounding trees brought a damp chill to the air. To Lex there had never been a more beautiful day. *I must be doing something right…'cause someone up there has certainly dropped a wonderful gift right into my lap.* "Yaaaaa!!!" She urged the horse on; both of them absorbed the brisk air around them with joy.

As they got within sight of the jeep, Lex reined in the large horse. She walked him around slowly to cool him off. "Doesn't look like we'll have much trouble here, huh big fella?" She aimed him towards the still-rushing creek. "Let's take a walk down there before we get started, okay?" She patted his neck, and they made their way slowly towards the loud roar.

****

Amanda walked into the kitchen, her cheeks slightly flushed and a big smile on her face. Martha turned around from the pantry and grinned. "Well, well...you must have had a good time feeding the stock. That's an interesting look on your face, honey." She watched as the younger woman blushed.

"Oh, yeah...I had a great time." Amanda realized what she said too late. She lowered her head trying to control her heated face.

Martha walked over to her and pulled a few errant stalks of hay from her hair. "Mmm... looks like it."

Amanda covered her face with her hands. "Oh, God..."

The housekeeper felt pity for her and relented. "Sweetheart, calm down. There's nothing to be ashamed of. I'm glad you two have hit it off so well." She wrapped her hand around Amanda's arm and pulled her towards the table. "Sit down while I get you some coffee." She grabbed a couple of mugs from the cabinet, filled the carafe, and then sat down at the table beside Amanda. "Did Lexie get off to the creek okay?" she asked as she poured them each a cup.

"Umm...yeah, she did. She told me that she would be checking the fence also, and not to expect her back before it got dark." The young blonde took a small sip of her coffee.

Martha appeared surprised. "She told you she'd be late?" She gave a slight shake of her graying head. "She never actually tells anyone when she'll be back. I usually just fix her a big breakfast and plan dinner for dusk on days when I know she'll be riding fence patrol."

Amanda just stared into her mug. "Well, maybe she just said that because she knew that we'd be worried, since she's still hurt."

"Honey, that's never bothered her before." The housekeeper patted her hand. "Not that she's unfeeling, it's just that she normally doesn't think about little things like that." She took a deep breath. "Not like she can, having to run this place all alone."

Amanda looked up. "But I thought her brother helped her." Her brow furrowed in confusion.

The heavyset woman scoffed. "Hubert? Help? Not in this lifetime, sweetheart. Sometimes I think his sole purpose in life is to aggravate poor Lexie, and, of course, to mooch money off her." She took a sip of coffee and sighed. "He's seven years older than she is and has never done an honest day's work in his life. Oh sure, Lexie lets him keep the ranch's books, and he has that accounting office he runs in town, but he's no good." Her lips twisted into a scowl. "He's hated Lexie ever since their daddy signed the ranch over to her. Not to mention he's just plain mean." She took another sip of coffee. "I normally wouldn't be telling anyone this, but I trust you, and I want you to be aware of just how nasty that man can be." Pausing, she studied the young woman across from her.

Amanda had a pretty good idea where Martha was heading with this conversation. She met the wise brown eyes across from her. "Lex told me about Linda." She saw the housekeeper's posture relax somewhat. "Hubert threatened Lex last night about my staying here. So she decided to tell me why he was so…hostile." A sad look crossed her face. "Did Linda actually dump Hubert for Lex?"

Martha took a deep breath. "Oh yes. You see, Hubert is quite handsome – tall, dark, with blue eyes like Lexie's…only his are crueler. Women just seem to throw themselves at his feet until they get to know him. The smart ones run like all get-out." She finished her coffee and began wiping the table with a damp dishcloth. "He's also got Lexie's temper. They both got that from their daddy, but he never learned to control it like she did." *Took her until she was almost twenty-five, but she finally did.* "I think Linda just got tired of Hubert taking his mad out on her, and, to get back at him, she latched onto Lexie."

Amanda frowned. "She didn't love Lex, did she Martha?"

"Oh, I think she did, in her own little way. She just wanted a little fancier lifestyle than what Lexie was willing to give her." Martha remembered grimly the month-long bender that Linda's desertion had wrought with the impressionable young woman.

Lex would get up before dawn, feed the livestock, and handle the general ranch business before the rest of the hands even stirred. Martha could sometimes coax the sullen woman to eat breakfast, but not often. Lex would lock herself in the office and drink until late afternoon, when usually a carload of 'friends' would pick her up and take her into town. They'd spend the rest of the afternoon and all of the evening bouncing from bar to bar, generally raising hell. Once or twice they had the law called on them. After the bars would close, these so-called friends would bring Lex home, and Martha would usually find her passed out on the porch swing the next morning.

After this had gone on for nearly a month, Martha quit pleading for Lex to come to her senses, and took direct action. One morning, after finding Lex once again sprawled unconscious on the front porch, the angry housekeeper mixed up a large bucket of extremely muddy water and dumped it on the unsuspecting rancher.

"Whoa!" Lex sputtered. "What the hell did you do that for?" Her head was spinning, and she imagined she was about to toss the contents of her stomach all over the porch.

"If you plan on letting this ranch run itself into the ground and sit out here smelling worse than a pig farm, I thought that maybe you'd want some mud to wallow around in." Martha dusted off her hands and walked towards the door. Turning around, she continued her tirade. "So either clean yourself up, or find a new baby-sitter – 'cause I'm not gonna tolerate one more minute of your self-pitying garbage, you hear me?!" She shook a finger at Lex.

"Yes ma'am," a chagrined Lex mumbled to the housekeeper as mud dripped down her face.

If the situation hadn't been so serious, Martha would have laughed out loud at the figure before her: bloodshot blue eyes standing out starkly from the mud-covered face, sodden clothes hanging loosely on the trembling frame. "I'm sorry, Martha." Lex took a couple of steps forward, until she was standing less than a foot away. "Please don't leave me," she whispered, her eyes filling with tears. "I'll get my act together, I promise."

She looked so much like a beaten child; Martha wrapped her arms around the younger woman and pulled her to her ample bosom. "Oh sweetheart...I was just so angry, watching you throw your life away like that." She rocked the now sobbing woman gently, then pulled back and used her ever-present dishtowel to wipe her charge's face. "Now get this porch cleaned up, go upstairs and take a long hot shower, and come into the kitchen for a big breakfast. I'll tell the boys to handle the chores for the next couple of days, 'cause you're gonna eat and then go straight to bed." She wiped a spot clean on Lex's forehead and gave her a gentle kiss. "Now go on, and be quick about it." As she turned and moved back into the house, Martha grumbled under her breath about crazy kids and how she had to go and change into a clean apron.

After that, Lex rarely drank, except for the occasional beer or two with the hands on poker night. But she never touched hard alcohol again. Martha knew the young woman had scared herself, and she was glad that Lex had promised her to stay sober. Hubert had teased her, saying she was too weak, not able to handle her alcohol. He tried to knock Lex off the wagon by constantly belittling her. But Lex just put up with his taunts. She said she had given her word, and that he wouldn't know anything about keeping a pledge to someone.

"Martha?" Amanda became concerned by the look on the older woman's face. "Are you all right?" She grasped the hand that had been absently wiping the table.

The housekeeper shook her head and gave Amanda a small smile. "Sorry 'bout that, dear...I got a little lost in my memories." She placed her other hand on Amanda's. "C'mon. Let's get to work on those cabinets."

****

Lex stood at the edge of the creek, mesmerized by the still rapidly flowing water. She shifted her gaze slightly downstream to see that the little Mustang was still in the same place. The car's rear bumper was just barely visible above the water line. Lex looked behind her to mentally calculate the path she would use to pull the car from the water. *How to get it from there to here... that's the sticking point. One of the chains from the jeep should be long enough, but how in the hell do I get the chain on the car?* She looked at the water, and then down at herself. *Well, I could just tell them I fell into the creek,* she smirked, imagining the looks on their faces. *Ah...no... not a good thing to do...Martha WOULD use a spoon on me then!* She relegated that problem to the back of her mind and decided to worry more about it when she got the jeep out of its muddy nest. Lex turned away from the churning waters and walked back over to the patiently waiting Thunder. She mounted the large horse and rode back towards priority number one.

An hour later, an angry and mud-covered Lex finally drove the jeep towards the creek. Even using the winch attached to the front of the vehicle, she still had to dig and push to extricate the buried jeep. Lex had removed her ever-present black cowboy hat and duster to save them. Now she was almost solid mud from the tip of her head to the soles of her boots, and she was mad enough to spit nails.

The tall rancher backed the equally mud-coated jeep to a large tree ten yards from the bank of the creek, until it was almost touching the heavy oak. Lex wound a length of chain around the trunk of the tree and the other end around the back axle. She then pulled a longer stretch of chain from the jeep and attached it to the steel cable that she unwound from the winch. Lex tied one end of rope to the chain and the other around her waist. *That's it...I've got to be certifiable...jumping into this damn creek not once, but twice in one week. Martha is gonna have me committed.* She looked down at her clothes that were barely distinguishable under the grime. *At least I can use the excuse that I needed to get the mud off me, so I rinsed off my clothes – don't have to tell them it was in the creek.*

Lex slowly waded into the creek. She noticed how much the current had slowed down since Friday. "Damn, but that's cold!" she grumbled, as the water slowly made its way to her shoulders. She let the current move her downstream. When she got near the partially submerged car she took over. Her strong stroke cut through the water easily. Gently bumping the car, she grimaced. *Easy, Lexington...don't put any more dents in than it already has.* She pulled herself up on the trunk. Lex dragged the rope across the creek until she finally got the chain into her hands. *Great...now I get to play Jacques Cousteau and try to find the damn axle.* Taking a deep breath, Lex slid off the rear of the car and slipped under water. It only took her a minute to grope her way down, wrap the chain around her target and return to the surface. *All right...now to get back to the jeep.* The rancher pulled herself back across the creek, a strange sense of déjà vu invading her senses.

It took Lex over two hours to pull the small car from the creek. At times she feared the old oak would fall and crush the vehicles and her. The huge tree creaked and complained, but, in the end, stood strong. Her jeep didn't fare any better. Once the little Mustang was safely ashore, she patted the bedraggled jeep on the hood and promised it a nice cleaning. The old vehicle was Lex's pride and joy; she had rebuilt it herself while in high school.

Lex secured the waterlogged Mustang to the jeep and walked over to the patiently waiting Thunder. She removed his saddle and bridle and patted his strong shoulder. "Okay, old buddy, I'll race ya home!" He snorted and started towards the trees, content to take the shortcut back to the barn. The rancher returned to the jeep and fished her cell phone out of the pocket of her coat. She dialed the number for the ranch, hoping that Martha, and not Amanda, would answer.

On the third ring, her wish was answered. "Walters' residence."

"Martha, it's me," Lex smiled into the phone, imagining the shock on the older woman's face. She rarely used the cell phone, saying she'd rather speak to someone face to face.

"Lexie? Honey, is everything okay?" The housekeeper sounded a little nervous.

"Everything's wonderful, Martha. I got the jeep, and I'll be making a stop at the maintenance shed before I get back to the house," came the not-so-subtle hint.

"Good lord, sweetheart. Don't scare me like that! I thought for sure something was wrong when you called," Martha sighed heavily.

"Sorry. I wasn't trying to scare you. It's just that I sent Thunder on ahead, and I didn't want you to worry when you saw him and not me. The road's still pretty muddy, and I thought it would be too dangerous for him to be led behind the jeep." Lex tossed the saddle, blanket, and bridle in the back of the jeep. "I should be in sight of the house in about half an hour or so," she hinted, hoping Martha could keep a certain blonde away from the windows.

"That sounds great, Lexie. I thought Amanda and I would go over to my place for a while. I've got some pictures she might be interested in seeing," she laughed, knowing that Lex knew *exactly* what pictures she had in mind. Martha also knew that the road to the maintenance shed was not visible from her house. "We'll be back in a couple of hours, that should give you time to take care of your horse and get yourself cleaned up, too."

Lex laughed, too. "Uh...well, I was pretty muddy, but it's mostly cleaned off now." She climbed into the jeep. "I'll see you at the house later, then. Bye, Martha." She disconnected the call before the older woman figured out what she had said. *I'm gonna be in so much trouble for that,* she grinned to herself. It was one of her favorite pastimes – teasing the housekeeper to keep her on her toes. *But she gives as good as she gets, that's for damn sure.*

****

"Oh, Martha...those were priceless!" Amanda was seated in the den surrounded by several photo albums. They had spent the last hour or so talking about families, and just enjoying each other's companionship.

Martha looked at the clock on the mantle. *Been almost two*

hours since Lexie called...guess we should get back to the main house and get dinner finished up.* "Amanda? Do you want to help me with dinner tonight? Lexie should be back any time now."

The young blonde jumped to her feet and scooped several of the albums up. "I'd love to. What do you need me to do?" She practically beat the older woman to the door. "Oh...where do you want me to put these?" She indicated the books in her hands.

The older woman laughed and took the albums. "I'll take those, dear." She put the items on a nearby desk. "C'mon...I put a roast on earlier today. Let's see what we can find to go with it, shall we?"

****

Lex put the Mustang in the shed, telling herself she'd be back after Amanda went to bed to begin working on it. She was amazed at the lack of damage it had sustained. There was a medium-sized dent in the rear left panel, and, of course, the water damage, as well as the kicked-in back window. *But at least the window is still in one piece – shouldn't be too hard to put back in place.* She had even found Amanda's purse and laid it on the workbench to dry out. *Can't give it to her yet...she'd be too suspicious.*

Now the dark-haired woman was busily brushing down Thunder. The massive animal was munching contentedly on the hay she had given him. *He deserves some reward for beating me back to the barn,* she mused. Lex had actually finished his grooming some time ago, but had allowed the time to slip away from her as she daydreamed. *C'mon, Lexington...get your damn head on straight!* The rancher patted the horse on his broad shoulder. "Enjoy your snack, boy." She left the stable and walked towards the house.

Stepping up onto the porch, the tired and dirty rancher stopped and removed her boots. Lex slowly opened the door and peeked inside when she heard voices in the kitchen. *Let's just see if I can sneak upstairs before Martha gets a good look at me.* Though no longer dripping creek water, her jeans and tee shirt were still damp and heavily stained with mud. She could also feel small bits of mud and debris in her hair. *Thank God my hat covers up most of my head.* Her once white socks were now a reddish brown. Each step squished on the hardwood floor, causing Lex to wince. She eased her head slowly around the kitchen door, hoping to get past the housekeeper. *Good! They're both busy.* She continued walking quickly down the hallway.

"LEXINGTON MARIE!! What on earth have you done?!?" a very familiar voice boomed.

Uh-oh. Lex spun around in mid-stride, which caused her wet feet to slip out from under her. She landed on her rear end with a sodden thump. "OW!" The muck-covered rancher slowly stood up, rubbing her backside with her hands. "Hi, Martha. Did you get your cabinets all straightened out?" she asked, backing up towards the staircase. *That's it, Lex...act casual.*

"Don't you 'Hi Martha' me, Lexington! You're soaking wet! And I know for a fact that it hasn't rained at all today." The heavyset woman stomped up to Lex, placing her hands on her hips and cocking her head to one side.

"Ummm...well...you see, the jeep was really buried in the mud, and I, umm..." her voice trailed off as she saw the look in the older woman's eyes that said she meant business.

"Yeeesss?" Martha drew out the word, impatiently tapping her foot.

How does she do it? One look and I feel ten years old again! "Aw hell, Martha...I was covered in mud, and thought I'd better rinse off before I came into the house." She looked down at her soggy socks.

Martha relented. "I appreciate that, honey...but why all the sneaking around?"

The tall woman looked up, her eyes barely visible under her hat brim. "I wasn't actually 'sneaking'...just didn't want to disturb you while you were cooking dinner." She gave a small smile.

Amanda witnessed the entire scene from the kitchen doorway. She covered her mouth with her hand, not wanting to interrupt. The poor rancher looked so...cute, standing there with Martha chewing her out like a recalcitrant child.

The housekeeper yanked the black hat off the damp woman's head. "Good lord, child! What is all of that stuff in your hair?"

Lex closed her eyes and sighed. "I told you I got really muddy. Can I, *please*, go take a shower now?" She grabbed her hat from the older woman and made her way up the stairs.

"Dinner should be ready in about thirty minutes," Martha called after her.

"Thanks," Lex smiled as she squished her way up to her bedroom.

Martha turned back towards Amanda, who was barely containing her giggles. "I swear, that girl can get into trouble just climbing out of bed in the mornings!" she sighed, leading Amanda back into the kitchen.

The young blonde finally lost it. She had to sit down on a nearby stool to remain at least somewhat upright. "She looked so pitiful...does she do that often?" she wheezed in between her giggles.

"Unfortunately, yes. Mud must be one of her favorite accessories, because she's forever covered in it." The housekeeper stirred a pot of something on the stove. "I swear she could find mud in a drought!"

Amanda laughed. "She was rather grimy. But did you really have to fuss at her like that?"

Martha turned away from the stove and met the younger woman's eyes. "No...but if I don't throw at least a token fit, she'll think I don't love her anymore. I think she secretly enjoys the attention."

"Well, I don't think it's hurt her any. She speaks of you with the utmost respect and love." Amanda sobered. She wanted this sweet woman to realize just how devoted the young rancher was to her. "She told me the night I met her how much she cared for you, and that you were the only mother she'd ever had."

Martha wiped an errant tear from her eye. "That goes double for me. She's one of the main reasons I never married. I had the only family I ever needed right here," Martha smiled. "I've had several offers over the years, but I never could bring myself to leave her. And I couldn't see me ever having a child I would love half as much."

Amanda walked over and gave Martha a hug. "Well, for

what it's worth, I think you've done a fine job of raising her. Lex is a wonderful person."

"Thank you. I'm very proud of the woman she has become, although I think she had more to do with it than I did." She took a deep breath. "Now...let's get dinner on the table. She should be straggling down anytime."

"Martha," Lex admonished, leaning in the doorway, "you talking 'bout me again?" Her hair was wet and combed back from her face. She was wearing jeans and the ever-present tee shirt, which for once actually had a design on it.

Jake's John Deere? Amanda smirked. *Bet ol' Jake would sell more tractors if his billboards looked like that!* She helped Martha move the food to the table. "So, how did the fence by the creek look? Did you have to make any repairs?"

"No, not at all." Lex reached for a bowl on the cabinet, only to have her hand slapped by Martha. "Hey! I was just trying to help!" She yanked her hand away quickly.

The housekeeper shooed her away. "We have it all under control. Now go sit down." The rancher affected a hurt expression. Martha turned her around and slapped her gently on the rear. "Don't give me that look. You've been out working all day, and you need to sit down."

Lex raised an eyebrow, but did as she was told. "You two have been working all day, too. What's the difference?"

Amanda looked at the perplexed housekeeper, who was trying to think of a good comeback. "Because we actually sat down once in a while and took a break," the blonde replied, "And we know you didn't."

The dark woman frowned. "What makes you think I didn't?"

Martha butted in. "Two reasons: One...you *never* take a break when you work in the field. Two...you look like you can barely stand up."

Lex opened her mouth, but promptly shut it at the housekeeper's upraised hand. "No...don't you argue with me. I've known you far too long," she smiled triumphantly. "So just sit there quietly while we get dinner on the table."

Lex smiled. She knew when she'd been beaten. "Yes ma'am."

After dinner Martha once again refused any help with the dishes. She chased the two younger women out of the kitchen, popping her dishtowel at them with glee.

Lex grabbed Amanda's hand and laughingly dragged her from the mock battle, threatening to return similarly armed. She pulled the blonde down the long hallway to the den door. "Want to watch a movie?" she suggested to her companion with a gentle smile.

Amanda squeezed the hand that held hers. "I think I'd like that very much. But I need to call my grandmother first, if that's okay with you."

"Sure...you know you can use the phone anytime." She pulled the young woman's hand to her lips with a courtly bow. "My castle is yours to do with as you wish." She gave Amanda a slight nudge towards the office. "G'wan. Take all the time you need." Lex sat down on the sofa and propped her bare feet on the coffee table. "I'll save ya a spot," she grinned.

Amanda looked towards the office, and then back at the lazily sprawled rancher. "You know, it is getting late..." she started towards the sofa, "and I'd hate to disturb them. My grandfather really needs his rest." She sat down next to the older woman and snuggled up close. "Besides, I called them from Martha's house today. I'm sure they're okay."

"How's your grandfather doing? I haven't seen him since he got out of the hospital." Lex asked. She put her arm around the blonde, who gave her a puzzled look.

"You saw him at the hospital? Why didn't I ever see you?" Amanda edged just a little bit closer.

Lex looked down at her with a fond smile. "Well, I'd only visit once or twice a week, mainly to make sure Mrs. Cauble was doing okay, and it was always first thing in the morning."

"Oh, well that explains it. I normally wouldn't get to the hospital until nine or ten, since I would stay so late the night before." She stopped and thought for a moment. "Waitaminute! It was you, wasn't it?"

Lex met her gaze. "What?" she asked quietly.

"Monday and Thursday mornings there were always fresh flowers by Grandpa Jake's bed," the young woman smiled. "You were the one who brought them, right?"

Lex looked somewhat embarrassed. "Uh, yeah…well…the florist was on my way in." She felt small arms slightly constrict around her. "And, Mr. Cauble had always been really nice to me." She motioned to the entertainment center. "He made that, you know." Trying to change the subject a little, she asked her original question again. "How's his leg? Has he gotten his cast off yet?"

"Yep…he's almost back to his old self, but he's got a pretty heavy limp. Although he's told us that it's only temporary." Amanda leaned up close to Lex's ear. "But he's doing much…" she kissed the tender skin, "much…" a slight nibble on the nearby lobe, "better."

Lex moaned and turned her head. She met Amanda's teasing mouth passionately. They took their time as they both enjoyed the contact. Lex pulled Amanda into her lap, and the blonde reciprocated by tangling her hands in Lex's dark locks, gently kneading the strong neck.

The rancher was the first one to break away with a slightly glazed look in her eyes. "Wow…" She cleared her throat. "That was…"

Amanda placed a soft kiss on her chin. "Oh yeah…it most certainly was," she smiled. "But you know, that may have been a fluke." She nibbled on the dark woman's lower lip. "Shall we try again just to be sure?"

Lex answered her with a quiet growl. She began a fierce exploration of the blonde's pale throat. Working her way up to a small ear, Lex gave it a gentle tug. "Sounds like a plan to me," she whispered, enjoying the little shiver she could feel running through the young woman.

They continued almost hesitantly, neither in any hurry to push the other too far. *Feels so good!* Amanda used her small hands to map out the strong muscles in the older woman's back. She was feeling almost overwhelmed by the incredible sensations coursing through her body. *I've never felt anything like this before.* She had thought that what she had with Judith was special, at least until now. *No, that was friendship, or maybe even infatuation…this is…*a low moan escaped her as Lex found a particularly tender spot on her neck. *This is incredible!*

Lex couldn't seem to get enough of the tender throat under her lips. She bit down gently on the pulse point, eliciting a low moan from the woman sprawled in her lap. Even though her heart was pounding in her ears, the dark woman had never felt such a complete feeling of peace before. When Amanda began running her hands up and down the rancher's broad back, Lex knew deep in her soul that she'd come home at last.

By unspoken agreement neither woman took the activities any farther. They both wanted to savor the moment. Lex regretfully pulled back. "It's getting pretty late...why don't we continue this...conversation...tomorrow?"

Amanda ran a trembling finger down the rancher's flushed face. "Probably a good idea." She could feel the older woman's chest heaving with effort. "Why don't we go upstairs and get some sleep?" She climbed off Lex's lap, grabbed one of her hands, and pulled the still seated woman to her feet. "C'mon...I'll tuck you in." A wicked smile was her answer. Amanda blushed. "Lex!" She slapped her arm, "You know what I mean!"

The tall woman smiled and pulled the red-faced Amanda into a strong hug. "Sorry...it's just that you're so cute when you blush." Lex kissed the blonde head under her chin. "But you're right...it's been a pretty long day." She allowed the younger woman to step back, but caught her small hand. "Can I walk you home?" Lex gave her a wink and a smirk.

Amanda chuckled. "Hmmm...I dunno. What would my parents say?"

Lex grinned. "They'd say I was incredibly lucky." She pulled the blonde to the door. "Let's go...I don't want you turning into a pumpkin, or some other such nonsense."

Navigating the stairs had been an experience. Lex took the opportunity to stop at almost every step, citing some unknown house rule about a kiss per step. Amanda obliged because she didn't want to jinx the house. Fifteen minutes later, they finally found themselves at Amanda's bedroom door. Lex pulled a small hand to her lips and kissed it gently. "Goodnight..." she whispered, her blue eyes locked with Amanda's.

The smaller woman released the hand in hers and put her arms around Lex's neck. She stood up on her tiptoes and zeroed in on a pair of slightly bruised lips. "Goodnight." She kissed Lex with abandon, wanting to send the older woman to bed with something to remember her by. "Sleep well." Amanda placed a final peck on Lex's lower lip, then released her and turned towards her door. "See you in the morning." She smiled and closed the door behind her, leaving a stunned - but grinning - rancher staring after her.

"Oh, boy..." Lex turned and headed across the hall, "maybe I need a cold shower," she laughed to herself as she crossed the room towards the dresser. "Nah...I'll just put on my boots, and go check out the car." *That should calm me down. Yeah, right!*

Chapter
9

Amanda had been awakened by another bad dream. No matter how hard she tried, she could not go back to sleep. She tiptoed to the bedroom across the hall, needing the presence of the dark-haired rancher to soothe her frazzled nerves.

Standing in the doorway, Amanda peered towards the bed. She tried to see if the older woman was asleep. "Lex?" she whispered, not hearing any sounds from the bed. "Are you asleep?"

Total silence. Amanda crept towards the bed and found it empty. *Now where on earth could she be?* She looked in the bathroom and found it deserted as well. *Maybe she went downstairs for a snack or something.* The young blonde made her way to the far side of the bed and sat down. *I'll just wait here for her.* A few minutes later, a completely worn-out Amanda curled up on her side and fell asleep.

Lex crept down the dark stairway. *I feel like a teenager sneaking out away from my parents.* She carried her boots in her hand, not wanting to make any noise that could awaken Amanda. Once outside, she slipped the boots on, suppressing a shiver as a cold wind ruffled her hair. Looking off to the right of the house, she was thankful that Martha's little cottage was completely dark. *Good. Maybe she'll get a little rest.* Growing up, Lex wondered if the ever-present housekeeper slept at all. Any time of the day or night the young girl could always count on seeing Martha about, usually in the kitchen.

Lex smiled to herself as she looked up at the cloudless late-night sky. The full moon illuminated the path in front of her. *Maybe, with Amanda's help, I can try and get Martha to take it easier.* Upon reaching the shed, the dark woman opened the door and slipped inside. Turning on the light, she pulled a pair of worn coveralls from their hook and quickly stepped into them. *At least they'll keep me warm,* she sighed, and moved towards the still-dripping little car.

Three hours later, a dirty and exhausted Lex sneaked back through the silent house. She had spent most of the night taking the Mustang apart and had found that the water damage was not as severe as she had imagined. *Once it dries out completely, it shouldn't take too much work to get it running again.* She undressed in the dark and padded silently into the bathroom to start the shower. Not even bothering with turning on the lights, Lex pulled open the glass door and stepped inside. She moaned with relief when the hot spray hit her exhausted body. Almost falling asleep in the shower, she quickly rinsed off and climbed out, wrapping a large towel around her body. Sliding between the sheets, Lex was asleep before she realized that she did not put on any pajamas, and that she was not alone in the large bed.

****

Lex awoke to gentle sunlight streaming through the windows and a heavy weight on her upper body. She opened her eyes and saw light blonde hair spread across her chest. *Wha...?* Sometime during the night Amanda had not only found her way into Lex's bed, but had snuggled up against the naked woman under the sheets. Her left arm was casually slung across the older woman's chest, and her left leg was tangled with the rancher's own long limbs. *Oh boy.... This could get...interesting. Damn, what time is it, anyway?* She glanced at the clock on the nightstand, surprised to see it was a little after seven in the morning. With a quiet sigh, Lex slipped out from under the smaller woman. She quickly made her way to the dresser to find some clothes for the day.

Amanda felt her mattress move. *Move? What gives?* She slid one sleepy eye open, and spotted Lex moving towards the dresser. *Mmmm...nice body, s*he mused. Amanda jerked awake when she realized what she was seeing. *Naked?!?! What is she doing in my bedroom naked?* The young woman blinked. Amanda realized with a start that she was in Lex's bedroom. Peeking under the sheet, she was somewhat relieved to note that she had on an oversized tee shirt. *Whew! Don't know if I am more relieved or disappointed. Hmmm...definitely disappointed.*

Amanda saw Lex open a drawer and remove a handful of clothes. She slammed her eyes shut before Lex turned around. The rancher silently spun on her heel, then made her way to the bathroom and quietly closed the door behind her. *Okay...let's just think about this for a minute.* Amanda racked her brain. *Ah, that's right. I was waiting for her to come back to her room, and I must have fallen asleep.* She frowned to herself. *But why would she get into bed with me if she were naked?* She bit her lower lip. *Maybe she didn't realize I was here...but that still doesn't explain the fact that she had NO clothes on!!*

The bathroom door opened and Lex tip-toed out. "I'm awake," Amanda said quietly.

The tall woman sat gently on the edge of the bed. "Good morning...I hope I didn't wake you," she smiled.

"No, not at all..." Amanda would not meet her eyes. "Sorry...I didn't mean to fall asleep here. I had another bad dream and couldn't sleep. So I came in here to talk to you, but you were gone." She gave Lex a questioning glance. "Where were you?"

"I couldn't sleep, so I went down to the barn," Lex told her quietly. *Not a complete lie, anyway.*

"Oh. Anyway, I guess I fell asleep waiting for you. Didn't mean to take over your bed like this."

Lex patted the young woman on the leg. "Hey, no problem. I was so tired when I came in, I just took a quick shower and fell into bed."

Amanda covered the hand on her leg with one of her own. "What time did you get to sleep? I know it was pretty late when I wandered in here."

Lex stood up. "It wasn't that late...probably right after you came in." She gently pulled Amanda up on the bed. "C'mon. Why don't you get up and get dressed, and I'll meet you downstairs for breakfast."

Amanda stood up on her knees on the edge of the bed. She linked her hands behind the tall woman's neck and pulled her close. "I've got a better idea."

Lex quirked an eyebrow, but didn't complain as the young woman took her time exploring her mouth. She found her hands drifting to Amanda's hips, unconsciously pulling her closer.

"Ahem."

They broke apart quickly, each shooting an embarrassed look towards the door. Lex found her voice first. "Good morning, Martha." She directed a grin at the housekeeper, who was standing in the doorway with her arms crossed.

"Obviously," the heavyset woman snorted, causing Amanda's blush to deepen.

"It's...ummm...not what it looks like, exactly," the young blonde stammered to explain.

"Right..." Martha turned to leave. "Just wanted to let you both know that breakfast is ready," she winked. "I'm sure you've both worked up an appetite." Shaking her head, she left the room and closed the door behind her.

Amanda fell back on the bed laughing. "Oh, God...she's not going to let us live this down, is she?"

Lex put her hands on her hips and grinned. "Nope..." she offered the now giggling woman a hand. "C'mon...let's go face the music." She pulled Amanda up. "Does that bother you?"

The younger woman stood up, wrapping an arm around Lex's waist. "Nope. And I hope it doesn't bother Martha too much either...'cause I'm not gonna stop anytime soon."

Lex laughed as they made their way out of the bedroom.

****

The only sound at the table was when silverware would touch a plate. Amanda was too embarrassed to speak, and Lex was still tired from being up most of the night. Martha had a knowing smile on her face. She was enjoying the younger women's discomfort. *They are just so cute.* "Okay, would you two please relax?" she laughed. "I'm sorry I teased you, but I just couldn't resist." She looked over at Amanda, who smiled at her shyly. "I know not much was going on, because Lexie was completely dressed."

"Huh?" Lex blinked, coming back to the conversation with a start. "What did I do?"

"What's the matter, honey? Are you not feeling well?" The housekeeper touched her wrist.

"No...I'm fine." Lex took a deep pull from her cup of coffee. *I hope the caffeine kicks in soon, or this is gonna be one helluva long day!*

Amanda finished swallowing a mouthful of food. "Actually, I think someone's just tired. She told me she was having trouble getting to sleep last night."

Trouble sleeping, huh? Martha had a pretty good idea why the rancher looked so worn out. *Probably spent all night messing with that car!* She glared at the exhausted woman, who gave her an answering shrug. "Uh-huh. So does that mean that you're going to take it easy today?"

Lex shook her dark head. "Nope. I've got to begin working on the bridge. We're going to start running out of supplies pretty soon."

"WHAT?!?" two surprised voices chimed in at once.

"Lexie, we have enough things to get by on for at least another week, maybe two," Martha exclaimed. "I really don't think you should be messing around with that old bridge. It may not be very stable."

Amanda agreed. "She's right. There's no telling what kind of shape it's actually in. Can't you wait until the creek slows down some more?" She smiled at the rancher. "I'm certainly not in any big hurry to leave."

Lex returned her smile. "I'm not trying to get rid of you either. But I would like to have that bridge serviceable by the end of the week...and I don't know what the extent of the damage is."

Amanda nodded. "Okay, but I'll go with you."

Lex started to argue, but couldn't seem to get past those bright green eyes. "Sure. I'd appreciate the company."

Martha's jaw nearly hit the table. *Ooh...she's got it bad. I've never seen Lexie give up without a serious fight.* She just sat there and grinned.

The rancher noticed the silly smile on the housekeeper's face. "What?" she asked, feeling a little irritable. "Something wrong?"

"Nope...just peachy, dear."

Amanda laughed, nearly inhaling her juice.

Lex glared at her. "You too? Do I have food on my face or something?" Anger colored her tone. *What the hell is their problem?*

Martha laughed as she covered her mouth with a pudgy hand. "Sorry..." she stifled a giggle. "I can't help it!" She burst out laughing again as she watched the rancher's face darken.

The young blonde placed a hand on Lex's arm. "Hey," she snorted. "Sorry...I'm not sure why I'm laughing. I guess Martha's good humor is contagious!" she smiled brightly.

Martha was busy wiping the tears from her eyes. "Oh Lexie...you're just so cute when you get a little flustered. It reminds me of when you were about twelve and your daddy wouldn't let you go out of town with all the hands to the auction."

Lex smiled at this little memory. "Yeah...I didn't realize little girls didn't stay overnight with a group of grown men. I was so angry," she laughed. "Sorry about losing my temper." Lex rubbed her eyes. "Must not be completely awake yet."

Martha stood up, stepped behind the rancher, and rubbed her strong back. "Honey, don't worry about it." She began carrying the dishes to the sink. "Are you going to get started on the bridge right away?"

Lex nodded as she stood up and brought her plate to the sink as well. "Uh-huh...thought I would load up the truck with lumber right after feeding the stock, so I..." She paused when Amanda cleared her throat with a frown. "I mean we, probably won't be back until dinner."

The housekeeper turned away from the sink. "After you get finished feeding, come back to the house first. I'll have a nice lunch packed for you both." The look on her face dared the tall woman to argue with her.

Lex thought about brushing her off, but considered the young woman with her. *Even if I don't usually eat lunch, there's no point in making Amanda suffer,* she grinned to herself. *Besides, it's always a good idea to keep Martha just a little bit off-stride.* "That would be great, Martha...I'd really appreciate it." She nearly laughed out loud at the expression on the older woman's face. *Gotcha! Teach her to tease me!*

Amanda snickered. *Poor Martha...she doesn't have a snappy comeback for that one.* "So would I. Do you need any help putting lunch together?"

The older woman scoffed. "No dear...you would be more help if you could keep an eye on Grumpy over there." She ignored Lex's outraged look. "Try and keep her out of trouble, if you can."

Lex threw up her hands in disgust. "Okay...I can take a hint." She gave Amanda a look. "C'mon. Let's go take care of the stock." She stomped out of the kitchen without another word.

The young blonde exchanged amused glances with Martha, then followed the angry rancher out of the kitchen.

****

As they drove the old truck back to the barn, Lex glanced at Amanda with a contrite look on her dark features. The younger woman had picked up on her moodiness and had been uncharacteristically silent for the entire morning. "Hey."

Amanda pulled her glance away from the window where she had been studying the passing terrain. "Hmm?"

"I'm sorry I've been such an ass this morning." Lex was floundering on unfamiliar ground. She was completely out of her element, and wasn't really sure how to make things right.

The blonde woman studied the shadowed features across from her. She opened her mouth to reply when Lex's upraised hand halted her.

"No...I'm tired and cranky, and I shouldn't have taken it out on you." She gave Amanda a small smile. "And to top it all off, I have got to go back to the house and beg Martha's forgiveness. She's gonna make me pay, let me tell you."

Amanda smiled back. "Yeah, well...I don't think you'll have to work too hard. She's pretty sweet." She reached over to latch onto Lex's spare hand and tangled their fingers together. "And you really don't owe me an apology. I can see how tired you are."

Lex shook her head. "That doesn't excuse my behavior. Martha would be the first one to tell you that she raised me better than that." She shook her head. "I would probably be in jail or dead if she hadn't straightened me out years ago." She pulled the truck up behind the hay barn, where a large stack of boards lay. "You want to help me load some stuff up?"

"Wouldn't miss it." Amanda pulled her gloves back onto her hands and hopped out of the truck. She waited until Lex stepped out from the other side, then walked to the back of the vehicle to meet the rancher. "Is there any special size or type of these things you want us to load?"

Lex had removed her coat and stepped over to the neat waist-high stack of lumber. "I figure we could take a little bit of everything so we don't have to make extra trips." She opened a small door that led into the back of the barn. "Let me get some tools, and then we'll begin piling some of this stuff into the truck, okay?"

Amanda opened the tailgate and sat down. "Works for me. I'll just keep Ol' Rusty Blue here company." She swung her legs back and forth, giving the taller woman a cute smile.

"What did you call my truck?" Lex asked, mock outrage in her tone. She turned away from the door with her hands on her hips.

"Ummm...Ol' Rusty Blue?" Amanda gave her an innocent look.

Lex stalked back over to the truck to step neatly in between the younger woman's legs. Placing her hands on the slim hips, she pulled the small body closer. "Rusty Blue, huh?"

The blonde leaned back on her hands with an evil grin.

"Don't forget OLD..." She was about to continue when she felt soft lips nibble on her own. Amanda took the initiative and deepened the kiss. She wrapped her legs tightly around Lex's back and pulled the older woman into her with a strong need.

Minutes later the rancher broke off the kiss reluctantly and cleared her throat. "Great name for the truck..." She stepped back, gently untangling herself from the beautiful woman below her. "I'll just go get the...umm...tools now." She stumbled into the barn on shaky legs.

****

Lex pulled the truck to a stop several yards from the bridge. She was afraid of getting too close in case the structure wasn't stable, or the edge of the creek crumbled. She stepped out of the vehicle and watched as Amanda did the same. The young woman had a strange look on her face as she followed suit. The rancher moved to the passenger's side of the truck and reached out to Amanda. "Are you..." Before she could finish her question, she found her arms full of a crying woman.

"Oh, God..." Amanda latched onto the tall woman, sobbing.

"Shhh..." Lex gently rubbed her back, "You're okay..." She gently rocked Amanda, not knowing what to do or say.

The small blonde buried her face in Lex's chest, sniffling. "S..sorry...I guess seeing all this in the daylight kinda brought it all back." She looked up into concerned blue eyes. "I could have been killed."

"Yeah, but you weren't. Everything turned out okay." Lex brought a gentle hand to the tear-stained face, wiping under Amanda's brimming eyes. "Do you want to go back to the house?"

Amanda took a deep breath and sighed. "No. I'm all right. I just had one heck of a wicked flashback, that's all." She hugged the tall frame. "Thanks..." She released a shaky breath as she stepped back and wiped her face with her hands. "Let's get started, shall we?"

"Are you sure? I can always come back later if you're uncomfortable." Lex took a step forward and captured a small shaking hand. Bringing it to her lips, she kissed it tenderly. "I don't like to see you hurting like this."

Amanda brought their linked hands to her face. She rubbed the large palm against her cheek. "I think it was just shock; I'm okay now." She kissed the inside of Lex's wrist. "Thanks." She released the hand and stepped back again. "Let's go see what the bridge looks like. It's not going to repair itself." She looked downstream. *No sign of my car. Probably miles away by now. Oh, well...*

Lex shook her head in wonder. "You are an amazing woman, Amanda Cauble." She gave the small woman a smile. "C'mon."

They stood at the road where it met the bridge and looked down at the rapidly moving water. Lex took a few more steps forward until she was directly on the edge of the old wooden structure. She peered down at the shattered boards and sat down on the edge, and then started swinging her booted feet below her.

"Lex? Do you really think you should be that close? What if the edge breaks off?" Amanda took a few tentative steps forward, not quite reaching the rancher. *One of us falling in is more than enough – I'm not about to tempt fate that way!*

The older woman looked over her shoulder and grinned. "Then I guess I'll be going for a swim, huh?" She cocked her head and swung her long body down, disappearing from sight.

"LEX!!!" Amanda screamed, running towards the bridge. Before she could reach the edge, a pair of hands appeared, followed by a hat-covered head.

"What?" The rancher pulled herself back up on the bridge. She saw the panic in the younger woman's eyes and cursed herself. *Idiot! She just got calmed down, and you go and scare the hell out of her. What are you using for brains?* Lex stood up and crossed over to Amanda, pulling the shaking woman into her arms. "I'm sorry...I wasn't thinking." She kissed the blonde head.

Amanda accepted the hug, then stepped back and slapped the taller woman on the arm. "You could have warned me before you went diving off the end...I thought you fell!" She grabbed a handful of the rancher's jacket and pulled hard. "Don't you *ever* do anything like that again, do you hear me?"

"I hear you...I didn't mean to scare you." Lex looked into the younger woman's eyes, almost losing herself completely in a sea of green. "Forgive me?" she entreated, her voice trembling with uncertainty. *Would serve me right if she wouldn't...*

Amanda raised a gentle hand and caressed the dark cheek. "Oh, Lex. You don't have to ask for my forgiveness. You just scared me, that's all." She stood on her tiptoes and placed a tender kiss on Lex's chin.

Lex took a relieved breath and smiled. "I'm sorry. It won't happen again, promise." She led the smaller woman away from the bridge and back towards the truck. "If you don't mind helping me dig out some of this lumber, we'll get started, okay?"

****

The next few hours were spent reinforcing the remaining patch of bridge on their side of the creek. Lex was pleased to find very little structural damage other than the eight missing feet from the center of the bridge. She decided it would be easier to build a walkway across to the other side of the creek first, and then worry about driving across later.

It was late afternoon before Lex agreed to quit for the day. She had been tirelessly sawing and hammering for several hours. She stopped only when Amanda insisted that they have lunch. Her green tee shirt was darkened with perspiration, though the slight breeze stirring was quite cool. The tall woman stood up from where she had just hammered in yet another board and pulled her battered black hat from her head. Looking up at the sky, she took a deep breath and wiped her sweaty forehead on her shoulder. *Might as well start cleaning up – not much daylight left.* She turned to Amanda, who was picking up the leftover pieces of lumber and tossing them into the truck, as she had been doing most of the day. "You about ready to go back to the house?" Lex asked the younger woman as she walked over to stand beside her.

Amanda leaned back against the battered truck. "Oh, yeah. I think my aches have aches, now." She gestured around the area. "I've kept things pretty well picked up. You just say the word, and I'll be ready to leave."

Lex laughed, and tossed the hammer into the back of the truck. "Consider the word given." She stepped back over to where she had been working and finished picking up the odd assortment of tools. She carried them back over to where Amanda still stood and tossed them into the back of the truck. Opening the passenger side door of the vehicle, Lex gave a mock bow to the young blonde. "Shall we?"

Amanda bent into a somewhat stiff curtsy. "Why, thank you ever so much! And here I thought chivalry was dead!" she drawled, as she slid into the seat, giggling.

Lex tipped her hat as she closed the door. "Nope. Just dead tired!" She crossed to the driver's side and tumbled in. "Let's go home."

****

As they trudged up the rear steps to the house, Amanda couldn't remember the last time she was so tired. *And Lex did most of the hard work. I just cleaned up behind her and brought the lumber.* She spared a quick glance to the tall woman beside her. *She looks worse than I feel. Maybe I can talk her into taking a quick shower, and then going straight to bed.* A slight blush stained her cheeks after that thought. *Uh, no. Don't think I'll say it quite that way.*

Lex was about to open the door when she noticed the younger woman's face. *Don't tell me she got sunburned today.* "Amanda? You okay?" she asked, opening the door and motioning for the blonde to precede her. "You didn't get too much sun today, did you?"

Oh, crap! Now what do I say to avoid further embarrassment? "Maybe, I'm not sure. I guess I'm just tired." Amanda took a deep breath and almost moaned with pleasure at the smells emanating from the kitchen. "And hungry."

Lex laughed at that statement. "Newsflash!" After blocking the expected slap, she poked her head through the kitchen door. "Martha, we're back!"

The housekeeper ambled out of the kitchen, wiping her hands on the ever-present dishtowel. "Yes, I can see that dear."

She wrinkled her nose. "You *are* planning on taking a shower before dinner, aren't you?" She reached up and pulled the dusty hat from the rancher's head and swatted Lex with it. "How many times have I told you to take your hat off when you come into the house? Now go on upstairs and get cleaned up. Dinner should be ready in about thirty minutes." Martha turned quickly and moved back into the kitchen, not giving Lex a chance to argue.

"I can never get the last word in with her," Lex mumbled as she walked towards the stairs. She turned and looked at Amanda, who giggled. "Well, I don't think you're exactly smelling like daisies yourself," Lex grinned, and then darted up the stairs with a very aggravated blonde on her heels.

Lex and Amanda were sitting in front of a roaring fire, Martha having chased them out of the kitchen after dinner. The housekeeper had refused their help with the dishes, citing her inability to find anything after they put stuff away yesterday."Amanda?" Lex broke the comfortable silence. "I've got to ride to one of the back pastures tomorrow and check out a few things. Would you like to come along?" The young blonde was sitting in the floor at the rancher's feet, one arm wrapped possessively around a strong leg. Lex was unconsciously playing with the golden hair tangled in her fingertips. "I remember you saying that you don't like to ride, but..."

The smaller woman craned her head at an angle, so she could see the rancher's face. "It's not that I don't like to ride, I'm just afraid of falling off." Her eyes met Lex's and she smiled. "Could we go double?"

Lex returned her smile. "I was just about to suggest the same thing." She slipped out of the chair she was sitting in and landed beside Amanda. "So is that a yes?" Lex pulled the young woman into her lap. "Or should I try to convince you?"

"Well..." Amanda wrapped her arms around the older woman's neck. "Your horse is pretty tall..." she leaned in for a kiss. "I think you'd better start trying to sway my vote," she whispered, as Lex captured her lips.

After Amanda was thoroughly convinced, she led a tired Lex upstairs. Stopping at the guestroom door she whispered, "Goodnight," and gave the callused hand she held a gentle squeeze.

Lex pulled the smaller woman into her arms and kissed her
with a tender intensity. When both of them became breathless,
she slowly broke away. "Yeah." She cleared her throat. "See you
in the morning." She turned and crossed to her own room, trying
to calm her own pounding heart. Stepping inside, Lex closed the
door and then moved over to the dresser. *Better get changed, so
as soon as she's asleep, I can go check out the car.*

Half an hour later, the tall woman was once again sneaking
out of the house. She stopped at Amanda's door and listened for
a moment. *Good.* Then rubbing her eyes, Lex began tiptoeing
down the stairway with her boots in hand.

It took the weary rancher almost three hours to put the small
car back together. She was more than certain that she could have
it running within the next night or two. *Can't wait to see her face
when I pull this little baby around to the front of the house,* Lex
grinned to herself. *I'll finish cleaning up the engine tomorrow
night. Maybe a long ride will wear her out, so I can get started
earlier.*

The mantle clock in her bedroom chimed twice when Lex
finally dragged herself back into the room. *At least I'm getting to
bed at a decent hour tonight,* she mused, stripping off her clothes
as she made her way into the bathroom. Lex sneaked back into
her her bed, she looked around carefully. *Can't be too careful.*
Seeing that she was indeed alone, the exhausted woman pulled a
sleepshirt over her head and collapsed under the sheets.

Chapter
10

Lex had just finished saddling up Thunder when Amanda strolled into the barn. The younger woman leaned up against the stall door with a small backpack tossed over one shoulder. "Are you about ready?" she asked, looking quite smug.

The rancher turned and looked at her. Faded jeans, worn denim shirt and Lex's old leather jacket from her high school days made the small blonde look like a teenager. *She certainly fills out those clothes better than Louis ever did.* "Are you propositioning me?" She quirked an eyebrow at the now blushing woman.

"Maybe," Amanda retorted, "Are you accepting?"

Lex laughed and led the large stallion out of the stall. "Maybe," she tossed the word playfully back to her companion. "Whatcha got there?" the older woman asked, pointing to the backpack. "Homework?" she grinned.

"Nope." Amanda walked towards her, swinging her hips. "Lunch," she winked. "And maybe I'll share if you're real nice to me."

"*Maybe* you'll share?" Lex asked as she dropped the reins and pulled the younger woman close. "Just how *nice* do I have to be?" She leaned down and gently nipped a nearby ear. "And exactly what will you be sharing?" she whispered into the same ear.

Amanda felt her legs go weak beneath her, and she stumbled forward slightly. "Ah..." she couldn't seem to form a complete thought, since the older woman decided to forsake her ear and work directly on her throat. Letting the backpack slide gently to the floor, Amanda groaned softly as Lex finally captured her lips. She was on the verge of an all out collapse when the rancher finally relented and gave her a chance to breathe. "God, Lex...are you trying to kill me?" she whispered, fighting to regain her equilibrium.

"Hmm?" Lex mumbled, burying her face in the sweet-smelling blonde hair. "Oh, sorry about that. I guess we should be getting on our way, huh?" She stepped back regretfully.

"Yeah... just give me a minute to get my legs back," Amanda joked. "Although... I would like to continue this little chat later." She ran a shaky hand through her hair and picked up the discarded backpack.

The dark-haired woman smiled. "I'd like that too." She grabbed the reins once again and started for the door. "C'mon, boy. Let's take Amanda for a little tour."

Once outside, Lex easily mounted the prancing horse and reached down for Amanda. "Up ya go." She pulled the small woman up in front of her. "Thought you'd like to be able to see where we're going. Just hang on to the saddle horn, and I'll hang on to you."

"Now that's the best offer I've had in a long time." Amanda leaned back into the warm body behind her. One strong arm circled her waist, as Lex gripped the reins loosely in her right hand.

"Don't worry. I won't let you fall," Lex whispered in the small woman's ear, enjoying the little tremble she felt run through Amanda's body. *C'mon, Lexington...try and control yourself, or it's gonna be one helluva long day,* she chided herself, giving the body in front of her a gentle squeeze.

****

They rode slowly for a couple of hours, Lex taking the scenic route towards their destination. She wanted to prolong the pleasant ride as long as possible. They slowly made their way into heavy woods, following a slightly worn path that the rancher explained was her favorite. "I usually ride up here to get away from everything," she told Amanda. "Been known to take a sleeping bag and supplies and just spend the weekend relaxing."

The terrain had become steadily steeper, until Amanda realized they were actually in the hills just north of the ranch. "You have stock that stay in this? What are they, mountain goats?" She felt the body behind her chuckle.

"No. There's a small pass just ahead that opens up into a valley...that's where we keep a small herd of wild horses and cattle. The grazing is much better in the valley, so we don't have to bother feeding. But we only keep a small amount of the cattle there," Lex explained. "We normally take the road from the north, but we would have to drive through the creek, and that's kinda impossible to do right now." She felt the stomach under her hand rumble. "I guess you're trying to tell me that you're hungry?"

Amanda laughed. "Uh...yeah. I guess so." She reached back and patted the muscular leg behind hers. "Does that mean we're stopping for lunch soon?"

Lex pulled her close again. "Yep. And I know of just the right place." She led Thunder off the beaten path as they worked their way through the dense trees.

Amanda's breath caught in her throat. The clearing Lex had led them to was absolutely beautiful. Silence prevailed, and the sun fought its way through the treetops to shed its light on a small pond. Lex dropped down from the powerful horse and pulled Amanda gently from the saddle. "I hope this is okay. It's one of my favorite spots." She led the smaller woman to a fallen tree and dropped the backpack beside it, then continued on towards the small body of water. A small pit ringed with rocks nearby was the only sign that anyone had ever been there.

"Lex, it's beautiful. This is your hideaway?" Amanda looked around them, absorbing the beauty and solitude.

The dark-haired woman turned back away from the pond. "Yeah. I come up here to clear my mind. It's not too far from the ranch in case they need me, but it's far enough away that they don't know where it is."

Amanda sat down in front of the log and patted the ground beside her. "Why don't you come over here and we'll see what Martha packed us for lunch?" She opened the backpack, pulling out a couple of foil wrapped packages.

"Sure." Lex ambled back over to where Amanda was sprawled, and dropped down casually beside her. She accepted the package that the smaller woman handed her, and began to open it. "Mmm...smells like a roast sandwich. She knows it's my favorite."

"Oh, yum. This is wonderful," Amanda agreed, taking a bite of hers. "I can see why it's your favorite." She reached into the backpack with her free hand and pulled out a bottle of water, then handed it to Lex. "Here...she doesn't forget anything, does she?" She set her sandwich on her leg and opened another bottle from the bag.

Lex nodded her head as she happily munched away. She swallowed. "Nope. She probably thought I'd forget the canteen, which I didn't," she smiled.

"So...why are we checking the stock? Are you afraid the heavy rains may have done something to them?" Amanda asked after they finished their lunch. "Could the creek have flooded them out?" She was lightly running her hand up and down the rancher's denim-clad leg as they looked out over the water.

Lex took a deep breath and sighed. "No, nothing like that." She looked into the younger woman's eyes. "The other night, while I was checking the books, it looked like we were missing an unusually high amount of animals."

"Okay, but isn't that somewhat normal on a ranch this size?" Amanda asked, a little confused.

"Usually, yes. But not only are we beginning to lose cattle, but sometime recently we've begun to lose money, as well." Lex felt a small hand grasp hers. "I don't normally do the books, that's Hubert's job. But I just had this strange feeling that something was wrong, and it looks like I was right."

Amanda leaned over until her head was on the rancher's broad shoulder. "So what are we going to do about it?"

"We." I think I like the sound of that, Lex grinned inwardly. "We," she paused, smiling into the other woman's eyes, "are going to do a quick headcount in the back pasture. I can compare what we find with what had been reported at the beginning of the summer. That should give us an idea of what's going on." She stood up and pulled Amanda up with their linked hands. "C'mon. It's only about another twenty minutes from here."

****

Lex maneuvered Thunder through the narrow pass, which was only wide enough for perhaps two horses at a time to go through comfortably. Amanda shivered and the arm around her waist tightened.

"You okay?" Lex whispered in her ear.

She leaned back and enjoyed the protective grasp. "Yeah...it's just kinda spooky. I guess because it's so quiet." The only sound was the sodden clump of the horse's hooves echoing eerily along the jagged walls. Amanda squeezed the strong leg behind her, feeling the muscle jump.

"Don't worry, it's perfectly safe. I ride through here all the time." Lex buried her nose in the fragrant blonde hair. "We're almost through."

The path suddenly opened up, making way for the more dense foliage. They rode through the thick forest in silence until Lex suddenly pulled Thunder to a stop.

Amanda, who had been daydreaming, came back to herself with a start. "What?" She looked around. "Why are we stopping?"

Lex pointed off to their right. "Smoke." They were on a slight rise and could see over the treetops easily.

The younger woman strained her eyes. "Where?" she squinted. "Are you sure?" She still couldn't see anything.

"Yeah. It looks like it's not too far away, either. We'd better go check it out." She gently kneed the black horse into a faster pace. "Hang on, this may be a little bumpy!"

The closer they got to the smoke, the more uncomfortable Lex became. *I don't like the look of this. There's not enough smoke for anything more than a campfire.* She slowed Thunder down to a walk.

Amanda felt Lex continue to tense up the closer they got to the mysterious smoke. She turned around in the saddle to look up at the rancher's face. "Lex?" She gave the hand on her stomach a soft squeeze. "What's the matter?" She looked at where the smoke was coming from. "It doesn't look like a very big fire."

Lex frowned, then looked down at the younger woman. "It looks like a campfire. Only, no one should be out here." She swung down from the horse, then reached up to help Amanda dismount. "We're gonna walk the rest of the way." She loosely tied the horse's reins to a nearby tree. "Stay here, boy. We'll be right back." She rubbed his nose, then reached over and captured Amanda's hand. "Let's go check this out."

They walked through the heavy trees for almost a quarter of an hour before Lex stopped. When Amanda opened her mouth to speak, the older woman placed a gentle finger on her lips. At the young blonde's questioning glance Lex pointed through a gap in the trees towards a clearing. There was a truck with a large trailer in the middle of the clearing and several figures were milling around. It looked like they had been there for several days by the condition of the area and of the men.

Sonofabitch! So this is what has been happening to our stock! They had apparently driven the truck through the creek and become stranded after the heavy rains. She looked around carefully. *I count six men – that looks about right.* Lex motioned for Amanda to follow her.

They made their way back to Thunder quickly. Lex hurried over and began digging through the saddlebags. Pulling out the little-used cell phone, she turned it on, then swore.

"Damn!! I was afraid of this!" She crammed the phone back into the bag, buckling the cover angrily.

Amanda placed a gentle hand on the agitated rancher's arm. "What's wrong?"

Lex bit back an angry reply and took a deep breath instead. "Those guys are stealing my stock, and I can't get a signal with the damn cell phone." She looked Amanda in the eye. "I need you to ride back to the ranch and call the sheriff."

"Umm, okay. But what are you going to do?" The younger woman seemed confused.

Lex gave her a smile that didn't quite reach her eyes. "Teach them it's not nice to steal."

Amanda took a firm grip on her arm. "What?!" She pulled the tall woman closer, getting right up into her face. "You can't be serious! There are at least six men, possibly more." She tangled her hands in Lex's coat. "It's too dangerous." Her green eyes sparkled with unshed tears.

Lex framed the young woman's face with her callused hands. "I have to do something. They look like they're getting ready to move out soon." She caressed a soft cheek. "I'm just going to slow them down until help gets here." She bent down and briefly captured Amanda's lips with her own. "You need to hurry." Lex lifted the small woman into the saddle and took a moment to adjust the stirrups. Handing the reins to the blonde, she patted the small leg. "Be careful."

Amanda stretched out her hand waiting for Lex to grasp it. "I will." She kissed the larger hand that was in hers. "You, too. Please don't take any unnecessary risks. We still have a conversation to finish." She gave Lex a watery smile.

The rancher squeezed her hand. "Don't worry, I won't." She released the hand and stepped back away from the huge horse. "Tell the sheriff they're at the back clearing, he'll understand."

Amanda nodded and turned the big horse around. She led him back up the path and turned back in the saddle before they got to the main stand of trees. She felt an irrational urge to race back to Lex. *I have this horrible feeling something is going to go terribly wrong.* Wiping her eyes, she gave a shaky wave and then turned Thunder towards the trail.

****

The big stallion must have picked up on Amanda's distress. He moved quickly through the trees once they had made their way through the pass. Oak and cedar trees flew by the small woman too quickly for her to distinguish as she hung onto the saddlehorn for dear life. Breaking through the dense trees at last,

Amanda heaved a huge sigh of relief as the barns came into view. They charged past the isolated buildings and headed straight for the ranch house itself.

Amanda practically jumped out of the saddle and fell to her knees as her legs gave out near the back porch. Thunder snorted, slung his head, and pounded the ground with his front hoof. "Thanks, boy. I appreciate you getting me here so fast." She patted his neck before she attempted to climb the steps with shaky legs. She almost screamed when the back door swung open before she could reach it.

"Good lord, child..." Martha pulled the young woman into the house. "What on earth happened? And where is Lexie?" she asked. She guided Amanda into the kitchen and assisted her into a nearby chair.

"Lex," Amanda wheezed, "is okay." She took a deep breath, "stealing," a wheeze, "cattle," another breath, "call...the sheriff." She coughed and took another deep breath.

Martha sat down next to her and held the small hands, trying to warm them up. "Okay. You say someone is stealing our stock?" The young woman nodded as she tried to catch her breath. "And we need to call the sheriff?" Another nod. "Where is Lexie?"

"She's still out there, keeping her eye on them," Amanda gasped out, her breathing almost under control. "She said to tell the sheriff they were in the back clearing," she paused, "and she was afraid that they were getting ready to leave." Tears formed in her eyes. "She said she was going to teach them not to steal." She turned a pleading look to the housekeeper. "You don't think she'd do anything rash, do you?"

Martha released her hands and moved over to the phone. Dialing, she looked back over at Amanda. "That's exactly what I'm afraid of." She paused, listening to the phone. "Yes, I need to speak to Sheriff Bristol...this is Martha Rollins." She listened again. "Yes, I'll hold."

****

Lex watched Amanda ride away until she disappeared into

the dense foliage. *Now let's go have some fun.* Her mind ran through several different scenarios as she jogged back to the clearing.

Sitting in the tangled underbrush, the hidden rancher had a very good view of the entire clearing. A dark shadow passed over her that made the watching woman jump slightly. She looked up sheepishly. *Just a damn cloud.* A slight grin quirked her lips. *Cloud? Hmm...looks like rain again. If I can just keep these fools busy for a while, hopefully they'll be stuck here until Amanda can get the sheriff out here.* Lex's mind wandered as she waited patiently for an opportunity...

Charlie Bristol had been the sheriff for longer than Lex could remember. He had a knack for always being around when she needed him, especially after her father had left. The sheriff would show up for breakfast at least once a week, ostensibly to make sure everything was okay. But only Charlie and Lex knew the main reason – Martha Rollins.

The tall and lanky man was several years older than the heavyset housekeeper, but he followed her around like a little boy with his first crush. He'd bring her flowers, ask her out to the movies on Saturday night, and plead with the sweet woman to marry him at least once a month. Every time she gently turned him down with the excuse that she could never leave her "little Lexie" to work the massive ranch alone. Charlie respected that, and in truth, it made the gentle woman even greater in his eyes.

It took a couple of years, but poor Charlie finally got the hint. Martha cared for him but she just couldn't bring herself to leave the ranch and settle down. Charlie understood, and he stayed close friends with Martha. He would take her to various dances and picnics, but he never gave up the hope that someday she'd tire of the ranch life and agree to become his wife. But until that day arrived, he was more than happy to have Martha as a good friend. And the lovestruck lawman never stopped dreaming about settling down with the sweet housekeeper that ran the Rocking W Ranch.

Lex circled around the clearing until she was behind the

large truck and trailer. Looking around, she noticed that several of the men were arguing. She pulled out her pocketknife, then began crawling towards the apparently empty vehicles. After she made her way under the trailer, Lex positioned herself near the wheels on the farthest side. *Oh yeah...face down in the mud is so much fun.* She grimaced and slowly poked a small hole on the inside of the tire, which began to loudly hiss. *Damn!* She quickly wiped a small amount of mud on the neat slice. The mud quieted the sound and slowed the speed that the air was leaking out. Lex proceeded to take care of the remaining tires in the same manner, then stealthily made her way back to her hiding place.

The clouds quickly overtook the late afternoon sky, and thunder rumbled ominously in the distance. Lex smiled. She could see the trailer slowly sinking to the ground. *Only a matter of time before these morons notice.* She decided to take care of the attached truck next. *I wonder how Amanda's doing. I hope she made it to the ranch all right.*

Martha hung up the phone with a grim smile. "Charlie's on his way. He said he'd take the back way in." She crossed back over to where Amanda sat nervously, tearing a paper napkin into tiny bits. "Honey?" She touched the younger woman's shoulder.

Amanda jumped, startled. "What?" She looked down at the mess on the table. "Sorry..." Then she raised her eyes to the older woman. "Did you say the sheriff is on his way?" The small blonde stood, pushing her chair up against the table. "I've got to get back. Thunder should be rested enough by now." She began to walk towards the kitchen door when Martha grabbed her arm.

"Now you wait just a darn minute! If you think I'm going to let you go back to..." Martha was interrupted by the anxious blonde.

"I've got to...she may need me," Amanda appealed to the older woman. "Please don't ask me to leave her out there all alone, Martha. I just can't do it."

The housekeeper released the young woman's arm with a heavy sigh. "All right..." she motioned with her hand, "But you're not going anywhere without a radio." She made her way through the house into Lex's office. She pulled a handheld radio out of its charging base and handed it to the younger woman. "I'll sit here by the base radio, and you can call me if you need anything, okay?" She was about to say more when a rumble of thunder interrupted her.

They both looked up, as if to see something through the ceiling. "Great. Now Lexie will have an excuse to play in the mud again." Martha shook a finger in Amanda's direction. "And you're gonna put on a raincoat before you take off again, right?"

Amanda ducked her head and smiled quietly. "Yes ma'am." Suddenly she was enveloped in a strong hug, which she happily returned.

"Honey, I want you to be extra special careful. Don't take any crazy chances." Martha rubbed the younger woman's back. "I have enough to worry about with Lexie always going off half-cocked." She turned around and led Amanda out of the room. "C'mon...let's get you bundled up and ready to go."

****

Lex had just returned to her hiding spot after sabotaging the truck, when the first raindrops began to fall. *Great. I knew I should have brought my coat.* The flannel shirt she had on had felt great earlier in the day. Now that the sudden cloud cover hid the sun, the wind was decidedly cooler. She rubbed her hands briskly up and down her arms, trying to keep warm. Lex almost laughed out loud at the scene unfolding in front of her.

The rain started coming down in earnest, causing the would-be thieves to rush around picking up their belongings. A short and stocky dark-haired man had almost made it back to the truck when he noticed that something was wrong. "Hey, Matt!" he yelled to the tall lanky man near the campfire, "Looks like we got a couple of flat tires!"

Lex nearly gave herself away laughing. *Oh, we've got a regular Einstein among us,* she shook her head. *Wonder what his first clue was?* She blinked away an errant raindrop, thankful for the dark cowboy hat that kept most of the rain out of her face.

Another man checked the other side of the trailer. "This side's flat too!" The man they called Matt walked over to the truck and pulled a rifle from inside. "You guys keep a close watch. I don't like the looks of this."

The rancher crept slowly back from her vantage point. *Uh-oh...I think he means business.* She crept back farther into the brush.

Matt tossed the rifle over to the short stocky man. "Darrell...take this and do a perimeter check. If anything moves, SHOOT IT!" He turned to face the older man who had checked the far side of the trailer. "Randall, get the other rifle out of the truck and check the other side of the clearing." The gray-headed man nodded and complied.

Lex looked around. *Where did the other three go?* Suddenly, the bushes to the left of her began to rustle. *Shit!* She ducked down lower, practically lying face down in the rapidly building mud. Man number four stepped out of the shrubbery almost on top of her.

"Matt! What the hell's goin' on?" he asked as he zipped up his mud-covered pants.

The rancher slowly lifted her head. *Two left...*She decided not to move until she knew where the other men were. Looking around, Lex noticed a slight movement in the trailer. *I thought that thing was empty.* She watched as a young teenager climbed out of the trailer and approached the leader.

"Aw, Matt. It's starting to rain again. Are we gonna get out of here pretty soon?" He ran a hand through his shoulder-length brown hair. "I really want to go home."

Matt put his hand on the boy's shoulder. "Yeah...we'll just leave the trailer for now. Why don't you go on and get into the truck? We'll be there in a little bit." The young man nodded and started towards the vehicle.

Lex looked at her watch. *Charlie should be here before too much longer...and knowing Amanda, she's probably on her way back by now.* She moved slowly backwards. *Better get back to the pass and wait for her.* The rancher started making her way slowly around the clearing trying to stay out of sight.

She was more than halfway there when she nearly ran into man number six, who was making good use of the nearby thick bushes. He had long blonde hair that was partially tied into a ponytail and did not look at all happy to be squatting in the rain.

Lex edged around until she was directly behind him, waiting patiently. *Hurry up, buddy...* she thought to herself, *I really don't want to be watching this.*

The man stood up and turned. He came face-to-face with a tall drenched woman in a black cowboy hat, who had a very *not nice* expression on her face. "Wha...?" he started.

"Say nighty-night!" She punched him hard in the face, getting an intense amount of pleasure in watching the man crumple to the ground. Lex pulled off the man's shirt and tore it into two strips. She used one for a gag and the other to tie his feet together. She used his belt to tie his hands and smiled down at her handiwork. Lex grimaced as she flexed her right hand. *Damn hardheaded thief.* Then she continued her journey towards the pass. Suddenly, she heard one of the men in the camp shout.

"Hey, guys! I think I see something!!" He took careful aim and fired.

****

Amanda was almost back to the pass when she heard the first gunshots. *Oh my God! LEX!* She pressed her heels to Thunder's sides, urging him to move even faster. Amanda knew that the rancher was unarmed and she was terrified of what she might find. *Hang on, I'm on my way!*

Tearing through the pass, Amanda had to pull the huge horse up quickly. They almost collided with the solitary figure on the path.

"Hey! Slow down!" Lex said, reaching up to grasp the heaving animal's reins.

Amanda slid off the exhausted horse. She stumbled over her feet and almost tackled the older woman.

"Amanda? What's wrong? Are you okay?" Lex wrapped her arms around the younger woman, who buried her face in the damp material of the rancher's chest.

The smaller woman choked back a sob. "Am I okay?" She squeezed tighter. "I heard gunshots." She pulled away from the taller woman, using her hands to inspect the muscular form. "Are you okay?"

Lex grinned. "Oh, yeah...I'm just fine." She took her hat off and shook the excess water from it even though the rain still fell heavily. "A little damp, but fine."

The younger woman was not completely convinced. "Are you sure? You're not hiding anything from me, are you?" She continued to search the tall woman for any signs of injury.

Lex grasped her hands and smiled. "No. They weren't shooting at me," she laughed. "But I'm not sure if that rabbit will ever be the same again."

Amanda smiled through her tears. "God. I heard the shots, and I thought..." she sniffed as she tried to regain some composure.

The older woman gathered Amanda into her strong arms. Lex bent down to place a gentle kiss on the blonde forehead, which was partially hidden by her hood. "Were you able to contact the sheriff?" she asked, pulling back slightly. "I don't think those guys will be going too far right now."

"Yeah...Martha talked to him. He said that he'd come in the back way." She paused. "What do you mean, they won't be going very far? What have you done?"

Lex gave her a devious little grin. "Seems the tires on their trailer went flat..." She pulled a piece of wire out of her back pocket and laughed, "and this accidentally fell off their truck."

"How did..." Amanda shook her head. "Never mind. I don't think I want to know." She walked back over to Thunder, untying something from behind the saddle. "Here, you look half-frozen," she declared, handing the rancher her duster. She then grabbed the saddlebag and began to dig through it. "Oh, and Martha sent this." She pulled out the handheld radio and tossed it to Lex.

"Great. Now I don't feel so damned isolated." Lex stuffed the radio into an inner pocket of the large coat. Holding out her hand, she silently requested that Amanda move closer to her.

The small woman quickly complied, tucking herself comfortably up against the rancher's ribs. "Now what are we going to do?" she asked as she gratefully absorbed the taller woman's warmth.

Lex looked down at her with a serious look. "I don't suppose I could talk you into going back to the house?"

"I don't think so," Amanda said seriously.

"That's what I thought." She gave the younger woman a gentle smile. "We," she hugged her close, "are going to find a good spot to watch the fun." She sobered. "But we have to be very careful, since these idiots have guns." She held up a warning hand. "And, you have to do exactly as I say. No questions asked, okay?"

Amanda gave her an equally serious nod. "Okay. As long as you realize that I'm not completely helpless, right?" she countered.

"Gotcha," Lex agreed and led her down the trail back towards the clearing.

****

It took them almost an hour to walk back to the clearing, their progress hampered by the heavy rain. Lex placed Amanda in the dense shrubbery then settled down behind her. She wrapped her long arms around the small waist. They watched in amusement as the man Lex identified as Matt looked under the hood of the truck. He apparently had no success in getting it to start.

Lex leaned into Amanda and placed her mouth next to a small ear. "I wonder what his problem is?" she whispered, an evil chuckle coloring her tone.

The younger woman giggled and squeezed the hands that were wrapped securely around her stomach.

Another man walked up to the truck to say something to Matt. The leader looked around the clearing and pointed in the opposite direction from where Lex and Amanda were sitting. Darrell started walking in their direction carrying his rifle.

Lex whispered, "Uh-oh. They must have finally figured out that one of them is missing."

Amanda turned slightly in the older woman's arms so that she could speak. "Missing?"

The rancher nodded. "Yeah, he's tied up over in those trees to the right." She pointed.

Amanda frowned at her. "You?"

Lex gave her a sheepish shrug. "Yeah. I practically tripped over him on my way back to meet you," she grinned. "He was, uh...somewhat indisposed."

Amanda's brow creased in a thoughtful manner, then suddenly cleared. "Oh...eww..."

"Yeah," Lex agreed. "But now that they've figured out that he's missing, things could start to get a little rough." She gave the smaller woman a concerned look. "We may have to get out of here in a hurry, so be ready."

Amanda nodded then reached a hand up to cup Lex's cheek. "As long as we leave together." She pulled the rancher's face down for a gentle kiss. "No heroics, right?" she managed to ask after they finally broke apart.

Lex placed a quick kiss on the tip of her nose. "Right." Then she became instantly alert. "Get ready to move. It looks like they're beginning to search for their missing buddy." She released Amanda's waist and captured her hand. "C'mon. We'll be safer back by the pass." Lex pulled Amanda behind her as she crawled through the bushes.

They decided to circle around to the left of the clearing in hope that the longer path would be free of the searching men. Lex suddenly came to a halt, causing Amanda to slam into her back.

"What...?" the smaller woman whispered, fearing detection.

The rancher turned halfway around, placing a gentle hand over Amanda's mouth. "Shh..." She motioned with her other hand to the right of where they were standing.

Darrell was searching the underbrush. He used the barrel of his rifle to move the heavy shrubbery out of the way. In his other hand, he carried a flashlight to help cut the gloom of the heavy rain and early evening stormy sky. He was swinging the light in a wide arc, coming dangerously close to the two women.

Lex pulled Amanda to stand directly behind her and hoped that the dark duster she wore would camouflage them. "If we happen to get separated, take Thunder and meet me back at the pond. They'll never find us there," she whispered. A strong squeeze of her hand and an emphatic shake of Amanda's head were her only answer. Lex spun around to face the young woman. "I'm not planning on it happening, but we need to be prepared just in case!"

The small woman sighed, then nodded. Lex turned back around to watch the man search, slowly backing the two of them away from him. She froze as the light panned across her body. Lex could feel small hands clench tightly on the back of her coat. The light kept going and Lex released a breath she didn't even realize she had been holding. The tall woman slowly backed up again, gently pushing Amanda back as well.

The light suddenly hit her in the face, and the man let out a yell of surprise. "Hey!" He lifted the nose of his rifle, trying to aim it and the flashlight at the dark apparition in front of him.

Lex spun around quickly, still using her body to block his view of her companion. "RUN!!!" she hissed, pushing Amanda forward roughly.

The small woman stumbled, but regained her footing and began to move quickly through the heavy trees with Lex right behind her.

'CRACK!'

Bark exploded off a tree near Amanda's head. *Oh, God!* She willed her body to move faster. Through the pouring rain she could hear men shouting. *Great! Now he's gotten help!* She risked a glance behind her, seeing Lex a few steps back.

'CRACK!'

'CRACK!'

More shots rang out, and Amanda could hear several bodies crashing through the brush right after them.

"To the right!" Lex hissed. She tugged the small woman's arm in that direction, as they veered off the slight path they were on and pushed through even denser foliage.

'CRACK!'

'CRACK!'

Those shots sounded further away this time, Amanda thought as Lex pulled her down into some heavy bushes. Panting hard, the young woman squinted in the dim light. They seemed to be inside a small burrow that was so thickly concealed that the falling rain could hardly break through. It was too dark for Amanda to see anything past the large form in front of her, so they sat silently for what seemed like hours, just waiting and listening, trying to hear any noise over the rumbling thunder. Each of them was too tired and afraid to utter a sound. After a while, Lex finally broke the silence.

"Stay put. I'm going to take a quick look around," she whispered.

Amanda grabbed her arm. "Please, don't!" she begged, fear evident in her tone.

Lex leaned into the young woman's ear. "We can't stay here all night." She reached into her pocket and pulled out the radio. "Call Martha and find out where the sheriff is." She placed a soft kiss on Amanda's cold lips. "If I'm not back in thirty minutes, get to the house."

Amanda wrapped her arms around Lex's neck, pulling her close. She gave the rancher a searing kiss, finally breaking off to catch her breath. "No! You *will* come back to me!" she insisted with a trembling voice. "This is non-negotiable, got it?"

Lex cleared her throat. "Yeah, I got it." She leaned forward and kissed the smaller woman's damp forehead. "I'll be right back." She turned and crawled out of their hideaway.

The young blonde wiped her eyes and turned on the radio. Holding the button down she whispered, "Martha, can you hear me?" Amanda released the button, hearing a small burst of static.

"Amanda? Sweetheart, is that you? I can barely hear you." Martha's voice broke through the static loudly, making the young woman wince and hurry to turn down the volume.

She placed her mouth as close as possible to the microphone. "Yes, it's me. I have to be quiet, though. Have you heard from the sheriff?"

"Yes I have, honey. He should be at the site any time now. He's got three deputies with him."

Amanda breathed a sigh of relief. "Martha, you have to warn him that they have guns." She mentally added up what she had seen. "Two rifles that we're aware of. And there's…"

She was abruptly cut off by the sounds of gunfire. It sounded like it was quite some distance away. *NO!!!* She almost sprang out of her hiding place, her heart pounding.

"Amanda? Honey, are you still there?" Martha's concerned

voice broke through her racing thoughts.

"Uh, yeah. I'm here." She took a deep breath. "Look, I've got to go, Martha. I'll talk to you later, okay?" She turned off the radio then sat in the dark, straining to hear anything over the thunder and pounding rain that punctured the stillness.

The thirty-minute time limit was almost up and the young blonde was a nervous wreck. *I can't believe I let her talk me into staying here. Where could she be? Is she okay? Oh, God...* She stifled a scream as a dark form broke through the dense brush and almost landed on top of her. "Lex?" Amanda reached out blindly.

"Yeah, it's me," the older woman wheezed, trying to catch her breath. "I led them back towards the clearing. Those fools will be chasing each other in a big circle for hours."

Amanda let out a deep breath. "Good. Martha said the sheriff should be there with his deputies any time now." She placed her hand on the rancher's shoulder. "Is it safe for us to get out of here?" She was more than a little concerned about her friend. Lex was still breathing hard. "Are you okay? I heard more gunshots while you were gone."

The older woman was silent for a few moments, trying to get her breathing under control. "Yeah, I'm fine. It's just real hard to run in the driving rain wearing boots and a heavy duster," she chuckled. "Guess I'm a little out of shape."

Amanda crawled closer until she was almost sitting in the dark woman's lap. "Yeah, right. You're still recovering from broken ribs, remember?" She snuggled into the welcoming arms. "Ooh...this feels really good. I'm a little chilled." She looked up, barely able to make out the outline of Lex's face. "I imagine you're freezing, since you've been out in this cold rain longer than I have."

"I've been warmer, that's for sure," Lex whispered as she nuzzled the sweet neck below her. "But to tell you the truth, I'm pretty warm right now," she chuckled, then fought back a small cough.

The small woman lifted a hand and placed it on the shadowed face above her. "You're feeling a bit warm. We need to get you back to the house and into bed."

Lex gave the hand a small kiss. "I'm fine. Just out of breath from all that damn running." She cocked her head to listen outside their hideaway. "But you're right. I think it's safe for us to try to leave now." Climbing to her feet, Lex pulled the younger woman up to stand beside her.

****

The walk back was slow since Lex was cautiously keeping them off any real paths. The rain also hampered their progress, even though the heavy tree cover blocked out most of the downpour.

How on earth does she know where we are going? Amanda wondered as she kept her eyes locked on the tall figure a bare step ahead of her. Lex doggedly made her way through the thick foliage, not hesitating about which direction to take. *She must have some kind of built-in radar,* the blonde mused. The object of her thoughts must have felt her scrutiny. Lex turned her head and gave the younger woman a weary smile. Amanda returned it with a smile of her own. *I'm really worried about her. She seems so...washed out.*

They had been traveling for close to an hour when Amanda reached forward and captured a muscular arm. "I hate to sound like an annoying kid on a trip, but how much further?" she asked quietly.

"Do you need to stop and rest?" Lex questioned. "I'm sorry it's taking so long, but I thought it would be a good idea to take the roundabout way, in case those guys are still trying to find us. Let's take a quick breather." She sank to the ground gracelessly, propping her back up against the nearest tree. "We've still got about thirty minutes of walking to do."

Amanda dropped down beside her and linked her hand with one of Lex's larger ones. "Sounds good to me." Leaning her head on the nearby broad shoulder she sighed, "Is your life always this...interesting?"

The older woman chuckled. "No. Well, at least not until recently." She glanced down and between quick flashes of lightning could just barely make out the young woman's features.

"I've had more things happen in the last week than in the past couple of years." Lex squeezed the small hand in hers. "Guess you brought the excitement with you."

"Oh, yeah. I love driving my car off into flooded creeks, then running around in the cold rain getting shot at," Amanda laughed. "All part of my big plan to bring some thrills into my otherwise boring existence."

"Got more than you bargained for, huh?" Lex released the delicate hand and wrapped her arm around Amanda's shoulder, pulling the smaller woman close. "Me too." She gave the damp head a gentle kiss.

They sat there quietly listening to the sounds around them. The intermittent thunder rumbled and punctuated the bright flashes of lightning. Lex let her body relax and her eyes slowly drifted shut.

Amanda felt the body next to hers go limp, and she looked up in alarm. The older woman's head was tipped forward with her chin resting lightly on her chest. Reaching up with her free hand, the young woman lightly touched the still face, which appeared unnaturally pale in the flashes of light.

"What?" Lex blinked, opening her eyes wide in an effort to become more alert. "Sorry...all this exercise must have worn me out." She wiped a hand over her face.

"Uh-huh." The small blonde pulled Lex's face towards her with her hand. "Are you getting sick?" she asked. Amanda peered intently into the somewhat glazed eyes.

The older woman blinked again and shook her head slightly. "No...really, I'm okay. Just a little tired." *And I think my ribs decided to shift apart again...but she doesn't need to know that just yet.* Lex tried to take a deep breath and felt a sharp pain along her side. *Oh, yeah...I'm not gonna hear the end of this for quite a while. Martha's going to whip my butt.* She glanced over at her companion and saw the exhaustion on her fair features. Lex gathered up what little stamina she had left and stood up, pulling Amanda up with her. "C'mon. We're almost back to the pass, and then we can ride the rest of the way home."

Amanda allowed herself to be hoisted to her feet, not missing the slight tremor in the hand pulling her up. "Now that's the best idea I've heard all day." She brushed herself off and resumed her place behind Lex, as the dark woman began blazing a trail through the thick trees.

They found Thunder standing under a canopy of leaves, happily munching shoots of tender grass. The big stallion looked up and nickered a greeting as the two weary women approached.

Amanda expelled a huge sigh. "I never thought I would be so happy to see a humongous horse." She walked over to the still animal and patted his neck in relief.

Lex followed her and checked Thunder's saddle. "Hey, boy. You about ready to go home?" She leaned against him heavily.

The small blonde wrapped an arm around the weary rancher. "C'mon, honey...let's get you home, too." The endearment had slipped out before Amanda could take it back. Lex didn't say anything, but the happy smile on her face said it all.

"Sounds like a hell of an idea." Lex climbed up on the tall horse and pulled the smaller woman up behind her. "Thought I'd drive this time."

Amanda wrapped her arms carefully around the rancher. "Sure. I've always been told what a great back-seat driver I am, anyway." She felt a chuckle rumble through the tall woman. The young woman wriggled her hands into the heavy coat and gave the flat stomach a gentle tickle. "Home, James," she commanded regally. Snuggling up to the strong back, Amanda placed her cheek against Lex's shoulderblade.

The exhausted woman unconsciously leaned back against Amanda. "Yes ma'am." She gently kneed the big horse. Lex led him back up the path to the pass and let the large animal find his way cautiously through the dark.

Chapter
11

The ride back to the ranch house was uneventful. The rain took pity on the two tired, damp women and slowed to a light drizzle. The moon was trying to break out of the clouds as Lex pulled Thunder up to the stables.

Swinging her leg over his massive neck, the rancher slowly dismounted and turned to pull Amanda down to the ground. "C'mon, buddy. Let's get you cleaned up and fed." Lex led Thunder into the building. She walked the dark horse to his stall while Amanda went to get a bucket of feed.

When Amanda returned with the oats, she noticed that the older woman had already pulled the saddle and blanket from the animal. Lex was in the process of brushing Thunder down. She poured the contents of the bucket into his trough and then stepped into the stall. "Here," she said, taking the brush from Lex's hands, "let me finish this. Why don't you go on up to the house, and I'll meet you there?"

Lex looked down into earnest green eyes. "I'll make you a deal. You can finish with the grooming and I'll clean up the tack. Fair enough?" When the smaller woman opened her mouth to argue, Lex continued, "that way we can walk back up to the house together. Deal?" She placed a grubby hand on the small shoulder. *Let's try this a different way.* "Besides," she hesitated looking down at the ground, "I could kind of use a little help with the walk up there. I'm so tired I'm about to fall down," she finished in a near whisper.

Amanda placed a concerned hand on the rancher's arm. "What's wrong?"

Lex shook her head. "Nothing much, I'm just really tired." She leaned heavily against the side of the stall.

"If you're admitting to that, it's time to take you up to the house." Amanda wrapped a small hand around Lex's arm and began pulling her out of the stall. "I'll come back after a while and finish up with the tack."

Lex meekly let the small blonde drag her from the stable, a tiny grin on the edge of her mouth. *I can't believe I let her get away with this sort of thing. She is certainly something else.*

Amanda swung open the back door practically dragging the exhausted rancher behind her. "Martha! Where are you?" she yelled, pulling the tall form towards the kitchen. "Here." She pushed Lex into the nearest chair. "Sit down before you fall down." She gave Lex's shoulder a gentle squeeze. "I'm going to go find..."

"What on earth happened to you two?" Martha bellowed, standing in the kitchen doorway. "I swear, Lexie...I can't leave you alone for a minute!" She stomped over to where Lex was sitting slumped in her chair. The housekeeper scowled as she pulled the battered black hat from her head. "Good lord! You're as white as a sheet!" she exclaimed, running a pudgy hand across the mud-spattered brow. Turning her attention to the young blonde woman, she asked, "are you okay, sweetheart?"

Amanda sighed, and dropped into a nearby chair. "I'm fine. Just tired, and a little damp." She pushed the wet hood off her head with a grim smile.

Martha, who had begun helping the rancher take off her coat, gasped, "Is this blood?" She gently touched Lex's side.

"Ow!" Lex flinched. "Probably just mud." She tried to bat away the hands that were pulling at the damp shirt. "Ow! Hey, Martha! Cut that out!"

Amanda stood up and walked over and squatted down beside the beleaguered woman. "Blood?" She put a small hand on the dirty denim-covered thigh to balance herself. "Lex?" The young blonde forced the rancher to look her in the eye. "What happened?"

"I dunno...I think it's just mud," she scowled.

Martha shook her head and gave a derisive snort. "Honey, if that's mud, I'm a size 6!" She pulled the coat off the rest of the way then began unbuttoning the filthy shirt. "Let's just take a look, okay?" She turned to Amanda. "Sweetheart, could you go upstairs and get the salve and some clean towels out of the master bathroom?"

Amanda nodded, a worried look on her face. "Sure." She hopped up and patted Lex on the shoulder. "Be right back." She kissed the dark-haired woman on the top of her head then hurried from the room.

The housekeeper turned her attention back to the rancher, who was fighting to keep her eyes open. "Now, Lexie," she tapped her leg, "would you care to tell me what happened out there? I didn't want to upset Amanda, but Charlie radioed about twenty minutes ago. He said that by the time he got there all he could find was an abandoned trailer, and a stolen truck." She pulled the shirt open, and away from the rancher's side. "What happened to you?" The older woman used a corner of the wet fabric to wipe at the blood on Lex's side. "This looks like a mighty wicked gash on your side here, honey."

Lex tried to shift away from what Martha was doing. "Ouch! Would you please stop that!" She found her hands captured by smaller, older ones. "Okay, okay." She cleared her throat. "I think it's a bullet wound." She looked into the concerned brown eyes of the woman who was like a mother to her. "Musta happened when they were chasing me." Lex shot a questioning look at Martha. "Wait. Are you trying to tell me that Charlie didn't catch those idiots out there?" She tried to stand up, but was quickly pushed back down. "Damn! How could he let those fools get away? They could barely take a crap by themselves."

"Now you listen to me, young lady! Last I heard he was still looking for them, so you just calm down." She began pulling the shirt off Lex, who began fighting her again. "Would you please let me take a look at that?"

Lex held the shirt closed stubbornly. "Wait…" she took a deep breath, "can we compromise?" She gave the older woman a pout. "I really want to take a shower. It feels like I'm wearing at least half of the back pasture."

Martha shook her head. "I don't know what I'm going to do with you, Lexie." Then she nodded. "Okay. Compromise it is. But," she held up a warning hand, "it will be a quick shower and then you're going to bed. You've spent too many nights staying up late."

Amanda was standing in the doorway. She had the requested items in hand and a cute grin on her face. "I bet it was almost impossible to get her to take medicine as a child, wasn't it?"

Lex scowled while Martha burst out laughing. "As a child?" Another chuckle. "Sweetheart, I'd rather pull my own teeth than try to get this one to do something that may actually be good for her." She held out a hand to the rancher, who had a grumpy look on her face. "All right, let's get upstairs and get you cleaned up."

"I can do it myself, you know," she complained, but accepted the help up anyway. "You're not gonna bathe me too, are you?" Hearing a giggle from the doorway, she glared at Amanda. "Aw, not you, too!"

The young blonde smiled and shook her head. "Sorry. You're just too cute when you act like an overgrown child." Seeing the outraged look on Lex's face, she backed up. "Umm…I'll just go upstairs and get the shower ready for you." Amanda turned and took off down the hallway, laughing.

"You'd better run, blondie!" Lex called after her. "I'll get you back for that little remark!"

****

It took her a little longer than usual, but Lex finally finished taking her shower. She walked into the master bedroom, wearing her flannel pajama bottoms and a large towel draped over her shoulders. *Wow, even after the day she's been through, she's still absolutely beautiful.* Amanda had returned from her own clean up effort and was sitting on the bed with Martha when Lex made her entrance.

Martha stood up. "Lexie! Where's your nightshirt? Are you trying to catch pneumonia, or just drive me insane?" She grabbed the rancher's arm and pulled her over to the bed.

"I didn't see any sense in putting it on until you were finished clucking over me." Lex sat down slowly. "It's right here on the bed...would have bitten you on the butt if it had been a snake," she teased the older woman.

"Hrumpph. We'll just see about that, won't we, Little Miss Smarty Pants?" Martha gently pushed her onto her back. She turned to address the young woman now standing beside her. "Amanda, don't let this one here get away with anything. She really is impossible sometimes."

"Hey!" Lex pouted, trying to regain some dignity as the housekeeper began spreading salve over the long gash across her ribs. "Ow! Careful there, I'd like to keep myself in one piece, if you don't mind." She slapped at Martha's hands.

Amanda sat down next to the rancher's legs. "What on earth happened there?" She looked carefully at the wound. "If I didn't know any better..." Her face took on an angry edge. "You were shot?!?" She stood up and paced the length of the room. "I don't believe you! You got shot, and didn't tell me?!" The young woman stomped back over to the opposite side of the bed. "How could you not tell me something like this?" She sat on the edge, glaring at the dark-haired woman.

"No! It's not like that...really." Lex stretched her arm across the bed, beckoning for Amanda's hand. "I didn't know." Seeing the storm clouds gathering on the fair brow, she continued, "honestly...I didn't. I though my ribs were just acting up again. And it's really just a slight scrape." She gave Amanda her best pitiful look.

Martha listened quietly to the young women argue. *Poor Lexie...looks like she's finally found someone who's not afraid to stand up to her. Good!* she smiled to herself.

Amanda took a calming breath and grasped Lex's hand. She looked the rancher in the eyes and saw nothing but the truth. "Okay, I believe you." She pulled the hand to her lips and gave it a small kiss. "But," she squeezed it a little tighter, "next time, tell me when you're hurting, okay?"

The rancher nodded. "Promise." Then she flinched. "Dammit, Martha! I think you're enjoying this a little too much!" she gasped as the housekeeper taped a large square of gauze on the wound. "Easy, there...Hey!" She squirmed as the older woman tickled her good side.

"Hush up, you! Now sit up and I'll wrap these ribs again." She smiled as Amanda crawled over to help her patient into a sitting position. "If you would keep these wrapped for more than a day, they'd heal a heck of a lot faster, you know." She pulled the large elastic bandage from behind her back.

"Where did you...?" Lex asked, her face flushing slightly.

Martha laughed. "Honey, I do the laundry around here, you know?" She began wrapping the wide bandage around Lex. "And I know all about the last time you broke your ribs." She laughed at the look of surprise and embarrassment on Lex's face. "Teach you to try and keep anything from me," the housekeeper snickered.

Lex rolled her eyes, but stayed silent. *Figures...damn woman has eyes in the back of her head, and can read minds, too!* She glanced over at Amanda, who was covering her mouth with one hand. "What?"

The younger woman shook her head, but the sparkle in her eyes gave her away. She sputtered, then finally laughed out loud. "Sorry, Lex. But she's right. You shouldn't try to hide things like that."

"There. All done." Martha fastened the bandage with safety pins. She picked up the nightshirt and started slipping it on the injured woman's body. "By the way, Roy called while you were out. He said that he and the boys are bringing out a truck tomorrow and they're going to finish the work on the bridge. He said that they had to wait until all the supplies came in, that's why it's taken them so long." She began buttoning the shirt, much to the rancher's dismay.

"I can dress myself, Martha," Lex argued but let the older woman finish. "I'm glad they're coming out tomorrow. The six of them can have it finished in no time." She sat back, exhausted.

Amanda brushed the hair out of those blue eyes. "I was wondering, where do the hands stay? I've seen Martha's house, the stables, and the hay barn, but..." She stopped when Lex squeezed her hand.

"The hands stay at the bunkhouse, which is just up the road from here. It's closer to the main cattle pens." She took a pained breath and closed her eyes. "It can hold up to fifteen men, but there's only six of them right now. We hire extra help when we start tagging in the spring."

Martha chuckled. "Actually, there're only five real hands. Lester is mainly the cook, right, Lexie?" She looked up when there was no answer and saw that Lex had fallen asleep. Shaking her head, the housekeeper smiled at Amanda. "C'mon honey, let's go get you something to eat. I still have some roast and potatoes left." She stood up and covered the sleeping woman with a blanket.

Amanda regretfully let go of Lex's hand, and climbed off the bed. "Okay, then I'll come back and sit with her for a while." She followed the older woman from the room, glancing back at the doorway at the woman asleep on the bed. *She looks so fragile when she's asleep.* "I'll be right back," she whispered.

****

Amanda finished at the stables and ate a quick dinner. She raced back up the stairs, after being chased out of the kitchen by Martha. "Just see that she stays in bed tonight. Don't let her take any more trips out to the stables, okay?" the housekeeper commanded, then sent the young woman on her way.

Amanda leaned against the doorframe to the master bedroom and sighed. The rancher was sleeping peacefully. Lex had kicked off the blanket and was now curled up on her good side, facing away from the door. The small blonde tiptoed into the room and made her way quietly to the bed. She picked up the blanket from the floor to cover the older woman with it when Lex rolled over and sat straight up in bed, sweat dripping from her body.

"Damn!" she muttered, visibly trembling. "Amanda?" She looked at the smaller woman in dazed surprise.

Amanda placed the blanket around her shoulders and then

felt of her forehead. "You're burning up, Lex. I'd better go..."

Lex grabbed her hand. "Don't leave me," she asked in a hoarse whisper. "I'll be okay." She trembled again. "Could you just stay with me for a while, please?"

Amanda smiled. "Of course I can. Just let me get you some aspirin for that fever, okay?" Seeing the older woman nod, she quickly stepped into the bathroom. Amanda brought a glass of water with several white tablets. Sitting next to the rancher, she gave her a teasing smile. "Here. Take these, then I'll get you tucked in. I seem to be doing that a lot, huh?"

Lex took the aspirin and finished the water. She leaned over and placed the glass on the side table. "Yeah." She fell back into her pillow. "Does that bother you?"

"No...in fact, it makes me feel really good that you let me." Amanda pulled the covers over the still trembling woman. She ran her hand gently through the dark hair.

Lex partially closed her eyes and smiled softly. "Thanks." The feel of Amanda's fingers combing through her hair was very relaxing. "Mmm..." She closed her eyes the rest of the way and drifted off to sleep.

Amanda sat by her side for a long while, running her fingers through Lex's thick hair. *Guess I should go to bed myself, now,* she thought. She laid a gentle hand along the strong jawline, noticing with relief that the fever seemed to be easing. Amanda stood up and was about to walk towards the door when she heard Lex moan slightly in her sleep. *I really don't want to leave her, though.* She compromised with herself, crossing to the other side of the bed and crawling under the covers. *Oh yeah...this feels great!* Lex moaned again and the younger woman turned on her side and took a callused hand in hers. "Shh...it's okay. I'm here," she whispered, which calmed the rancher down immediately. Amanda pulled Lex's hand up to her face and tucked it under her own cheek. She continued to watch Lex sleep, murmuring to her quietly.

****

Martha walked into the master bedroom with a tray in her hand. *It's going to be a beautiful day!* she thought, humming softly to herself. Looking towards the bed, she stopped dead in her tracks, a big grin breaking out over her round features. *That's just too cute!*

They were still sound asleep, although it was almost eight o'clock in the morning. Lex was lying flat on her back with Amanda curled up beside her. The blonde's head was nestled under Lex's chin, and her arm embraced Lex's shoulder protectively; the rancher's left arm was uncovered as well, wrapped securely across the young woman's back...

The housekeeper walked over to the bed and set the tray down on the side table. She could see that both women were still deeply asleep. Martha reached over and placed her hand gently on Lex's forehead. *Thank the good Lord that she's not running any fever this morning. I was a little concerned about that bullet wound, but I guess I cleaned it up okay.* Not wanting the sleeping women disturbed, she reached over to the telephone on the table and turned off the ringer. *Heh. There's more than one way to skin a cat!* She quietly sneaked out of the room, closing the door behind her.

****

She was lying on her back in a sunny field of wildflowers, the gentle fragrance of the flowers around her, a warm breeze stirring her hair. She knew she should get up, but her body rebelled, embracing the warmth of the quiet spring day with decadent pleasure.

Lex took a deep breath, inhaling another lung full of the sweet smell of flowers and opened her eyes. She was somewhat surprised that she was indoors, and even more surprised to find herself in bed. *But I could swear that I smelled fresh flowers.* Her brow creased in confusion and then she noticed the source of the delightful smell. A tousled blonde head was ensconced comfortably against her shoulder directly under her chin. *Gotta compliment Martha on her choice of shampoo for the guest room,* Lex smirked. *That dream was nice, but reality is so much better.* She didn't want to disturb Amanda but her body demanded that she get up. The rancher carefully shifted the smaller woman off her, which got her a small sigh in return. She was finally able to maneuver herself into a sitting position, and was charmed when Amanda rolled back over and snuggled into her pillow. Lex eased herself off the bed, biting her lower lip to stifle a groan. *Getting too old to play all day in the rain, Lexington,* she admonished herself as she made her way slowly into the bathroom.

Mmm...something smells tasty. Amanda woke up, concerned to see that she was lying in the big bed alone, and...*hugging Lex's pillow?* She turned her eyes towards the bedside table, seeing a large tray sitting on it. "So that's where that wonderful smell is coming from," she mumbled, taking another deep breath and closing her eyes blissfully.

"Gee...thanks," Lex drawled as she stepped out of the bathroom.

Amanda blushed and pulled the pillow over her head. "Oh, good grief," she giggled. "I can't believe you heard that."

The tall woman walked over to the bed and sat down. "Good morning to you, too," she grinned.

One green eye peeked out from under the pillow. "Morning," Amanda grumbled, then sat up. "How are you feeling?" She reached towards the older woman. "You look a lot better this morning."

Lex accepted the small hand and pulled it to her lips for a little kiss. "Must be the company I'm keeping."

Amanda blushed to the roots of her hair. "Umm..." she pointed to the tray, "isn't that breakfast?" She tried desperately to change the subject.

Lex raised an eyebrow, but relented. "Yeah. Martha must have just brought it up a few minutes ago. The food is still steaming." She grinned when the younger woman blushed again.

"Oh, God. She was in here when we were asleep?" Amanda stuttered.

The older woman winked at her. "Yep. And now she probably realizes that I didn't need any extra blankets last night." *Ooh...bad, Lexington, very bad. But she's just so damn cute when she blushes!*

To her surprise, the blonde grinned. "That's funny...neither did I." She crawled over to Lex and wrapped her arms around the older woman's neck. "Good morning," Amanda whispered, leaning in and planting a sensuous kiss on Lex's mouth.

The rancher moaned and deepened the kiss almost instantly. Lex put her hands on the small of Amanda's back. She pulled the smaller woman closer, melding their bodies together.

Amanda leaned into the taller woman, burying her hands in the thick dark hair. She gasped when Lex finally broke away. Her heart was pounding so hard she just knew the rancher could hear it.

"Goo..." Lex had to clear her throat before she could continue. "Good morning." She pulled back a small bit. "Certainly makes waking up worthwhile."

Amanda giggled and leaned forward until her forehead was on Lex's chest. "Oh yeah. I think I've just become a morning person."

Lex chuckled and pulled the smaller woman close. Nibbling the nearest ear, she whispered suggestively, "I'm more of a night person, myself." She felt Amanda tremble. "You cold?" she teased, squeezing the small body a little tighter.

"Umm..." the blonde stammered," nnn... no... as a matter of fact, I'm pretty darn warm right now." She tilted her head back, as the older woman worked her way down the slim neck. "Ahh...oh..." She couldn't seem to put together a coherent thought, with Lex taking tender bites of her throat. "Oh, God..." she whispered, as she ran her hands down the strong back. Amanda found that she couldn't sit up any longer as she fell back gracelessly to the bed.

Lex followed her, never giving up on her quest to know every inch of the young blonde's throat. "So sweet..." she mumbled, then turned on her side to get more comfortable. The tall woman's ribs complained and she let out a pained gasp.

Amanda pushed her back to get a look at her companion's face. "Lex? What's the matter?" She could see the pain in those blue depths, and she grasped the paled face with gentle hands.

Lex felt herself guided onto her back against the bed. "Sorry...guess I turned wrong or something," she mumbled. "Just give me a minute to catch my breath." Closing her eyes, she concentrated on trying to will the pain away.

Amanda brushed her hands slowly across the strained face and leaned down to kiss Lex on the forehead. "Shh...just lie still for a little while. Let me go get Martha." She started to get off the bed, but Lex grasped her arm.

"No." The barely heard plea slipped through Lex's lips before she could stop it. "Stay, please," she murmured so faintly, the younger woman sensed it more than heard it.

"Okay, I'll stay." Amanda positioned herself with Lex's head in her lap. She gently stroked the older woman's face and ran her hands through the dark hair. "Shh..." She continued her soothing motions, trying to keep the rancher calm.

A quiet knock at the door made Amanda look up. "Come in," she responded quietly. Lex's eyes were closed, and she finally had a peaceful look on her face.

Martha came into the room slowly, apprehensive about what she would find. *Hope I'm not interrupting anything.* "What's going on, sweetheart?" She saw the look on the young blonde's face, with Lex apparently asleep in her lap. "How's Lexie this morning?" *She looks pale...* The housekeeper walked over to the bed and could now see tears forming in the young woman's misty-green eyes.

"Umm...she was doing pretty good earlier." She flushed at the double meaning. "I mean, she was feeling better than she was last night." Amanda looked down at the still face in her lap.

Martha sat gently on the edge of the bed. She placed a light hand under Amanda's chin, forcing the younger woman to look at her. "And...?"

Amanda's tears threatened to spill as she looked into Martha's caring brown eyes. "We were...uh...just..." She bit her lower lip, "She turned wrong, and I think her ribs moved, or something." Her shaking hands kept up their gentle tracing.

"Oh honey..." The older woman wiped a stray tear from Amanda's cheek. "Everything's going to be just fine." She looked down at Lex, who now looked completely relaxed in sleep. "Darn fool kid..." Martha smiled. "Why don't you come downstairs with me, and we'll let Lexie get some rest?"

"No, I can't." Amanda shook her head. "I promised Lex I would stay with her, and I don't want her to wake up alone."

Martha was about to argue with her when she heard the phone downstairs ringing. She reached over to the bedside table and plucked the cordless phone off the base. "Walters' residence, Martha speaking."

"Martha, this is Charlie. Is Lex around?"

"I'm sorry, but she's resting right now. Is there something I can do?" Martha asked.

"Sweetheart, I hate to be the bearer of bad news, but we've lost track of those damned thieves...the last trail we had, they looked like they were headed towards the house." The sheriff's deep voice sounded regretful.

Martha's face lost some of its color. "What exactly does that mean?"

"It means that you need to get everything locked up tight. I had to send most of my men back to town because of some trouble there. But don't you worry...me and Joseph will keep looking until we find them." Charlie was sounding tired, but resolute.

"Are you sure, Charlie?" The housekeeper's normally strong voice sounded a little nervous.

"I'm sorry to be calling with this so late, but I just wanted to make you aware of what was going on," he apologized.

"No, I appreciate you calling. I'll let Lexie know."

"Are you sure you'll be okay? I really wish I could be there with you, but I think I'll have better luck out here searching, instead of sitting around the house waiting." He paused. "Besides, I know Lex is more than able to handle whatever comes her way."

Martha took a deep breath and then released it. "We'll be just fine. The boys will be back by late this evening, hopefully."

"Okay, then. You take care, and call me if you need anything. I'll still have the radio on the same channel," the sheriff promised.

Martha looked down at the sleeping rancher's peaceful face. "Yes, we will, Charlie. Thank you." She hung up the phone with a shaky hand.

"What was that all about, Martha?" Amanda noticed the slight tremble to the older woman's actions. "Was that the sheriff?" She gave the chubby arm a gentle squeeze.

"Yes sweetheart, that was Sheriff Bristol. He wanted us to know that they haven't been able to find those thieves yet. They lost their trail earlier this morning." She looked down again at Lex.

Amanda's brows knit in confusion. "Well, that's rotten luck and all, but why do you look so upset? I mean, he's going to keep looking, isn't he? And they weren't able to get away with anything, right?"

Martha swallowed hard. "The last trail they found was headed in the direction of the ranch house." Her voice shook a little bit. "And, unfortunately, there's been a big ruckus in town, and Charlie had to send some of his men back. So he and one deputy are the only ones still searching."

"But..." Amanda shook her head, "these men have guns, and they're running around loose!" She stopped a moment, when a thought suddenly occurred to her. "What if they realized that Lex was the one who sabotaged their truck? Do you think they would be stupid enough to come up here?"

"I don't know, honey. That's why Charlie wanted me to tell Lexie. He said she's more capable of defending this house than most of his deputies are." Martha gave her a rueful grin. "He tried for several years to get Lexie to join his department...said she was stronger, smarter, and a heck of a lot better shot than those college boys that work for him." She reached down and brushed the tangled bangs from the sleeping woman's face. "Let's let her get some rest, and I'll tell her about Charlie's phone call when she wakes up." She was about to stand up when the ominous rumble of thunder caught her attention. "That's just dandy. Just what we need, more rain!" Martha stood up and then spotted the untouched tray. "Ahem." She gave Amanda a stern glance. "Honey, next time you two decide to get involved in something, eat your breakfast first."

The younger woman closed her eyes in embarrassment. "Oh, good lord..."

Martha walked to the doorway, then turned back. "Might as well get started on it...breakfast, I mean. You can feed Lexie when she wakes up." She grinned and sauntered out the door.

Amanda scowled down at the sleeping rancher. "You are in

so much trouble when you wake up!" She kissed Lex softly on the lips, then eased out from under her. "She's not going to let us live this one down, and you made me face her alone," she whispered in Lex's ear as she covered the injured woman with a blanket. "And I think we're about to run into some more trouble, so you had better get to feeling better, pronto!"

Another deep roll of thunder rattled the windows, punctuating her observation.

****

Martha spent the remainder of the morning busying herself with housework. She proudly smiled from time to time over her parting shot when leaving the master bedroom. *Oh, the look on Amanda's face...absolutely priceless! I really should be ashamed of myself.* She had just finished dusting the sitting room and was making her way back towards the kitchen when there was a knock on the back door. *Now who could that be?* The housekeeper grabbed the nearest weapon, in this case a mop out of the utility room. She went to the back door and peeked through the curtains that covered the small glass windows in the door. *Ah.* "Charlie! Get yourself in here before you catch your death!" she exclaimed as she swung open the door, pulling the tall man inside.

"Thanks, Martha...I just wanted to stop by and give you a report." Charlie shook the drenched hat outside before closing the door, then followed the heavyset woman into the kitchen.

She placed the mop in a corner, daring him to say anything. "Let me fix you something to eat," Martha offered as she bustled towards the stove.

Charlie Bristol had been coming out to the ranch long enough to know when to keep his mouth shut. "That would be great, Martha. Thanks." He took off his coat, put his hat in a nearby chair and then dropped down into a seat. "Damn...it's been a long night. Is Lex doing okay? You told me earlier that she was resting."

Martha began cooking, turning every so often to talk. "I guess you could say that. She got shot, but it just grazed her side.

She's upstairs now, sleeping." She tried to sound nonchalant, but the lawman could hear the tremble in her voice.

Charlie got up from his seat and walked over to the stove to gently wrap his arms around the trembling woman. "Shh...it's okay, sweetheart. Let it out," he whispered in her ear.

Martha spun around, tucking her head into the tall man's chest, sobbing quietly. "Dammit, Charlie...I could have lost her!" She felt his arms wrap tightly around her as she let the stress of the last few days break free.

The quiet lawman just stood there, loaning his strength to a woman who rarely needed any. *She's the strongest woman I know...yet she lets me see this side of her. God, I want to take care of her for the rest of our lives.* He bent his head down and placed a tender kiss on her graying head. "I know, honey...she'll be fine. Our Lex can handle just about anything." *Oops...that kinda slipped out.* He always thought of the young rancher as his adopted daughter, and he knew she was the child Martha never had. *Oh well... it's not like she doesn't know how I feel, right?*

Martha enjoyed the embrace for a few more moments then stepped back, wiping her eyes with the edge of her apron. "Thanks, Charlie. I guess I musta needed that." She gave him a light kiss on the chin and turned back to her cooking. "So...any luck in finding those thieves? We had to practically sit on Lexie to keep her home last night."

Charlie moved back to the table and sat down. "Not really. Seems they broke up into two different groups, and then went in opposite directions. Joseph went after one group, and I'm looking for the other." He waited until Martha turned around to face him. "One group may be coming this way. That's why I'm here," he said quietly, not wanting to upset the woman he loved.

"I was a little afraid of something like that. Amanda told me what Lexie had done to them. They'd have to be totally stupid not to figure out who did it." She carried a plate of food over to the table and sat it down in front of the sheriff. "Do you think they'd really come after her?" She grabbed the carafe of coffee and brought it to the table along with two mugs.

"I'm not sure. Part of me thinks they'll just try to get transportation out of here. But I don't think they know that the bridge is out." He began dutifully spearing the food, speaking between bites. "What bothers me most is the fact that they are so good at hiding. They could be right outside and I may never find them." He was one of the best trackers in the area. As a teenager, Charlie would hire himself out to out-of-town hunters, making his spare money helping them find game, while most of his friends worked at the local Dairy Queen or lumberyard. And for these thieves to have the skill to elude him, it made him justifiably nervous.

Martha sat down looking into her coffee mug. "I'm afraid," she whispered.

"Honey, I'm not gonna rest until I catch these bastards! And you can take that to the bank!" He reached over and grasped her hand. "No matter how long it takes. I will not let them hurt you!"

The housekeeper looked at him with sad eyes. "I'm not afraid for me, but for Lexie. She's so stubborn. I don't want anything else to happen to her. This week has nearly killed me!" *There...I finally got it out... I don't know how much more I can take.*

"This week? What else has happened, Martha?" he asked, forgetting his food and scooting his chair closer to hers.

Martha sighed. "Friday night, she was down by the creek checking the fence, when she saw a car get washed from the bridge. Damn fool child could have drowned, jumping in like she did," she smiled. "But she did bring us a blessing in disguise..." *Not expected, but certainly welcome.*

"Good God! I thought you raised her with more brains than that! I knew that the bridge was washed out, but..." Charlie squeezed the hand in his. "What kind of blessing are you talking about? Who did she pull from the creek?"

"You know Jacob and Anna Leigh Cauble, right? Well, their granddaughter Amanda was in the car that was knocked into the creek. She's such a sweet girl, too."

Charlie knew that look. *Uh-oh. She's got that Martha Matchmaker face on again.* "Really? I've never met her. Old Jacob talks about her all the time, and she sounds like a wonderful person." *Tread lightly, Charles...don't want to encourage her too much. She was so disappointed after that 'Linda thing' a few years back.* "Is she still here?"

"Oh yes. She's upstairs right now, taking care of Lexie," Martha smiled fondly.

The sheriff's eyebrows rose at that statement. "Taking care of Lex? You've got to be kidding me! We are talking about the same person, right? Tall, dark, and brooding? The Lex I know wouldn't allow that," he laughed.

Martha squeezed his hand again. "You'd be surprised what Lexie has allowed that young woman to do. She even lets her win arguments! I never thought I'd see the day when that would happen!" She chuckled, then got serious again. "I just hope Lexie will stay in bed for a day or so, to get her strength back. She's been so tired lately, and this last little adventure has about worn her out."

"I don't know if that will be possible, Martha. If my suspicions are right, half of that group of thieves could be on their way to the house as we speak...and they could be looking for trouble," he said, looking her directly in the eye.

"They're headed here? Are you going to leave us some protection?" a voice from the kitchen doorway asked.

Both people at the table looked up. A young blonde woman was standing in the doorway with a very concerned look on her face. Amanda looked somewhat disheveled in the oversized maroon sweats she was wearing. She walked into the room and sat down at the table next to Martha.

"Amanda honey, what are you doing downstairs?" Martha asked as she stood up to grab another coffee cup from the cabinet.

The young woman smiled. "I can't stay long, I just came downstairs to get Lex something to eat." She gave the housekeeper a sneaky grin. "I made her promise to stay in bed today." She blushed slightly, remembering what the rancher had told her. *'Only if you keep me company...I tend to get bored, otherwise.'* This had been said with a diabolical smile, which had sent shivers of excitement up and down Amanda's spine.

Charlie looked at the young woman with a tired smile. "Miss Cauble, I really wish I could stay here and personally guarantee your safety, but the truth is I can't even justify keeping a man on this case."

"Please, call me Amanda." She looked at him closely. "And who says you can't stay on the case?" She looked somewhat confused.

The sheriff shook his head sadly. "City politics, Miss..." he saw her frown and amended, "Amanda. The county commissioners don't much care for Lex. She really hacked them off a few years ago, and the bast...err...excuse me, old coots haven't gotten over it yet."

Amanda was shocked. "And, because of their hurt feelings, they won't allow you to help? That's absolutely ridiculous!" She slapped her hand down hard on the table.

Martha stopped working on the tray for Lex and walked over to stand behind the upset young woman. "Yes, it is, sweetheart." She looked at the lawman. "Charlie, don't lose your job over this. I'm sure Lexie can handle things just fine."

He smiled. "It just so happens my vacation starts today. And Joseph just happened to get 'sick' last night. He said he owed Lex a favor, and he'll keep looking for as long as he needs to." He stood up and picked his hat off the extra chair. "Martha, if you wouldn't mind, we'll keep in touch with you on the radio – channel six."

The housekeeper handed the sheriff two thermal containers full of coffee. "I'll carry the portable with me. Now you be careful out there. We've got a date next Saturday night, and I hate to be stood up!" She gave him a gentle kiss on the cheek.

Charlie blushed, but smiled. "You know I'd never stand you up, sweetheart." He gestured with a thermos. "Thanks for the coffee. I'll keep in touch." The lawman stepped out of the kitchen with a happy grin on his face.

Martha looked over at Amanda, who was smiling knowingly. "Now don't you look at me like that." She shook a pudgy finger at the now giggling blonde. "We've been friends for years!"

Amanda covered her mouth with her hand. "I didn't say a word." She shook her head solemnly. The housekeeper swatted her on the arm, then moved back towards the counter. "Hey! It's not my fault your boyfriend is so cute," she chortled again when

Martha actually blushed. *Heh. Paybacks!*

The housekeeper rolled her eyes. "I guess I deserved that." She finished her work on the breakfast tray. "How is Lexie feeling?" Martha opened the refrigerator and poured a glass of orange juice.

"Much better, I think. She's only running a slight fever this afternoon, and her coloring is almost back to normal." Amanda stood up and checked out the tray. "Fruit wedges? Can you actually get her to eat something that's good for her?"

Martha shook her head. "Not usually, but you tell her she had better finish every bite, or I'll come upstairs and feed it to her personally!" She handed the tray to Amanda and turned her towards the doorway. "Good luck, honey. You're gonna need it!" she laughed, as Amanda left the kitchen.

Chapter
12

Lex was standing in the bathroom with her nightshirt unbuttoned and opened. She was turned to one side so that she could
examine her right side in the bathroom mirror. The rancher had
removed the elastic bandage from her body and was gingerly trying to peel off the tape covering the wound. "Ah...damn! When
will someone invent tape that can be taken off without ripping all
your hide off in the process?" she grumbled as she continued to
slowly pull the tape from her skin, wincing with every tug.

"Ahem."

Lex jumped, spinning her head towards the open doorway.
"Oh. Hi," she smiled guiltily at the small blonde standing in the
doorway. Amanda's hands were on her hips and one foot tapped
impatiently.

"What do you think you're doing?" Amanda frowned, purs-
ing her lips.

"Um...well...I had to go to the bathroom?" she rationalized,
as if that explained what she was doing.

The younger woman scowled as she stepped into the room.
"And you had to unwrap your ribs to do that?" She stood directly
in front of the rancher, looking up into somewhat embarrassed
blue eyes.

"No." Lex gave her a sarcastic rolling of those same eyes.

"But my side was aching a little bit, so I thought I'd change the bandage."

Amanda pulled the shirt aside and glanced at the gauze taped over the wound. "Okay. But the bandage is still on. Do you need some help reaching it?" She ran a light hand over the area in question and looked back up at the rancher.

"Uh, sure." Lex gave her a sheepish grin. "I was having some trouble removing the tape."

The smaller woman knelt down so that she was at eye level to Lex's waist. "Hold this." She pulled the shirt back, handing the edge to the older woman. Amanda placed one hand on the rancher's hip for balance and began to gently pull the tape back. "Hold still," she admonished the flinching woman.

"Ow!" Lex jumped again. "I'm not gonna have any skin left at this rate!" she hissed.

The young woman looked up at her and laughed. "Broken ribs don't bother you. Gunshot wounds don't slow you down." She shook her blonde head, "But putting medicine or bandages on…" She patted the flat stomach softly. "You are such a big baby." Amanda paused as she placed a gentle kiss on the bare abdomen. "I really like that." She stood up, the tape forgotten. "I really like you." The blonde wrapped her arms around Lex's neck slowly and pulled the dark head down. Amanda gave the rancher a sweet gentle kiss as she tried to show what her heart desperately wanted to say.

Lex accepted the kiss and the feelings that went along with it. She pulled back slightly, noticing the sparkle of emotion on Amanda's face, emotion that was reflecting how she was feeling too. "Yeah? I really like you, too." She leaned down and captured soft lips again. Lex prolonged the contact until they both broke away breathless.

Amanda leaned into the strong chest and took a deep breath. "Whew…okay. Let's get you taken care of, and then I'll serve you lunch in bed." She dropped back to her knees and reached for the tape again. "And if you're a really good girl, I'll tuck you in." She started to pull on the tape and felt Lex tense up. "Easy. It'll be over soon, I promise." She removed the tape and slowly tried to pull the gauze away from the wound. "Ouch," she whispered, noticing that the gauze was stuck to the wound. "Oh, Lex. This looks like it bled quite a lot." Amanda looked up, and saw the pain in the tall woman's eyes. "I don't think I can get this off without hurting you more."

Lex took a deep breath and closed her eyes. "Yeah, I know." She leaned up against the counter. "I need to clean up anyway. Let me just get into the shower."

The younger woman stood up and placed a hand on her arm. "I've got a better idea. Why don't you let me run you a nice warm bath? Kinda soak for a while and rest?"

Lex opened her eyes slowly. "That sounds like a great idea." She rubbed her eyes. "I'm still pretty beat."

Amanda ran her hand across the strong jaw gently. "I can tell. Why don't you go sit down for a minute, and I'll start the water." She pulled Lex slowly into the bedroom and directed her to the edge of the bed. "Be right back." Amanda kissed the dark head and disappeared into the bathroom again.

****

Amanda stood on the balcony, leaning on the railing and enjoying the break in the rainfall. Heavy clouds still filled the late-afternoon sky but the lightning had stopped. Only an occasional rumble of thunder shattered the still silence.

Lex had been sleeping for several hours after Amanda had managed to wake her and get the still-tired woman out of the tub.

Amanda had stepped into the bathroom over an hour after the older woman had begun soaking in the tub. She had become concerned when Lex had been in there so long without so much as a peep. When she saw the rancher sound asleep among the bubbles, she couldn't help but smile. Just like Sleeping Beauty...she marveled as she stepped to the side of the tub. Well, it worked for Prince Charming, she thought. The small blonde leaned over and placed a gentle kiss on the lips of the sleeping woman, who almost slipped under the water in surprise.

They had a brief argument over the re-bandaging of Lex's wound (which Amanda had won), and then the young blonde had forced the rancher to take some medication that Martha had brought upstairs to combat infection. The housekeeper and the smaller woman had made a good team, practically browbeating poor Lex into submission. They got the injured woman settled and Martha left soon after Lex fell back asleep. The older woman had admonished Amanda to get some rest as well.

But Amanda was too full of energy to sleep, so she called her grandmother to assure the older woman that she was doing fine.

"Hello," Anna Leigh's soft but strong voice answered the phone.

"Gramma? How are you? How's Grandpa?" Amanda felt tears burn her eyes for no reason.

The older woman chuckled. "We're fine, Mandy. How are you? I was a little concerned when we didn't hear from you last night. Jacob said that you were probably worn out from your horseback ride."

Amanda choked back a sob. "It was a long day, that's for sure," she sniffled as she tried to get her emotions under control.

Anna Leigh heard the small sound and became instantly alert. "What happened? You and Lexington didn't have a fight, did you? I know she can be a little abrupt sometimes, but she really is a dear girl."

"No, no. Nothing like that. We just ran into some trouble when we were out riding yesterday. We stumbled onto some thieves, and..." Here, she lost the last shreds of her composure. Amanda began crying uncontrollably, scaring the older woman half to death.

"Mandy, honey...calm down." She paused to gather her thoughts. "That does it. We're driving out there right now! I don't care if I have to swim across that damnable creek!" Anna Leigh raised her voice, something that Amanda had not ever heard before.

"NO!" Amanda said sharply. She then softened her tone. "No, Gramma, I'm okay. It's just been a bad week that's all. And with Lex getting hurt like that, I guess I'm just a little on edge."

"Hurt? Was she thrown from her horse or something?" Anna Leigh guessed.

"Ummm...no," Amanda hedged, knowing her grandmother would panic for sure if she knew what had happened. But she had never lied to the older woman, and was not about to start now. "She was shot." Then she added, "but it only grazed her side. It's just that her ribs are acting up and..." she didn't get any farther.

"SHOT?!?" Anna Leigh practically yelled through the phone. "Are you okay, sweetheart? Dear God, is she okay? Do we need to send a doctor out there?" She stopped her questions when the phone was taken away from her.

"Peanut? What's going on? Your grandmother is white as a sheet. Are you okay? Did I hear her correctly — was someone shot?" Jacob Cauble's deep voice took over the phone, causing a wave of relief to wash over the young woman.

"Grandpa?" Amanda felt her anxiety drop away immediately. "I'm fine. Lex got a little hurt, but she's okay now."

Jacob sighed. "A little hurt? If she was shot, that's more than a little hurt, Peanut. Do you want to talk about it?"

Amanda ran her hand through her hair. "Yeah, actually I would. Got a few minutes? Maybe get Gramma on the other phone?" She had to tell someone about this. Her emotions were still too raw.

"Sweetheart, we have all the time in the world for you," Anna Leigh spoke from the other phone. "Talk to us."

Amanda wiped the tears from her eyes and told her grandparents everything. She began with the wonderful tour of the ranch on horseback, then recounted finding the thieves and the frightening ride back to the clearing after she had alerted Martha and the sheriff. She conveyed the fear she'd felt while hiding in the thick bushes waiting for Lex to return. And finally, she related to them her alarm when she found that the older woman had been shot, and of the fear she had of losing something that was quickly becoming quite special.

Jacob and Anna Leigh had been very supportive, talking the young woman through her bouts of tears and laughter. She told of meeting Sheriff Bristol and of her finally being able to catch the unflappable Martha off guard. And she expressed to them how deep her feelings were becoming for the beautiful rancher

*and of her hopes for a long-term relationship with the tall
woman.*

Amanda was so wrapped up in her thoughts that she didn't
hear when another person joined her on the balcony. Strong arms
wrapped themselves around her waist as large hands rested
lightly on her stomach.

"Penny for your thoughts," a deep voice whispered in her
ear as gentle lips nipped at the soft lobe.

"Mmmm..." She leaned back into the warm body behind her
and covered the hands on her abdomen with her own. "Just daydreaming."

"About anything in particular?" Lex whispered, while she
nibbled a path down the smooth neck.

Amanda leaned her head to one side to give the rancher better access. "Uh..." her knees were beginning to weaken.
"Hmmm?" She turned around and wrapped her arms around the
tall woman's neck.

Lex took this opportunity to blaze a fiery trail down the
younger woman's throat and felt small hands clench in her hair.
The body that she was holding trembled. "Cold?" she murmured,
a slight smile on her face as she continued her assault.

"N...n...no," Amanda breathed. "It just...ahhh..." She
released a deep breath. "C...can we take this inside? I seem to be
having trouble standing."

Lex halted her exploration of the soft throat under her lips,
leaning back just enough to look into slightly glazed green eyes.
"Really?" She gave the young woman a sexy smile. "Think
you're coming down with something?"

"Could be." Amanda unlocked her hands from the silky dark
hair and grasped the large hands that were settled on her waist.
"Maybe you should tuck me into bed." She pulled the older
woman back inside.

Lex followed, as her legs felt suddenly weak. *Must be contagious.* "Sounds serious," she whispered, trying to keep the
playful banter alive. She allowed the young blonde to seat her on
the edge of the bed.

Amanda slowly unbuttoned Lex's nightshirt and pushed the

rancher gently onto her back. "Oh, yeah. I'm going to need lots of special attention." She pulled her own shirt off. "Think you can handle it?" She watched as the blue eyes darkened. "Let me demonstrate." Amanda leaned down and covered the mouth under hers with a searing kiss.

When they finally broke apart, Lex pulled in a shuddering breath. "Let me see what I can do," she murmured, as her hands explored the supple young body with tender caresses. Taking her time, Lex slid her callused hands across the dips and curves, mapping out her intentions with gentle desire.

Amanda felt a burning fire course through her veins as the older woman memorized her body by touch. Lex stopped at different points to leave a heated kiss or a gentle nip. *Oh. It was never like this before,* was her last coherent thought before she rode out a wave of ecstasy as brightly colored lights exploded beneath her closed eyes.

****

Amanda awoke much later with a strong body wrapped around hers. A dark head was pillowed on her stomach and two long arms were stretched protectively across her body. She unconsciously ran a hand though the disheveled dark hair, while her other hand was softly clasped around a tan arm. *I don't know what got into me. But I don't think Lex is going to complain,* she smiled in remembrance. *That was so intense. But I don't think I've ever felt so...loved before,* she sighed. *That's what this is, I think,* she considered, looking down fondly at the sleeping woman in her arms. *No. I KNOW that's what this is.* She felt a strong surge of emotion hit her deeply. *I wonder how Lex feels about it?*

The object of her affection stirred and tightened her hold slightly. Lex nuzzled the smooth skin under her cheek. She opened one blue eye and focused on the shining green eyes above her. The rancher reached up with one hand to wipe the single tear that trickled down Amanda's cheek. "What's wrong?" she asked, attempting to sit up.

The young woman held her down gently with an arm.

"Nothing. I'm just being stupid." She sniffled as she tried to get her roiling emotions under control.

Lex kissed the flat abdomen. "Are you regretting..." her voice broke.

"Oh God, no!!" Amanda lifted the rancher's face upward until they were inches apart. Placing a trembling kiss on Lex's lips she whispered, "no regrets. I'm just a little overwhelmed." Another gentle kiss. "Okay, a lot overwhelmed. I've never felt anything like this before." She touched her forehead to Lex's.

The older woman smiled as tears formed in her eyes as well. "I never thought I'd feel anything like this...ever." She swallowed hard and brought a large hand to cup Amanda's cheek and wipe away another stray tear with her thumb. "I..." she paused as she searched her heart to find words to express the incredible feelings coursing through her body. Unable to find any, Lex gave Amanda a soft kiss. The blonde promptly deepened the kiss to add her own unspoken feelings.

Their bodies were able to articulate what their voices couldn't. Amanda pulled back far enough to gaze into blue eyes that had deepened almost to indigo. Swearing that she could see directly into the other woman's soul, Amanda matched her intensity. Her green eyes sparkled with unshed tears. "I love you." Three words spoken so softly, she barely heard them leave her mouth.

But Lex heard them. Her eyes widened and she stopped breathing. Then those blue eyes closed as silent tears tracked over her chiseled features. She opened her mouth to speak but was unable to utter a sound. Finally taking a large gulp of air, Lex opened her eyes again.

Amanda placed concerned hands on the older woman's face and searched her eyes intently. "Lex?" she whispered, her heart aching. "Honey, what's the matter?" The young woman used her thumbs to brush the tears from Lex's face. "Please, talk to me." She could feel the rancher's body begin to tremble, still not able to speak.

Lex pulled Amanda tightly to her and buried her face in the tangled blonde hair. "No one has ever said that to me before," she rasped, her throat thick with emotion. "And," she pulled back until she could look the smaller woman directly in the eyes, "just so there's no confusion..." Lex placed a soft kiss on Amanda's lips, "I love you, too." She pulled the smaller woman into her arms and then rolled over to lean back against the headboard.

Amanda snuggled happily into the strong arms. She was content to just sit and absorb the warm feeling that was bubbling up between the two of them. Even the now loud rumbling of thunder couldn't ruin the euphoria that Amanda was feeling. She felt a soft kiss on the top of her head, and the arms holding her tightened.

"I hate to disturb you," the familiar deep voice rumbled in her ear, "but if we don't get downstairs pretty soon, Martha's gonna come looking for us."

The small blonde took a small bite out of the conveniently located nearby shoulder. "And this would be a bad thing?" She nibbled her way over to the tan throat. "Would it bother you? Her seeing us like this?"

Lex laughed. "Hell, no! I just didn't want you to get embarrassed, that's all."

"Well, I don't think she's going to pick on me much, at least for a little while anyway. We sorta called a truce this morning," Amanda smiled under the rancher's chin.

Lex pulled the young woman's face up so she could see her eyes. "Truce? Did you two have an argument?" she asked, concerned. *Please, no. I thought they liked each other.*

"No. Nothing like that." Amanda gave her an impish grin. "I caught her in the kitchen with her boyfriend."

Lex laughed. "Charlie was here?"

"Yeah, early this morning." Amanda went on to explain everything that he had told Martha and her, and how he refused to stop looking until the thieves were caught.

The rancher released a heavy sigh. "Damn. I was afraid of something like that." She kissed the top of Amanda's head. "C'mon. Let's get cleaned up and go downstairs. I'm starving."

Amanda climbed off Lex with a regretful sigh. "And I thought that noise was thunder. I didn't know it was your stomach growling," she smirked at the older woman. "Wanna conserve some water?" She held her hand out to Lex who took it immediately.

"Sure." Lex allowed the smaller woman to pull her off the bed and lead her into the bathroom. "Although I don't know how much we'll conserve. This could take a while," she laughed, following the cute blonde.

****

Martha was standing at the kitchen window, staring silently out at the darkened sky. Amanda was about to call out a greeting when Lex covered her mouth with a large hand. Giving the younger woman a devilish grin, the rancher sneaked up behind the housekeeper and wrapped her arms around the ample waist.

"Evenin' Martha!" she boomed, squeezing her quarry tight.

"Aaaarrgghh!" the older woman screamed, then spun around quickly. "Blast it!" She slapped the taller woman on the arm. "I swear I'm going to keel over dead one of these days!"

Amanda stood a few steps behind Lex, bent over laughing. "Good one, Lex!" She finally stopped long enough to catch her breath.

The housekeeper glared at the young blonde. "You know," she said with her hands on her hips, "I can get my spoon after you, too!" She swatted Lex on the rear. "And you..." she pushed the tall woman towards the table, "sit down and I'll get you something to eat." Noticing that they both had damp hair, she let a wicked smile cross her face. "You too, Amanda." Then making sure she could see their faces added, "I'm sure you both worked up quite an appetite." She enjoyed the very dark blush that graced both younger women's faces. *Heh. Teach them to mess with me.*

Lex looked up and smiled as her blush faded. "As a matter of fact..." She raised an eyebrow at Martha. "You'd better give me double helpings." She winked at Amanda, who just covered her face with her hands. "Right, Amanda?"

The young blonde uncovered her face and stuck her tongue out at the rancher. "I'll get you for that!"

"I certainly hope so!" Lex gave her a sexy smile. "I'll be

looking forward to it."

Martha walked up to the table and lightly tapped the dark head. "Behave yourself, Lexie." She then gently ran her hand through the damp hair. "You look like you're feeling better, sweetheart."

"I am, Martha. Guess all that sleep did the trick. I feel almost as good as new." She leaned back into the caress and guiltily enjoyed the attention. "And I had a really good nurse." She smiled tenderly at Amanda.

The housekeeper softly touched Lex's forehead, relieved to find it cool. "How's your side? Do you want me to change the bandage?"

With a shake of her head, Lex captured the small hand and squeezed it. "It's great. Amanda took care of it earlier."

The older woman looked over at Amanda who nodded. "Yep. It had bled quite a bit during the night, but other than that it looked pretty good." She gave Martha an impish smile. "I just re-bandaged it a few minutes ago. It seems to be healing just fine."

Lex reached across the table and grabbed a small hand. "Must be all the good care I've been getting."

"How're your ribs?" Martha asked as she placed the platters of food on the table and sat down to join the younger women.

"Good as new," Lex said between bites of food. She raised her head quickly when a loud crash of thunder rumbled outside.

Martha laughed. "Teach you to try and fib to me!"

Lex moaned. "Yeah, right." Then she turned serious. "Not to try and change the subject, but have you heard anything else from Charlie?"

The housekeeper gave her a grim look. "He radioed in a couple of hours ago. No luck so far, but a couple of deputies rode in by horseback, and they were going to take over while he and Joseph went up to the bunkhouse for a rest."

"Good. I didn't want him to stay out there indefinitely. He's begging for pneumonia as it is," Lex frowned. "Any word on how the work on the bridge is coming along? Have you heard from the boys?" She continued to eat, not realizing just how hungry she was until the food began to hit her stomach.

Martha shook her head. "They called right after lunch, and said that the bridge should be finished by sometime tomorrow." She looked at Amanda. "I'm sure Lexie will give you a ride back into town."

Amanda looked up from her plate with a surprised look on her face. She saw the mischievous grin on the housekeeper's face and smiled. "Well, I really do need to check on my grandparents." She saw Lex's face fall. "But, I'd like to just go and pick up some clothes and things, and come back here to help out. At least until someone is completely healed." Amanda smiled at Lex who gave her a relieved look.

The rancher picked up her glass of ice tea and tried to look nonchalant. *God, that scared me. I was afraid that she was going to leave me as soon as she was able to.* She lifted the glass to her lips. "You don't have to work here. You know you're welcome to stay as long as you want."

"I know, it's just that..." Amanda paused when she saw the glass shake slightly in the dark-haired woman's hand. *Why is her hand trembling like that?* She looked into Lex's eyes and noticed a thinly veiled fear in those blue depths. *She thought I'd leave? After today?* The blonde felt a sharp jab of pain in her chest with this realization. *We're going to have a nice long chat later, my friend.*

"Amanda?" Lex called her out of her reverie. "You with us?"

Amanda blinked then shook her head. "Uh, yeah. Sorry about that." She stood up and took her now-empty plate to the sink. "I need to go call my grandmother, if that's okay with you." She looked at Lex, whose face was impassive.

"Sure, go ahead. I was going to go down and check on the horses." Lex stood up as well and placed her hand on the empty chair back.

The blonde woman crossed the kitchen to lay her hand on Lex's. "Martha and I fed them this morning, so they should be okay." She pulled the callused hand to her lips and kissed it softly. "Don't be gone too long, all right?"

Lex finally allowed a smile to cross her face. "Right. Give your grandparents my best." She gave the small hand a gentle squeeze then made her way to the door. "Martha, lock the door behind me just in case, okay?"

The housekeeper was running water into the sink. "Amanda, honey, could you do that for me? I've already gotten my hands stuck in this dishwater." She gave them both an innocent look.

Amanda walked over and placed a light kiss on the round cheek. "Okay... but I think you should work on your subtlety," she laughed and followed Lex out of the kitchen.

They walked silently down the hallway hand in hand until they reached the back door. "Do you need any help? I could wait to call my grandmother." Amanda watched as Lex put on her heavy duster and placed the battered black cowboy hat on her head. "Do you ever leave the house without that hat?" She reached up and pushed it back off the rancher's head, getting a smile in response.

"Well, actually, no I don't. Guess it's like my security blanket. My dad gave it to me right before he left." Lex paused. "Makes me feel like he's here with me, watching."

Amanda began to button the coat closed. "How long has it been since you've spoken to him?" She looked up and saw a fleeting sadness in Lex's eyes.

The rancher took a deep breath and released it slowly. "'Bout a year, I guess. He called asking for some money, said the circuit was pretty tough." She let her gaze turn inward for a long moment. "Haven't heard from him since, so I guess things are going better for him." She shook her head. "Anyway, guess I'd better go check on the horses." Lex pulled the younger woman into her arms. "See you in a little bit." She leaned down and slowly captured Amanda's lips. Small arms wrapped tightly around her neck.

"Hurry back," Amanda whispered when they finally broke apart. Thunder interrupted her, followed by a nearby flash of lightning. "Be careful." She ran a loving hand across her strong jaw.

Lex leaned into the caress and closed her eyes. She took a shuddering breath, then looked down into green pools of light that were Amanda's eyes. "I love you." Lex saw those eyes sparkle and a smile cover the blonde's face.

"I love you, too." Amanda stood up on her tiptoes and placed a very soft kiss on the tall woman's lips. She deepened the kiss and poured her heart and soul into the connection.

Lex opened the door and stepped out. Turning, she said, "I've got a key, so go ahead and lock the door." She started down the steps. "I'll be back in about an hour or so. Just want to look around."

Amanda stood at the open doorway with a sweet smile on her face. "Don't be too long, or I'll come out after you," she winked at the older woman. "I know of several better activities than messing around with a bunch of horses."

Lex bit her bottom lip. "Hmmm...hold that thought. I may have a surprise for you later," she grinned, and started towards the barn.

****

Lex made a short check of the horses and then moved quickly into the maintenance barn. The little Mustang was still sitting there waiting patiently. She slipped off her coat and hat and stepped into the greasy coveralls that she had left hanging by the door.

An hour later, Lex was certain that the little car had suffered no serious damage due to the flood. She put a couple of gallons of gas in the tank and then sat down in the drivers' seat to turn the key. The engine grumbled then finally sputtered to life. "YES!!!" she yelled out loud and pumped a hand into the air in triumph. Leaving the engine running, Lex walked over to the telephone that was hanging on the wall.

Two rings later, Martha answered. "Walters' residence, Martha speaking."

Lex mischievously lowered her voice to a rumbling growl. "Hey, baby...you sound hot. Whatcha wearing?" She covered up the mouthpiece to try to muffle her laughter.

"Oooh...you sound absolutely marvelous. What are *you* wearing?" the housekeeper countered when she recognized the voice immediately.

Lex lost it. Laughing hard she replied, "Greasy overalls, sweetie..."

Martha laughed as well. "Hmm...a little too kinky for me, I think. But let me ask my friend in the other room. I think she's into nutcases like you!"

"Wait!" Lex yelled. "Don't get Amanda just yet. I need you to do me a favor." She used her best pleading voice on the phone. "Ask her to stand at the window in the sitting room, looking out the front. I want to show her something."

Martha chuckled. "Got it running, did you?" She knew how much the young blonde treasured the classic car. "She's going to fall to pieces, you realize that, right?"

Lex smiled. "That's okay. I'll pick them up." She began stripping the coveralls off with one hand. "I should be up there in about 5 minutes, okay?"

"Okay, sweetheart. I'll make sure she's ready." Martha hung up the phone, then went in search of the young woman in question.

****

While Lex was busy getting the Mustang in running condition, Amanda had gone into the office to call her grandparents.

"Hello, Grandpa Jake," she greeted the deep voice that answered the phone.

"Hey there, Peanut! How's everything going?" Jacob chortled, thrilled to be speaking to his favorite granddaughter.

"Great! How are you feeling? Is your leg still bothering you?" She remembered how badly Jacob limped. He was barely able to walk on his newly healed leg without discomfort.

"Not bad at all now, sweetheart. I'll be back on the jogging track in no time!" Jacob chuckled as another voice broke in on the conversation.

"I'll second that, Mandy. Your grandpa has been chasing me all over the house!" Anna Leigh laughed. "How's Lexington feeling?"

Amanda laughed as well. "Much better, Gramma. She's gone out to check the horses right now." She took a deep breath. "Once everything gets back to normal, I'd like to invite her home for dinner, if that's okay with both of you."

Anna Leigh crossed the living room to sit next to Jacob on

the sofa. "Does this mean what I hope it means?" she asked as her husband grasped her hand gently.

"Yes, I think it does, Gramma. I've never felt like this with anyone else before." Amanda paused. "I love her."

Jacob chuckled. "Wonderful! I've always liked her. Especially after the way she took care of my Anna Leigh during that whole escapade with the Taylor house."

"Oh really? Guess I'll have to get her to tell me all about that, huh?" Amanda laughed. "Anyway, I just wanted to call and let you know that the bridge work should be finished sometime tomorrow. So I'll probably be home in the next day or so." To cut off any other questions the young woman continued, "I told Lex I wanted to stay out here for another week or so, just until she's healed up from this past week's activities. I just want to pick up a few things, and see both of you."

They spent the next half-hour or so talking about inconsequential things. Amanda had to promise to bring *her* rancher to dinner in the next couple of days. *They sound almost as thrilled about all of this as I am. I wonder if that's possible? I wonder what my own parents will think? Uh, don't think I want to know the answer to that one right now.* Her grandparents had always been very supportive of her life's choices. Her parents couldn't seem to comprehend what she tried very hard to tell them. She always felt more loved and happy during the summers of her childhood since they were spent with the two most important people in her life. Jacob and Anna Leigh had treated her as their own child, with all the love and support she had been missing at home.

Amanda hung up the phone, feeling a bittersweet pang in her chest. Her grandfather's recent accident had reminded her of their mortality and she always became a little sad after these types of thoughts. *Stop it! Don't dwell on the bad things, just think about all the good things!* she repeated her grandmother's mantra, which kept her sane during those long nights at the hospital.

Amanda was still drifting in her thoughts when the phone rang. Martha must have picked it up immediately, because it only rang one time. A few moments later the housekeeper bustled into the room with a big smile on her face.

"Amanda! I'm sure glad I found you! Lexie wants you to look out the front window. She has a surprise for you." The older woman grasped her arm and led the blonde into the sitting room.

The room was feminine, Amanda noticed. It was filled with Queen Anne furniture, and a beautiful baby grand piano standing proudly in one of the only rooms she had not been into. The large bay window had delicate lace curtains and soft watercolor paintings graced the room.

"Martha, it's beautiful!" she whispered as she looked around the room in awe.

The housekeeper sighed with a sad look on her face. "This was Mrs. Walters favorite room. I remember when she used to sit at the piano and play for little Lexie." She wiped an errant tear from her cheek. "Lexie used to sit in here for hours, practicing. She was really good at it, too. Until her father told her it was useless to play the piano when she should spend her time learning how to run a ranch." Taking a deep breath, the housekeeper continued, "she still comes in here every once in a while and plays. I think it relaxes her."

"Lex plays the piano?" Amanda was somewhat surprised. The rancher didn't seem like the type to spend time with something that had to be done indoors.

"Oh, yes. She even used to write compositions when she was in school." Martha's face took on an angry tint. "But that no-good father of hers teased her until she quit." She was about to comment further when a honk from outside interrupted her.

Amanda rushed to the window, then gasped, "oh my God!" She rushed out of the room and through the front door before the housekeeper could say a word.

Martha peeked through the front window and saw a light blue Mustang sitting in the circular drive. "Well, I'll be..." she muttered, then laughed and headed towards the kitchen.

****

Amanda stood on the front porch with tears streaming down her face. Lex had stepped out of the vehicle and was standing on the driver's side with the door still open. The young blonde walked slowly down the steps, unable to say a word.

The rancher smiled. *Oh, this was definitely worth a few sleepless nights.* She barely had time to brace herself before Amanda wrapped her small body around the taller woman.

"I can't believe this! I thought it was lost forever!" Amanda murmured with her face tucked securely in Lex's shoulder. "Was this what you were doing all those nights?"

Lex buried her face in the soft blonde locks. "Yeah. Surprised?" She smiled when the younger woman squeezed tighter. "It's got a small dent on the left rear panel and the upholstery needs to be cleaned, but other than that it's okay." She pulled away from the small blonde momentarily and reached into the back seat. "I found this in the front floorboard." Lex handed over a purse and briefcase dotted with dirt, but reasonably intact. "I didn't look at anything, but I laid everything out on a workbench to dry."

Amanda looked at the items, then back at Lex. She grabbed the tall woman around the neck and kissed her soundly. "Thank you!" Amanda couldn't begin to explain the emotions thrumming through her. "You have no idea what this means to me!" she began to cry.

Lex held her close and kissed the top of the blonde head. "I have a pretty good idea. I know that you and your grandfather found this car and rebuilt it together. But you never complained about it when you thought it was gone."

The younger woman stepped back to look her directly in the eyes. "The car is very important to me, that's true. But as long as I was alive, I knew that things always have a way of working themselves out. My grandparents taught me that." She framed the strong face with her hands. "And as long as I have you, nothing else matters." Amanda leaned up and placed a soft kiss on Lex's chin.

Lex closed the car door and led the young woman back towards the house. "I'm just glad you dropped into my life." She opened the front door then handed Amanda the keys to the car. "Here...you can drive us into town tomorrow." Lex locked the door behind them.

Chapter
13

The two young women were sitting in front of a roaring fire in the den. Lex was comfortably ensconced in a chair with Amanda relaxed in her lap. "Are you sure I'm not hurting you?" Amanda asked the older woman. Lex had a very tight hold on her and they had been snuggling for well over an hour.

"Are you kidding me?" The rancher nibbled on a convenient ear. "I've never felt better." She was about to get a little more serious about it when Martha walked into the room.

"Excuse me, Lexie. But I've gotten dinner ready, if you can tear yourself away from what you are doing." The housekeeper worked hard to keep the grin off her face. "If not, I guess I can just throw it out."

Amanda practically jumped out of the dark-haired woman's lap. "Wait! You wouldn't throw out perfectly good food, would you?" She seemed horrified by the thought.

Lex laughed and stood up as well. "Please. This is the same woman who would save my plate and make me finish it later when I was growing up." She shook her head. "She never throws food away!"

Martha popped her dishcloth at the dark-haired woman as she walked through the door. "That's only because you would barely stand still long enough to eat, then you'd come back an hour later whining about being hungry."

The trio laughed their way into the kitchen. Martha pushed the younger women gently into chairs and joined them as they passed platters of food back and forth.

"I've been meaning to ask you Martha, when do you find time to cook all these wonderful meals?" Amanda asked as she devoured her food with gusto.

"It's not really that big of a deal, honey, and it doesn't take that long at all." The housekeeper jumped when thunder rumbled a little too close by.

Lex looked up at the ceiling and shook her head. "I swear, I'd almost welcome a drought after this past week." Another crack of thunder shook the house.

"Sounds like it's getting closer," Amanda stated and unconsciously scooted closer to the rancher.

"It's only weather. Nothing to be worried about." Lex wrapped her arm around Amanda's shoulders and pulled her close. Then she quieted and listened carefully. "Did you hear something?"

Martha looked at her quizzically. "I hear another storm approaching, why?" She couldn't hear anything out of the ordinary.

"Shhh..." Lex warned as she got up and stepped over to the kitchen window. "Something isn't right out there."

Suddenly another crash of thunder rumbled, and the lights went off in the house.

"Damn!" The rancher cursed and groped around in the darkness. She reached into a nearby drawer and pulled out a flashlight. "Amanda? Martha? You two okay?" She aimed the beam of light towards the table to highlight two pale faces. Walking over to the frightened women, Lex squatted down between them. "I don't like the feel of this." She saw the small blonde tremble slightly. Lex grasped a nearby hand and squeezed it gently. "Hey...it's okay. Probably just the storm."

Amanda knew that Lex was only saying that to make her feel better. *I think we're in some serious trouble here,* she mused as she looked into concerned blue eyes. "Yeah, sure." She looked over at Martha who had a concerned look on her face as well.

Amanda was about to reassure the housekeeper when the sound of breaking glass assaulted their ears.

Lex jumped up and looked at Martha. "You two get into the storm cellar, I'll go see what I can find." She started towards the door when two sets of hands caught her from behind.

"Are you crazy? C'mon down into the cellar with us. I've got the portable radio here in my apron. We'll call Charlie," Martha begged Lex, as she was suddenly afraid for the young rancher.

Amanda waited patiently for the older woman to finish. "She's right. If it is those thieves, they have guns, and you don't. Please don't do this," she pleaded quietly. Amanda knew in her heart that Lex couldn't and wouldn't do as she asked.

Lex kissed the small blonde gently on the lips. "Go with Martha. I've got to check this out." She turned to look at the housekeeper. "Go to the cellar...please." She stared at the older woman for a very long moment. "Call Charlie. Tell him to come in through the back door." She walked over and grabbed a nearby skillet. "You always said I was dangerous in the kitchen," she smiled.

Martha smiled grimly and grabbed the younger woman. "C'mon, honey. The cellar is very well hidden. We'll be safer there." She looked up at the rancher as tears floated in her dark eyes. "Join us soon, okay, sweetheart?" She squatted down beside the table and moved the small rug underneath.

Lex followed her lead, scooting the table off to one side so that the housekeeper could open a trap door. "You two go on in, I'll cover your tracks." She bent down next to the older woman and gave her a strong hug. "I'll see you in a little bit."

Martha smiled as she stepped down into the dark passage. "You'd better." She continued down until she reached the bottom. The housekeeper picked up a lantern and lit it with a nearby book of matches. "Thank the good Lord I clean this place up on a weekly basis."

Amanda looked at Lex with tears running down her face. "I'd rather be with you." She leaned into the strong hand that caressed her face. "I don't think I can stay anywhere without you."

Lex pulled her close for a deep kiss. "I need you to take care of Martha for me." She jumped as the back door was forcibly opened. "Hurry. I'll see you soon." Another quick kiss. "I love you," she whispered as she sent the small woman down the stairs. Lex closed the trap door behind her.

The rancher rearranged the rug and placed the table back over it. She started towards the doorway armed with only a flashlight and a cast iron frying pan. Lex could hear voices in the hall as she raised her makeshift weapon and stood against the wall.

"Shut up, dammit!" a deep voice barked low, just inside the house. "They know we're here now."

A younger voice broke though the silence. "Why do we have to do this, Matt? Wouldn't it be easier to just steal a car or something?"

"Because I don't like being made a fool of, and that damn woman did just that!" the deeper voice intoned as they walked carefully down the hall. "You still with us, Darrell?" he whispered behind him.

"Yeah...I'm here. Why, I don't know," another annoyed voice grumbled. He cocked the rifle to make sure a round was in the chamber.

Lex leaned closer against the wall as she heard the three men move nearer and nearer to the kitchen doorway.

****

Amanda watched with a growing sense of dread as the trapdoor closed. She turned to look around the small room. The lantern's flickering light painted the walls that were covered with open shelves. Canned goods and other items nestled neatly in several rows. With a heavy sigh, Martha had sat down on a wooden bench that ran down the middle of the room.

"C'mere, honey." The housekeeper patted a spot on the bench. She pulled the small radio from her apron pocket as Amanda sat down beside her. "Charlie? Do you read me?" the older woman spoke into the small radio quietly.

A small burst of static answered as a faint voice replied, "Martha? Read you loud and clear. What's up?"

The housekeeper glanced at the young woman and a relieved smile broke out on both of their faces. "You need to get to the house, pronto. We've got some unexpected visitors."

"Roger that..." a short pause, "where are you, hon? Are you okay?"

Martha exchanged a worried glance with Amanda. *Better not give too much away, just in case.* She thought a moment before replying, "Amanda and I are *weathering* it out just fine." She paused again, giving that time to sink in. "Lexie said for you to come in the back way. The electricity is off, so be careful."

There was a short pause, then the sheriff spoke. "Gotcha. I'm at the previously discussed location. I'm on my way now." He understood the need for caution. The thieves could listen in on their conversation far too easily. "Sit tight, sweetheart," he signed off.

Light thumping from above caught the two women's attention. Martha looked at the ceiling and chewed on her bottom lip. "Sounds like they're in the hallway now." She glanced over at Amanda, whose shadowed face held a look of alarm.

"I hate just sitting here!" the young woman exclaimed. Amanda stood up and paced the length of the small room. "There's got to be something we can do!"

The housekeeper stood up and took a firm grasp on the surprisingly strong shoulders. "I don't like it much either, but we are helping in a way." Martha saw Amanda take a breath to argue. "With us safe down here, Lexie can concentrate on those men and not have to worry about us." She pulled the young woman back over to the bench to sit down. "The best thing we can do is stay calm, in case she needs our help." She held Amanda's hand and squeezed it firmly.

Amanda took a deep breath and wiped a stray tear from her cheek. "I know that what you're saying makes sense, but I can't help but feel that I should be doing more." Another loud thump from above made her look up at the ceiling. She was about to say more when a sharp bang came from above. *Oh, God, no!* "LEX!!!" she screamed.

****

Lex leaned up against the wall next to the doorway and listened as the three men continued to argue.

"Okay, listen. If we split up, it won't take as long to search."

"Matt," the younger voice interrupted, "I don't wanna do this. It ain't right."

"Shut up, Ronnie," the older man snapped, then sighed. "Fine. You stick with me, and we'll check upstairs. Darrell, you look around down here. Shoot anything that moves, got it?"

A resigned sigh was his answer. "Yeah, yeah. I got it." He watched as the other two moved towards the stairs. Flashes of lightning through the windows and broken back door were the only illumination in the silent house.

Lex hugged the wall tighter. She heard two of the men move past the door and step towards the darkened stairway. The third man stood in the hallway grumbling to himself.

"'Check the downstairs,' he says," he mumbled, "'shoot anything,' he says." He peeked into the kitchen.

The rancher raised the frying pan over her head and prepared to swing downwards as soon as the thief entered the room.

Darrell stood in the doorway, holding his breath and listening carefully. A close strike of lightning lit up the entire room. He could see that the room was empty except for the abandoned food sitting on the table. The thief shook his head and continued down the hallway towards the front of the house.

Lex let out the breath she had been holding, angry that the man didn't walk into the kitchen. *Guess I'll just have to follow him.* She eased into the doorway and slowly looked out with one eye. The rancher could barely make out the dark form that was creeping into the den. *Time to play hide-and-seek,* she smiled, as she sneaked down the long hallway.

Darrell crossed into the den, waving the rifle back and forth as he peeked around the heavy furniture. Lex slowly crept up behind him as he made his way to the office. She raised the frying pan over her head. The nervous man sensed another presence in the room and he started to turn around. Another flash of lightning lit up the room, highlighting a tall form barely two feet away from him. He raised his rifle to fire at the apparition that appeared to be swinging something towards his head.

'CRACK!'

The gunshot echoed throughout the silent house, leaving a deathly still quiet behind it.

****

Amanda jumped to her feet to race up the stairs when a strong hand on her arm stopped her. "Let go of me!!" she cried, as she struggled to break free.

Martha held the squirming young woman tightly. "No, sweetheart. We've got to stay here." She wrapped Amanda in a firm hug. "We don't know what's going on up there."

Amanda tried to twist out of the strong grasp, then finally relented. "But she may need me!" she sniffled as she buried her face into a strong shoulder. "She could be hurt..." A shudder ran through her body, "or..." She couldn't even finish such a horrible thought.

The housekeeper hugged the younger woman. "Honey, you can't think like that." She placed a gentle kiss on the blonde head. "Our Lexie is one of the strongest people I've ever known." She led the smaller woman over to the bench to sit down.

Amanda calmed down, thinking about what the older woman had said. *She is very capable. I'm not giving Lex enough credit.* Amanda could read the fear in Martha's eyes as well. *I never thought about what this is doing to her. Lex is practically her daughter. I've been pretty selfish here.* She linked her hands with the older woman's and squeezed gently. "You're right, as usual. I guess I'm just a little on edge. It's been a pretty wild week."

Martha was about to reply when the radio crackled.

"Martha? You there?"

She hurriedly pulled the device once again from her apron. "We're here, Charlie."

"I'm right outside. Did I hear a gunshot just now?" Nervousness was quite evident in the sheriff's tone. "Are y'all okay?"

Martha took a trembling breath then looked over at Amanda. The young woman was chewing on her lower lip. "Amanda and I are fine. We're still hidden." Her voice broke, "I'm not sure about Lexie, though." She felt a small arm wrap around her shoulder in support.

"She's fine, I'm sure of it," Charlie assured her. "I've got reinforcements on the way. We caught one group of those damn thieves, hiding near the stolen vehicles."

Amanda pulled the older woman close with relief. "That means there's only three left." She gave a forced little laugh. "No contest."

****

The silence hung heavily in the air upstairs as a crumpled body lay sprawled in the center of the office floor. The tall figure stood over the still form for a moment, then squatted down beside it to check for a pulse. *Still breathing. Guess that's a good sign.* Lex tossed the frying pan off to one side. She removed the laces from the unconscious man's work boots and tied up his hands and feet. She picked up the rifle and was about to leave the room when she heard heavy footsteps on the stairs. *Good. One down and two to go.* The rancher crossed stealthily across the den, ending up next to the doorway. Lex peeked around the corner and could barely see two forms. One was at the foot of the stairs and the other was standing in the kitchen doorway.

"Matt, I'm scared!" the younger man whimpered softly as the older man stepped into the kitchen. A moment later he returned and walked towards the partially opened back door.

"Shut up! I swear to God, if you don't quit whining, I'll shoot you myself!" he growled as he opened up the door to the utility room and quickly looked inside.

The smaller man sat down on the bottom step and wrapped his arms around his knees. A large clap of thunder startled him and he began to cry, rocking back and forth. "Matt. I wanna go home!"

Lex watched as the taller form moved quickly back towards the stairs.

SMACK! The sound of the slap shattered the silence.

"Sssshhhh! Quit being such a damned baby! You're fifteen years old. Grow up!" He shook the younger man's shoulder. "Now c'mon! Stay behind me and keep your mouth shut!" Matt started walking down the hallway towards the den where Lex stood waiting.

C'mon, you bastard. Just a little closer. She silently urged him on. *Dragging a poor kid into this mess. I'm gonna enjoy this!* She turned the rifle around in her hands to hold it like a club.

The back door swung open as another peal of thunder rolled, and lightning illuminated the sky once again.

"Hold it!!" A man's voice yelled as he flashed a beam of light down the hallway. "Sheriff's department!"

Matt whirled, keeping the young man between him and the deputy. The lawman raised his gun and aimed.

"NO!!!" Lex screamed to keep the boy from being shot. She jumped out of the den, brandishing her rifle like a club. "Hold your fire!!" She yelled at the deputy as she swung the gun downward towards the thief's head.

'CRACK!'

'CRACK!'

The lights came on just as the shots rang out.

****

"Okay. I've got men at all of the doors and I've found where they threw the outside electrical switch. As soon as everyone is in position, I'll turn the lights back on, and we'll go in."

Amanda quickly pulled the radio from Martha's now shaking hands. "Do you really think that's wise? We don't know where Lex is, or what the situation is up there."

"Normally I'd agree with you. But I don't want my men to be shooting at shadows. Someone could get hurt." He paused, trying to get his point across without upsetting either woman unduly. "And, if Lex is hurt, it'll be easier to find her if the lights are on."

Before Amanda could reply to that dark thought, two more gunshots rang out upstairs. The electricity flickered on moments later. "Charlie? What's going on?" she practically screamed into the radio. "Charlie?!?!" Amanda handed the radio to Martha and started towards the stairs. "That's it! I'm not spending a single second longer down here!!"

Before she could reach the stairs, the trapdoor opened. The bright light from above blinded the two women momentarily. Amanda had to shade her eyes from the glare, since there was only one weak bulb in the storm cellar. "Lex?" she whispered, begging in her heart for it to be true. She charged up the stairway with Martha quickly at her heels.

Lex was practically bowled over by the overexcited women. She found herself almost flat on the floor. "Hey, hey! Take it easy!" she chuckled.

Charlie stood in the doorway with a big grin on his face. "Damn, Lex. I've been meaning to ask you how you're able to attract the most beautiful women!"

Martha got up off her knees and took a near-leap at the lawman. "Oh, Charlie! You've always been such a sweet-talker!" She gave him a passionate kiss.

Lex looked up at Amanda who was leaning over her prone body. "I guess this means you missed me?" she asked with a devilish smile on her face.

The younger woman bent down and gave her a sweet kiss. "Yeah, I guess you could say that." Amanda sat up, looking Lex's body over carefully. "Are you okay? We heard several gunshots." She ran her shaking hands across the beautiful body beneath her.

The rancher sat up and wrapped her arms around the lovely blonde. "Not a scratch. How are you holding up?"

Amanda enjoyed the sensation of strong arms holding her close. "Just great...now." She placed a gentle kiss on the strong neck. "But I guess I should get you off the kitchen floor." She stood up and hauled the rancher up with her. Amanda wrapped her arms around Lex and squeezed tightly. "I really don't want to go through anything like that again." She tucked her head under the strong chin and exhaled with a great sigh of relief.

Lex kissed the blonde head as she brought her arms protectively around the smaller woman. "C'mon. Let's see if they need any help with the cleanup." She led Amanda towards the hall-way.

Charlie and Martha were already there, the housekeeper not releasing the strong grasp she had on the sheriff's hand. He stood there with a tired smile on his weathered face. The couple watched silently as his men finished up their business.

Amanda's eyes popped open wide. There were deputies everywhere! One was checking the back door while another was speaking to a young teenager who was seated on the stairway. Several more were leading away two men in handcuffs. One of the men was bleeding from a head injury, and he glared at Lex as he was led out through the front door. The other man was complaining about a gunshot wound to his leg and a headache. He, too glared at the rancher and questioned her parentage under his breath as he was led outside.

One deputy stepped up to Lex with his hat in his hands. "Uh." He looked down at his feet. "Lex, I want to apologize again for shooting at you." The young man looked like he was about to cry.

Amanda stiffened, and would have probably attacked the poor man had the taller woman not tightened her hold on the blonde's shoulders. "Jeremy, I don't blame you. All you could see was a person with a gun." She gave him a devilish grin. "I'm just glad you can't shoot worth a damn!"

He shook his head and smiled. "Yeah. Me, too." They all looked towards the front door as a loud rumble assaulted their ears. Jeremy grinned at the rancher. "That would probably be your men. It took two of our guys with riot gear to keep them away after they finished the bridge." He was about to say more when six muddy men stomped into the house.

The man in the lead was older with a scraggly dark beard that was liberally sprinkled with gray. The evident leader of the group, he limped up to Lex with worry in his eyes. "Miz Lexington." He looked her over carefully, not even noticing the beautiful young woman tucked up against her side. "You look like you're still in one piece. We'd heard on the radio there'd been some shooting." He finished his careful perusal and blushed slightly when he noticed the young blonde standing next to the rancher. The older man yanked his hat off his head and mumbled, "'scuse me...I...umm..."

Lex took pity on the grizzled man and smiled. "Lester, I'd like you to meet Amanda Cauble. Amanda, this is Lester. He takes care of the boys down at the bunkhouse."

The smaller woman held out a hand to give the older man a strong handshake. "Nice to meet you, Lester. Martha has spoken highly of you." She smiled brightly and ignored the mud liberally covering his bent form.

This caused his blush to darken. "Ah, now I know you're pullin' my leg." He gave the housekeeper a wry grin. "I'm just glad y'all are all right. Me and the boys are gonna go on up to the bunkhouse and get cleaned up." Lester smiled at Lex as he put his hat on and shuffled towards the door. He turned and tipped his hat at Amanda, "Real pleasure to meet you, miss. Hope we'll be seeing more of you around." He started back towards the door again, ushering the other men outside. "C'mon, ya damn fools, let's get out of these folks' way."

Amanda burst out laughing as soon as the door was closed. "He's cute." She looked up at Lex who gave her a tired smile. *She looks exhausted. Hmm...what should I do? Subtle? Yeah, why not?* She turned her attention to the sheriff and smiled. "Do you think anyone would mind if we went upstairs?" She gave the rancher a pleading look. "I really need to go sit down. My legs won't stop shaking." *True.* Amanda knew that this was the only way to get her tall friend to take a break. "Could you give me a hand up the stairs?"

Lex scanned the young woman's face worriedly. "Are you okay? Should I call a doctor?" She felt a small hand pat her stomach gently.

"No. I'm just tired. And more than a little shaken up, I guess. I'm not used to so much excitement." Amanda looked at Charlie and Martha who both grinned knowingly. "Well?"

"Uh, yeah. You go ahead and get some rest, we'll get this all straightened up down here." Charlie felt Martha's hand tighten around his. The smile on the lawman's face grew.

The small blonde began pulling Lex up the stairs. "Thanks, Charlie. We'll see you both in the morning." She gave a little wave, then smiled as she felt the rancher lean against her slightly. "C'mon, honey," she whispered. "Let's get you into bed."

The tall woman pulled her closer. "Now that's the best offer I've had all day." She leaned down and gave Amanda's ear a light nip. "Or at least all evening."

They made their way up to the master bedroom where Lex went straight to the bed and sat down. "Damn. I feel like I could sleep for days." She ran a hand through her tangled dark hair.

Amanda knelt at her feet and gently pulled off Lex's boots. "Sounds like a great idea to me." She stood up and unbuttoned the rancher's shirt. Amanda pulled it off and touched the bandage wrapped around Lex's ribs. "Let me go get something to..." Amanda found herself sprawled across the tall woman's body.

"I thought you were tired," a raspy whisper tickled her ear, then a soft nibble started across her throat.

The smaller woman sat up and moved back slightly. "Well, I...umm..." She lost her train of thought as electric blue eyes captured hers.

Lex ran a hand down the younger woman's cheek. "Sorry. I really shouldn't tease you like that, but you're so cute when you get flustered."

Amanda leaned into the touch and turned to place a soft kiss on the callused palm. "Yeah well, normally I don't like it when people tease me." She gave Lex a sweet look. "But with you, it's different, somehow." She smiled and reached down to unbutton the older woman's jeans. Seeing Lex raise an eyebrow, she blushed. "Now don't be getting any ideas. I just want you to be comfortable before we go to sleep."

The dark-haired woman gave her another look. Lex didn't argue as Amanda gently removed the jeans and pulled the sheet and comforter over her prone form. She fought to keep her eyes open to watch as Amanda removed her own clothes then crawled into bed. "Damn, but you're beautiful," she mumbled, as her eyes closed against her will.

Amanda blushed and rolled over on her side with her head propped up with one hand. "Obviously you are so tired that your eyesight has been affected." She brushed dark bangs off the resting woman's forehead. "Lex?" No answer. Amanda sighed. "Sleep well, my friend." She edged over and snuggled up against the rancher. Amanda kissed the tan cheek, then joined the rancher in sleep.

Chapter
14

Lex opened her eyes slowly, unsure of why she was awake. It was still dark outside. A glance at the bedside alarm clock showed that it was just a little after five o'clock in the morning. She started to get up and then realized that she had been effectively pinned to the bed by a small muscular body. *And my left arm is numb,* she grimaced. She realized that the lack of feeling in her arm must be the reason she was awake. A devilish smile crossed her face. *Oh, I could really have some fun here.* Using her free hand, Lex slowly pulled the covers back, exposing their upper bodies to the cool air in the room. Amanda moaned slightly and snuggled up even closer, which allowed the older woman to free her arm. Lex was quite proud of herself until the extremity began to tingle painfully.

Amanda woke up as she felt a definite cool draft. She opened her eyes and saw that somehow the comforter and sheet had been pushed down around her waist, leaving her upper body bare to the room. The young woman glanced up and saw that Lex was awake as well, biting her lower lip with a pained expression on her face. Amanda shivered slightly and pulled the covers up over them both. She ran her hand along the clenched jaw. "Lex? What's the matter? Is it your side?"

The older woman shook her head and tried to relax. She flexed her left hand with a small grimace. "No...my arm had fallen asleep," she gave Amanda a small grin, "and now I'm trying to wake it up."

The young woman sat up to lean comfortably against the headboard, and reached under the covers for Lex's arm. Amanda began to gently massage the strong muscles, enjoying the feel of Lex's smooth skin. She finished up and leaned over to give the rancher a tender kiss. "How's that?"

Lex pulled the smaller woman over until she was lying on top. "Mmm...seems to be working just fine," she murmured as she wrapped both arms securely around Amanda and squeezed. "But it may need extensive physical therapy." She rolled over until the young woman was under her. Lex began placing tender bites on Amanda's neck. "Better safe than sorry," she whispered in a nearby ear, leaving a soft kiss behind.

"Ooohh...yeah," Amanda gasped as she threaded her fingers in the thick hair above her. "I'll be glad to...oh, boy..." she trembled as the older woman began tracing a fiery path down her body with small bites and gentle kisses.

****

Lex and Amanda strolled into the kitchen hours later, looking quite happy and rested. Charlie was sitting at the table talking with Martha, who was at the stove cooking the morning meal.

"Well, well. Look who finally decided to get up," she teased the young women, who both had the decency to blush.

Lex recovered first as she sat down next to Amanda. "Well, we woke up earlier, and just decided to take it easy for a while."

Charlie snickered into his coffee cup, while the young blonde next to Lex blushed again. "Roy stopped by earlier. Said he and the boys were going to take care of the horses for you for the next week or so." He smiled at the housekeeper who had a smug look on her face. "They felt bad that you had to do all the chores lately, and they want to make it up to you."

Lex looked at Martha. "Sounds like a certain someone has

been busy this morning."

The housekeeper turned away from the stove with her hands on her hips. "Now you just listen to me, Lexie." She stalked over to the table and put one hand under the rancher's chin to tilt her face upwards. "You *are* going to take it easy for a few days. At least until these dark circles disappear from under your eyes." Seeing a stormy look appear on Lex's face, she leaned over and placed a gentle kiss on the young woman's forehead. "Please? For me?"

Lex's face lightened immediately. "Aw, Martha. Don't look at me that way." She glanced over at her blonde companion who tried to control herself. "What's so funny?"

Amanda was sitting next to the tall woman with one hand covering her mouth. "Nothing!" But her eyes were sparkling.

Lex leaned over until she was inches away from Amanda's face. She waited until the younger woman's eyes were locked with her own and said in a quiet voice, "I have ways of making you talk, my dear."

The younger woman's eyes widened, then glinted with something other than humor. "I'm looking forward to seeing you try." She leaned over and placed a quick kiss on the surprised rancher's nose.

"She gotcha there, Lexie!" Martha chortled as she went back to the stove. "I'm sure you girls are hungry, right?" She started piling two plates with food.

Charlie looked at them, then at his watch. "Wow. It's almost ten o'clock! Getting closer to lunch, isn't it?"

Lex glared at him. "You really don't want to go there." She looked down at the plate the housekeeper had placed in front of her. "Good Lord, Martha. Do you actually expect me to eat all of this?"

The older woman sat back down at the table after she placed a similarly laden plate in front of Amanda. "As a matter of fact, I do." She gave the rancher a long stare. "You haven't been eating enough to keep a bird alive...and I'm putting a stop to it!"

Amanda giggled. "I was wondering how she could run a ranch on what she ate. Now I know." She ignored the nasty look the tall woman was giving her.

Lex rolled her eyes. "Fine. But don't blame me for the mess in the kitchen when I explode from eating all of this," she grumbled as she started on her breakfast.

"Poor baby. You'll probably be bedridden for days." Amanda patted her leg in mock sympathy.

"Hrumpph," Lex grumped again, but she couldn't disguise the affection in her eyes. "And this would be a bad thing?" She winked at her companion.

The younger woman ducked her head, but prudently didn't answer. She continued to eat her breakfast with a large smile on her face.

Charlie looked at Martha who smiled happily. *Time to change the subject, I think.* The lawman cleared his throat and looked over at Lex. "Since you don't have any chores to do, what are your plans for what's left of today?" he asked with a twinkle in his eyes.

Lex placed her coffee mug back on the table and glanced over at the young blonde. "Well, I thought that if Amanda felt up to it, we'd make a trip to town." Seeing the younger woman's answering smile, she continued, "I need to pick up my other truck, and I thought that we could put her car in the shop to get the interior cleaned up."

"That would be great!" the young woman enthused, "my grandparents will be so excited!" Amanda took Lex's hand in hers. "Think I could talk you into staying there for a few days?" She looked into Lex's eyes and felt the room recede until only the two of them were there. "I realize that you know Gramma and Grandpa Jake, but I'd really like to introduce you to them, if you know what I mean."

Lex was so absorbed in the green eyes across from hers, she didn't notice when Martha and Charlie made their silent exit. She swallowed hard and tried to put her thoughts into words. "Are you sure about that?" She saw shock and then sadness cross Amanda's expressive face.

"What?" Amanda looked into sad blue eyes. "Why wouldn't I want to show you off?" She used shaky hands to cradle the older woman's face. Leaning forward, she placed a gentle kiss on Lex's trembling lips. "I love you," she whispered, "and I want the entire world to know it."

Lex felt the sadness squeeze her heart painfully. "I love you too," she spoke quietly, "but I don't want to see you get hurt." Taking a deep breath, she continued, "people in town have very long memories, and I've got a pretty checkered past." Her voice broke as she felt the soft touch of Amanda's fingertips brushing the tears that had fallen from her eyes.

Amanda stood up, then sat down again, this time in the older woman's lap. She wrapped one arm around Lex's shoulders and used her free hand to capture the rancher's callused hand. She brought the large hand to her lips, placed a tender kiss on the knuckles, and pulled their linked hands to rest between their bodies. "I've already told my grandparents about us," she whispered as she made eye contact with Lex, "and they couldn't be happier." She kissed the older woman's forehead. "And I really don't give a damn what anyone else thinks. So get used to it."

Lex started to speak. "Are..." She cleared her throat and tried again. "Are you sure about this? You're going to hear a lot of nasty stuff, and most of it's probably true." Seeing the fierce determination in those very green eyes, she relented, "I just want you to know what you are getting into." She was interrupted when Amanda's lips found her own.

Amanda poured everything she had into that kiss. She transferred all of her hopes, dreams, and love to the dark-haired rancher. When she pulled back, Amanda could see the love shining in Lex's eyes and she felt her own begin to fill with tears of happiness. "You're stuck with me....'cause I'm not going anywhere," she murmured as she leaned up until their foreheads touched.

Lex took a shuddering breath and closed her eyes. She pulled the young woman against her with all the strength left in her shaking arms. The rancher buried her face in the soft golden hair as she tried to come up with something – anything – to express the feeling in her heart. "Oh God, Amanda," she whispered hoarsely, "I love you with all that I am." She felt the return squeeze and allowed her heart to come home at last.

****

They had sat in the kitchen tangled together silently for what seemed like hours, neither woman speaking, and not quite ready to let the other go. Amanda finally pulled back slightly and ran her hand down the tan cheek of the taller woman. "Well, now that we've gotten that settled, are you ready to drive into town so I can show you off?"

Lex blushed. "Not much to show, but yeah, I guess so. Let me go get a bag together, since we'll be there for a few days." She waited until the smaller woman climbed off her lap with a reluctant sigh. "I've also got a few errands to run while we're there, if you don't mind." She stood and wrapped a long arm around Amanda's shoulder.

The young blonde grinned. "Sure. I've got some things to take care of, too." *Like requesting some more vacation time, and of course thanking that slimeball Rick for sending me out here,* she mused. *I can't wait to see his face!* A small giggle escaped from her.

"What's so funny?" Lex asked as they headed towards the stairs.

"I was just thinking about Rick." Amanda couldn't help herself; she chuckled again.

"And...?"

"I'm just picturing the look on his face when I stand up in front of the entire office and thank him for sending me on a wild goose chase." She shook her blonde head ruefully.

Lex stopped in the middle of the stairway and looked at her as if she had completely lost her mind. "Thank him?!?"

"Yep," Amanda nodded as she prodded the rancher forward once again. "I'm gonna say, 'Rick, if it weren't for you, I may have never met the love of my life. So thank you!' And then watch him pass out from the shock," she laughed.

Lex finally laughed as well. "That would certainly do it." She allowed Amanda to enter the master bedroom ahead of her. "But when he gets up, he's mine." This was said in a low growl. "The bastard nearly got you killed. And I have a few choice words of my own for him." She was walking towards the closet when the light touch on her back stopped her. Lex turned around and saw a quiet look of determination on the younger woman's face.

"No. Please don't." She tried to explain when she saw the confusion on Lex's face, "I would gladly go through all of that again for what I have gained this past week." She enjoyed the look of comprehension and then pure joy that suddenly covered the older woman's face.

Lex grinned and scooped the small woman up into her arms. "Funny. I feel the same way." She spun Amanda around and enjoyed the startled laughter that floated through the air around them.

"Lex! You nut! Put me down before you hurt yourself!" Amanda exclaimed as she wrapped her arms around the taller woman's neck. The younger woman realized that she was in the unique position of finally being able to physically see eye-to-eye with the rancher. Amanda took advantage of the opportunity presented to her and captured the older woman's lips with a vengeance.

Lex happily returned her offering and accepted the deepened kiss wholeheartedly. She slightly loosened her grip on the smaller woman when she felt her own legs begin to weaken. "God, Amanda," she whispered huskily. "It's amazing what you make me feel with just one kiss."

The younger woman smiled against her mouth. "It's only fair...considering what you can do to me with just one look," she murmured. "You in much of a hurry to get into town?" She slid down the long form slowly. "I thought we could leave sometime after lunch." Amanda stepped away carefully and captured the large hands as she backed up towards the bed.

Lex smiled, her eyes slightly glazed with desire. "You're the boss," she laughed as she allowed the younger woman to pull her forward onto the bed.

****

Amanda drove the little Mustang towards the bridge with a growing sense of unease. The closer they got the more she began to shake. *Oh, God...I don't know if I can do this.* She was starting to feel physically ill, until a strong hand covered hers.

"Stop the car for a minute, Amanda." Lex spoke quietly, but with authority, and the younger woman was unable to deny the request.

"No. It's okay," she managed to get out, even as she stopped the car.

Lex stepped out of the car as it rolled to a stop a few yards from the edge of the newly reconstructed bridge. She walked over to the driver's side, opened the door and offered Amanda her hand. "C'mere," she beckoned and felt the cold clammy hand of her companion as it grasped hers. "We're gonna take this slow and easy, okay? Just let me know when it gets to be too much." Lex pulled Amanda tightly against her as she began to slowly lead the younger woman towards the bridge.

Amanda took a deep breath and walked with Lex up to the edge of the bridge. Before she could feel any panic, the strong arm around her shoulder tightened slightly, and she felt the fear melt away. As she placed one foot on the wooden surface, she trembled. *Stop it! Lex is here, and she won't let anything happen. Just get over it!!* Amanda berated herself, angry that an inanimate object could instill such fear into her.

"Shhh...easy, sweetheart," Lex spoke quietly into Amanda's ear as she would a spooked horse. "Everything's going to be okay, I promise." They walked halfway across the bridge before she felt the smaller woman begin to relax.

Feeling her heartbeat begin to calm, Amanda sneaked a peek up at her protector. *Just like a security blanket, right Mandy?* She stopped in the middle of the bridge and returned the taller woman's embrace. "Thank you." She placed a soft kiss on the chest her face was buried in. "I'm going to be okay now." Amanda looked up at the shadowed face above her and smiled. "Let's go get the car and get out of here."

∗∗∗∗∗∗∗∗∗∗∗∗∗∗∗

The rest of the drive into town was uneventful as the two women shared humorous childhood anecdotes.

"And then he said, 'How in the hell did that calf end up wearing my boots?'" Lex watched the younger woman wipe her eyes from too much laughter.

The young blonde shook her head. "Stop it, please! I'll never get that picture out of my head. Poor Charlie!" she chuckled, then turned the car onto a beautifully landscaped street that had trees draped overhead. Amanda glanced over at the rancher who looked a little spooked. "We're almost there. You okay?"

Lex had been looking out of the window as she remembered the last time she had driven down this street. *Been almost eight months,* she thought, *not much has changed.* "Yeah, I'm fine. Just feel a little bit intimidated, I guess." She glanced back over at her companion.

"Really? So you've been over here before?" Amanda remembered that her grandmother had said that Lex was on the Historical Committee. She hadn't realized that the rancher had been to their house.

"Yeah, a couple of months before you moved back here, there was a meeting of the Committee at Mrs. Cauble's home...and I happened to attend." She took a deep breath to gain the courage to tell her story. "Anyway, the ladies were chatting about some old barn north of town, when some of the alarms on their cars went off. We all went outside to look, and there were a couple of kids trying to break into the vehicles." She looked down at her lap, unable to meet the startling green gaze across from her. "I wasn't really thinking. Just ran outside while Mrs. Cauble called the police. I caught them, but they tried to get away, and I..." Lex stopped, unable to continue.

Amanda had pulled the car over when she realized that the older woman was having more trouble than she cared to admit telling her tale. "You don't have to..."

Lex finally looked at her with shame-filled eyes. "Yes, I do. You really need to know what kind of person I can be." She took another deep breath. "They were just a couple of punks, trying to get a little extra money from stuff they could steal." She rubbed her eyes. "I lost it. Here they were, two dirty teenagers stealing from ladies I considered friends." Now Lex closed her eyes. "I beat the hell out of them. It took five deputies to pull me off them, and they both spent weeks in the hospital." She slumped down farther into her seat. "I've been ashamed to show my face in town ever since. I'd just get done what I needed to, and get out of town quickly, hoping not too many people noticed me when I was here."

"Oh, Lex." Amanda felt sympathetic tears welling up in her eyes. "You have nothing to be ashamed of. You protected people you cared about." She reached a hand over and clasped the rancher's arm.

The older woman opened her eyes and looked at Amanda. "I'm not sure I can agree with you. If you could have just seen the looks on those ladies' faces." A single tear slipped down her angular face. "I see them almost every night in my dreams. They were horrified, and for good reason." She ran a hand through her hair nervously. "I guess I'm just afraid of seeing that look on your grandmother's face when you show up with me on her doorstep. I don't think I could handle that."

Amanda unbuckled her seat belt and crawled into Lex's lap. "NO! My grandmother thinks the world of you. We've spoken on the phone quite a few times since I've been staying with you and she has said nothing but wonderful things about you." She gave the older woman a light kiss. "And if she felt any different, you know she would have told me!" Her tone dared the rancher to contradict her.

Lex sat quietly for a minute to absorb what the younger woman was saying. *She's right. Mrs. Cauble is certainly no wilting flower. She would have told Amanda about any misgivings she had about me already. Time to quit feeling so sorry for myself.* "Yeah, you're right." She gave the smaller woman a sweet kiss. "You wanna take me home, now? I think I want to tell your grandparents my true intentions towards you."

Amanda gave her a puzzled look. "Intentions? Why do I have this sudden vision of you standing under my window serenading me?" she laughed, then became somewhat alarmed when Lex gave her a grin.

"Damn! You figured me out!" Lex chuckled when she saw the shock on her companion's face. "Don't worry. I'll cancel the Mariachi Band."

Amanda slid back over into the driver's seat and laughed again. "You wouldn't..." She looked at Lex's semi-innocent face, "You would! Don't you dare!" She buckled up then, and pulled the small car back onto the street, laughing all the while.

****

Amanda pulled into the tree-lined drive and parked behind a shining red Suburban. "Looks like they're home." She got out of the car then strolled to the passenger's side and waited for the tall woman to climb out. "C'mon. Let's go give 'em a big surprise." She took Lex's hand and practically ran up the walkway to the door.

Before the young woman could open the door, it swung wide open. An older, more petite version of Amanda stood in the doorway smiling. "Mandy! You're home!" She rushed outside and wrapped her arms around Amanda in breathless abandon.

"Urk! Gramma, calm down!" Amanda gasped as the older woman squeezed the breath out of her.

Jacob Cauble stood just inside the doorway and watched with an amused air. "Well, Peanut, we can never accuse you of not making an entrance!" he joked, until the young woman released her grandmother and came at him full force. "Ugh! Okay, I'm happy to see you, too."

Anna Leigh looked at Lex who was standing back with a bemused look on her face. "Lexington? Are you just going to stand there, or are you going to say hello?" She stepped towards the tall woman.

Lex gave her a gentle smile. "Hello, Mrs. Cauble. It's been a while, hasn't it?"

"You scamp! Get over here!" Anna Leigh pulled the young rancher into a strong embrace. She whispered into Lex's ear, "I could never thank you enough for what you have given us. And I'm glad you're here."

Amanda and Jacob stood together and watched the scene on the front porch with glee. "I'm glad you got her to come back with you, Peanut. Your grandmother has been very worried about her since your last talk." He leaned down and placed a gentle kiss on the blonde head.

"Is the guest room still available? I actually got her to agree to stay in town for a few days, and I want to get her to visit Dr. Anderson while she's here." She smiled at the rancher when Anna Leigh brought her to the doorway.

Jacob let go of his granddaughter and reached for the tall woman standing next to his wife. He pulled her into a powerful hug and kissed the top of her head. "Welcome back, Lexington. I hope you will stay with us a few days so we can get caught up." He led Lex into the house with Amanda and Anna Leigh close behind.

The dark-haired woman followed him into the living room and sat in the loveseat he pointed her towards. "Well, if you don't mind me hanging around, I'd like that. I have some business to attend to here in town that will take a couple of days, if that's okay with you."

Amanda plopped down onto the loveseat, almost sitting in the rancher's lap. She grabbed Lex's hand and laughed. "Like I would let you out of my sight for any amount of time."

Jacob sat in the large recliner with Anna Leigh perched on the arm. "Looks like our little Amanda has gotten her hooks into you, Lexington." He laughed at the blush that colored both of the young women's faces. "Not that I'm complaining, mind you. As long as Mandy is happy, we're happy. Right, Anna?" He grasped his wife's hand and pulled it to his lips for a kiss.

Anna Leigh looked at her granddaughter and then at the woman seated next to her. "I couldn't agree more, Jacob."

"That's good, because I've fallen completely, totally, and irreversibly in love with Lex, and I couldn't be happier." Amanda snuggled closer to the completely embarrassed rancher.

Jacob and Anna Leigh exchanged amused glances. "So, Lexington," he drawled as he tried to keep a straight face, "What are your intentions towards our granddaughter?" When Jacob saw the shocked look on Amanda's face, he nearly lost his composure. He almost laughed out loud when he noticed the tall rancher struggling with her thoughts. "Well?"

Lex looked at Amanda, then at Jacob and Anna Leigh. She stood up to address the two older people. "Mr. Cauble, Mrs. Cauble, my intentions are purely honorable. I love Amanda with my entire being, and if I were able, I would ask you for her hand." She looked back at the young blonde, who had tears floating in her eyes. "But since I can't, I want to stand here right now and give you my word that I will treat Amanda with the greatest respect, and honor her for as long as she will have me." She felt a small hand grasp hers. "We've only known each other less than a week, yet it feels like a lifetime. She brings out the best in me, and I will do everything in my power to make her happy." *God, that was hard!*

Anna Leigh stood up, followed by Jacob. "Lexington..." she began sternly as she watched the emotions flicker across the angular features, "Welcome to our family." She walked over and pulled the dark-haired woman into a strong hug. "And call me Anna Leigh. Mrs. Cauble sounds so...impersonal, don't you think?" She felt the body she was holding shake with silent sobs. "Shhh. It's okay, sweetheart." She rubbed Lex's back comfortingly.

Lex drew a deep breath and slowly pulled away. "Thanks, Anna Leigh. You have no idea what it means to me to hear that." Embarrassed, she ran a hand over her eyes.

Amanda stepped up beside her and gave the tall woman a hug. "That was beautiful, Lex. I didn't know you were quite that eloquent." She leaned on the nearby shoulder.

"Well, Lexington, seems like you're stuck with us." Jacob walked over and embraced the young woman. "And if you call me Mr. Cauble again, I'll have to get tough! You can call me Jacob, Grandpa, or old fart. I'll answer to just about anything." He chuckled at her look of surprise. "Although I usually reserve 'old fart' for my Anna Leigh to call me." He flinched as the older woman slapped his arm lightly. "See what these Cauble women are capable of? Are you sure you want to be subjected to this?"

Lex laughed as she looked down at Amanda. "Yeah, I know. She's already popped me a couple of times... guess it's in the genes." She winced as the anticipated smack came her way. "See what I mean?" Her comment eased the seriousness of the conversation, for which she was glad. *Damn...that was harder than breaking a wild horse. Glad I'll never have to go through this again.* Then her thoughts sobered. *Oh, shit! I've still got to meet her parents!*

****

It was late evening as Lex and Amanda snuggled up on the sofa in front of a roaring fire. "You know," Lex chuckled, "I always knew your grandparents were special. I just never really realized just how special they were until today." She felt a light kiss on her collarbone, where Amanda's face was comfortably tucked.

"Yeah. It may sound strange but they're closer to me than my own parents," Amanda agreed as she snuggled closer in the dark woman's lap. "I love my mom and dad, but we were never as close. I've always felt like I could tell Gramma and Grandpa Jake anything."

Lex kissed the top of her head. "I know what you mean. I feel the same way about Martha. She's always been there for me."

They sat there for a while longer enjoying the quiet company of each other as they stared at the dwindling flames. Amanda had dozed off while Lex contemplated her visit to the bank the next day. The rancher also realized she would have to go to the county jail to sign the complaint against the five thieves. Lex had refused to press charges against the teenager when Charlie told her he was an orphan under the care of his older brother, Matt. When she asked him what they were going to do with the boy, the sheriff said they would probably have to put him in juvenile hall. Lex was going to see the boy tomorrow and ask him if he'd like to work on the ranch. *I hope I'm making the right decision here. But I can't let a boy go to jail for following his brother.*

Anna Leigh glided quietly into the room, in case the two younger women were asleep. She noticed her granddaughter was sound asleep on the rancher's lap and the dark-haired woman was staring pensively into the dying fireplace. She edged over to the arm of the sofa and perched atop it. "Lexington? Is everything all right, honey?"

Lex looked up at the older woman and saw where Amanda

got her beauty. "Yeah, just fine. I was just going over in my head the things I have to do tomorrow," she spoke quietly to keep from waking the sleeping bundle in her arms.

"From what I hear, that means a trip to the doctor as well, doesn't it?" Anna Leigh didn't know how else to bring such a subject up. "Amanda said over the phone that you have broken ribs, and had been shot?"

The rancher sighed and ran her free hand through her hair. "Yeah. She'll badger me 'til I go, I guess." Lex looked up at the older woman. "It's really not that bad. I'm sure she made it sound worse than it actually was."

Anna Leigh grinned and gave the dark head a gentle pat. "Uh-huh. You forget how well I know you." Then her face took on a pensive look. "Why haven't you been by recently? I've missed the conversations we used to have on the patio Saturday evenings." The two women would sit outside and drink iced tea and discuss everything from politics to the price of cattle after the Historical Committee meetings. But Lex had stopped coming by after the incident eight months ago.

"I...I..." Lex stammered as one of her worse fears stared her in the face. "I just figured you didn't need me around your little gatherings. I'm not exactly tea party material." She couldn't look the older woman in the eye.

"Lexington. I was never so proud of you as I was that day you stopped those horrible thieves! What if one of the ladies had decided to leave early? Do you think they would have just run away?" She forced the younger woman to look her in the eye. "I don't think so. I believe that they would have seriously hurt someone. And you jumped to our defense immediately." She gave the young rancher a gentle smile. "Don't be ashamed of the fact that you protected us from an unknown danger. Yes, they were just boys. But you know as well as I do how vicious young men can be. Don't underestimate what you did that day. The ladies still talk about how very proud of you they are."

Lex was caught speechless. *I never realized...* "Mrs., ummm... Anna Leigh," she smiled at the look the older woman gave her. "Thank you. I've been worried all this time about what happened back then. I'll still worry about it, but you've helped me put it more in perspective."

Anna Leigh leaned over and kissed the dark head. "Honey, there's nothing in this world I wouldn't do for you. Now why don't you get yourselves upstairs and into bed?" She gave the young woman a sneaky grin. "Unfortunately, the guest room is under repairs, so you'll have to share with Amanda. I do hope that's all right." She patted the nearby arm. "Get some rest, we'll see you in the morning." She got up and left the room as a chuckle escaped her lips.

Lex looked after the older woman with a fond smile. *Oh yeah. She's subtle.* She glanced down at the sleeping woman in her arms. *Wonder if I can keep her awake long enough to make it upstairs?* "Amanda?" she whispered, as she gently shook the small body.

"Mmmm?" The blonde head tucked itself tighter into her chest.

The rancher shook her head in defeat. *Can't say I didn't try.* She stood up and cradled the sleeping form gently. *Okay, now where the hell is her bedroom?* Lex started walking up the stairs. She remembered from a previous tour of the house that all the bedrooms were on the back area of the second floor. Just as she reached the top, Amanda woke up slightly.

"Lex?" She looked up into the blue eyes and then realized where they were. "You didn't carry me up the stairs, did you?" Amanda used one hand to push the dark bangs from the rancher's eyes.

"Yep," the tall woman smiled. "And your grandmother told me the guestroom was being repaired, so we'll have to share." She shifted her grip on the small form in her arms. "So where should I take you?"

Amanda grinned. "Anywhere you want to."

Faith's Crossing

Chapter
1

Lex awoke at her usual time – before the sun had the opportunity to rise. Groaning slightly to herself, the dark-haired woman used her right hand to rub her weary eyes, and debated with her more practical side, which was telling her to get out of bed. Just when she had decided to listen to that annoying little internal voice, she felt the small body that was partially draped across her snuggle even more tightly to her side. Lex sighed. *Not like I have a good reason to leave this.* Her lips turned up in a small smile. *Not like I'd leave this even if I* did *have a good reason.* She pulled the small woman closer, feeling the blonde head turn upwards.

"Morning," a sleep-roughened voice grumbled, and then soft lips kissed Lex's tanned throat. "I've got to figure out a way to make you sleep in until at least sunrise – just once." Green eyes tracked up the sharp planes of the rancher's face, and absorbed the relaxed look on her companion.

Lex smiled, working her hand under the soft material of the younger woman's sleep shirt, gently scratching the smooth back. "I dunno if you can, but it will certainly be fun watching you try."

Amanda crawled up the long body until their faces were inches apart. "You're on." She dropped her head slightly, brushing her lips gently against Lex's. Feeling strong hands running along the inside of her shirt, gently mapping the route of her spine, Amanda deepened the kiss, and noticed that the body under hers trembled. "Mmm..." She smiled against the older woman's lips. "Cold?" She loved the way Lex responded to her touch, knowing that she reacted to the taller woman in much the same way.

"N... n... no... not... at all," Lex stammered, unable to control her voice when she felt small hands exploring under her shirt – hands that knowingly found just the right places to touch, leaving behind an almost electric charge. "Amanda..." she cleared her throat, "we shouldn't..." But her body was happily rebelling – arching towards the younger woman's touch. "Your... ah... grandparents..." she mumbled, losing the battle as small, soft hands began tracing down towards her stomach, closely followed by insistent bites and small licks from the amused blonde's mouth. "They might... oh, God..." Her eyes closed as Amanda found a particularly sensitive spot just below her ribs.

"Shhh..." the younger woman murmured. "It's okay, sweetheart... they're at the other end of the hall, and won't be up for hours." She slowly worked the soft shirt up the quivering body below her. "Besides," she chuckled, "the risk of getting caught is half the fun." Then she stopped talking, and concentrated on the enjoyable task at hand.

****

Lex had a small smile on her face as she followed the young blonde down the stairway a few hours later. It had taken all of her considerable willpower to *not* climb into the shower with Amanda after their pre-dawn activities, especially after the younger woman had gone into great detail about what she would be missing. *She is such a little tease,* she smirked, unable to take her eyes off the gently swaying hips in front of her. She was so engrossed in her perusal that she didn't realize the small body had stopped, and she had to grab the railing to keep them both from falling when she bumped into the lithe form.

Amanda turned around to peer into the rancher's deep blue

eyes. "Hey there. Everything okay?"

Lex snapped back to reality and nodded. "Yeah, sure." Her brows creased into a questioning gaze when the smaller woman grasped her arms and exchanged places with her, putting Lex on the step below her. "What?"

Giving her companion a mischievous smile, Amanda leaned forward and wrapped her arms around the older woman's neck. "Much better," she whispered, looking directly into Lex's eyes before she captured the rancher's lips in a sweet possessive embrace.

"Ahem."

Reluctantly breaking off the kiss, Lex slowly turned around to find the source of the interruption. "Oops." She felt Amanda giggle.

At the bottom of the stairs stood Anna Leigh, a gentle smile on her face. "Good morning, you two." Her smile widened as she watched her granddaughter wrap her arms around the tall woman. "I trust you both slept well."

Amanda propped her chin on the broad shoulder in front of her. "Oh, yeah... like a baby." She gently pulled the dark-haired woman closer. "But, then again, I had a pretty good nap on the sofa last night."

"Sorry, but you looked so peaceful, I didn't have the heart to disturb you." Lex unconsciously leaned into the embrace.

Amanda felt large hands entwine with hers, which were splayed across Lex's flat stomach. "Yeah, but you could have made me get up, instead of carrying me up the stairs."

Anna Leigh saw the taller woman blush slightly. "C'mon. I was just on my way up to tell you two that breakfast is ready."

"Great! I'm starving!" Amanda skipped down the stairs, stopping next to the smiling woman and capturing her hand, then dragging the grinning rancher into the kitchen.

"There's a big surprise!" Lex mumbled to Anna Leigh, who laughed as the small blonde backhanded the tall woman on the stomach.

They all entered the kitchen laughing, which caused Jacob to turn around from the counter where he was pouring a cup of coffee. "Good morning, ladies." He pulled two more mugs from the cabinet. "Coffee?" Hearing thankful groans, he smiled and filled the cups, and then turned towards the women.

"Good morning, Grandpa Jake!" Amanda wrapped her arms around his waist and squeezed tight. Snuggling her face into his chest, she released a heavy sigh. "I've really missed this."

Jacob enveloped her in his arms, returning the hug. He kissed the blonde head beneath his chin and smiled. "Me too, sweetie. Did you sleep well, Peanut?" Looking to Lex and Anna Leigh he nodded. "Hey there...have a seat, ladies. Breakfast is ready." With a final hug and kiss to his granddaughter, Jacob turned towards the stove. "Wanna help, Peanut?"

Lex looked questioningly at the older woman. Anna Leigh shook her head. "Better do as he says: sit down, or he'll never serve us!" She pointed at a chair opposite her, and watched the younger woman ease into it.

While the two women got comfortable at the table, Jacob and Amanda brought over several platters of food. The small blonde handed Lex a steaming cup of coffee and gave her shoulder a gentle squeeze. "Here you go! Hope you're hungry. Grandpa makes the best omelets I've ever tasted!" She winked at Jacob as he sat down next to his wife.

They spent the majority of the meal talking of the events at the ranch during the past week, with both of the elder Caubles expressing their shock and concern.

"...And then, after we get to the house, Martha and I discover that tough-stuff over there," she pointed at Lex with her fork, "got shot sometime during all that running, and never said a word to either one of us."

Lex sat her coffee mug down on the table. "You're getting it all out of proportion." She looked helplessly at Jacob. "I really didn't notice – it was barely a scratch."

"Yeah, right! A scratch that even now, several days later, is still bleeding." The young blonde gave her companion a dirty look. "Which is why we're going to see Dr. Anderson right after breakfast, right?"

Rolling her eyes, Lex let out a heavy sigh. "Amanda."

Anna Leigh looked across the table at the dark-haired woman. "Is that true?" Not waiting for an answer, she expelled a long breath. "Lexington, you run the risk of a wound like that getting infected."

"That's what I've been trying to tell her, but she's just so darn stubborn!" Amanda added, sensing another ally in this ongoing battle. "She wouldn't even let me change the dressing on it this morning!" she said in a strained voice.

The tall woman looked over at Jacob, begging with her eyes for some help. Since he was keeping silent, she decided to change the subject. "Mr.... ah, Jacob – do you know of a good detail shop around here?"

"Sure, Lex. Shuman's on Fourth does excellent work, why?" He had finished his breakfast and was relaxing in his seat, one arm casually draped across the back of his wife's chair.

Amanda leaned forward a bit. "Oh, that's right...you can't see the driveway from here." She grinned broadly. "C'mon, let's go out front and I'll show you!" She jumped to her feet and pulled the equally smiling rancher with her through the house.

As soon as they reached the door, she turned around to face her grandparents. "How did you know we were here yesterday, since you can't see the driveway? You opened the door before we could even get to it."

Anna Leigh laughed. "You did call and say you were on your way, so we were expecting you. And when we heard the slamming of car doors, we figured it had to be you!" Hand in hand, she and Jacob followed the young women outside, stopping in shock when they saw the little Mustang sitting in the driveway, muddy, but whole. "Oh, my...." She placed her free hand over her heart. "How...?"

Jacob turned to look at his granddaughter. "But I thought you said..." He noticed that Lex was turning a very unusual shade of pink.

"Lex pulled it out of the creek and got it running again. She gave it to me the night all the excitement happened." Amanda wrapped an arm around the embarrassed rancher.

"Didn't do that much, really... just let it dry out," she mumbled, not at all enjoying the attention that was being focused on her.

Jacob came up on her other side, giving her a hug. "Uh-huh... and just how *did* you get the car out of the creek? Whistle, and it followed?" He enjoyed the look on both of the women's faces – Lex's, which was one of pure embarrassment, and Amanda's, which told the others that the idea had never crossed her mind.

"He's right." Amanda looked up at the rancher, who wouldn't meet her gaze. "The car was on the far side of the creek...how did..." she paused, understanding dawning on her features. "You didn't," she whispered, the closing of Lex's eyes telling her everything. "You went *back* into that cold, heavily running stream, *after* you had your ribs broken? Are you *nuts*?" She spun around to get face-to-face with the taller woman, her voice quivering.

Jacob moved over to where Anna Leigh was standing. "I think we should go in and take care of the breakfast dishes, don't you, sweetheart?" Seeing her nod, he gently grasped her hand and limped into the house.

Lex opened her eyes, hearing the upset in the younger woman's voice. "I... um... you were just so sad about losing that car, and I wanted to do something to cheer you up. Especially after the story you told me about how you got it..." She regarded the shining green eyes that took her breath away.

"But, God, Lex... you could have asked me to help you." Amanda felt her control slipping, then the callused hands cradled her face gently. "When did you...?"

"The day I went to get the jeep. I used the winch on it to pull the Mustang out of the water." She kissed Amanda on the nose. "Piece of cake."

Amanda moved her arms up until they were wrapped around the dark-haired woman's neck. "Yeah, right. And just how did you attach the winch to the Mustang?" She saw Lex trying to think up a good answer. "Magic?"

"How'd you guess?" Lex smirked. She felt her head being pulled downwards. "Not buying that, huh?" the tall woman asked, as she leaned in to meet Amanda halfway. Their lips touched, and to Lex time ceased to matter – it was as if all the sounds around them stopped, and all she could hear was the rapid beating of her own heart. A motorcycle suddenly roared by, causing the dark woman to realize where they were standing, so she slowly broke off the kiss.

Amanda brought her arms down and placed one around the tapered waist. "Don't think for a minute that I've been distracted from our little discussion — we'll finish it later." She led the older woman inside. "But right now, we've got a doctor's appointment to keep."

Chapter
2

Even though she protested about having to go, Lex really liked Dr. Anderson – the elderly physician had taken care of her assorted injuries and illnesses her entire life, and was one of the few people she trusted completely. She and Amanda arrived at his office shortly after the doors were unlocked, so they were the only people sitting in the painfully cheerful waiting room. Since Dr. Anderson was a family practitioner, his office had brightly colored scenes adorning every wall: one wall had a circus theme, creating the feel of being inside the Big Top; another had a large mural of hot-air balloons; and the last looked like a corral, complete with several horses. Lex chose to sit in this last area, to her companion's amusement.

"Always the little cowgirl, huh?" Amanda chuckled as she sat down beside her.

The rancher looked around and smiled sheepishly. "Uh, well actually, I just like looking at the balloons." She pointed to the colorful wall across from them.

Before they could continue their conversation, the interior door next to the receptionist's window opened, and a small, gray-haired man, bent with age, stepped into the main room. "Little Lexington Marie! It's been a while, hasn't it, child?" he greeted with a strong voice. "Now get yourself in here, and bring your little friend, too." He turned and headed down a brightly tiled hallway, gesturing to a door on his left.

Amanda chuckled at the chagrined look on the rancher's face, as she followed after the old doctor. Lex stopped at the door and waited for the younger woman to enter the room before her. "Don't you start," she whispered, getting a giggle in response.

"Come in, come in... Close the door behind you," the small bespectacled doctor offered, sitting on a small rolling stool. "Now hop up on the examination bed, Lexington." He chuckled at her rolled eyes. "And don't give me that look, or I'll have to call Martha."

Lex sighed, and gingerly hoisted herself up on the padded table. "It's probably just a waste of your time, Dr. A., but..."

Ignoring her protestations, he turned towards the young blonde still standing by the door. "Come over here and sit down, honey..." He cocked his head at her and smiled. "I don't believe we've met before, have we?" he said, holding out a wrinkled hand.

Amanda grasped the offered hand, faintly surprised at the strength in it. "No, I don't think so. My name is Amanda Cauble." She gave him an earnest smile.

The doctor held her hand in both of his. "Jacob and Anna Leigh's little Amanda?" Seeing her blush and nod, he laughed. "That's grand! They speak of you all the time. They are so proud of you, my dear." He allowed her to sit down, and then turned his attention to his patient, checking the clipboard his nurse had left in the room. "So... what have you gotten yourself into now, honey?" He laid the paperwork on the stool and adjusted his glasses. "Broken ribs and a gunshot wound?" Dr. Anderson held the end of his stethoscope to warm it up a bit. "I'll bet you really set Martha off with that!" He waited patiently as Lex unbuttoned her shirt, and then gently placed the listening device to her chest. "Have you made her mad? You look like you've lost a bit of weight."

"No, just been real busy. She'll fatten me up again in no time." Lex sighed, then flinched when he began to probe the bandage on her side.

"Hurts, huh?" He shook his head. "Got a nasty scrape here, too..." he said, poking the muscular side gently. "Why aren't your ribs wrapped up? Do you want another punctured lung?" The old man began pulling the taped bandage from her side.

"Ow!" Lex jumped sideways slightly. "Could you please leave me some skin?"

The elderly doctor ignored the tall woman's complaints and finished removing the gauze, letting out a low whistle. "That doesn't look good at all," he mumbled, shaking his head in dismay.

Amanda jumped up from her chair to stand next to him. "What? What's wrong?" She peered around the small man, trying to see what he was looking at.

Running a hand down his face, Dr. Anderson pushed Lex onto her back, then lifted her legs until she was lying flat on the bed. "Might as well get comfortable, girl. We're going to have to open it up to take care of the infection." He patted her leg. "Let me go get Laura – she's going to have to help me." He left the room to search for his nurse.

The small blonde took a close look at Lex's side. She could see that the area around the wound was very swollen, and the skin had an unhealthy red shine to it. The bruising on her chest was fading, only showing mottled yellow and light purple, and the gash she received in the creek was almost completely healed. The older woman was lying still, her eyes closed. Amanda brushed the dark bangs off her forehead. "Are you in much pain?"

Blue eyes opened, meeting her concerned gaze. "No...that's what's so strange. It's only a slight ache." She captured the small hand running through her hair and brought it to her lips. "Is this where you tell me, 'I told you so'?" she teased, trying to get a smile from the worried young woman.

"No, Lex, this is where I say, 'I wish I wasn't right', because I hate seeing you go through this." Amanda looked at the wound again. "That looks really bad. I can't believe it's not hurting you! I hurt just looking at it."

Dr. Anderson came back in the room, followed by a young woman about the same age as Lex. "See? I told you we wouldn't be long." He told the waiting women. "Laura, this is…" He was about to introduce Amanda when the small red-haired nurse spoke up.

"Amanda? How's your grandfather?" She gave the young blonde a hug and a huge smile.

"He's doing great, thanks." Amanda stepped back, but kept one hand on the nurse's arm. "Talks about you quite a bit… says you're the best nurse he ever had."

Laura laughed. "That's just because I sneaked him a milk-shake every now and then." She looked over at the exam table. "Lex… it's been a while, hasn't it?" She gave Amanda's hand a gentle pat, and walked over to the table. "What have you done to yourself this time? Wreck a car? Fall off a horse?"

Doctor Anderson had put on rubber gloves, and pulled a rolling tray next to Laura. "No, actually something different, this time. Gunshot." He grinned as his nurse paled slightly.

"*Gunshot*?" She looked at the wound. "Dear Lord, Lex… do you thrive on trouble?" She gave the rancher's shoulder a slight squeeze. Turning to Amanda, she offered, "You don't have to watch… we'll come get you as soon as we're done."

The young blonde shook her head. "I'd rather stay, for moral support. If I won't be in the way." She saw the grateful look on the rancher's face.

"No… not at all." Laura pulled on her own gloves. "You can sit right over there." She pointed to a chair by Lex's head. "Maybe with you here, we won't be subjected to your friend's bad language." She almost laughed out loud at the nasty look the woman on the bed was giving her.

"Hey! It wasn't my fault! That needle was huge!" Lex countered, glad that Laura was helping her in the effort to distract the young blonde.

Laura reached over to the rolling cart and grinned. "You think that one was big…?" She took the protective cap off the syringe that she was holding. "I get to give you three of these!"

The doctor laughed. "Laura, don't tease my patient." He gave Lex a friendly pat on the leg. "Now, we're going to give you a local anesthetic, so try not to kick my nurse, okay?"

Rolling her eyes, Lex nodded. "Okay. But she could at least

pretend not to enjoy it so much," she countered, with a mock glare to the redhead. "I don't remember you being this sadistic in school."

"That's just because you didn't know me like you do now," the nurse retorted. "Now *you* be still, and *I'll* try to be gentle."

****

"Do you really think that's such a good idea, Lex? The doctor said you should just lie down and take it easy for the rest of the day." Amanda sat up straighter, straining to see over the tall steering wheel. They had dropped off the Mustang at the detail shop and picked up Lex's truck before going to the doctor's office, and the young blonde felt somewhat dwarfed by the large customized Dodge pickup.

Lex turned her head to look at Amanda, who was sitting with one leg tucked under her so that she could see over the steering wheel. "The bank is on the same street as the pharmacy; it won't take me but a minute to go in."

When she stopped at a light, Amanda looked over at her passenger. Lex was unusually pale, and her eyes had a slightly glazed look to them. "Why don't you let me take you home, and then I'll go pick up your prescription?"

"I really need to get that paperwork at the bank – I called Mr. Collins yesterday, and said I would be in today to meet with him." Shifting in the seat, she closed her eyes as another wave of dizziness washed over her.

Amanda grasped the shaky arm near her. "I'm sure he'd understand…"

"Maybe. But I won't be able to get any rest until I can look at those papers." She maneuvered her arm until she was holding Amanda's hand. "Please, Amanda, I promise to make it quick." Seeing the younger woman begin to waver, she added, "you can come in with me to make sure, okay?"

Amanda didn't say anything, but she pulled the large truck up to the bank and turned it off. "Five minutes, Lex… then we're going to pick up your prescriptions, and I'm taking you home and putting you to bed." Seeing the smirk on the older woman's face, she groaned, "you know what I mean."

Lex laughed, then slowly got out of the truck. "What? I didn't say a word." She held the door open for her companion.

A short heavyset man in an expensive suit met them just inside the door. "Ms. Walters! What a pleasure to see you again." He grabbed her hand and began to shake it wildly. "Please, come into my office." Pausing, he looked at the young woman standing next to the tall rancher. "Oh, excuse me, miss...?"

Lex turned slightly towards the smaller woman. "Sorry... Mr. Collins, this is a very good friend of mine, Amanda Cauble." She gestured towards the banker. "Amanda, this is Mr. Collins, the president of this fine institution." She smiled as the banker blushed.

"That is too kind of you to say, Ms. Walters." He led them to a glassed-in office in the corner of the building, and motioned them inside. "Please, make yourselves comfortable." After Lex and Amanda were settled, the slightly balding man closed the door, and then sat down behind an ornate oak desk. "I received your email, Ms. Walters, and personally gathered up the information you requested. And..." he pulled out a small attaché case from under the desk, "not only was I careful in my research, but I put everything in this case for you." His pudgy hands shook slightly. "You don't believe that anyone here at the bank would be involved in any illegal activities, do you?"

Lex waved a hand in the air to cut him off. "No, of course not, Mr. Collins. I just felt that the fewer people who knew about this, the better off we would all be."

The bank president visibly relaxed. "Ah, that's fine... just fine. We will do anything to keep one of our best customers happy."

Amanda cleared her throat discreetly, and casually looked over at the dark-haired woman sitting beside her.

Lex smirked, then slowly stood up, extending her hand across the desk. "Mr. Collins, it's been a pleasure doing business with you, but I'm afraid I have another appointment to get to."

"No problem, Ms. Walters...you have my home number if you need anything else, right?" He pumped her hand enthusiastically.

Lex winced, then disentangled her hand from the beaming banker and picked up the attaché case. "You'll be the first one I call, Mr. Collins." The tall woman turned and ushered Amanda out of the room.

****

Amanda rushed out of the pharmacy as soon as she was given Lex's prescriptions. So intent was she on her thoughts, she didn't see the large man about to go through the door. "Ooof! Excuse me..." Stumbling back, she glanced up and saw who she had run into.

"Well, well. Hello there, sweet thing." The deep voice drawled. "Fancy meeting you here – come in to pick up your birth control pills?" Rick Thompson blocked her exit, standing in front of Amanda with his thick arms crossed over his chest. "No, wait... I guess that you don't need to worry about that sort of thing anymore, do you?"

Why do I have the sudden urge to go home and shower? Yuck! "It's really none of your business, Rick...so if you'll excuse me, I have someone waiting for me." She tried to edge past the big man, who grabbed her arm to stop her.

"Wait! I just want to talk to you for a minute. When will you be coming back to work?" He let the small woman wriggle out of his grasp, confident that she wouldn't go anywhere. Amused, Rick decided to see just how far he could push the little blonde. "So... have you had a nice *vacation*?" he sneered.

"You bastard!" Amanda slapped him hard, knocking Rick back a step.

"Why you little bitch! I'll..." Stepping forward, he reached for Amanda, only to be stopped by a strong grip on his shoulder. "What?!?" He spun around, ready to pound on whoever had decided to interfere.

Ice blue eyes glared into his. "Problem?" Lex inquired coolly, even though it took all that she had not to smash the large man into next week.

"Mind your own damned business, Walters," he ranted, "the little whore slapped me!" His tirade was stopped when Lex grabbed two handfuls of his suit coat, pulling him into her face.

"So? Knowing you, you probably deserved it!" Lex growled. "Wanna try picking on someone your own size?"

"Why? What's it to you?" His bravado fading, Rick's tone turned more wheedling.

"She's a friend of mine, asshole!" Lex could feel her heart pounding in anger, which in turn caused her newly stitched wound to throb painfully.

Amanda took the opportunity to step around Rick, and moved to stand behind the agitated rancher. Placing a cautious hand on Lex's back, she whispered, "let it go. He's not worth it."

Lex released her hold on his jacket and took a deep breath. Seeing the big man begin to smile, she leaned close to him again. "And…" she dropped her voice to a menacing drawl, "if I *EVER* hear of you speaking about her that way again, they're gonna have to use Velcro to put you back together." She turned away from him to leave.

"This ain't over yet, by a long shot!" he yelled halfheartedly after realizing a small crowd had gathered. "You'd better be careful who you're threatening around here!" Rick waved a fist at the departing women.

Neither woman turned around, but Lex waved a bored hand over her head. "Yeah, right." She followed the small blonde to the truck, climbing inside.

Amanda closed her door and leaned on the steering wheel. She looked over at Lex, who was slumped in her seat, eyes closed. "Are you all right?"

The rancher pulled herself together and sighed. "Yeah… that jerk has always been able to yank my chain." She looked at the younger woman closely. "He didn't hurt you, did he?"

Amanda gave her a strained smile and started the truck. "Only the inside of my hand when I slapped him." She flexed the hand in question, and then pulled the large vehicle out of the parking lot. "Let's go home." She gave her passenger a real smile, "so I can tuck you into bed."

"Mmm… I think I can handle that," Lex returned her smile. Then her eyes closed, almost against her will. "Damn, Laura musta given me some sort of sedative. I can barely stay awake," she mumbled, her head falling against the seat.

"Yeah, she did say that she was going to give you something to help you relax..." Amanda's voice trailed off when she saw that the older woman had fallen asleep. She felt a strong protective urge come over her. *Rick's real lucky he didn't start anything with her... or I would have done more than just slap him.* She drove the rest of the way home in contemplative silence, taking her time and avoiding the main streets, since they were normally rougher riding, and she didn't want her companion jarred anymore than necessary.

As she pulled up into the driveway, Amanda noticed that her grandparents were walking out to the Suburban. Climbing out of the truck, she met them halfway.

"Mandy! Sweetheart ..." Anna Leigh wrapped her granddaughter up in a loving hug. "We were getting concerned. You've been gone for hours." She looked towards the truck. "Is Lexington going to come inside?"

Jacob had made his way over to where the two women were standing. "You just caught us on our way to the car dealership. They called to say Anna Leigh's new car is ready." He had been driving his wife's car when a drunk driver hit him six months ago. They had waited until last month to order her a new one, since the doctor had not cleared Jacob to drive until recently.

"Hi, Grandpa." Amanda stepped into his welcoming arms. "I take it you've finally been given a clean bill of health?" She relinquished her hold on him and smiled at her grandmother. "Lex fell asleep on the drive home. They had to reopen the bullet wound because it was infected, and Laura," she smiled towards Jacob, "gave her a sedative to keep her calm."

Jacob smiled. "How is Laura? She was such a sweetheart to me...although I think I gained a few pounds from those contraband milkshakes she kept sneaking in to me." He looked at the sleeping figure in the truck. "Do you need any help getting Lex into the house?"

Amanda followed his gaze, her eyes softening as she looked at the dozing rancher. "No, I'll wake her up in a minute. At least I should be able to get her to rest today." She gave them both a hug. "You two go ahead and pick up that new car. I can't wait to see it!" She ushered them to the Suburban.

Once Jacob and Anna Leigh had driven off, Amanda walked over to the hunter green 4x4. She opened the passenger door slowly so she wouldn't startle the sleeping woman. "Lex?" she asked quietly. "Honey, it's time to wake up." She brushed the bangs out of the dark woman's eyes, which slowly opened at her touch. "Hey there."

Lex looked around, somewhat disoriented. "Umm..." she cleared her throat, "hi." Blinking a couple of times, she finally recognized where they were. "Sorry... didn't mean to drop off like that." She wiped a shaky hand across her face.

"Don't worry about it." Amanda unclipped the seat belt holding her in. "Think you can make it into the house?"

Lex rolled her eyes and sighed. "Relax, I'm fine...just a little drugged up." She sat up and swung her legs out of the truck.

Amanda took a step away, but stayed within an arm's reach. "Okay... well, I'm staying right here, just in case," she insisted, daring the other woman to argue with her.

"Waste of time..." Lex stepped down from the truck, but her legs began to buckle as soon as she put her weight on them. "Whoa!"

Amanda jumped forward and caught Lex before she fell. Wrapping her arm around the taller woman, she chastised, "Teach you to not listen to me!" She started towards the house slowly. "Of all the stubborn, pig-headed..."

"Hey!" Lex complained, but held on tightly to the small blonde, "I just wasn't awake yet," she grumbled, allowing Amanda to guide her into the house, and then up the stairs into their bedroom. Amanda wordlessly directed Lex to the bed, pulled the comforter down and pushed Lex down gently. She lifted the rancher's feet up, removed her boots, and began to unsnap her jeans.

"If you were trying to get me into bed, all you had to do was say so," Lex teased, trying to gauge the other woman's mood. Reaching down to help, she was startled when her hands were batted away. "What?"

Amanda pulled the jeans off the long legs, folded them neatly and placed them on a nearby chair. "Hush." She pulled a well-worn nightshirt from Lex's suitcase, and draped it over the bemused rancher. After smoothing the covers over the tall form, the small blonde went into the adjoining bathroom and brought out a glass of water, stopping to grab the prescription bottles from her purse.

"Here – take these. I'm going to go downstairs and get you something to eat."

Puzzled, Lex did as she was told. "Okay... are you mad at me?" She sat the glass down on the bedside table.

Stopping at the doorway, Amanda realized how she must have looked to the other woman. "No, honey, I'm not." She walked over to the bed and sat next to the older woman. "I'm sorry. I just wanted to get you settled before you fell asleep again." She brought a hand up and caressed the tanned cheek. "I'll be right back." Standing up, Amanda leaned over and kissed Lex on the top of her head. "Behave yourself for a few minutes."

"Yes ma'am." Lex realized that she wasn't going to win any arguments today. "Could you do me a favor and bring the bank papers with you? I'd really like to start looking over them." She gave Amanda her best pleading smile.

"Sure... if you promise to get some rest first," Amanda countered, standing at the doorway. "I'll even help you, if you want."

Lex leaned against the pillows. "It's a deal." She felt another wave of lethargy wash over her. *What in the hell did they give me? I feel like I could sleep for a week!* Closing her eyes, the exhausted woman didn't even notice when Amanda sneaked from the room.

Chapter
3

Amanda was sitting at the kitchen table nursing a cup of coffee when Jacob and Anna Leigh returned from the dealership some time later.

"Peanut, is everything okay?" Jacob sat down next to her, concern etched on his strong face.

"Hmm? Oh, sure, Grandpa." She released a heavy sigh. "Just thinking." Looking across the room to her grandmother, she gave a wry smile. "Mother called while you were gone."

Anna Leigh sat down on the other side of the young woman. "Oh...is there anything wrong, dear?"

Amanda shook her head. "No... she called to see how Grandpa was feeling, and to find out why I haven't called her for so long. I told her that everything was great, and that you'd gone to pick up your new car." Taking a deep breath, she almost whispered, "Mother says since I'm 'not needed' here anymore, she wants me to come to Los Angeles and help her with the gallery."

Jacob put a strong arm around his granddaughter's shoulders. "Help with the gallery? She rarely spends any time there herself these days." He looked at his wife. "I wonder what she's up to now?"

"Maybe she just misses you, Mandy." Anna Leigh tried to

be tactful. Fact was, Elizabeth Cauble only seemed interested in her children when she needed something from them. "Did she give you any other reason for wanting you to come back?"

Amanda ran her hand through her long blonde hair in agitation. "Not really...she did say that she and Dad were about to go out of the country again. But she usually leaves Jeannie in charge of the gallery, so I don't know why she wants me there." Her older sister had rarely come here to visit, spending most of her time traveling, much to Jacob and Anna Leigh's dismay. Amanda wiped a tear from her eye. "I told her I wanted to stay here permanently, because I've found someone that I truly care about, and that I am happy for the first time in a very long time."

Anna Leigh squeezed her hand. "What did Elizabeth say about that?"

"She said that I was too young to know what I wanted." She sat up straighter. "And that this was just a 'phase' I'm going through." Amanda gave her grandmother a resolved look. "It's not a phase, Gramma. I've never felt anything more... right. And I'm not giving this up."

Jacob pulled her close. "We're both behind you one hundred percent, sweetheart." He looked over at his wife. "Funny thing is, I think your grandmother was told the same thing when we first started dating."

"C'mon, Anna... hurry up!" the diminutive redhead yelled, jogging towards the lake.

Anna Leigh laughed and followed her best friend. She didn't notice the young man carrying an armful of wood across the path in front of her. "Ooof!" She knocked him down, scattering the wood everywhere. "Oh, my... I'm so sorry!" she apologized, helping the boy to his feet. Taking a close look, Anna realized that this was no boy... he was probably seventeen, a good year older than she was. Tall, and very nice looking, the young man was now covered with a layer of dirt from the path. "Are you okay?"

Jacob Cauble looked at the young woman that he had fallen for, literally. "Uh, yeah. I'm sorry I was in your way. Are you all right?" He dusted himself off, caught in her bright green eyes.

Anna laughed. "I'm fine." She looked up into his shining blue eyes, "Where are my manners? My name is Anna Leigh." She reached out with a slender hand.

He wiped his hand on his shirt before shaking her hand. "Jacob Cauble. Pleased to meet you."

They spent the entire summer together, since both of them were staying at the lake, she with her high society friends, and he with his job as assistant to the maintenance man. Jacob thought that Anna must work around the cabins, and Anna assumed that he was there as a guest. As the summer came to a close, each found that they had been wrong about the other's background, but didn't seem to care.

"Anna Leigh," Jacob felt her snuggle closer to him as they watched the moon over the lake one evening, "I love you with all my heart and soul...I just wish I could offer you more."

She kissed his strong jaw. "Jacob, my love... you have given me more this summer than I ever dreamed possible."

He bent to one knee. "I can't give you much, but I would be honored if you would consent to become my wife." He pulled out a small silver ring, which normally graced his pinkie on his right hand. "This was my great-grandmother's wedding ring, and it would make me proud if you would wear it until I could get you a proper engagement ring."

"Oh, Jacob..." She pulled him close. "I would be proud to be your wife." She allowed him to place the small ring on her finger; it was a perfect fit. "And if you dare try to replace this with something else, I may have to thump you!"

They went to tell her parents together, hoping that their obvious love would override any objections they may have.

"Absolutely not! No daughter of mine is going to marry some money-grubbing carpenter!" Robert Winston roared, pulling the young woman from Jacob's arms. "Get up to your room this minute!" He pushed her towards the stairs.

"With all due respect, sir..." Jacob began, trying to reach his beloved.

"Get out of my house!" Robert pushed the young man away, waiting for the butler to grab him. "And stay away from my daughter!"

*Jacob struggled, then stopped as he saw Anna Leigh begin
to cry. "I love you, Anna Leigh. Don't give up on us!" he yelled,
as he was dragged bodily from the house.*

*The next day, her father, who hoped that a vacation would
bring the young woman to her senses, put a weeping Anna Leigh
on a passenger ship to Paris.*

Anna Leigh laughed. "I'd forgotten all about that." She
looked down at the small silver band on her right hand. Seeing
Amanda's questioning look, she explained, "My family was considered to be in the upper echelon of Austin society at that
time... Daddy thought your grandfather was 'beneath my station'
– he even went so far as to send me to Paris for one summer."
She smiled in remembrance. "I had been there for six miserable
weeks, when a certain young gentleman showed up on my doorstep."

"Grandpa?" Amanda whispered, mesmerized by the story.
"How did...?" She looked at her grandfather, who had a slight
blush on his face – much to the delight of his wife.

"Well, since Jacob didn't have the kind of money needed for
passage, he worked his way across on a ship. I believe it was a
cattle ship, wasn't it dear?" She smiled.

Jacob finally laughed. "Oh yeah... shoveling sh... er, by-
product for almost five weeks – talk about an adventure!" Seeing
the delighted smile on his granddaughter's face, he knew that
they had successfully sidetracked her from her previous depres-
sion. "To this day, I can't even look at a bag of fertilizer without
traumatic flashbacks!" he joked.

"Guess that means you won't be out to visit the ranch anytime soon, huh?" A sultry voice teased from the doorway.

"Lex! What are you doing up?" Amanda jumped up from the
table and hurried over to the rancher. "You should be in bed!"
she chastised.

The tall woman allowed herself to be steered to the table and
guided into a chair. "I feel much better now, especially since I've
finally got all that medication out of my system." She grinned at
Jacob and Anna Leigh. "Remind me to get even with Laura the
next time I see her."

Jacob chuckled. "She's pretty good at that, I remember." He gave the dark-haired woman a stern look. "You really should be in bed resting, Lex. You still look pretty pale."

"Oh, no... I hate lying in bed – makes me feel like I'm sick or something." Lex raised a hand to stop Amanda before she could add anything. "I really feel fine. Besides, I've got some paperwork to start looking over." She quirked a brow at the young blonde.

Amanda sighed, realizing she would not win this round. "Okay, but only for a little while – then you're going to get some more rest, or else."

"Or else what?" Lex smirked, glancing over at Jacob, who was trying not to laugh.

Watch out, my young friend... little Amanda's a lot tougher than she looks. He grinned, looking at his wife.

The small blonde put her hand on Lex's shoulder, giving it a gentle squeeze. "Or else I'll call Martha, and tell her you're not taking care of yourself..." She loved the scowl that replaced the cocky smile on the rancher's face. "And I'm sure she'll be glad to haul you out to the ranch for a little TLC."

"You wouldn't... you would!" Lex countered, seeing the gleefully evil grin that covered Amanda's face. "All right, all right!" She let out a long breath. "You win... for now, anyway."

Trying to stop the battle, Anna Leigh decided on another tack. "Lexington, you are quite welcome to use our office – the desk is more than large enough to work on, I believe."

The rancher gave the older woman a relieved smile. "Thank you, Mrs. Cauble, uh, I mean Anna Leigh," she said with an apologetic quirk of her lips. *That's going to take some getting used to, I think.* "I really appreciate you allowing me to stay here while I get some business taken care of, especially since my brother and I are not getting along right now, and I couldn't very well stay at his house." *Yeah, that's an understatement.*

"C'mon." Amanda grabbed her hand and pulled the taller woman to her feet. "I'll show you where the office is, and help you get settled." She smiled at her grandparents as she tugged the rancher out of the room.

****

Amanda led the taller woman through the house, pulling her into a spacious room off the main hall. Large bay windows with cheery curtains brightened the room, which had a large antique cherry wood desk sitting in front of the windows, and several oversized chairs were scattered around the room.

"This is where Gramma keeps track of things at the real estate office, even though she officially retired a couple of years ago," Amanda explained, showing Lex the large computer which occupied one whole side of the desk. "She wants me to take over for her, but until recently, I really didn't have any good reason to live here permanently." She gave a sweet smile to the rancher. "C'mon, let's sit down for a minute before you get too engrossed in paperwork." She helped the taller woman sit down on the sofa, and dropped down beside her with a sigh.

Lex watched as the younger woman nervously played with their still-clasped hands, a small tremor of fear running through her. *Something's bothering her... bite the bullet time, I think.* "Amanda?" She used her free hand to lift the small woman's chin up, so that they were looking eye-to-eye. "What's the matter?" Seeing a small sparkle of tears in those sea-green eyes, a lump formed in her throat. "You know you can tell me, right?"

"I know, but it's just kind of hard to explain. I'm twenty-three years old, and yet every time my mother calls, I feel like I'm sixteen again." She felt the reassuring grip on her hand tighten slightly. "I spoke to my mother earlier today. She wants me to come to Los Angeles and work in her art gallery."

Lex stiffened. "And..." she had to clear her throat, "what do *you* want?" Feeling her heart pound, the older woman tried valiantly to appear calm. The woman sitting next to her must have noticed, because she scooted closer, almost sitting in her lap.

"I want..." she pulled their linked hands up to her lips, "to stay here." She kissed the large hand in hers. "I want to tell my grandmother that I would be glad to run her office for her, and..." Amanda was unable to finish her thought, as she was pulled up into Lex's arms, and her mouth was captured in a passionate kiss. The young woman tangled her hands in ebony waves, pulling Lex to her with almost inhuman strength. She trembled as she felt strong hands begin to roam across her back, sliding across her shirt with sweet urgency. Amanda pulled away to look at Lex's face and whispered, "I just found you." Seeing answering tears shine in those incredible blue eyes, she continued, "and I'm not ready to give you up...not for my mother; not for anyone."

Lex looked into the younger woman's eyes, and saw a fierce determination there. *She really means this.* Feeling her misgivings crumble beneath that gaze, Lex tried to think of words to convey what she was feeling in her heart. "I love you," she whispered, believing the sentiment to be totally inadequate, until she saw the answering smile break across Amanda's face.

"I love you too," Amanda murmured, leaning forward to place a gentle kiss on the rancher's mouth. Breaking off, she snuggled her face into the tanned neck, happy to simply absorb the feeling of love that seemed to surround her.

They sat quietly for a while, each content to just hold the other, until a ringing phone made them both jump. Amanda regretfully slipped off Lex's lap, and had just curled up next to her when Anna Leigh came into the room.

"I'm sorry to disturb you, Mandy...but your father is on the phone, and he wants to talk to you." The older woman looked upset

"Gramma? Are you okay?" Amanda stood and walked over to her grandmother. "Did Daddy say something to upset you?" She felt Lex come up behind her and place a comforting hand on the small of her back.

Anna Leigh took a deep breath. "I'm fine, sweetheart." She gave her granddaughter a wry smile. "God knows I love my son, but he can be so small-minded at times. I've often wondered where we went wrong with him." But she did know. Her parents, trying to make up for losing their daughter to a 'working man', gave young Michael the best of everything, even when Jacob and Anna Leigh strenuously argued against it. He was showered with expensive clothes and fancy cars, and had decided at an early age that money was the most important thing in the world, no matter how much his parents tried to tell him otherwise. And when his grandparents introduced him to a young socialite from a wealthy family, Michael immediately saw his opportunity and proposed. *How on earth did our sweet little Amanda come from such a business-like merger?* Anna Leigh often wondered to herself.

"Guess I'd better get this over with." Amanda walked over to the desk and picked up the phone. "Hello, Daddy." She listened for a few minutes, her normally cheerful demeanor becoming more clouded by the minute. Looking across the room, she saw that Lex and her grandmother were in a deep discussion. She placed her hand over the mouthpiece and whispered, "Lex..." No other words were necessary, as the tall woman crossed the room quickly to pull the small blonde into her arms.

Looks like she's in good hands now. Anna Leigh left the room quietly, closing the door behind her.

"I know what Mother wants, but as I told her earlier today, I'm staying here in Somerville." Tears welled up in her eyes as she listened to her father's tirade. "I'm a grown woman, Dad... I love you and Mother, but there's nothing there for me anymore." She took a deep breath as Lex pulled her tight, kissing her lightly on top of her head. "I've found someone I love very much, and I'm very happy here." She leaned into the strong arms now supporting her. "Yes, Gramma and Grandpa know about it. She's staying here with us now." Amanda pulled the phone away from her ear as her father began to rant in earnest now. "NO! She's not like that! They have accepted my choices, why can't you?" Amanda felt tears of frustration fall down her face. "I'm sorry you feel that way, *Father*." She slowly lay the phone on its base, and then turned and tucked herself into the strong body behind her. "Oh, God..." she began to cry.

Lex was at a loss. *What can I say to her without sounding like a selfish fool?* "Shhh...it's gonna be all right, sweetheart," she whispered into the nearby ear.

Amanda cried herself out, feeling a deep sense of loss. "He doesn't want anything to do with me until I 'come to my senses'," she sighed. "He says all you want is my money, and that you're just using me." She looked up, expecting to see anger.

Laughing out loud, Lex gave Amanda a strong squeeze.

"You can't be serious!" She continued to chuckle, released her grasp on the younger woman and stepped over to a small table, where the attaché case from the bank lay. Pulling out an envelope, she handed the smaller woman a piece of paper. "Read the balance on the statement." She grinned.

Amanda gave her a questioning gaze, but did as she asked and looked down at the bank statement. *No wonder she's smiling... she has more money than* both *my parents have combined!* "You're kidding, right?" she questioned, looking up at the grin stretched across the rancher's face.

Lex shook her head. "Nope. My mother was from a very well-to-do family, and with the investments I've made in the past few years, it's safe to say that I won't be trying to clean out your bank accounts in the middle of the night." She smiled.

"Not that I ever had any worries in that regard, Lex. I don't use my parents' money, which has also caused quite a few arguments." Amanda crossed to where the taller woman was standing and stepped into her arms. "I wouldn't care if you were just a poor ranch hand, I'd still be hopelessly in love with you."

Lex kissed her temple. "I know... and you should know that I fell in love with you the moment I pulled you out of the creek. I had no idea who you were, but there was something about you..." She pulled the smaller woman closer. "So, are you going to help me read all these damned reports? Maybe you can figure out where all the money is going."

Amanda allowed herself to be led over to the desk and sat in a nearby chair. "Sure. I help with the bookwork at the office all the time – I love numbers."

Grinning at the younger woman, Lex handed her a pile of papers. "Maybe I should hire you to do my paperwork at the ranch? I hate sitting in an office when I can be outside doing something instead."

"I'd love to." Amanda smiled. "What are you willing to pay?" she asked, sorting the papers into some semblance of order.

Lex gave her a sexy smile. "I think we could work something out." She started dividing the papers she had into neat little piles.

****

They worked quietly for almost two hours, each woman studying the papers before her. Amanda finally found a pattern to the losses, pointing it out to the older woman. "Look. This is the third time I've seen this." She handed the paper to Lex.

"Now that you mentioned it, I've seen it a couple of times myself." Lex dug through a pile, then jumped to her feet. "That sonofabitch!" She threw the papers down and began to stomp through the room. "I'll kill him!"

"Lex! Wait!" Amanda jumped up from her chair and caught the tall woman before she could reach the door. Latching onto a strong arm, she forced Lex to turn and face her.

The angry rancher was almost to the door when she felt a small hand grab her arm. Spinning around, she was about to sling off the annoyance when a quiet voice cut through the red haze of her fury.

"Lex?" Amanda spoke quietly, hoping to calm the angry woman as one would a wild animal. "Hey, come over here and sit down, please?" She thought at first Lex was just going to brush her aside and continue out the door, but the piercing blue eyes softened, and the older woman allowed herself to be guided to the sofa.

Leaning back on the sofa, Lex closed her eyes and took a shaky breath. "I'm sorry," she murmured, feeling the anger ebb away, leaving only weariness in its place.

Amanda sat down next to her, feeling her own heart slowly return to its normal rhythm. She watched as the older woman finally calmed down, seeing the tense lines on her face slowly soften. Picking up the hand that was clenched into a tight fist, she coaxed it open, entwining their fingers. "Shhh...there's nothing to be sorry about."

Lex pulled their joined hands up until they were against her chest. She bent her face down and placed a very soft kiss on Amanda's knuckles. "I'm sorry that you had to witness that." Lex opened her eyes and looked down at their hands, still unable to bring herself to meet the younger woman's gaze. "But better that you know now how I can be, I guess."

"Look at me," Amanda quietly demanded. Taking a deep breath, Lex slowly raised her eyes to look into the green ones before her. Expecting to see fear or disgust, the rancher was somewhat shocked at the amount of love and understanding she was receiving instead. When she opened her mouth to speak, Lex found her lips gently covered with a soft fingertip.

"If that's the best you can do to scare me off, you're in big trouble." Seeing the older woman taking a breath to speak, Amanda shook her head. "No, wait... I know you have a temper," she said with a wry smile, "and if you ask anyone in my family, they'll tell you I have a pretty short fuse myself." She took her hand away from Lex's mouth and used it instead to caress the tanned cheek. "So, between the two of us, everyone else had better watch out!" Noticing that Lex's blue eyes were turning watery, Amanda threaded her fingers behind the older woman's neck, pulling her head forward. She gave Lex a gentle kiss, then pulled away and smiled. "Would it help you to talk about it?"

Lex leaned forward again until their foreheads were touching. "There's not much to say..." her voice dropped to a hoarse whisper as her eyes involuntarily closed. "It's about the missing money." Her hand was released, and she felt a heavy weight descend onto her chest... until small, strong arms wrapped themselves around her comfortingly. Pulling the smaller woman into her lap, Lex buried her face in the soft reddish-blonde hair. "It's not the amount of money that bothers me," she mumbled, feeling the younger woman squeeze her tighter.

Amanda stroked the dark head tenderly. "Shhh... I know that, honey." She felt the body under hers tremble slightly.

"My own brother..." Lex sniffed, trying to control her emotions. "How can my own brother be embezzling money from the ranch?"

Dear God... no wonder she's so upset. Amanda could feel the quiet sobs wracking the slender form beneath her. "Sweetheart...maybe there's another explanation."

Pulling herself together, the older woman leaned back so she could look into Amanda's face. "I could probably handle the fact that he's taking money from the ranch, since he really never got over the fact that Dad signed it over to me." She gave the younger woman a weak smile, as soft fingertips wiped the tears from her face. "But the way he's done it... I really never thought the slimy bastard was that smart."

"He can't be too smart... since you've caught him at it," Amanda remarked, relieved to see that her companion was feeling more like herself.

Lex shook her head sadly. "That's just it, Amanda. Looking at the statements and receipts, we haven't caught him..." She helped the young woman off her lap, picking up some papers from the desk. "Look right here..." She showed the smaller woman the signature on the withdrawal slip. It read, 'Lexington M. Walters'. "We've caught *me*."

Chapter
4

Later that evening, Amanda convinced Lex to tell Anna Leigh and Jacob what was going on, since they had been running their own business for years. She was hoping their different perspectives would help them find an easier solution – one that didn't include Lex having to testify against her only living sibling, and possibly sending him to prison. *I don't think she could handle that kind of guilt – not to mention dragging all of this out in public,* Amanda reasoned.

"So, he's been withdrawing money by signing your name to the slips for the last few months?" Anna Leigh asked, looking at the receipts from the bank. "And since all the statements had been sent to him, you're just now finding out about it?"

Lex was sitting in a nearby chair with her head propped in her hands. "I know... it was totally irresponsible of me not to have copies of the statements sent to the ranch every month." She was feeling more and more foolish by the minute.

Amanda, perched on the arm of Lex's chair, rubbed her back comfortingly. "I think what Gramma is wondering is why the bank hadn't figured out that something unusual was happening." She looked at her grandmother, who nodded in agreement.

"Goodness, Lexington! I never meant for you to think that!"

She waited until the young rancher looked up at her. "It's just that the only time I can see that you've withdrawn money without using a check is when your brother has done it, and it was for fairly large amounts. I just can't believe they actually allowed this to happen without some sort of verification."

Jacob looked up from the papers he was studying. "She's right... those idiots at the bank should have realized something was wrong a long time ago... unless someone there is in on it too."

Lex closed her eyes, suddenly feeling exhausted. "I've already called Mr. Collins and told him not to allow any more withdrawals from this account without visual verification." She leaned her head against the chair. "I'm going to take your advice and go down tomorrow to open a new account, so Hubert won't have any more access to the ranch funds."

Anna Leigh looked at Jacob, and they both looked at the rancher in concern. Amanda looked down, seeing that Lex had closed her eyes. "Lex?" She ran a hand gently through the dark hair. "I think you've done all you can today." She waited for the older woman to look up at her. "It's getting pretty late, so why don't we go upstairs and go to bed?"

"Yeah, I think you're right. I'm beat," Lex sighed, then slowly stood up. She smiled tiredly at the older couple sitting at the desk. "I really appreciate all of your help today. I don't know what I would have done without you." She looked down at her feet self-consciously. "I think I was just so shocked when I found out who was behind all of this, I couldn't think straight."

Anna Leigh walked over to the taller woman and wrapped her arms around Lex's broad shoulders. "Oh, sweetheart... you're part of the family. We'll always be here for you."

Jacob stood beside them, giving Lex's shoulder a gentle squeeze. "That's right, honey. Now get yourself upstairs and get some rest."

Lex stepped back and gave them both a heartfelt smile. "Thank you...I wish I had known my own grandparents – but I have a feeling they couldn't have held a candle to you two." She then allowed Amanda to steer her out of the office and up the stairs, leaning slightly against the smaller woman.

"Lex, are you all right?" Amanda asked, as the rancher placed an arm around her shoulders.

"Yeah, I'm fine. Just enjoying the company," she chuckled, feeling Amanda swat her on the rear. "And I am a little tired...it's been one hell of a long day." She patiently let the younger woman guide her to the bed, sitting down with a grin.

Amanda began to unbutton Lex's shirt, not noticing the smirk she was receiving. "Have you taken your medicine this evening, Lex?" Not waiting for an answer, she efficiently disrobed the rancher, and picked up a soft cotton nightshirt from a nearby suitcase for Lex to wear. "Here... put this on." She dressed the older woman as if she were a child. Before she could finish buttoning the shirt, she felt her hands gently captured.

"Amanda...?" Lex spoke softly; causing sea-green eyes to focus on her, "please stop fussing so much...you're going to wear yourself out." She brought the small hands to her lips and placed a soft kiss on the delicate knuckles. "Why don't you join me?"

Amanda blinked. "Oh." She gave Lex an embarrassed smile. "I didn't even realize what I was doing." She pulled away slowly, grabbing her own nightshirt from a nearby dresser. Stripping quickly, Amanda didn't notice the appreciative eyes watching her until she had slipped the long tee shirt over her head. "What?"

"Have I ever told you how beautiful you are?" Lex asked, in a reverent tone. "Just looking at you makes my heart stop."

"Oh, c'mon... I think that medication you're on is affecting your eyes..." Amanda chuckled, and then looked into Lex's face, seeing that the older woman was quite serious. "You really think so?" She walked over to the bed and sat down.

Lex pulled her close, then rolled over onto her back, tucking the younger woman against her left side. "Oh, yeah..." She gave her a light kiss on top of her golden head.

Amanda felt an unexpected surge of happiness flow through her with that thought. *Wow...* "Thank you," she murmured, absorbing the feeling with joy.

"You're welcome." Lex pulled her even closer, if that were possible. "Love you," she managed to say before sleep claimed her.

"I love you too," the fair-haired woman whispered, as she kissed the strong shoulder underneath her cheek.

****

The early morning sun was shining brightly through the windows when Amanda opened her eyes, which caused her to groan and attempt to bury her face into her pillow. Feeling the pillow move, she reopened one eye and realized the surface her head was propped up on was actually breathing. *Amazing... I actually woke up first.* She reached for Lex's forehead with one hand. *No fever... that's a good sign.* She thought about getting up, but the older woman had her arm wrapped possessively around Amanda's shoulder, and she really didn't want to disturb her. *So I guess I'll just suffer here in bed,* she smiled to herself. *What a hardship.* She wrapped her arms tightly around the strong body beneath her and drifted off to sleep again.

Lex woke up sometime later, pleased to note that the fuzzy feeling from the medication was gone, and the wound in her side didn't hurt at all. Amanda was still sprawled against her, tousled blonde head snuggled up under her chin. Looking towards the window, Lex could see the late morning sun streaming in. *I can't believe I slept so long.* Peering down fondly at her companion, she smiled. *She's not gonna let me live this down for a while, I'll bet.* She pulled the younger woman close and softly kissed the top of her head. "Amanda..." She felt a small arm squeeze her tighter. "C'mon, sweetheart, time to get up. We can't lounge around in bed all day."

"Mmm... no," the smaller woman grumbled, "don't wanna." She buried her head deeper into Lex's shoulder.

Desperate times call for desperate measures, Lex grinned to herself, as she slowly edged a hand under Amanda's nightshirt, tickling her ribs.

"Hey!" the young blonde squealed, jumping. "Not nice!" Sitting up, she rearranged her shirt. "You look like you're feeling better today," she observed.

Lex rolled over onto her left side, and propped her head up

with her hand. "Yep... good as new."

Amanda mirrored her posture with a sweet smile. "I wouldn't go that far...you still need to take it easy for a few days – doctor's orders!" Seeing the decidedly evil grin that broke out across the rancher's face, Amanda quickly rolled out of bed and started towards the bathroom. *I don't know what she's thinking, but I don't think I'll like it,* she thought to herself. "Don't give me that look..." she warned, not turning around. Amanda was almost to the doorway when she was caught from behind. Strong hands reached under her shirt and began tracing a gentle pattern on her stomach.

"Want me to scrub your back?" a soft voice growled in her ear.

Amanda felt her legs start to weaken as Lex began a tender assault on her neck. "Uhmmm..." She lifted her arms over her head to tangle her hands in the dark woman's hair. The large hands began to drift upwards, taking a firm grasp on responsive flesh. "Ohh... yeah... sharing is good..." she murmured, then allowed a chuckling Lex to guide her gently into the bathroom.

****

By the time they made it downstairs the kitchen was strangely quiet. Amanda steered Lex into a chair at the table and smiled. "Looks like I finally get to cook you some breakfast." She brought over a mug of coffee and placed it in front of the taller woman. "Here, you can start with this." She stepped over to the stove and turned the griddle on to heat.

Lex took a sip of the coffee gratefully. "Thanks, but you really don't have to wait on me hand and foot, or cook my breakfast. We can always stop and get some doughnuts, or something."

"Oh, no... those things will kill you! Besides, I like taking care of you... I've never had anyone to pamper before – so get used to it." Amanda shook a finger at her, indicating that no more arguments would be heard, then turned and started pulling items out of the refrigerator.

Anna Leigh walked into the kitchen to refill her coffee cup. "Good morning, girls." She gave Amanda a hug, then kissed Lex on top of the head as she joined her at the table. "What kind of trouble are you two planning on getting into today?"

Amanda turned away from the counter where she was stirring pancake batter. "Funny you should ask, Gramma. I was going to talk to you about that."

"Really?" The older woman winked at Lex. "Well, here I am, so ask away. Do you need me to do something for you?"

Pouring the batter onto the griddle, Amanda chuckled. "Actually, I was hoping it was something I could do for you." Keeping one eye on the griddle, she partially turned to look at her grandmother. "Since I've decided to live here in Somerville on a more permanent basis, I was wondering..." She didn't get the rest out before Anna Leigh leaped to her feet and wrapped the younger woman in an exuberant hug. "You're staying? That's wonderful, Mandy!" She pulled away to look her granddaughter in the eye. "Does this also mean I have a new office manager? Two people have called in the past week to give notice because of Rick." She felt bad that things had gotten this much out of hand – but her thoughts had been focused on Jacob's health, and the real estate office had been on the bottom of her priority list after her husband's accident.

Amanda gave her grandmother a squeeze, then returned her attention to the pancakes. "If you still want me to, then yes." Flipping them over, she turned to Anna Leigh. "*But...*" she pointed the spatula, "only if you think I'd be the best person for the job."

"Absolutely! When can you start?" Anna Leigh laughed, then sat down at the table across from Lex. "Would you two mind meeting me at the office this afternoon? I can't wait to get rid of that sorry excuse for a human being."

Lex grinned. "I can't speak for Amanda, but I would love to be there when you give that worthless son of a ... goat the axe." Looking at the back of the small blonde, she smirked. "Did Amanda tell you she had a run-in with him yesterday? He probably has a nice little bruise to show for it, too."

"Really? What happened?" Anna Leigh smiled back at her granddaughter, who groaned.

"I couldn't help it... he started mouthing off, and I just lost my temper." Amanda placed the pancakes on plates and brought them to the table.

"Aaand?" The older woman drew out the word, expectantly.

"I slapped him." Amanda sat down next to the rancher, embarrassed.

Lex snorted. "More like knocked him silly! He nearly fell over!" she teased.

"Good Lord, Mandy! That man is huge! He could have seriously hurt you!" her grandmother scolded.

Looking over at Lex, the fair-haired woman smiled. "I wasn't worried – Lex got in his face and nearly made him wet his pants!" They all laughed. "But please, Gramma, wait until we get there before you do anything, okay? I really don't trust him."

"Certainly, sweetheart. That would work out better, anyway. Jacob has been going stir crazy, so he's decided to work in his shop for a little while, and he's gone now to get supplies." She smiled. "He's just so glad to be able to drive himself around again."

Lex laughed again. "I can sympathize, since I nearly drove Martha crazy when I broke my leg a couple of years ago."

"How did...?" Amanda shook her head. "Never mind. I don't think I want to know."

Anna Leigh gave Lex a sympathetic look. "Wasn't that when you rolled your truck during that nasty ice storm?"

"Yeah... that whole mess is the reason Martha insisted that I start carrying a cell phone with me. She gets pretty upset when I forget to take it." *Like the night I went to check the fence in a thunderstorm... Well, at least that worked out.* Seeing Amanda's questioning look, she shrugged. "It happened on a Friday afternoon, and they didn't find me until Saturday night."

"I remember... I swear, she nearly called out the National Guard!" Anna Leigh looked at Amanda. "Martha called everyone on the Historical Committee, and had nearly every able-bodied man in the county combing every inch of the roads between here and the ranch."

Amanda looked at Lex, aghast. "Dear God! That must have been horrible for you!"

"It really wasn't that bad. I don't remember much about it."

Lex tried for nonchalance.

Anna Leigh slapped her on the arm. "That's because you were unconscious for most of it, silly!"

The tall woman rolled her eyes. "See? I told you it wasn't that bad." She gave them both a smirk, then stood up and put her plate in the dishwasher. "You about ready?" she asked the younger woman. "I'd like to get my business with the bank done as soon as possible."

"Yeah, I'm done." Amanda put her dishes away, then kissed her grandmother's cheek. "See you at the office around one o'clock, Gramma?"

"That will be perfect, sweetheart. You two try to stay out of trouble until then, okay?" Twin sets of rolled eyes caused Anna Leigh to chuckle. "I know it's a lot to ask..." she said as they left, laughing.

****

They were sitting in Mr. Collins' office, the pudgy man sweating profusely as Lex sat there, silently glaring at him.

"I... I... swear to you, Ms. Walters," he stammered, wiping his forehead with an already damp handkerchief, "I honestly don't see how this could have happened!" His face was getting redder by the minute, and Amanda was afraid the poor man was on the verge of passing out.

"Are you doubting my word, Mr. Collins?" Lex asked quietly, her intense blue eyes boring into the bank president's face.

"No!" he practically shouted. "I mean, of course not!" he clarified, more quietly. "But our policy on any withdrawal is to get a visual identification – especially with such large amounts."

Lex leaned forward in her chair. "Then," she paused, lowering her voice even more, "unless my brother has changed drastically," she looked down at her own body, "I suggest that one of your employees is either not following policy, or they are in on his little scheme." She glanced up, catching the sweating banker staring at her breasts.

He flushed scarlet, and began to stammer, "M... m... m... Ms. W...ww... Walters..." He pulled his collar away from his throat. "I can assure you that we will be investigating this matter thoroughly. And these papers," he held up several documents, "will insure that only you..." He looked somewhat puzzled at one page, "and Miss Cauble here..." not hearing Amanda's gasp of surprise, "will be the only people who have access to this account."

Lex nodded and stood up. "Very good... and if anything happens to this account," she gave him an icy stare, "I will hold *you* personally responsible." She got a certain enjoyment out of seeing the banker's face suddenly pale. "Good day, Mr. Collins." Lex gestured for Amanda to precede her through the office door.

After Amanda signed the necessary papers, Lex ushered her out of the bank and into the truck. The younger woman was unusually quiet as the rancher helped her into the passenger seat and closed the door after her.

Getting in behind the wheel, Lex sighed. She looked over at her silent friend with concern. "Are you all right? You seem awfully quiet."

Amanda blinked, then turned her gaze towards the dark-haired woman. "You didn't tell me you were going to do that."

"What?" Lex asked, puzzled. "Oh... that." She met the green eyes with a hopeful look. "I'm sorry, I guess I wasn't really thinking. Does it bother you?"

The younger woman wrinkled her brow thoughtfully. "No! I mean it's not that... I was just really surprised, that's all." She offered her hand to Lex. "But why put anyone else on the account, after all the trouble it's already caused? And why me?"

"Because I know you would make sure Martha was taken care of if anything ever happened to me..." Lex squeezed her hand.

"Please don't talk like that. I don't think I could survive if anything ever happened to you." Amanda took a deep breath, willing herself not to start crying. "Why not put Martha's name on it, then?"

Lex pulled Amanda's hand up and held it to her cheek. "I'm afraid if I do, Hubert will find out somehow, but he'd never suspect that I would give authorization to someone I've only known for a short while, " she kissed the small hand, "and because I'm totally in love with you, and want to share all I have..."

"You know that I have all I really need right here, right now, don't you?" Amanda tenderly cupped the rancher's cheek. Resisting the urge to crawl across the seats and wrap herself around Lex's body, she smiled. "I'll try not to ever break this trust you have in me." Removing her hand, the younger woman sat back and buckled her seatbelt. "It's almost time to meet Gramma at the office. You ready?" She knew that this was not the time or place for such a deep conversation, and could also see that her companion was more than a little off balance by the whole thing.

Lex nodded, somewhat at a loss for words. "Yeah... this ought to be fun, huh?" She backed the truck out of the parking space in front of the bank and drove towards the real estate office.

Chapter
5

Lex followed Amanda into the small building, ignoring the curious looks that passed her way. The younger woman led her into a brightly lit room with several partitioned cubicles, guiding her to a comfortable chair next to a cluttered desk.

"I would apologize for the mess and try telling you it normally doesn't look like this, but I refuse to lie." Amanda grinned, sitting down at the desk.

Lex leaned back in the chair, crossing her legs at the ankles and resting her entwined hands on her flat stomach. "They say a cluttered desk is the sign of a busy mind..." she grinned. "When do you find time to sleep?"

Amanda stopped her cleaning efforts, and wadded up a piece of paper – throwing it at the smirking rancher. "Oh, you!"

Lex caught the paper in mid air, tossing it back, only to have it hit the smaller woman on top of her head and then ricochet over the partition. "Oops!" She tried to look innocent as a small woman peeked over the wall, glaring. She had short, sandy-blonde curls framing her round face, and appeared to be a few years older than Lex. Her almost gray eyes flicked to the desk with a scowl.

Her demeanor instantly changed when she saw who was sitting at the desk. "Amanda! 'Bout time you got back!" She disappeared, and then reappeared a moment later in Amanda's cubicle, encircling the younger woman in a hug. "You look great!" She noticed for the first time that they weren't alone and gave Lex a tentative smile. "Oh, sorry... I didn't know you had company." She studied the silent woman from head to toe – extremely blue eyes, denim shirt, pressed jeans and worn but well cared-for boots. "You must be Lexington... the whole office has been buzzing about you."

"Really?" The tall woman stood and held out a hand. "You can call me Lex."

The older woman smiled, more genuinely this time. "Lord, my manners are horrible! I'm Wanda Skimmerly. It's really nice to meet you." She shook the rancher's hand.

"Wanda?" Amanda interrupted her babbling. "What do you mean, the whole office is buzzing?"

"Well, when your grandmother called to say you weren't coming in for a while, she said something about how you were literally pulled from the jaws of death – that's Janet talking, not me." She looked at Lex. "She's the one who spoke to Anna Leigh when she called in."

Lex laughed, then sat down in her chair. "I'm afraid it wasn't that exciting... I just helped Amanda out of the creek, and then held her hostage until the bridge was rebuilt." She winked at the older woman.

Wanda shook her head. "Uh-huh... if you say so." She looked at Amanda, who was sitting on the edge of her desk. "Well, I'll let you get back to it, then...nice to finally meet you, Lex."

"Yeah... nice to meet you, too," the dark-haired woman replied, waving a hand at her retreating form. She glanced over at her companion, who had a smirk on her face. "The 'jaws of death'? Good grief! These people need to quit watching so many talk shows."

Amanda chuckled, but was kept from answering by the buzzing phone on her desk. "Amanda Cauble..." She listened for a moment, then broke into a wide smile. "Hi, Gramma... sure. We'll be right there." She looked at Lex as she hung up the phone. "Showtime." Offering her hand to the reclining woman, Amanda pulled the rancher up out of her chair and led her towards the office.

****

When they walked into the manager's office, Lex and Amanda noticed that Anna Leigh was sitting behind the desk, and Rick was lounging in a visitor's chair with a sullen look on his face. Hearing the door open, the large man turned, then jumped to his feet. "I should have known," he sneered as Amanda walked by him to sit on the corner of the desk. "This is about yesterday, right?" The large man glared at the young blonde. "You went crying to grandma because I hurt your little feelings?" Not getting a response from the small woman, Rick looked over at Lex, who was casually leaning by the door with her arms folded across her chest. "She's got you on a pretty short leash... eh, Kentucky?" he said, using the old school nickname to taunt the tall woman. "Maybe you'll do a few tricks for us, huh?"

Before Lex could reply, Anna Leigh spoke up. "That's quite enough, Mr. Thompson. Now please have a seat."

Lex gave him a fake smile, but wisely kept quiet. *I'm really gonna enjoy this.* She looked over at her companion and saw the angry set to Amanda's face. *It's nice to have someone take up for me, for a change.* Wanting to ease the tense lines on the younger woman's face, Lex winked, and got a small smile in return. *That's better.*

Anna Leigh stood up, walking around the desk. "Mr. Thompson... first, let me assure you this meeting has nothing to do with the events of yesterday – that was outside of this office, and I feel that my granddaughter is more than capable of taking care of herself." Seeing him relax, she continued. "However, it has been brought to my attention that of late, you have been abusing your position."

"Abusing, my ass!" he sputtered, ready to jump to his feet once again.

"Mr. Thompson!" Anna Leigh held out a hand to forestall

his outburst. When he sat down again, she returned to the desk and sat down. "I have had several complaints about your treatment of the employees of this office." She pulled some sheets of paper from her briefcase. "These are the complaints from this past week." Handing the papers to Rick, she watched as he read over them.

"Harassment? Lewd comments? Intimidation?" He looked up at the older woman, his face reddening with anger. "What the hell is this? Some sort of freakin' witch hunt?"

Anna Leigh shook her head sadly. "No, Mr. Thompson, it isn't. And we're not even going to go over what you did to Amanda last Friday."

"What? I sent her on a call...it's not my fault the little brat can't read directions!" he blustered.

Pulling a discolored paper from her purse, Amanda finally spoke. "Funny...even though it's kind of water-stained, you can still make out the client's name... 'L. Walters', and in the space below are the directions, in your handwriting."

"Mr. Thompson, as a woman who almost lost her granddaughter due to your petty games, I am furious. And, as the owner of this business who nearly lost a very valuable employee, I have no other recourse than to terminate your employment with this agency."

"What?!?" Rick jumped to his feet, incensed. Glaring at the young blonde, he yelled, "it's all your fault! Things were just fine around here until you showed up!" He pointed his finger at Anna Leigh and continued his tirade. "You old biddy! Always looking down your nose at me − well, I'm not gonna sit still for this!" He took a step towards the desk when a hand on his arm stopped him.

"That's far enough," Lex spoke quietly.

"Get your damned hands off me, you meddling bitch!" Rick spun, slamming an elbow into the unsuspecting rancher's side.

Lex grunted and fell to her knees, her arms wrapped around herself in agony.

Turning his murderous gaze on Anna Leigh he growled, "you're next, old woman."

When Amanda saw Lex fall to the floor, everything around

her slowed. Rick started walking towards the desk, when suddenly his head snapped upwards, the imprint of the young woman's shoe on his chin. Amanda readied herself for another kick when the big man fell backwards, his eyes rolling back in his head.

Lex was able to look up just as Amanda knocked Rick out. Kneeling on one knee, she concentrated all her attention on fighting unconsciousness herself. She closed her eyes and swallowed several times, fighting a wave of nausea that was brought on by the excruciating pain from her abused ribs. *This hurts worse than when they were first broken.* She focused on taking very small breaths, when she felt a gentle hand on her shoulder.

"Lex? C'mon sweetheart, look at me." Amanda brushed the dark hair away from the rancher's bowed head, frightened by the loss of color on the normally tanned features.

Anna Leigh was on the phone, calling the sheriff to come clean up the office. "Mandy? Should I ask for an ambulance?" She was worried, especially since Lex hadn't moved since she had dropped to the ground.

"Honey? Do you want to go to the hospital?" Amanda was still running her hand nervously through the dark hair.

Lex shook her head. "No," she managed to get out, hoarsely. Finally able to look up into worried green eyes, she gave a slight smile. "Just... let me... catch my breath."

"Let's get you off the floor." Amanda waved her grandmother over, and the two of them helped the still pale rancher into the nearby chair.

The sheriff and two deputies stepped into the room, seeing the big man still out cold on the floor. "Damn..." He looked over at Lex. "Did you do this?"

The dark-haired woman shook her head and inclined it towards Amanda.

"Amanda?" He took off his hat and scratched his gray head. "Well, I'll be damned... what did you use? A two-by-four?"

The young woman blushed, and looked down at Lex. "Ummm... no." She felt the rancher grasp her hand, which had been resting on the tall woman's shoulder. "I, uh... kicked him."

Anna Leigh joined in. "That's right! Mandy took kickboxing

lessons during the summers when she stayed with us. Even won a few tournaments."

Charlie laughed. "Damn! Remind me never to make you mad..." he teased, watching the deputies pull a groggy Rick to his feet and out of the room. "I know he's a jerk, but do you have any other charges to press? I'll need something to put down on the report."

"Assault." Amanda spoke quietly, and with a touch of anger, still looking down at Lex. "He hit Lex in the side, unprovoked."

The dark-haired woman shook her head. "No. I'm not pressing charges," she whispered, still in agony.

"But..." Amanda started, confused.

"No!" The rancher turned her pain-filled eyes towards the sheriff. "Tell him if he'll leave Mrs. Cauble and Amanda alone, I won't press charges."

Charlie nodded. "Gotcha." He looked at her still-pale face closely. "You gonna be okay?"

"Yeah, fine. Do you need me to sign anything?" She sat up a little.

"Nah... I'll take care of it." He put his hat on and walked to the door. "Take care of yourself, Lex." Tipping his hat to Anna Leigh and Amanda, he said, "you ladies just give me a holler if you need anything."

Anna Leigh walked to the door and shook his hand. "Thank you, Sheriff. I certainly appreciate your quick response. Let me walk you out."

"Thanks, Mrs. Cauble. Take care, Amanda," he said as he waved and walked out the door.

Amanda returned his wave, then squatted down beside Lex. "You feeling any better?" She was relieved to see the color beginning to reappear on the older woman's face.

Lex smiled. "My hero," she said, enjoying the blush on the younger woman's face.

"I really don't know what came over me...I saw you go down, and then he was coming towards Gramma." She pulled Lex's hand up to her face. "I guess I just snapped." *The idea that I could easily take down someone that size without thinking scares me,* she mused. "What kind of person am I to do something like that?" she whispered aloud.

"A very brave person, who will stand up for her family when they are being threatened," Lex answered. Seeing the serious green eyes still distant, she added, "but damn, Amanda... you're something else! Wanna be my bodyguard?"

That did it. The smaller woman finally broke out of her mood and chuckled. "Oh Lex..." She laid her head down on the rancher's lap, wrapping both arms around the strong legs and squeezing.

Anna Leigh walked back into the room. "Lexington... are you certain you're going to be okay?" She stopped next to the dark-haired woman and placed a gentle hand on her shoulder.

Lex looked up into the kindly eyes that looked so much like Amanda's, and smiled. "I'm okay, now. Just sort of got my attention, that's all." She looked down, seeing her hand running unconsciously through the long blonde hair in her lap.

The older woman gave her shoulder a tender squeeze. Taking a look down as well, she saw her granddaughter's head comfortably pillowed on the rancher's legs. "Mandy? Honey, I hate to disturb you, but everyone is in the conference room... it's time to make the announcement."

Amanda lifted her head with a wry smile. "Well, it's got to be easier than what we just went through, right?" She climbed to her feet and stretched. "You want to sit in? I'm sure the boss won't mind," she asked Lex, and then looked to her grandmother for confirmation.

Lex shook her head. "Actually, I need to make a few phone calls, if you don't mind me 'borrowing' your office."

"My office?" Amanda laughed. "Oh, yeah... sure." She kissed the dark head. "I'll be back in a little while." Entangling her arm with Anna Leigh's, she said, "c'mon, Gramma. Let's go harass the help."

✳✳✳✳✳✳✳✳✳✳✳✳✳✳✳

Amanda sat through the endless congratulations with a smile on her face, but even her normally good nature was beginning to slip as the boundaries of her personal space continued to shrink.

If one more person pats me on the head, I swear I'll bark! The meeting itself only lasted about ten minutes, but the group of employees had circled their new office manager afterwards, and showed no signs of leaving – even though it was almost an hour later.

Anna Leigh heard her granddaughter sigh for the third time in the last five minutes. *I think it's time to save Mandy from our well-wishing friends.* She stood up and cleared her throat, getting everyone's attention immediately. "Everyone, I realize how excited we all are, but let's give your new boss a break." Accepting the grateful smile from the young woman, she continued, "With all that has happened in the past week, I'm still going to insist that my granddaughter take another week or two off to get some things settled. I know I can count on you all to continue on without her for a little longer." Agreeing murmurs were heard, and the happy employees began filing out of the room.

Amanda stood up and stretched, making her way over to Anna Leigh and wrapping her arms around the older woman. "Thank you...I know they meant well, but the walls were beginning to close in on me." She pulled away to look her grandmother in the eye. "Are you sure you want me to take more time off? I don't really need to..."

"Yes, I'm sure." Anna Leigh placed a hand under the younger woman's chin, looking carefully into her shadowed green eyes. "Honey, you've been through more in the past week than some folks handle in years...and I think you need an extended vacation to sort through it all." She kissed her granddaughter's forehead and pulled the young woman into another hug. "You have a lot of issues to work through, even if you don't realize it."

Amanda sighed. "Yeah, I know... guess the first thing I need to do is go to LA, pack up all my stuff, and get it shipped here."

"What's the rush?" The older woman pulled away slightly, but kept an arm looped around Amanda's waist. "It's been there for over six months already. What difference would a little longer make?"

The smaller blonde allowed Anna Leigh to escort her out of the conference room and back towards 'her' office. *That's going*

to take some getting used to. "Well, after my last couple of conversations with Mother and Father, I wouldn't put it past them to
either throw it all away, or give it to charity...they were pretty
upset with me."

They had just walked up to the open office door when Anna
Leigh asked, "so, when are you leaving for Los Angeles?"

"Probably next week." Amanda answered casually, not seeing the stricken look on Lex's face as she stood up from the desk.
"Lex, did you get your phone calls taken care of?" She gave the
rancher a smile. "I thought we'd never get out of that meeting."

"Yeah..." The tall woman looked around uncomfortably.
"Umm... I've got a couple of errands to run..." She ran a shaky
hand through her hair, "you wanna stay here for a little while and
get settled?"

Amanda looked at her quizzically. The rancher was looking
pale and shaky. *What's up with her?* She stepped a little closer
and put her hand on Lex's arm, causing the older woman to jump
slightly. "Okay... when you get back, I have something to talk to
you about." Feeling the arm under her hand tense, Amanda
looked up into Lex's face. "Are you okay? You're not looking
too well."

Lex took a breath to speak and shook her head. *She's right...
I heard the tail end of the conversation and panicked.* "Sorry...
ummm..." She looked down at the floor. "Did I hear right?
You're going to California?" she inquired, willing her voice not
to quiver.

Amanda mentally slapped her forehead. *Idiot! She's already
shook up, and then hears that?* Getting inside Lex's guard,
Amanda snuggled up to her and wrapped her arms around the tall
woman gently. "Yeah...that's what I wanted to talk to you about.
You feel up to taking a trip with me sometime next week? I want
to go get the rest of my stuff packed up and shipped here, before
my parents throw it out." She felt the older woman instantly
relax.

"You want me to go to your parents' house with you?" Lex
asked, unsure. "Do you really think that's such a good idea?"

Hearing the office door quietly close, Amanda smiled to
herself. *Gramma always seems to know.* She pulled away

slightly, then threaded her hands through the taller woman's hair, pulling the dark head down gently. "I want them to meet you... so that they can see why I love you so." Amanda felt the rancher tremble as she brushed Lex's lips softly with her own, so she gently deepened the kiss until a warmth began to spread throughout her own body.

Strong hands that had been wrapped around her waist slowly migrated downward, pulling the smaller woman nearer. Groaning into the older woman's mouth, Amanda squeezed closer, until their bodies melded almost into one.

Lex broke off the kiss to breathe and nuzzled the blonde woman's ear. "You'd better stop now, or your new office is going to get more of a christening than you can imagine." She felt the small body shake with laughter.

"Oh God, Lex... I think that would be a little hard to explain, don't you?" Small chills ran down her spine as Lex nibbled on her earlobe. "Uhhh... L... Lex... ah... you'd better stop, or you're gonna... mmmm... end up on my... ah... desk."

Kissing the tip of Amanda's nose, Lex grinned, then backed off. "Heh... don't tempt me." She took a deep breath, pleased to note that her ribs didn't seem to have been damaged in the earlier scuffle. "So... when are we leaving?" she asked, seeing a large smile cover her companion's face.

"Really? You'll go?" Amanda wrapped her arms around Lex's body exuberantly. The sharp intake of breath caused her to pull away quickly. "Oh no, Lex... your ribs! I'm so sorry..."

"Sshh... they're fine... just a little tender." Lex pulled the small woman close again. "And of course I'll go. Do you actually think I could stand to be without you for what... three, four days? Uh-uh... you're stuck with me, sweetheart." She kissed the soft blonde hair lightly.

"Cool – I think I can handle that," Amanda murmured. She was about to say more when a knock on the door interrupted her. "Come in," she answered, giving Lex one final quick kiss on the chin before backing away a step.

Anna Leigh poked her head into the office. "Sorry to disturb you Mandy, but Elizabeth is on the phone, asking for you." The older woman gave her granddaughter a somewhat disgusted look. "Sounds like your mother is in another one of her little 'moods'."

Amanda shook her head sadly. "I'm sorry, Gramma... might as well send her on through." She walked over and sat down behind the large desk as the older woman left the room again.

"I'll, uh... give you some privacy." Lex started towards the door.

"No!" the younger woman almost shouted. "Please stay? For moral support?" she begged, as the phone buzzed. Amanda waited until the tall woman sat down in the chair across from her before she picked up the handset. "This is Amanda. Hello, Mother."

"Amanda Lorraine Cauble! I've been calling all over town looking for you..." Elizabeth's pinched voice whined.

"I'm fine, thank you for asking," the young woman replied, annoyed. "Is there something I can do for you, Mother?"

"Don't take that tone with me, young lady. I'm still your mother – even though you never bother to call me anymore," Elizabeth berated. "When are you coming home? I fail to see how you can be happy in that horribly small town. They don't even have a proper museum."

Amanda rolled her eyes. *Well, we do have the Texas Oak Tree Museum, but I guess she's probably not interested in that.* "Mother, believe it or not, the world does not revolve around museums and the cultural arts."

Elizabeth gasped. "Dear Lord! Don't say things like that! I do believe living with your grandparents is ruining you! They never did appreciate the finer things – I have no idea how your father turned out the way he did."

"I've often wondered that myself," Amanda murmured. "Is there a reason you called, other than to belittle Gramma and Grandpa?"

"See? You made me so upset that I almost forgot the reason I was looking for you..." the older woman sighed. "You have to come home next week...we are having our annual Fall Dinner for your father's business associates, and he would like for you to be here."

"Mother, I have a job and responsibilities here. I can't just drop everything to fly halfway across the country for a dinner party!" Even though she had planned to go to California next week, the younger woman did not want to give her mother the satisfaction. Seeing Lex smile, she crooked a finger at her, beckoning the rancher towards her.

Lex raised an eyebrow, but got up and walked behind the desk. Amanda stood up wordlessly, then pushed the lanky form of her lover into the chair, gently sliding into the taller woman's lap. Amanda listened to her mother's ranting as strong arms pulled her close.

"I think we've been too lenient with you, Amanda. You didn't used to act this way with us." Her mother's tone was harsh. "I told your father that it was not a good idea for you to spend so much time down there..."

Amanda tensed. "Why? Because I'm actually thinking for myself?" Lex gave her a squeeze, and her anger dissipated, replaced by an aching sadness. "I'm sorry I'm such a disappointment to you, Mother."

Her mother sighed. "Amanda dear... it's not that you're a disappointment, you've just gotten so headstrong. What happened to my little girl?"

She's still in Los Angeles, working in the gallery, Amanda thought. *Jeannie was always her little girl... I was always her disappointment.* "I guess I grew up," the young woman sighed.

"Thank God!" Lex whispered in her ear, making Amanda chuckle.

"I'm sorry, what was that, Mother?"

"I said, it would mean a lot to your father and me if you could make it for this dinner." She paused, then added, "you can even bring your new friend if you want to. We'd really like to see you, dear."

"Oooh... an invitation... guess I'd better starch my jeans," Lex whispered into the nearby ear.

Amanda swatted the large hands resting on her stomach. "Actually, Mother, that would work just fine. I need to come and pack up the rest of my stuff anyway." She leaned back as soft lips nibbled lightly on her neck. "What night is the dinner?"

Elizabeth breathed a sigh of relief. "Next Friday. Could you come a day or two early? Jeannie and Frank will be staying at the house next week, and I know they would love to see you."

Amanda turned slightly to give Lex a questioning glance.

"Sure...whatever you want," the rancher murmured.

Amanda gave her lover a light peck on the lips. "Mother? We can fly out early Wednesday – but I have to be back here Sunday, all right?"

The older woman tsked. "Four days? Well, I guess it's better than nothing. Call us Tuesday with your itinerary, and we'll have the driver pick you up."

Frowning, the young woman shook her head. "No, Mother, that won't be necessary. We'll just rent a car." She hated the limousine.

"Fine. I won't bother to do anything for you," Elizabeth muttered. "Your father would feel better if you acted more to your upbringing. We worked very hard to get where we are, and I really don't want you to embarrass him by acting so lower class. At least rent a decent car, not like that old junker you drive now."

Oh yeah, they worked terribly hard, waiting until certain family members died to get at their inheritance. "Yes, Mother." It was hard to stay angry with her mother with Lex kissing the nape of her neck. "I'll see you on Wednesday." She hung up the phone before the older woman could complain any more. "Aarrgh! She's so infuriating!"

Lex squeezed her tighter, and then kissed her on top of the head. "Mmm... think of it this way – you'll get your revenge when you show up with me," she chuckled.

"What do you mean?" The younger woman shifted in the rancher's lap so she could look the rancher in the eye.

"Well, I don't think I'll fit in too well – but don't worry. I'll try not to spit on the floors or anything." She gave Amanda a wry smile.

Stroking the tanned cheek, Amanda smiled gently. "Do you actually think that I would be ashamed or embarrassed of you?" She gave the older woman a sad look. "Why?"

"No... I don't think you would feel that way – but I can't help but feel a little 'common' around folks like that." Then she grinned. "I guess this means I have an occasion to wear my new boots."

Amanda wrapped her arms around the dark-haired woman's neck. "Honey, they probably could call you a lot of things, but common certainly isn't one of them... gorgeous, sweet, funny, wonderful..."

Lex covered her mouth with a large hand. "Hush! I get your point, but I don't have anything to wear to something like that. I'd do anything for you, you know, but..." she lowered her gaze, a slight blush creeping onto her face, "I hope I don't have to wear one of those slinky-looking numbers. I haven't worn a dress since I was four years old."

Lifting the older woman's chin, Amanda gazed into her eyes. "Sweetheart, I would never ask you to be something you're not. You can wear cutoffs and an old dirty tee shirt, and I'd still be proud to walk in with you."

Lex laughed. "Now *that* would be a picture!" She gave the younger woman a tender kiss. "But I think I should probably find something to wear – I really don't have anything but jeans." A shy smile. "You want to help me pick something out?"

"Oooh! Shopping! My favorite hobby!" Amanda looked at Lex with a sexy grin. "Well, it *was* my favorite hobby, until recently." She climbed off the rancher's lap. "We'll pick something up when we get to LA... C'mon... let's go get something to eat, I'm starved."

"Newsflash," Lex grinned, getting to her feet as well.

Chapter
6

After telling Anna Leigh goodbye and not to expect them for dinner, Amanda and Lex found themselves sitting at a secluded table in a nearby restaurant.

Amanda was attacking the chips and salsa with gusto. "This is great!" she mumbled between mouthfuls. Glancing across the table, she noticed Lex was staring at her with an amused look on her face. "What?"

"Amazing." The older woman grinned, shaking her head.

"What?!" Amanda stopped and studied the smiling face across from her.

Lex unsuccessfully tried to lose the silly smile she knew had to be on her face. "Umm..." She took a sip of her iced tea, then cleared her throat. "I was just wondering... how does someone as small as you enjoy food so much, and still have such a fantastic figure?"

Amanda blushed, ducking her head. "I don't know about the figure, but I've always enjoyed my food." The smaller woman's eyes grew large as a sizzling platter of fajitas was brought to their table. "Ooohhh..."

Lex partially choked on her tea. "Damn, Amanda... are you trying to kill me?" She laughed at the blush her comment caused. The dark-haired woman's brows knit in thought. "Hey – I just realized something."

Amanda looked up from her fajita construction. "What's that?" She added a dollop of guacamole, and then folded the tortilla over in triumph. "Heh."

"This is the first time we've gone out to eat together – kinda like a first date, huh?" Lex smiled at the obvious enjoyment her companion had at building her meal.

Chewing then quickly swallowing, Amanda nodded. "Hey, you're right. Want to do the entire clichéd first-date thing? How about a movie after dinner? We could make an evening of it."

"Sure! Do I have to get you home early?" Lex grinned. "How late is your curfew?" She lifted a forkful of Spanish rice to her mouth.

"Nothing to worry about there; my grandparents trust me. I've never had a curfew when I have stayed with them." She took a sip of her tea, and gave Lex a sexy smile. "Of course, I've never had such a good incentive to stay out late before, either." Watching the tall woman flush, she giggled.

Lex, finished with building her own fajita, shook her head. "Then I guess it's probably a good thing we didn't meet any sooner – I could have corrupted your tender sensibilities." She looked up with a devilish smile. "Although, I believe it would have been fun to try."

Amanda wiped her mouth with her napkin, then returned it to her lap. "You can say that again," she teased.

****

After flirting shamelessly with Amanda throughout the meal, Lex dropped her napkin to the table with a heavy sigh. "Hey, it's actually a pretty nice evening, not too cool. Could I interest you in a walk through the park instead of a movie?" she asked, adding, "I need to work off this dinner somehow." *I really need some fresh air. All this indoor activity is starting to make me a little stir-crazy.*

"Do you feel well enough to go on a walk?" Amanda looked into the blue eyes across from her. "How are your ribs?"

Lex leaned away from the table and sighed again. "I feel

fine... stuffed, but fine." She waved at the waiter for the check. "You about done?" she inquired, indicating Amanda's empty plate.

The younger woman placed her napkin on the table and groaned. "Mmm... I think a walk is a great idea! I won't be able to eat another bite for a least a week!" She glanced up sharply at Lex's stifled chuckle. "Don't you dare..." she declared, shaking her finger at Lex. "C'mon! There's a nice little park a few blocks from the house. It has a small lake and a path to walk on, too." She grabbed the check as soon as it hit the table. "My treat – I asked you to dinner, remember?"

Lex conceded with a nod. "Okay, next one's on me." Seeing the nasty smirk on the young blonde's face, she shook her head. "Uh-uh... don't you even *think* about going there!"

Amanda shrugged her shoulders, putting an innocent look on her face. "Who, me?" She left money on the table with the check, and stood up. "Let's go see what kind of trouble we can cause at the park. I'll get my dessert later." With a wink, Amanda strolled happily out of the restaurant, leaving her companion to pick up her jaw and scramble after her.

****

The last of the sun's rays reflected brightly off the small lake, as Lex pulled the dark truck into a nearby parking space. "Looks pretty deserted," the rancher commented, not seeing any other cars in the lot. As she stepped out of the tall vehicle, Lex pulled on her well-worn denim jacket, then closed the door and crossed to the other side.

"Yeah, but you should see this place in the spring and summer...you can rarely find a parking space then." Amanda pulled a folded paper napkin from her purse, then climbed down out of the truck. Handing the item to Lex, she slipped on the coat she had brought: the old leather jacket Lex had worn in high school that she had 'borrowed' from the rancher. "Brrr...that wind is getting pretty chilly." Pulling the taller woman towards a paved path, she grinned. "C'mon! Let's get moving, so I'll warm up."

Lex allowed herself to be guided down the well-traveled

path. "What's this?" she asked, handing the napkin to the smaller woman.

"Duck food," Amanda chuckled, opening it up to show two leftover flour tortillas. She linked her arm through the tall woman's and continued down the path that led to the lake.

Lex looked down at the young blonde fondly. "Do you come here often?" She felt the arm linked with hers tighten slightly.

"Yeah...this is kind of my thinking place – I usually bring old bread along and feed the ducks for hours at a time." She led the older woman through a stand of trees, which opened up to a small cove. "When I was in school, I always spent my summers here. Mother never understood why." She pulled Lex over to a large log that was close to the water, then sat down next to her. "Mother and Dad would go to Europe, Jeannie would travel with them, or spend her time at one type of camp or another. I would beg to come here to visit Gramma and Grandpa..."

Lex pulled her close with a strong arm. "I don't really remember much about any of my grandparents," she said quietly. "Dad's folks died when he was just a kid, leaving him the ranch. I vaguely remember my mother's father... tall and handsome. But after she died, I never saw him or my grandmother again." She straightened a little, then smiled. "They didn't care much for Dad – he's kinda rough around the edges."

Amanda put her arm around the older woman. "I'm sorry." She felt sympathetic tears filling her eyes.

Lex leaned over and kissed the top of the blonde head. "Don't be; I'm not. Martha and the guys at the ranch more than made up for it – I had more attention from all of them than most kids ever get from two sets of grandparents."

"Really?" Amanda peeked up at the taller woman's face, which wore a wistful smile.

"Oh, yeah," she laughed. "Of course, most of the hands usually helped me get into trouble. Poor Martha spent most of her time chasing me with a spoon and hollering, 'Get your filthy butt out of my kitchen and get into the tub!'" She paused thoughtfully. "Come to think about it, she still does that!"

Amanda giggled. "I bet you were a real handful growing up."

"I don't think so, but I'm sure Martha's opinion would differ." Lex watched as several ducks jumped out of the water and waddled towards them, quacking excitedly. "Looks like your friends missed you." She grinned at Amanda's delighted smile.

"Calm down, guys!" The younger woman was pulling the tortillas apart into very small pieces. After eyeing Lex cautiously, the ducks decided she didn't pose a threat, and continued their enthusiastic welcoming of her companion. "Sorry... they're a little excitable." Amanda looked over at Lex, who was watching a gray and white duck nibble on her boot tips.

"They're psycho – this crazy thing is trying to eat my boots!" She wiggled her feet slightly, causing her attacker to pause momentarily, then start up again.

Amanda laughed. "That's all I have, guys. I'll bring a loaf of bread next time." She showed the ducks her empty hands, which caused them to glare at her for a moment, wagging their tail feathers in agitation.

"I don't think they're real happy with you right now," Lex teased, and then stood up. "Let's continue our walk. Maybe they'll get the hint." She offered her hand to Amanda, who accepted it gracefully.

"Thanks, that sounds like a great idea." Amanda allowed herself to be pulled to her feet. "Let's not use the path. Do you mind if we just walk along the shoreline?" She held the hand in hers tightly as they began walking.

****

They were on their second circuit around the small lake when Lex's cell phone rang. Jumping slightly, she stopped and pulled the small device from her coat pocket. "Hello?" She listened for a moment, then frowned. "Martha, what's wrong?" She felt a small hand on her arm, and looked down into concerned green eyes.

"Lexie, I'm really sorry to bother you like this," Martha apologized, sounding very upset.

"Don't worry, we were just taking a walk...now tell me what's the matter." Lex forced herself to stay calm. *Martha never calls me...I've never even heard this damned phone ring before.* "Go on, tell me."

"Honey, it's your brother. He called the house a few minutes ago looking for you." The housekeeper sounded quite agitated.

"Okay... did you tell him I was in town?" Lex didn't like where this conversation was going.

"No, not at first. I didn't figure it was any of his business." The older woman sighed. "I told him you weren't available...that really upset him." She chuckled in remembrance.

Lex laughed. "I'll bet. Then what?"

"He told me it was very important that he talk to you immediately – I told him again that you couldn't come to the phone. That's when he really started getting upset."

Dammit! Lex felt a headache fast approaching. "What did he say to you, Martha?"

"Oh, well he yelled and whined quite a bit," she laughed, "then he said, 'Forget it! I'll just come out there myself!' and hung up."

"He's on his way to the ranch?" Lex ran a slim hand through her hair. "Shit!" She glanced at Amanda, who was looking at her with a worried expression. "How long ago did you talk to him?" Lex was already pulling Amanda down the path towards the parking lot.

"I just hung up with him right before I called you," Martha said, not quite as angry as before.

"Good... I'm on my way – lock all of the doors, in case he gets there before I do, okay? Don't let him in for any reason." Lex and Amanda were at the truck, the taller woman holding the passenger's door open for her companion. She closed the door, then quickly jogged around to the other side and climbed in.

"Why? Are you expecting him to cause trouble?" Martha sounded concerned. "What's going on, Lexie?"

Holding the phone with her shoulder, Lex put the truck in reverse and backed out of the parking space quickly. "I don't know what to expect. We found out that he's the one who's been taking money from the ranch." The rancher glanced at Amanda with a questioning look.

"Tell her to sit tight. We're on our way." The young woman

answered the unspoken question.

Lex smiled at her companion and turned the truck south on the road out of town. "Amanda says to hold tight..." she spoke into the phone.

"She's there? Let me talk to her, then." Martha perked up. "You shouldn't be talking on the phone while you're trying to drive, it's not safe." She could hear the roar of the truck engine over the phone.

"Yes, ma'am." Lex handed the phone to the smiling blonde sitting next to her. "She wants to talk to you."

"Martha! It's great to hear from you, although I'm sorry about the circumstances," Amanda chattered happily. She genuinely missed the older woman, even though it had only been a couple of days since she had last spoken to her.

"Amanda honey, how are you?" the housekeeper asked, sounding quite pleased with herself.

"Great! I've really got a lot to tell you when I see you again— so much has happened!" Amanda watched as Lex rolled her eyes.

Martha laughed. "Really? Well, I can't wait! Were you able to get Lexie to go see the doctor? I swear, that girl argues with me sometimes just for sport!"

"Yesterday morning, as a matter of fact; her side was terribly infected, but Dr. Anderson took care of that." The younger woman reached over and caressed a muscular leg, causing a slight smile on the rancher's serious face.

"Blast it! I knew that would happen. But you say she's okay?" Martha sighed. "She never takes care of herself..." the older woman muttered more to herself than to Amanda.

"She's fine; got a couple of stitches, and Dr. Anderson made her promise to keep her ribs wrapped for another week," Amanda chuckled, remembering the argument with the old doctor. "He says she's gotten a little too thin, though..." This little bit of news got her a glare from the subject in question. "Don't give me that look... and keep your eyes on the road," Amanda scolded.

The housekeeper laughed. "If I could get her to sit still long enough to eat!" She turned serious. "But I think that she's eaten more in the last week or so than the entire last month combined.

And I have you to thank for that – she's happier now than I can ever remember seeing her. So thank you, Amanda – for giving my little girl back her heart."

Lex had turned to glance at Amanda, who had stilled suddenly. Even in the fading sunlight, she could see a deep blush on the younger woman's fair skin. Reaching over with one hand, she touched the small blonde's shoulder. "Hey...you all right?" she asked, trying to keep one eye on the road and one on her companion.

Amanda blinked, and grasped Lex's hand. "Yep." She gave the large hand a strong squeeze and smiled. "Martha, I think I got the better end of the deal," she told the housekeeper.

"I think you both did," the older woman chuckled. "How far out are you now?"

Lex had just turned off the main road, and Amanda could see the old bridge up ahead. "We're almost to the bridge, so we should be at the house in about ten minutes or so."

"Great! I just started a fresh pot of coffee. I have a feeling we're gonna be needing it." Martha paused. "Hold on a minute, honey... I think I hear a car pulling up out front."

"Wait!! Martha? Are you there?" Amanda heard the phone being set down.

"What?" Lex looked over at the younger woman as they started across the bridge.

"She thought she heard a car drive up, and set the phone down to go look." Amanda listened intently to the phone, trying to hear any unusual noises.

"Dammit!" Lex sped up the truck, practically flying across the old wooden structure.

"Lex! Slow down! We're not going to be any help to Martha if you kill us!" Amanda had released the rancher's hand, and was bracing herself against the dash.

The older woman slowed the vehicle down reluctantly. "Has she come back to the phone yet?" Lex had a death grip on the steering wheel, the dash lights casting an eerie glow on her tense face.

"No... not – wait, I think I hear something." The younger woman chewed on her lower lip in concern.

"Amanda?" Martha sounded somewhat breathless. "You still there?"

"God, Martha, don't scare me like that! Are you okay? We're almost to the house." Amanda held her breath, waiting for the answer.

"Oh heavens yes, but I'm afraid Hubert is going to hurt himself trying to get in." She laughed. "Sounds like he's working his way around the house – banging on windows and doors as he goes."

The truck skidded to a stop in the long driveway, as Lex parked beside a grossly expensive BMW convertible. She looked over at Amanda and gave her a worried look. "Do you want to wait here, or..."

The young blonde frowned. "Do you really want me to?" She unbuckled her seatbelt, looking at the taller woman for an answer.

"No, I'd rather you stay with me; I'm less likely to strangle Hubert if there are witnesses." Lex gave her a wry grin. She unclipped her buckle and opened the door. "C'mon, let's go get this over with."

They were almost to the front door when they heard a man's voice screaming from the rear of the house, "Dammit, old woman! I know you're in there – open this friggin' door before I kick it in!"

Lex unlocked the front door and ushered Amanda inside, then closed and locked the door behind them. "Martha, we're here," she said in a normal voice, walking down the hallway.

The short, round housekeeper stepped out of the den, causing Amanda to yelp in alarm. "Oh sweetheart, I didn't mean to startle you." Turning towards the taller woman, she said, "Lexie, I think that Hubert has about worked his way around to the front of the house." Suddenly, a loud banging on the front door confirmed this.

"Goddammit!! Unlock this door, you old bitch, or I'll knock it down!" Hubert kicked the door ineffectually.

Lex opened the door, an angry set to her face. "Hubert! What in the hell is your problem?" She stood in the doorway, daring him to try and get by her. "And watch what you say about

Martha."

"Get the hell outta my way, Lex!" He tried to push past her, but was stopped when Lex put her hand in the middle of his chest. Hubert was only an inch or two taller than his younger sister, but he outweighed her by at least thirty pounds.

"Why?" Lex pushed her brother backwards a step. "What business do you have in this house?" She stepped out on the front porch with him. "I believe we settled that when I gave you the house in town – you didn't want anything to do with this 'old, dirty ranch', or so you said then."

Hubert stood quietly, remembering. He'd always hated the ranch, even as a child. Illogically, he felt that this place killed his mother, since she had started going into labor here at the ranch, and it took longer than it should have to get her into town to the hospital. Then, of course, his father bypassed him and taught his younger sister how to run it – it still hurt, all these years later. Looking at Lex now, he realized just how much he missed his mother. *She looks so much like her.* Shaking his head slightly, Hubert glared at his little sister. "I still don't, but I seem to be having some trouble accessing the bank records, and I thought I may have left some papers here last time I did the books."

"I should hope you're having trouble getting into the account. I changed it." Lex leaned against the doorframe, casually crossing her arms across her chest.

"What?!?" Hubert yelled, stepping up to the smirking woman, grabbing the front of her denim jacket with both hands, and pulling her towards him. "You can't do that!"

Lex reached up and grabbed the angry man's wrists, squeezing them painfully. "Let go of me," she muttered quietly, "or I'll break 'em... then we'll let the sheriff deal with you." A flicker of comprehension crossed his angry features.

Hubert released her, pushing the tall woman slightly. "Bitch." Taking a couple of steps backwards, he ran his hand through his dark hair. "Why didn't you call the law when you found out?"

"Because, no matter what else I think of you, you're family," Lex answered wearily. "Why did you do it? Couldn't you have just asked?"

The big man let out a derisive snort. "Yeah, right...so you could lord that over me like you have everything else?" He shook his head. "You're so damned high and mighty... always acting like you're better than everyone else. I don't have to explain anything to you – besides, you can't prove a thing."

"What do you want from me, Hubert?" Lex dropped down onto the porch swing gracelessly. Bracing her elbows on her knees, she sighed. "I'm not going to press charges, but I think it would be a good idea if you stayed away from the ranch for a while."

A movement in the doorway caught his eye. "Oh, you'd like that, wouldn't you?" Glancing at the small blonde moving towards them. "Is this your latest plaything? I'll have to hand it to you, she's... URK!"

Lex jumped up and pinned her brother against a nearby support post, her forearm against his throat. "Say what you want about me, you asshole, but NEVER let me hear you talk about Amanda that way again." She enjoyed the look of fear on the big man's face as she held him against the post, his face getting redder by the moment. She felt a gentle touch on her back.

"Lex? Let him go, please?" the soft voice pleaded behind her.

The tall woman flexed her arm, causing Hubert to stand up on his toes, gasping for air. "I've had it with you – I didn't want this ranch, but by God, I'm going to work it with everything I am, and no two-bit bean counter is going to change that." She felt Amanda place her small hand on her shoulder. "Especially not the likes of you!" Shifting slightly, Lex shoved her brother off the porch.

Hubert stumbled to the driveway, holding his throat and gasping for breath. "This isn't over, Lex," he panted, backing his way clumsily towards his car.

The rancher braced her hands against the porch rail, Amanda standing beside her. "Go home, Hubert," she sighed heavily, watching as her brother got into his car and drove away. Bowing her head, Lex closed her eyes against the exhaustion that was left behind, as her rage crumbled away.

"God, Lex..." Amanda whispered.

The older woman felt the words as if they were physical blows. Afraid to turn around, she took a deep breath. "Yeah, I completely lost it." She felt the smaller woman duck under her arm and snuggle close.

"Was he always such a jerk?" the young blonde asked, turning to look up into the anguished face above her.

"Huh?" Lex blinked, then wrapped her arms around the smaller woman in reflex.

Amanda smiled at the unconscious gesture. "Good grief! How you have kept from killing him before now is a complete mystery to me."

"Ahem."

Both women turned around to see Martha standing in the doorway, arms crossed. "You two gonna stand out there all evening mooning over each other, or are you coming inside for coffee?"

Smiling wearily, Lex wrapped an arm around Amanda and pulled her towards the door. "Well, how can we resist such a gracious invitation?" Allowing the younger woman to enter before her, Lex stopped in front of the smirking housekeeper.

Martha looked up into the twinkling blue eyes. "What?" Then she stopped in shock as the tall woman bent over and placed a gentle kiss on top of her graying head.

"Thanks." So softly uttered she almost didn't hear.

"For what, honey?" The older woman heard her own voice crack.

"Everything," Lex murmured, then followed Amanda into the house.

Martha watched them go, wiping a tear from her eye with the corner of her apron. "Rotten kid..." she grumbled, "Just when I think I have her figured out, she says something like that." She sighed heavily, then closed the door behind her.

****

The three women spent the next several hours sitting in the kitchen, with Amanda catching Martha up on the happenings of the last couple of days. She tried to gloss over her involvement in the incident with Rick, but Lex wouldn't let her.

"Wait... wait! Back up, Amanda!" The rancher looked over at Martha. "She neglected to tell you the best part." Watching the young woman blush, she continued. "Rick started towards Mrs. Cauble, so I stepped in behind him to try to get his attention." She gave a sheepish grin. "He, ah... elbowed me in the ribs," Lex cleared her throat, "and I dropped like a rock."

"Good lord, child!" Martha reached across the table and placed her hand on the tall woman's arm. "Are you all right?"

Lex nodded. "Yeah... just kinda took my breath away for a few minutes..." She gave the young blonde next to her a warning look. "Anyway, there I was, on my knees trying to catch my breath, when I see Rick moving towards the desk again. He got about two steps when he went flying backwards!"

Martha looked back and forth between the two younger women. "How?" She was practically on the edge of her seat.

"Amanda did some sort of karate, or something..." Lex looked at the younger woman for confirmation.

"Kickboxing, actually," the young woman muttered, embarrassed.

The housekeeper's jaw dropped. "You? Kicked him?"

"Nailed him right on the chin," Lex supplied helpfully. Amanda slapped her on the shoulder. "What?"

"I just wanna die..." the small blonde mumbled, covering her face with her hands.

Martha stood up, chuckling. "Don't feel bad, honey! I think it's great that you can defend yourself." She kissed the top of the young woman's head. "Now," she waited until she had both women's attention, "I think it would be best if you two stayed the night. It's been a long day, and there's no sense in your driving back to town this late."

Amanda looked at Lex, who shrugged her shoulders. "That sounds like a great idea. Let me give my grandparents a call so that they won't worry." She stood up. "I'll just use the phone upstairs, if that's okay."

Lex smiled. "Sure. I'll be up in a minute." Her eyes followed the young woman as she left the room.

"Lexie?" Martha was charmed by the smile on the dark

woman's face. "Honey?"

"Hmm?" Lex answered. "Oh! Umm... sorry about that." She straightened up in her chair. "What's up?"

Martha stepped over until she was standing next to the younger woman. Absently running her hand through the dark hair, she murmured, "I was so proud of you this evening, Lexie."

The rancher leaned into the contact unconsciously. "Really? I thought you would be disappointed. I almost strangled my brother on the front porch, Martha." She released a heavy sigh and closed her eyes wearily. "Dad was right."

"About what, sweetheart?" The housekeeper continued her gentle ministrations.

"He said my temper would cause nothing but trouble, and he was right – first Lou, and now Hubert." She fought the tears that threatened to fall when she thought about her youngest brother.

"How can you say that?" Martha sat down in the chair next to the anguished woman. "Louis was killed in a boating accident. You weren't even there!"

Lex looked at the housekeeper, tears threatening to spill from her shining blue eyes. "And if I hadn't lost my temper with him, he would have never gone in the first place."

It was the middle of summer, and Lex was angry because she was stuck in the office at the ranch, when she would much rather be down at the creek swimming. It had been over a year since her father had left her in charge, and the teenager was getting more and more stressed out every day. Running the ranch, putting up with the snide remarks of her older brother Hubert, and trying to keep one eye on her younger brother Louis, all combined to make the serious young woman a bundle of nerves.

After an especially trying argument with Hubert over the working of the latest herd of cattle, Lex had escaped to the office for some much-needed peace and quiet, when an excited Louis rushed into the room.

"Lex! There you are! I've been looking all over for you!" he exclaimed breathlessly. Where Lex and Hubert favored their mother with their dark good looks and blue eyes, Louis took after their father, Rawson – short, small frame, dark blonde hair, and

dark hazel eyes.

"Not too hard to figure out where I am," she muttered, "I seem to live in this damned office."

"Yeah," Louis agreed sadly. He missed his playful sister, who seemed to have disappeared in the past year or so. "Hey! I've got a great idea! A bunch of us are going to the lake this afternoon – why don't you come with us?"

Lex ran an impatient hand through her hair. "I can't... there's too much to do around here." She looked at her younger brother. "Just who is 'a bunch of us'?"

Louis couldn't meet her eyes. "Uh... well... five guys from school, and Jim's brother Randy, who's gonna drive us out there."

"Randy? The kid that just got out of juvenile detention? No way!" Lex stood up and paced around the desk. "He's what? Sixteen?" She looked at Louis, who was beginning to mirror her angry posture. "I absolutely forbid it!"

"You don't own me, Lex! I wasn't asking your permission – I just wanted to let you know where I'd be." He began to walk backwards towards the door.

"Dammit, Lou... use your head! You need a responsible adult around if you guys are going to the lake, not some kid who just got out of jail!" She was interrupted by a horn honking in the front of the house.

"They're here... I gotta go." Louis started for the door.

"Lou... I won't allow it!" She reached for his arm.

Jerking away from her, he cried, "You're NOT my mother, Lex! I don't need your permission to go anywhere – Hubert already said I could go!" He turned to face her. "I'll see you tonight." The young man raced out of the office.

Lex started after him, but the phone on the desk stopped her. "What!?" she yelled into the receiver, taking her anger out on a poor helpless salesman who happened to call at the wrong time.

The rancher was still simmering in the office when the phone rang again, several hours later. "Hello?"

A stranger's voice asked, "Lexington Walters?"

'Great, another salesman,' she thought. "Who wants to know?" Lex growled.

A short pause, then a sigh. "This is Richard Saylor. I'm one of the rangers that handles Somerville Lake."

'I knew it! They're in some sort of trouble,' she grumbled to herself. "Is this about my brother, Louis? What kind of trouble did he get into?" she asked resignedly.

The man cleared his throat uncomfortably. "Miss Walters, we need you to come down to the lake...there's been an... accident."

Lex jumped to her feet. "What kind of accident? Is my brother...?"

"The boat your brother was riding in capsized when another boat broad-sided it," the ranger spoke gently. "I'm afraid your brother was killed." He paused. "Do you have someone that can drive you to the lake? We need a relative to make a positive identification."

"I'll be right there." Lex hung up the phone numbly.

Looking back, Lex realized that was the day she had shut herself down – only going through the motions of day-to-day living, until Hubert brought Linda home. For a short while, Lex allowed herself to feel, until she was handed her heart back in pieces. Then it became easier to hide inside a bottle than to face the loneliness. After she sobered up, Lex decided to just quit caring – you couldn't get hurt if you didn't care. She never really mourned the death of Louis, choosing instead to shut off all of her emotions – until a certain green-eyed blonde entered her life.

Martha leaned over and pulled the younger woman into her arms. "Sweetheart, blaming yourself for that does no good. It was an accident, plain and simple. No one was to blame, especially you." The housekeeper kissed the top of the dark head. "Let it go." She held the rancher close to her as Lex sobbed, finally releasing all the grief she had held in for so many years.

Amanda stood quietly in the doorway, feeling guilty for witnessing such a private scene. *God... I vaguely remember that summer. I had no idea who that boy was that had been killed. Poor Lex.* Amanda wasn't very fond of the water, so she and her grandparents rarely went to the lake when she visited in the summer, but she remembered hearing them speak of the tragedy right after it happened. Sparing the women in the kitchen one final glance, she turned and walked silently up the stairs, tears of compassion in her eyes.

"Sorry, Martha, I don't know what came over me." Lex pulled away and wiped her eyes with her hand. "It's been almost ten years – why did I fall apart now?"

The housekeeper brushed the hair out of the younger woman's eyes. "Baby, you finally gave in to your feelings enough to grieve." *No sense in telling her how afraid I've been, wondering what would happen if she ever did open up... my poor little girl.* She picked up a napkin from the table and wiped Lex's face with it, like she used to do when the rancher was a child. "Now you go upstairs and get a good night's sleep."

Lex took a deep breath, then gave the older woman a shaky smile. "You're right, as usual. I'm pretty worn out." She leaned over and kissed the graying head. "Thanks."

Martha waved her off. "No need to thank me, child! That's what I'm here for." She stood up, embarrassed.

Smiling to herself, the tall woman stood up as well, then enveloped the stocky woman in a strong hug. "Well, thanks anyway." She felt the small arms give her a squeeze. "I love you, you know," the rancher whispered, just before she released the older woman.

"I love you too," Martha replied. She stepped away and turned Lex towards the doorway. "Now go on upstairs before Amanda thinks you've run off!" She swatted the smiling young woman on the rear.

"Yes ma'am." Lex hurried from the kitchen and up the stairs.

****

Taking and releasing a deep breath, Lex stood in the darkened doorway of the master bedroom, the only light in the room coming from the low burning fireplace.

"Amanda?" she called out quietly, unable to see if the younger woman was asleep on the bed. A movement near the fireplace caught her eye.

"Over here." Amanda sat up from her curled up position in

one of the overstuffed chairs.

Lex crossed the room quickly, dropping to her knees at the blonde woman's feet. "You okay?" she asked, placing her hands on the small legs.

Even in the dim light, Amanda could see the rancher's red and puffy eyes. Reaching out with a gentle hand, she brushed the unruly hair from Lex's face. "I'm fine, but you're looking a little rough around the edges. What say we take a quick shower and go to bed?" She continued to run her hand through the dark hair.

"Mmm..." Lex closed her eyes and absorbed the loving touch. "That's the best offer I've had all day." She gathered her wits about her and stood up. "C'mon... I'll scrub your back." She pulled Amanda up beside her, wrapping both arms around the smaller woman.

Amanda enjoyed the warm security of the strong arms she found herself in. Closing her eyes, she was content to stand and absorb the love that emanated from the older woman. "I could stay here forever," she mumbled, not realizing she had spoken out loud until she felt Lex squeeze her a little tighter.

"I hope so," Lex murmured in her ear, "because I have no intention of ever letting you go." She pulled her head back slightly so she could look into Amanda's eyes. "I love you." Leaning down, Lex gently covered the younger woman's lips with her own, placing a soft, re-affirming kiss on slightly parted lips.

Amanda leaned into the kiss, accepting the gentle, almost hesitant touch from the taller woman. Finally breaking off to breathe, she leaned her cheek against the rancher's heaving chest. "Let's go get that shower!" She gave Lex a quick kiss on the chin. "If you're real good," she led the dazed woman towards the bathroom, "I'll practice my massage techniques on you." She swatted Lex on the rear and closed the bathroom door.

Chapter
7

The sun was barely peeking over the horizon when Lex opened her eyes the next morning. She lifted her head from its warm nest, snuggled behind Amanda with her nose tucked in the sweetly fragrant blonde hair. Gently disentangling herself from the younger woman, Lex climbed out of bed, tucking the dark comforter around the small body. *Damn, I feel great!* she marveled to herself, unsure if it was due to the release of long-held in emotion or the wonderful full body massage she had received from Amanda's talented hands. She dressed quickly, left a short note on the pillow next to the sleeping woman, then crept quietly out of the room.

Bounding down the stairs, Lex saw a light coming from the kitchen, so she made a slight detour in that direction. She saw Martha at the counter humming to herself as she rolled out the biscuits; the rancher crept up behind the unsuspecting woman with an evil smile on her face.

"Good morning, Sunshine!" she bellowed, scooping up the shocked housekeeper and spinning her around the room.

"Aaaaahhh!!" Martha screamed, then reflexively grabbed the tall woman around the head, coating Lex's dark hair with flour and bits of dough. "Put me down, you crazy brat!" she huffed, "I'm getting airsick!"

Laughing, Lex stopped spinning the older woman, allowing her small feet to touch the ground. Realizing what Martha had been doing, she cringed when she saw the housekeeper remove her hands from where they had been clenched in her thick hair. "Ugh..." She gave the small woman another devious grin. "So, I'm guessing I look pretty good in white hair?" She casually reached behind her and rubbed her palms across the flour-covered countertop.

Martha snickered. "I'm sorry about that, Lexie... you just startled me." Seeing the look on the younger woman's face, she shook her head and pointed a finger directly at the tall woman's chest. "Now, wait just a minute..." She backed up several steps, with the rancher closing in on her.

"What's the matter, Martha?" Lex chuckled, hands still behind her back.

The older woman put her hands in front of herself defensively. "Don't be doing anything that you might regret!"

Lex laughed. "Me? Never!" She closed in on the smaller woman, cornering her against the stove. Just as Lex was about to raise her hands and rub flour in Martha's hair, she felt two small arms wrap around her from behind, trapping her arms to her sides.

"Can't leave you alone for a minute, can I?" a soft voice whispered in her ear.

Martha laughed, and wiped another blob of flour onto the rancher's nose. "Thanks, sweetie." She grinned at Amanda, then edged past the two women and went back to her biscuit making.

Lex twisted, then picked the young blonde up and cradled her in her arms. "Good morning, traitor."

Amanda looked up into sparkling blue eyes, then noticed the flour and dough in Lex's hair. "Umm... good morning?" She used one hand to brush flour out of the taller woman's hair. "You helping Martha cook breakfast again?" she teased.

Lex rolled her eyes. "No!" She mock-glared at the housekeeper's back. "This was completely unprovoked. All I did was come in and tell her good morning!" She gave the woman in her arms a slight pout.

"Ha!" Martha snorted. "Don't believe a word of it – the little brat sneaked up on me and started spinning me around the room!"

"You didn't!" Amanda looked up for confirmation.

"Well..." Lex blushed slightly.

"Ah... Lex?" Amanda grinned, her hands locked behind the rancher's neck.

"Mmm?" the older woman looked deeply into her eyes, a tender smile on her face.

"You wanna let me down now?" the smaller woman asked, seeing the look of total love on her companion's face.

"Not really..." Lex admitted. "I could do this for the rest of my life," she said quietly. "And I hope to." Even quieter.

Amanda stopped breathing. "Me too," she finally responded. "I can't think of anyplace I'd rather be."

Martha glanced at the two young women in the middle of the room. "Hey! Would you two either sit at the table, or go somewhere else right now? How am I supposed to cook with y'all giving each other puppy-dog eyes in the middle of my kitchen?" That got the intended response. Both young women blushed furiously.

Lex gently allowed Amanda to stand on her own feet. "Sorry about that. Sorta forgot what I was doing."

The younger woman gave her a gentle pat on her good side. "Don't be... It was fun." She saw that Martha was diligently working on the biscuits, with her back turned to the couple. Amanda reached up and pulled Lex's head down gently. "Let me give you a proper good morning." She gave the taller woman a long, passionate kiss, ending only when Martha cleared her throat.

"Excuse me, wouldn't you two be more comfortable upstairs?" the housekeeper asked.

"Oops!" Amanda chuckled. Then she looked directly at Martha and grinned. "Probably. But I'm so hungry I could eat some of Lex's pancakes!"

The housekeeper laughed, and Lex scowled. "Remind me to bring you breakfast in bed one morning – that'll teach you to tease me!" She gave the smaller woman a light pat on the rear, and then sat down at the table. "Need any help, Martha?"

"Oh yes, you could be a big help and go find something else to do for about twenty or thirty minutes!" the housekeeper hinted, trying to keep Lex out from under her feet.

Amanda walked over and pulled the tall woman out of her chair. "C'mon – let's go for a walk." She led Lex out of the room, with Martha's laughter floating after them. The young woman escorted the tall rancher down the long hallway, pulling her into the darkened den.

"I thought we were going for a walk?" Lex asked, as the small woman pushed her gently onto the couch.

Smirking, Amanda turned on the stereo and placed a CD in the player. "Changed my mind. It looks pretty chilly outside this morning, so I thought we could just sit in here and enjoy your wonderful stereo system." She pushed play, and turned the volume down until it became background sound. The lights from the stereo cast a soft glow in the room, allowing Amanda to see the gentle smile on her lover's face.

"Think so? Why don't you come over here and get comfortable?" Lex murmured, watching the pale lights flicker across the young woman's face.

Amanda grinned, then walked slowly across the room to climb into the rancher's lap, straddling her muscular legs. Wrapping her arms around Lex's neck, she whispered, "you're right. This is much more comfortable." She placed a soft kiss on the older woman's lips, then snuggled under her chin.

Lex chuckled and wrapped her arms around Amanda, pulling her close. "Happy to be of service, ma'am." Closing her eyes, Lex relaxed – somewhat shocked that she was able to sit still for such a long period of time, without the urge to be up and doing something. *You're a bad influence on me, Amanda...*she thought wryly, enjoying the feel of the young woman in her arms.

****

Half an hour later, Martha peeked into the den discreetly, finding them after hearing the sounds of The Corrs floating down the hallway. Seeing the two women curled up on the large sofa, she smiled to herself. *They look so darn cute, all snuggled up together like that.* She crept quietly into the room, trying not to startle them. "Lexie?"

The rancher opened her eyes slowly. "Hey, Martha," she whispered, trying to keep from disturbing her sleeping companion. "I guess breakfast is ready?"

"It sure is. Think you can tear yourself away?" Martha teased.

Lex grinned. "Well, if I have to, I guess." She looked at the older woman with a wry smile. "'Course, after breakfast I'm gonna need to wash my hair, for some strange reason."

Martha crossed her arms across her chest. "Not my fault. You shouldn't sneak up on an old woman like that!"

"You're not an old woman," Lex snorted, causing the bundle in her arms to moan, and snuggle closer. But the comment made her pause for a moment. Lex studied the older woman seriously, seeing for the first time the wrinkles on the once-smooth skin, and the hair that was becoming more gray than brown. *When did that happen? Have I been so self-absorbed that I never noticed?*

"Honey? Is everything okay?" The housekeeper noticed the far away look in the younger woman's eyes.

"Damn, Martha... it's been twenty-five years, hasn't it?" she asked, still a little shocked at the amount of time that had passed.

Martha perched on the other end of the sofa and chuckled. "Hard to believe, isn't it? I told you I was getting old."

"No, not old... but you've spent half of your life babysitting me...a little more than you bargained for, I'll bet." Lex gave her a sardonic smile.

"And well worth every single minute of it," the housekeeper replied. "Although, I could do with less excitement, if you don't mind. This past week or so has been a little bit too much, even for you." Martha stood up. "Now why don't you wake up Sleeping Beauty there, and come and get some breakfast?" she chuckled and left the room.

Lex let her eyes follow the older woman from the room, a fond smile on her face. *Gotta do something special for her. Maybe Amanda will have some ideas.* She looked down at the young woman securely attached to her. Leaning close to Amanda's ear, Lex whispered, "Amanda?"

"Mmm... no..." the small woman mumbled, burying her face deeper into Lex's chest.

The older woman grinned. "Sweetheart, you need to wake up." She kissed the blonde head.

"Don't wanna..." Amanda growled, squeezing her arms tighter around her captive.

"Breakfast is ready."

"What?" Amanda's eyes popped open, and her head lifted away from Lex's body.

The rancher laughed, pulling the small woman close. "You are absolutely priceless, Amanda."

"What's that supposed to mean?" She looked at Lex crossly.

"That means," the older woman placed a gentle kiss on Amanda's lips, "I don't know," another kiss, "what I would do," a longer, more passionate kiss, "without you."

"Mmm..." The younger woman curled up against her. She was about to continue when her stomach growled. Ignoring the loud rumble, Amanda threaded her hands through the dark hair, forcing the older woman against the sofa.

Lex sat back and enjoyed the gentle assault, until Amanda's stomach rumbled again. Seeing that the young woman had no intention of stopping, the rancher decided to take matters into her own hands, in a manner of speaking. She dropped her hands from the young blonde's shoulders, moving them down slowly until they came to rest on Amanda's hips. Leaning forward slightly, Lex stood up, carrying the small body with her.

"Whoa! The couch is moving!" Amanda exclaimed, opening her eyes and looking around. She had unconsciously wrapped her legs around the rancher's lean waist, and looked down at their entangled bodies with a flush of embarrassment. "Umm... guess I should let you go, huh?"

"Well, I could just carry you into the kitchen like this, if you want," the older woman told her with a sexy smile. "Or, I could carry you up the stairs, and give you a different kind of breakfast – although I would leave it to you to explain that one to Martha!" she smirked.

Amanda unwrapped her legs from the tall woman's body reluctantly. "As much as I would love to go upstairs with you, I don't think either one of us wants to face Martha's wrath if we don't have breakfast," she pouted slightly. "But, we may need some way to work off such a wonderful feast, don't you agree?"

****

"So, what kind of mischief are you girls going to stir up today?" Martha asked. The three women were sitting around the kitchen table after breakfast, relaxing with a cup of coffee.

Lex looked at Amanda, who shrugged good-naturedly. "Well, I thought we'd spend today and tonight here," seeing the younger woman smile in agreement, "then I have to get packed for our trip next week."

"A trip? Where are you going?" the housekeeper asked, secretly happy that they were staying at the ranch for another day. *It's just too quiet when Lexie's not around.*

Amanda placed her coffee mug on the table after draining it. "That's right! We haven't had a chance to tell you yet!" She smiled as Lex refilled both her and Martha's coffee cups with the professionalism of a seasoned waitress. "My parents are having this big dinner party next week in Los Angeles, and I've convinced Lex to go with me. Besides, I'm going to need some help packing up my stuff and sending it to my grandparents' house – since I've decided to move to Somerville for good."

"That's wonderful news, honey!" Martha laid a small hand on the young woman's forearm. She then looked over at Lex with a surprised grin. "How are you planning on getting there?"

The young blonde looked at Martha, confusion etching her lovely features. "Fly, of course... why do you ask?" She looked over at Lex, who had paled suddenly.

Oh, shit! I didn't even think about how *we were going to get there,* Lex panicked. "Yeah, Martha. You didn't think we'd walk, did you?" She tried to keep her tone light.

"Riiight... I guess it was a pretty silly question, wasn't it?" Martha spared a glance at Amanda, who was looking at the rancher with a concerned look on her face.

Lex sighed. "No, it wasn't silly. I hadn't really thought about the form of transportation that we would take to get there."

She looked at Amanda with an embarrassed smile. "I... uh... have a little... trouble... on airplanes."

"What kind of trouble?" The younger woman reached over and entwined their hands. "Do you get airsick?"

Martha chuckled. "We should be so lucky." She then quieted after the dark-haired woman glowered at her.

"No... it's not that." Feeling the gentle pressure on her hand, Lex continued, "I get a little... anxious... on airplanes." She looked at the housekeeper for help.

"I'd say more than anxious, sweetheart." The older woman looked at Amanda. "We had to practically knock Lexie out with tranquilizers the last time...not the best experience, let me tell you."

Amanda leaned in closer to the rancher. "What is it about flying that bothers you so much?"

Lex looked down at the table, unable to meet those intense green eyes. "I'm not sure. It could be one of several things: the enclosed space, the fact that we're thousands of feet in the air with nothing holding us up, or maybe it's just the sickeningly perky flight attendants. I don't know." She smiled at the younger woman.

"Maybe you just need something else to occupy your mind," the smaller woman offered.

"Such as?" she inquired with a wicked grin.

Amanda blushed. *Umm... let's try another tact.* She cleared her throat. "Maybe your anxiety is due to something that happened before. Have you had any bad experiences on an airplane?"

Lex smiled at the look on Amanda's face. "Hmm... you mean other than the food?" she teased, receiving the expected slap on the arm for that remark. "No, nothing that I can think of. I've only flown three times, and each time was more of a disaster than the last."

"And yet you're willing to put yourself through all of that again?" Amanda was shocked.

The rancher shrugged her shoulders. "Yeah. I figure it's about time to face my fears. Right, Martha?" She looked at the housekeeper, who had a perplexed look on her face.

She's certainly got it bad... "If you say so, sweetheart. I know you've really been bothered by this for a long time." Martha looked at Amanda. "She swore after the last time that she'd never fly again."

"Why? What happened the last time?" the small blonde asked, looking from Lex to Martha.

Lex rolled her eyes, as the housekeeper laughed. "They say..." she looked pointedly at the older woman, "that I hit a flight attendant, but I don't remember it. The medication I had been given to help me with my jitters was really something else."

Martha interrupted. "You did! They said it took three security guards to get you off the plane. You kept hollering that he..." laughing, she had to stop and catch her breath, "grabbed your... rear!" The housekeeper hooted. She looked over at Amanda, who had one hand over her mouth, trying to stifle her giggles. "The tranquilizers made Lexie really woozy, and when she stood up to grab something from one of the overhead compartments – they said she started to tumble backwards, and the flight attendant caught her."

Amanda lost it. "Oh, God... that poor man!"

Lex gave her an indignant look. "Hey! It was my butt he was groping!"

The housekeeper wiped the tears of mirth from her face and eyes. "And for that you broke his nose? I met the poor man later... believe me, honey, you weren't his type. I'm just thankful that he was so understanding, and didn't press charges against you."

"I've always wondered what you told him to keep me out of jail," Lex mumbled. To her amazement, the older woman blushed.

"Well, I... uh... appealed to his kind and generous nature," Martha stammered, somewhat embarrassed at the lengths to which she went to protect the young woman.

Lex put her elbow up on the table, and propped her chin on her open hand. "Oh, this I gotta hear!" She grinned at Amanda. "Please, continue." She waved her other hand regally.

"Brat," Martha snorted, then took a deep breath. "Okay... well, we got her settled in the car." She grinned at the young blonde across from her. "She slept like a baby for almost two days, too. Anyway, the poor man was in the airline security office, screaming about lawyers, court, and Amazon psycho women who should be locked away for the good of society." She gave Lex a knowing grin.

"So, how did you calm him down?" Now Amanda was curious as well.

"Well, for starters, I cried. Then I told him how Lexie was taking care of me in my decidedly waning years," she rolled her eyes at her audience, "and that she was all I had left in this world after her daddy up and left us." She gave them a devious smile. "After all, it really wasn't a lie now, was it?"

Lex laughed. "Martha, only you could make a man feel bad for getting beat up on an airplane."

The older woman stuck her tongue out at Lex. "Yeah, well... after I also explained to him that she was heavily tranquilized and had no idea what she was doing, he understood." Then she looked at the dark-haired woman with undisguised glee. "He told me his little poodle was the same way when they had to sedate her for long trips." Both she and Amanda cracked up.

Lex sat there looking at the two near-hysterical women, a deep blush on her face. Once they calmed down, she looked at Amanda with serious eyes. "Woof." Which set both women off again. Standing up, she tried to preserve as much dignity as possible. "I'm going upstairs for a shower, if you two ladies don't mind." She got to the doorway and turned towards them. "Try to stay out of trouble, okay?"

Amanda and Martha looked at each other, paused, then burst into laughter again.

****

The next few days were a whirlwind of activity for both women. They spent two days at the ranch with Martha, with Lex explaining to Amanda that she really wanted to do something special for the older woman, but was at a complete loss as to what.

"Let me see what I can do," the younger woman assured her. "Now, let's go get you packed." She dragged the unwilling rancher upstairs.

"Uh... Amanda?" Lex was ashamed of her wardrobe, or more to the point, the lack thereof. "Maybe we should just buy some clothes when we get there," she mumbled as the smaller woman made her way to the closet.

Amanda stopped at the closet door, her hand reaching for the knob. "Why?" She turned and looked at the taller woman with a tender smile. "Have you suddenly outgrown all of your clothes?"

Lex snorted. "Not yet... although I'm sure I will soon if Martha keeps stuffing me three times a day." With a resigned sigh, she walked over to the closet and opened the door, causing the light inside to come on.

"Whoa..." Amanda exclaimed. The closet itself was only ten feet deep and six feet wide – but it had two wooden poles on each side that went the length of the closet. The rear wall was covered by large oak shelves, which had folded shirts and sweaters in the individual cubbyholes. But what surprised the younger woman the most was how empty it was. Only the right side of the closet had any clothes hanging in it – and even these didn't fill the space all the way to the end. Shirts were on the top pole, with jeans and apparently a few pair of khaki slacks as well on the bottom pole.

Putting her hand on Amanda's shoulder, the tall woman sighed again. "Yeah. I told you I don't have many clothes – no sense in it, really." She shrugged. "Who's gonna see me, anyway?"

"Honey, I have yet to see you dressed badly. You've got to be the best dressed rancher that I have ever seen." Amanda winked. "Besides, I don't think Martha would let you out of the house if you weren't all clean and pressed."

The older woman laughed, and pulled Amanda into an one-armed hug. "Oh, yeah... we've argued about that for years – she keeps insisting on ironing my jeans and denim shirts. I keep telling her that the cattle really don't care what I look like." She followed the young woman into the closet. "And just how many ranchers have you seen?" Lex teased.

"Well, to be honest, you're the first one I've ever really met.

But," she turned and faced the older woman, "I've watched a lot
of TV – and you are most certainly the best looking cowhand
I've ever laid eyes on!" Amanda stood up on her tiptoes and
wrapped her arms around the tall woman's neck.

Lex unconsciously put her arms around the smaller woman
and bent her head to meet her halfway. "Why, thank you kindly,
ma'am," she drawled, placing her lips gently on Amanda's,
allowing the young woman to take the lead.

"Mmm..." Amanda murmured, leaning into the strong
embrace. She felt the large hands slide down her back slowly
then tuck themselves into the back pockets of her jeans. Breaking off the kiss, Amanda leaned her forehead into Lex's heaving
chest. "Much better..." She felt the chuckle rumble through the
rancher, and smiled to herself in response. After giving one last
squeeze to the lanky body, Amanda regretfully stepped back a
pace. "Whew... okay. Let's see about getting you packed." She
looked at the row of neatly pressed pants. "Most of these jeans
look brand-new. Have you been shopping lately?"

"Not exactly." Lex looked at her feet, embarrassed. She felt
a small hand lift her chin gently. Looking into the questioning
green eyes, she let a small smile appear. "I keep wearing the
same couple of pair because they're comfortable – it drives Martha crazy."

"You're so bad," Amanda chastised, then stepped away and
pulled several pairs of jeans off the pole, as well as one pair of
khakis. "Here... hold these..." She started shuffling through the
hanging shirts, then stopped. "Hey! Where did you get this?" she
asked, running her hand across the soft material. "Doesn't look
like something you'd wear chasing cattle."

"Oh... I forgot I had that shirt." Lex touched the fabric with
tentative fingertips.

Amanda grinned at her. "This is perfect! It'll go great with
these." She pulled a pair of pants from the rack, and handed them
to the rancher. Wandering to the rear of the closet, the young
woman grabbed a pair of shiny boots, and as an afterthought
snatched a pair of scuffed Nikes from a nearby shelf. "I didn't
know you owned anything like these," she teased, waving the
sneakers in the air.

The dark-haired woman scowled at her. "Smartass." Holding the items in her hands aloft, she asked, "are all of these clothes really necessary? We're gonna be there what? Four or five days at the most?"

"Absolutely! And you should consider yourself lucky..." the young woman walked past her, "I'm really packing light!" She stepped into the bedroom. "Do you have a bathing suit?"

Lex laughed as she grabbed a suitcase from one of the high shelves in the closet. "Yeah, somewhere. But I haven't worn it since high school... why?"

Amanda helped Lex carry the clothes and suitcase over to the bed. "My folks have a huge swimming pool with an attached hot tub – thought it might be fun to try it out with you."

"A hot tub, eh?" Lex stepped up behind the blonde, until her body was in complete contact with Amanda's. Moving the reddish-blonde hair to one side, Lex began placing small kisses on her lover's soft neck. "I don't think your family would approve of what I could do with you in a hot tub." She felt the petite woman tremble slightly.

Amanda felt her knees begin to weaken. "I really don't... care... mmm..." She raised an arm behind her head, taking a handful of thick dark hair in her fist and enjoying the sensation of gentle lips nibbling on her throat. "...what my family thinks... ahh..." she moaned, as strong hands began working their way underneath the front of her shirt.

"Ahem." Martha stood at the doorway, hands on her hips and an almost stern expression on her face. "You two are never going to get packed at this rate."

Lex sighed then turned around, pulling Amanda in front of her. "And this would be a bad thing?" She could feel Amanda's giggle where her hands were still splayed on the flat abdomen.

"Don't get sassy with me, Lexie. I can still take you over my knee." Martha stepped into the room, walking towards the couple.

"Watch it, lady... or I'll sic my bodyguard on you!" Lex threatened, ducking down behind the now-blushing Amanda.

"Hey! Don't get me involved here..." Amanda laughed, feeling the strong arms around her squeeze her tightly.

Martha grinned. "Looks to me like you're already pretty much involved, honey."

"Heh... she's got ya there, sweetheart!" Lex murmured in her ear, tickling her stomach.

Amanda slapped her hands. "Stop that!" she growled good-naturedly.

Lex propped her chin on Amanda's head. "Is there something we can do for you, Martha?"

"Actually, I came up here to tell you that Dr. Anderson called in your prescription of tranquilizers for your flight... he said that you can pick them up in the morning on your way to the airport."

"Thanks, Martha...but I'm going to try to do without them..." Lex sighed.

"Are you sure that's what you want?" the housekeeper asked.

The rancher released Amanda and sat down on the bed. "Yeah... I don't want to be drugged out when I meet Amanda's family." She ran a hand through her dark hair.

"Honey..." Amanda sat down next to her and grasped her hand. "I don't want you to put yourself through hell just because of them..." She gently stroked the strong arm with her free hand. "Believe me, they're really not worth it."

Martha sat down on the other side of Lex. "Okay...what about this?" She rubbed the rancher's back gently. "Why don't you take the medication with you and then you'll have it, just in case?"

Lex opened her mouth to argue.

"Sshhh... she's right." Amanda stopped her. "And," she linked her arm with the dark-haired woman's, "we both might need sedatives around my family – they tend to be a little high strung."

"Oh... so that's where you get it, huh?" Lex teased. "Ow!" She rubbed her arm where Amanda had punched her.

"Serves you right, Lexie," Martha chuckled, standing up. "You girls going to be ready for lunch soon?"

"I can always eat!" Amanda confessed gleefully, getting to her feet.

"Ha! Big surprise," Lex mumbled, then found herself pushed onto the bed. "What?" she asked the two retreating figures.

****

After lunch, Lex packed up the truck and then she and Amanda prepared to leave the ranch. Standing on the front porch, Martha tearfully hugged each woman.

"Now you girls try to stay out of trouble." She had just embraced Amanda, and stepped back to look into the shining green eyes of the younger woman. "Take care of yourself, okay, sweetheart?"

Amanda pulled the housekeeper into another strong hug. "I'll take good care of her, I promise," she whispered into the older woman's ear, and then kissed her on the cheek.

Lex rolled her eyes and grinned at Martha. "I'll call you as soon as our plane lands, don't worry." Seeing the tears on the round wrinkled face, she pulled the older woman into a fierce embrace of her own. "Hey, are you gonna be okay out here by yourself while I'm gone?"

"Heavens yes. I thought I'd get those new curtains made for my house while you were away." She stepped back and gave them both a devilish smile. "And it would be nice to have Charlie out for dinner a few nights this week – I know he must get tired of the food at the boarding house."

Lex winked at Amanda, then gave Martha a no-nonsense stare. "Maybe I should stop by there later tonight and find out what his intentions are."

"You wouldn't dare!" Martha yelped, not seeing Amanda quickly cover her mouth to hide a grin. "Lexington Marie! How could you even think about..." The housekeeper paused, hearing the slight giggle behind her. Seeing Amanda trying to control her laughter, she turned around in time to catch Lex grinning widely. "Oh, you!"

Laughing, the tall rancher pulled Martha into another hug. "Sorry, Martha. I just couldn't resist." She placed a gentle kiss on the older woman's forehead. "Charlie is like a second father to me. I hope you two will have some wonderful dinners while

I'm gone." She leaned down and whispered into Martha's ear, "I love you, you know, but try to behave yourself until I get back, okay?" She left another kiss, this one on a weathered cheek, and then stood up straight. "This isn't getting us any closer to town," Lex sighed, releasing Martha regretfully. "I'll also carry the cell phone. It'll be long distance, but call me if you need anything."

Martha practically pushed her off the porch. "Stop worrying! I'm a grown woman, Lexie. Now go on, and have a good time."

Amanda followed Lex down the steps. "Well, I can't guarantee fun, but I know for a fact it won't be boring!" she chuckled.

Lex opened the passenger's side door for Amanda, then helped her into the truck. "Guess I'll have to invest in one of those little steps for the truck," she teased, closing the door before Amanda could reply. "See ya in a few days, Martha!" she yelled, waving at the housekeeper as she crossed to the driver's side of the large vehicle.

The rancher watched through the rearview mirror as Martha waved at them, until they were out of sight of the house. Releasing a heavy sigh, she turned her attention to the road.

"Lex?" Amanda placed a small hand on her arm. "Honey? Are you okay?"

Blinking, the rancher looked towards her companion. "Yeah, I'm okay..." She gave Amanda a small smile.

Not to be deterred, Amanda let her hand drift down the strong forearm until she was able to intertwine their fingers. "Sure you are... now tell me what's bothering you."

Lex pulled their joined hands to her lips, and kissed the delicate knuckles. "I don't like the idea of Martha staying out at the ranch for so long all alone, especially with Hubert acting like such an ass."

Amanda chuckled. "Hmm... from what I've seen, I don't think she'll be alone, sweetheart."

"You think so?" Lex turned slightly, and gave Amanda a more genuine smile. "I sure hope so. He's been trying to get her to marry him for almost as long as I can remember." Turning her eyes to the road, she sobered. "I know she loves him, but she seems determined to stay with me."

"Why don't we call Charlie tonight and talk to him? Maybe he'll keep an eye on things while you're gone." Amanda was concerned at the look on Lex's face. *She's going to make herself sick worrying about all of this.* "I think she's just worried about you being alone," she gave the hand in hers a sturdy squeeze, "and I don't think that's going to be a problem anymore."

Lex smiled again. "Yeah?"

"Oh, yeah, most definitely," Amanda replied, love shining from her eyes.

Chapter
8

Once the truck had made it safely into town, Lex looked over at Amanda with a questioning glance. "Would you mind too terribly much if we went straight over to the boarding house? I can't concentrate on anything else until I know that Martha has been taken care of," she asked, with an apologetic smile. "I promise it won't take too long."

Amanda squeezed the hand she had been holding throughout the entire drive. "Good idea. I'd feel a lot better too."

Ten minutes later, they pulled onto a quiet residential street in one of the older sections of town. Large two story wood-framed homes populated the block, several of them sporting historical landmark signs in their front yards. Lex pulled the truck up to a house situated in the middle of the block, with a sheriff's department car sitting in the driveway.

"Wow," Amanda sighed, allowing Lex to help her from the truck. "It's beautiful!" She followed the rancher up the stone walkway to the front porch. "Charlie lives here?"

Lex stopped on the porch and smiled. "Yep. He lives here with Mrs. Wade and her son, David." Seeing the unasked question in the green eyes, she continued, "Mr. Wade passed away about ten years ago, and Mrs. Wade needed a boarder to help make ends meet, and take care of things around the house. Charlie was living in a tiny efficiency apartment on the other side of town, away from the Sheriff's Department – and he'd been good friends with the Wades forever - so he jumped at the chance for a nice room and home-cooked meals." Smiling, Lex knocked on the door.

Moments later, the door opened and a tall young man about twenty-five opened the door. "Lex!" he yelled, swinging the door inward and stepping out onto the porch, "It's been way too long!" He scooped her up in a bear hug, swinging the poor rancher around in a circle.

"Dammit, Dave... put me down!" Lex yelled, wriggling unsuccessfully to get out of his grasp.

He dropped her onto her feet and grinned, his white teeth shining against his ebony skin. Looking at Amanda, his smile faded a little. "Uh-oh...I didn't realize we had company."

Lex stood off to the side, watching as green eyes sparkled with amusement. "Sorry about that, Dave." She motioned the younger woman forward with a wave of her hand. "This is Amanda Cauble...Amanda, this brute is David Wade." She almost laughed at the chagrined look on the young man's face.

"Oh, shi... uh, I mean... hello, Amanda! It's nice to meet you." He held out a large hand tentatively.

Amanda grasped his hand firmly. "It's nice to meet you too, David. Have you known Lex very long?"

"Over half of my life, I think...and please call me Dave." He ushered the two women into the house, and into a spacious living room. "Have a seat, ladies. Can I get you something to drink?"

Lex waited until Amanda sat down on one end of a navy blue loveseat, then dropped down beside her. "Nah, we were hoping to chat with Charlie for a few minutes. Is he around?"

The young man leaned against the nearby sofa. "Yeah, I think he's upstairs getting cleaned up – he should be down in a few minutes." He was about to continue when a very petite older woman walked into the room.

"Lexie Walters! I thought my old ears heard your voice! Get yourself over here right now!" she demanded, opening her arms.

Lex dutifully rose from the loveseat and crossed the room, bending low to embrace the older woman. "Mama Wade, you just keep looking younger and prettier every time I see you."

The old woman swatted her arm. "Don't be spreading your bull around me, Lexie. I've had to hear it for too many years to be believing it."

Kissing the wrinkled cheek, Lex escorted the older woman to a chair. "I'm sorry it's been so long, but it's been pretty hectic at the ranch," she apologized.

Mrs. Wade slapped at her again. "You better quit treating me like some sort of senile invalid... I can still whip your fanny, young lady!" She noticed Amanda sitting quietly on the loveseat. "That your latest catch?" She pointed at the young blonde woman, who instantly blushed.

"What?!" Lex whirled around in surprise.

Dave laughed. "Charlie told us how you fished a young lady out of the creek – we figured this must be her," he explained, enjoying the several shades of red on Lex's face, as well.

"Where are your manners, girl?" the older woman queried. "Or should I just refer to her as 'the catch of the day'?"

God, where's a good rock to crawl under when you need one? "Sorry...Mama Wade, allow me to introduce you to Amanda Cauble. Amanda, this is Dave's mother, Mrs. Ida Wade."

Amanda stood up and walked over to the chair. "Pleasure to meet you, Mrs. Wade." She held out her hand.

"Good lord!" the older woman scoffed, standing up. "C'mere." She embraced the surprised blonde in a strong hug, which was enthusiastically returned. "Call me Mama, honey. Everyone else does."

Amanda laughed. *She's got to be one of the few adults I've ever found that is actually shorter than I am.* "Okay; thanks, Mama Wade. Dave tells me you've known Lex for a long time."

"Goodness, yes, ever since little Davey brought her home after school – must have been fifteen years ago. Have a seat, and I'll tell you all about it."

Lex stood up. "C'mon, Dave. I think that's our cue to leave. Want to show me how that work in the garage is coming along?" She pulled the poor man out of the room before he could respond.

"Mama! Mama!" ten-year-old David came running into the house, his clothes torn and blood running from his nose and split lip.

Ida stepped out of the kitchen, then ran to catch her young son in the hallway. *"Davey! What on earth happened to you?"* She dropped to her knees and began wiping the blood away with the edge of her apron.

Panting, he began, *"There were these boys... took my back-pack... started hitting me..."*

Ida clasped her son to her chest gently. *"Shh... calm down, baby. You're safe now."*

He struggled to get away from her. *"You don't... under-stand... Mama..."* He finally pulled free, and grabbed her hand. *"C'mon... you gotta help her..."* He started for the door, drag-ging Ida behind him. *"Please... I think they hurt her pretty bad..."*

Ida allowed her son to pull her out of the house, and down the street. *"Who are we going to go help, honey?"* she asked, as he practically ran down the sidewalk, pulling on her arm.

Half a block away, lying under the sparse shade of a half-dead tree, lay a young girl. She was curled up on one side, her knees pulled almost to her chest, and she wasn't moving. Davey yanked away from his mother's hand, and ran the rest of the way to where the girl lay. He squatted down beside her and began to run his hand gently over her dark hair.

"See? I told you I'd get some help! C'mon...wake up!" He brushed the hair out of her eyes, seeing the blood on her pale face. *"Mama? Please?"* The young boy turned around to plead with his mother.

Ida hurried over to the young girl, who looked to be twelve or thirteen years old. She was wearing jeans and a denim shirt, and well-worn cowboy boots. *"Davey, who is this girl?"* Ida dropped to her knees next to the unmoving form.

"I dunno, Mama... when those boys started hitting me, she stood up to them and told them to stop. So they started hitting her. She told me to run, and I told her I was gonna get help." Tears were running down his dark and dirty face, leaving muddy tracks behind. *"She's gonna be all right, isn't she?"* He bit his

lip to keep from crying out loud.

Turning the girl carefully onto her back, Ida frowned. "Davey, I want you to go to Mr. Conner's house, and get him over here right away. I'm going to need some help getting her to our house." Now I just have to figure out who this brave child is. I hope she'll be able to tell me soon. Seeing her son staring at the girl, she shook his shoulder. "David! Hurry!" She sighed as the young boy took off again.

They finally got the still-unconscious girl to their house, and comfortably ensconced in the guestroom. The dark-haired child hadn't moved; when they cleaned her up they found that she had a rather nasty gash on the back of her head, but no broken bones. She had called Sheriff Bristol to come over and see if he knew the girl, since Ida had never seen her before.

Charlie was understandably shocked when he saw the young girl sleeping in the Wade's guestroom. "Dear lord!! Lexington?" He stumbled over to the bed and sat down beside her.

Ida stood beside the lawman, seeing the tears in his eyes. "I guess you know our little hero here?"

He looked up at the small woman and smiled. "Hero? She looks like she's been in one hell of a fight. Martha's going to be furious!" He tenderly brushed the dark hair from the closed eyes, one of which was already sporting a dark bruise.

Ida patted him on the shoulder. "Well, she was. Several older boys were beginning to beat up my Davey when she came along and took them all on. Now my son has a serious case of hero worship."

The young girl began thrashing her head back and forth, and started to cry. Charlie scooped her up in his arms and held her tight. "Shhh, sweetheart, you're okay..." he whispered in her ear.

Lex opened her one good eye, confused. "Uncle Charlie?" she rasped, blinking to clear her vision.

"Yeah, it's me, honey. You feel okay?" He let her lie down on the bed, but still kept his arm under her shoulder.

"Umm... my head hurts, and I can't open my eye." Her lower lip quivered a little. "Where are we?" She saw the small dark-skinned woman behind Charlie. "Where's Martha?"

Ida stepped forward slowly, so as not to frighten the girl. "My name's Ida Wade, and you're in my house. Do you remember what happened?"

Lex shrugged her shoulders slightly. "Sorta. I saw some guys following a little boy home from school, so I decided to see what they were up to. I kinda got mad when they took his backpack away and started hitting him." She looked up at Ida. "Is the little boy okay? They got a few hits on him before I could stop them."

Ida laughed. "Oh honey, he's just fine." She stepped to the doorway and ushered in a small boy who was looking at the bed with wide-eyed wonder. "Lexington, I want you to meet my son, David." She gently pushed the young man towards the bed.

He stepped up to the bed and smiled. "Wow! You sure have a pretty eye!" he said, with the innocence of a child. "Your other eye probably looks real pretty too. Thanks for stopping those boys today."

Lex smiled at him. "You're welcome. Thanks for getting your mother to come and help me." She glanced up at Ida. "Thank you, Mrs. Wade. I'm real sorry I couldn't stop those guys from hurting David." She then looked at Charlie. "Can I go home now, Uncle Charlie? I really want to see Martha."

Charlie looked up at Ida with a grin. "Sure, sweetheart. Let's get you into the car. I'll even turn on the lights and siren, how's that?"

Ida looked up at Amanda, who had a gentle smile on her face. "After that, Lexie would walk Davey home from school... although I think the fresh baked cookies had as much to do with it as anything else," she laughed. "She even made sure he went to college, helped him get a scholarship and everything. Now he's got a business degree, and runs his own shop," she finished proudly.

Dave and Lex stepped back into the room. "Aw, Mama..." he grumbled.

Lex laughed, then walked over and sat down next to Amanda. "Mama Wade been telling her tall tales again?" She smirked at the look of outrage on the older woman's face.

"Hrumpph! I'll give you tall tales, young lady!" Ida grumped. Before she could continue her tirade, Charlie walked into the room.

"Well, well! Isn't this a pleasant surprise?" the lawman drawled, taking the chair nearest Ida. "Good evening, Ida. These kids giving you a hard time?"

Dave laughed. "She gives as good as she gets, you know that." He bent down and kissed her gray head. "I'd love to stay and visit, but I'm expecting a late delivery at the store." He gave a wave to the two women sitting on the loveseat. "Amanda, it was great meeting you – don't be a stranger around here. And Lex," he grinned, "you'd better start showing up a little more often, or else."

Amanda laughed. "Thanks, Dave. I'll get her over here more, I promise." She pointedly ignored the glare coming from her companion.

Ida stood up. "I'll walk you out, honey." She wrapped an arm around her son's waist as they left the room.

Charlie looked at Lex. "Everything okay out at the ranch?"

The rancher sighed, then stood up and walked over to the fireplace. Leaning on the hearth, she turned towards Charlie. "Yeah, pretty much. I do have a favor to ask of you, though."

Charlie could barely keep his jaw from dropping. *She's asking for help? Now that's a change!* "Sure, honey! Name it."

"Amanda and I are flying to California tomorrow to pack up her stuff, and I'd appreciate it if you would stay out at the ranch while we're gone."

The lawman watched as Amanda stood up and joined Lex by the fireplace, giving her a gentle rub on her back.

"Why? Not that I mind, but Martha has stayed out there by herself before." He looked at the undisguised sadness in the tall woman's blue eyes. "What is it?"

"Hubert is up to his usual tricks... although I really don't think he has the balls to do anything," Lex sighed. "But he was pretty pissed off when I chased him off the ranch the other day – so I'm not sure what he may do." She ran a hand through her dark hair nervously.

Uh-oh; they're at it again. Charlie remembered breaking up

several altercations between the siblings when they were growing up. "Umm...was there a particular reason you chased him
off? He's not going to try and press charges against you again, is
he?"

Lex laughed. "Ah... no." She shook her head. "I don't think
he'll come running to you this time..." She gave Amanda a grin.
"But I'd appreciate it if you'd stay out there, just in case."

Charlie grinned. "Well, it'll be a hardship, but I guess I can
do it. How long are you planning on being gone?"

Amanda gently pulled Lex over to the loveseat. "We fly out
tomorrow morning, and will be coming back Sunday afternoon.
I've got to be in the office on Monday."

"Have you picked up the sedatives yet?" Charlie teased. "Or
do you just need to borrow some handcuffs for the flight?"

"Charlie..." Lex growled.

He laughed, and winked at Amanda. "Or I could get someone from Animal Control to dart her before she boards..."

Lex stood up, glaring. "Charlie, I'd hate to make Martha a
widow before you could talk her into being a bride."

Looking surprised, the lawman blushed. "What makes you
think... she's never... ah, hell." He looked down at the floor.

Teach him to pick on me, Lex thought with a grin. "C'mon,
Charlie. Would it really be so bad to live at the ranch?"

Exhaling heavily, he looked up. "You wouldn't mind?"

"Mind?" Lex sputtered. "Why the hell would I mind?" She
looked at him in disbelief. "Martha is a grown woman, and I certainly have no hold on her."

"Well, yeah... I know, but... I mean, she's..." he continued
to stammer.

The rancher crossed the room quickly, then knelt at Charlie's feet. "You know, growing up, I had this recurring dream... a
fantasy, I guess." She waited until the flustered man's eyes met
hers. "In my head, and I guess in my heart too, Martha was my
mom – my real mom." She gave him a gentle smile. "And you
were my dad." Seeing the shocked happiness on his face, she
continued, "hell, Charlie, you two practically raised me anyway.
My own dad never really gave a damn about what I was doing. I
just wish Martha would quit worrying so much about me, and

take care of her own happiness."

Charlie smiled at her, a trace of tears in his gray eyes. "Honey…" he glanced at Amanda, "I don't think she has a thing to worry about anymore." He leaned forward and kissed her forehead. "Now I guess I'd better go on upstairs and pack a bag, since I'll be out of town on vacation for a few days." He winked at Lex. "And if I had ever had a daughter, I would hope she'd be like you." He enveloped the dark-haired woman in a fierce hug. "Have a safe trip, sweetheart." Charlie kissed the top of her head and turned to leave the room. "Take care of our girl, Amanda." He waved to the young blonde still seated on the loveseat as he left the room.

Lex sniffed, wiped her eyes, and then looked over at Amanda. "C'mon, let's go… we still have to get you packed."

****

Amanda sat in the den, watching the fire crackle in the fireplace, a gentle smile on her face. They had finished dinner over thirty minutes ago and Lex had apologetically left the house shortly thereafter, after receiving a mysterious phone call. *She was so cute about leaving, worried that I'd be upset,* she mused.

"Mandy? Where are you, dear?" Anna Leigh's voice echoed down the empty hallway.

"In here, Gramma," the young woman said in a normal tone. She turned around on the sofa as her grandmother stepped into the room. "Hi."

The older woman stepped over to the sofa and sat down beside Amanda. "Is everything all right, dear? Lexington certainly left in a hurry. You two didn't…" *Have a fight or argument,* she finished to herself, worried.

Amanda patted her grandmother's leg. "Oh, no. Lex just got a phone call, and left to take care of something. She said she would be back in an hour or so."

Anna Leigh leaned against the sofa with a sigh. "Thank goodness. I was afraid that you two had an argument about this trip."

"What would we have to disagree about? Lex seems really

excited about going." Amanda turned sideways, so that she could get a better look at her grandmother's face. "Has she said anything to you?"

The older woman gave her a gentle smile. "Well, she did mention she's a little afraid of embarrassing you." Seeing the look of shock on Amanda's face, she continued, "shhh... wait, let me try and explain." Anna Leigh chewed on her lower lip for a moment, thinking. "Earlier while you were upstairs, Lexington came into the kitchen, asking if I needed any help." Seeing Amanda's smile, she nodded. "Yes, I know. Anyway, I could tell that something was bothering her, so I asked."

"You look a little distracted, dear. Is something wrong?" Anna Leigh studied the quiet form leaning against the counter.

Lex looked up at the concerned tone, and saw only gentle understanding in the older woman's face. "Umm... actually, could I ask you a question? I'd really like your opinion on something." She dropped her eyes to the floor.

Sensing Lex's discomfort, Anna Leigh turned away from the stove and led the younger woman over to the table, guiding her into a chair. "Sure, sweetheart. What is it?"

"Well..." Unsure, Lex paused, until she felt the older woman squeeze her hands reassuringly. "I would ask Amanda, but I don't want to upset her. She's got enough on her mind right now." She looked down at their connected hands, startled at just how dainty Anna Leigh's looked in hers.

"Lexington, look at me please." Anna Leigh waited patiently until the shadowed blue eyes locked with hers. "Honey, there's nothing you could ask of me that you should be embarrassed about."

The rancher took a deep breath, momentarily closing her eyes. "I feel like such a hick." She opened her eyes and gave the older woman a shaky smile. "I don't want to worry Amanda, but I'm a little concerned about this damned dinner party we're supposed to attend."

Anna Leigh looked at the younger woman, confusion on her delicate features. "Concerned? Why should you be concerned, Lexington? It's just a dinner, not a Costume or Fashion Ball," she teased.

Lex snorted. "Oh God, that would be a real nightmare, wouldn't it? Although I'm gonna feel like I'm in some sort of costume, anyway." She looked into the green eyes that reminded her so much of Amanda's. "You know I love your granddaughter, right?" Seeing the older woman nod, she continued, "and that I'd do anything for her?"

"Of that, I have no doubt, dear." Anna Leigh squeezed the suddenly cold hands that were laced with hers. "But...?" she prompted.

Lex sighed, and looked down again. "I want to be there to support her, but I really don't have anything good enough to wear to this sort of thing. And..." another heavy sigh, "anything we buy I'm gonna be real uncomfortable in, and then they'll know what a bumpkin their daughter is hooked up with." She gave the older woman an intense look. "I don't care what they think about me, but I'll be damned if I'm the cause for even one second of embarrassment for Amanda." She released Anna Leigh's hands and stood up abruptly. "What am I going to do, Mrs.... uh, I mean, Anna Leigh?" She paced back and forth across the bright kitchen like a jungle cat. "I'd die before hurting her."

"Sweetheart, I don't think that's going to be necessary." Anna Leigh stood up and put her hand on the disturbed woman's arm. "Don't worry... we'll figure something out." She rubbed the tense arm soothingly. "Now, why don't you go on upstairs and drag my granddaughter down for dinner? It should be ready in about ten minutes."

The tall woman gave her a grateful smile. "Thanks for listening, Anna Leigh... now I know where Amanda got her heart from." Lex left the older woman standing in the kitchen before she could think of a reply.

Amanda felt tears well up in her eyes. "I thought she was just nervous about flying." *Oh, Lex, what am I going to do with you?*

Anna Leigh caught Amanda's hand. "Honey, I didn't mean to upset you. I just thought that you should know. Lexington was a little embarrassed about the whole thing."

"I can't believe she didn't trust me enough to talk to me about this," Amanda muttered, an errant tear making its way down her face.

"Oh, Mandy..." Her grandmother brushed the tear from Amanda's cheek. "It's not an issue of trust. Lexington was afraid of upsetting you. She knows how worried you are already about this trip, and she didn't want to add to your anxiety."

"That goofy cow-chaser. When is she going to figure out that she's a whole lot more important to me than any stupid dinner party?" the young woman whispered, more to herself than to her grandmother. Wiping her eyes with the back of one hand, Amanda sniffed. "That's it! I'm calling Mother right now and canceling. I refuse to make Lex feel this way." She started to stand, but found her progress halted by a strong grip on her arm.

Anna Leigh pulled the upset young woman down to the sofa. "Mandy, wait. I really don't think that's a good idea." She waited until she had Amanda's complete attention. "How do you think it will make Lexington feel if you cancel now?" When her granddaughter gave her a questioning look, she continued, "she'd probably feel that she was right, and that you're embarrassed because she's not used to being in that type of environment."

Amanda opened her mouth to disagree, and then understanding dawned on her face. "Oh God. She would, wouldn't she?" Knowing that her tall, dark, and brooding blue-eyed lover, for all her kiss-my-butt attitude, was emotionally very insecure. "Oh, Gramma, what can I do? I can't hurt her that way... but I don't want her to feel belittled or not good enough for my family, either." Then a devious smile broke out on her face. "Oooh... I think I've got an idea."

Uh-oh...Elizabeth had better watch out – Mandy's got that 'take no prisoners' look on her face. "Ah, sweetheart? You're not going to do anything that you might regret later, are you?"

Amanda laughed. "Of course not! I just have to plan my wardrobe, that's all." She leaned over and wrapped her arms around Anna Leigh's neck. "Thanks, Gramma! You're the best!" She kissed the older woman's cheek then stood up. "If you don't mind, I'm going to go upstairs and finish packing."

Anna Leigh stood up as well. "No, not at all. Do you need a ride to the airport in the morning?" The nearest airport was an hour and a half away, and she didn't know if the young women wanted to leave a car there for the entire week.

"No, Lex said she wanted to just leave her truck at the airport, so no one would have to make a three hour round trip drive to take us and then pick us up." Amanda stood at the doorway. "But I really appreciate the offer, and I know Lex would too. I'll see you and Grandpa in the morning, right?"

"Oh yes! Do you think we'd miss seeing you two off?" Anna Leigh scoffed. "Your grandfather would never forgive himself if we did." She crossed the room to meet the young woman at the door. "Try to get some rest tonight, sweetheart – the next few days will run you ragged, otherwise." She pulled her granddaughter into a strong embrace.

"I will, Gramma, I promise." Amanda returned the squeeze. "I love you." She felt a gentle kiss on the side of her head.

"I love you too, dearest. Goodnight." She watched as the beautiful young woman walked down the hall and then practically skipped up the stairs. *She's up to something,* Anna Leigh smiled to herself, *and I can't wait to see what it is.*

Chapter
9

Lex pulled the truck up to the Juvenile Detention Center, looking at her watch. *I really should have told Amanda where I was going, but then she would have insisted on coming with me – and I know that she wants to spend as much time as possible with her grandparents before we leave.* Releasing a heavy sigh, the tall woman stepped through the doors of the two-story brick structure, the white walls almost brown with the passage of time. The foyer was brightly lit, with several heavy doors sprinkled around, and a small Plexiglas service window off to the left of the entry doors. The rancher blinked a couple of times to adjust her eyes to the almost shining room, then quietly stepped up to the open window.

A middle-aged woman in a sheriff's department uniform smiled up at Lex from the desk stationed behind the window. "You must be Lexington Walters," she greeted. "Come on inside, Sergeant Roland is waiting for you in his office." She pointed to the heavy door to the right of the window. "Go on, I'll buzz you in."

Lex walked over to the door, cringing at the loud sound her boots made on the sparkling tile floor. She put her hand on the doorknob, then opened it when she heard the tinny buzz. Letting the steel door close behind her, the rancher got a slight chill down her back when she heard the click, knowing she was locked in until someone let her out. *Damn... I really hate this feeling.* She shook her head, trying to dispel the growing unease she felt.

"Ms. Walters! Thank you for getting here so quickly!" A deep voice jarred her from her thoughts, as a short heavy-set man in his mid-fifties stepped out of a nearby office. "Please, come in and have a seat." The smiling man escorted Lex into the office, pointing her towards a chair in front of a severely cluttered desk. "I'm Sergeant Roland, by the way. I'm in charge of this facility." He shook her hand before sitting down.

Lex smiled, and leaned back slightly in her chair. "Is this in reference to that boy that was with the cattle thieves we caught on my property?" she prodded, wanting to get out of this 'facility' and back to Amanda. *Oh, I've got it bad, all right. Can't even be out of her sight for more than a few minutes... totally disgusting,* she smiled to herself.

Sergeant Roland nodded. "Yes ma'am, as a matter of fact, it is." He spent a few moments digging through the multiple piles of paperwork on the desk. "Ah! Here we go!" He opened up a plain brown folder, shuffling through the papers in it. "Sheriff Bristol said you were interested in putting the boy to work at the Rocking W, is that correct?"

Lex nodded. "That's right, but only if he is interested. I have no desire to force the kid to work for me if he doesn't want to." She ran a hand through her hair. "And..." she leaned forward in her chair, "I don't think anyone should be judged or punished for something that someone else in his or her family has done."

Having heard the town gossip about the Walters family, the lawman could only nod his head. *Having that skunk Hubert for kin certainly is proof of that theory,* he mused to himself. Reading a page from the file, he said, "well, it looks like Ronnie is an average student, quiet, and has never been in any type of trouble before – would you like to talk to him before you make your decision? If you both agree, we'll have to get him assigned as your ward, so that you both would be covered legally." He closed the folder.

"I'd be appointed his legal guardian?" Lex questioned,

unsure of her feelings. *I didn't do a very good job with the last boy in my care,* she berated herself.

"Yep." Sergeant Roland stood up. "Why don't we go talk to Ronnie, and then we can discuss all the boring legalities." He escorted a silent Lex out of the room, guiding her down the eerie hallway until they reached another steel door. "Do you have any weapons that need to be checked?"

Making a show of patting her pockets, Lex smirked. "Hmm... I seemed to have left my sword in my other pants."

Sergeant Roland shook his head. "Charlie warned me about you," he grinned, "and he said to give him a call if you caused too much trouble." Using a key, he opened the door. "Come with me, please."

Lex followed the still chuckling man into another hallway, suppressing a shudder as the door clicked behind them. *Good thing I never went in for a life of crime. I'd never survive being locked away like this,* she thought.

Understanding what was keeping his 'guest' quiet, the good sergeant decided to play tour guide. "Most of the boys we have stay in what we refer to as the Clubhouse. It's an open bunk area that can hold up to twenty kids at once – right now we only have seven," he smiled proudly. "And they're all pretty good boys, mostly just got in with the wrong crowd, or their families didn't have time for them – sorta like Ronnie." He opened a door on their left-hand side, a few steps before the end of the hallway. "Here's one of the visitation rooms – make yourself comfortable, and I'll go fetch the boy."

Lex was pleased that this door didn't automatically lock when it closed. *Yeah, like it matters... where in the hell can you go from here?* She wandered around the small room, which had a table, two wooden chairs, and a comfortable looking loveseat that hugged one wall. The walls were unadorned, but she was able to look out a small glass and wire-meshed window, seeing the dark and empty street outside.

She was still staring out of the window when the door opened. Turning slightly, she quietly studied the young man who stepped in ahead of Sergeant Roland. *He's not much bigger than Amanda is,* she mused. Slight of frame, his sandy blonde hair was much shorter than she remembered, only coming down to the top of his collar. He was wearing what appeared to be new jeans, and a clean white button-down shirt.

Lifting his head, Ronnie finally gathered enough courage to look this strange woman in the eyes. *Whoa, she's tall,* was his first thought. He felt the sergeant's gentle hand on his shoulder guide him to a chair.

"Why don't we all have a seat and get acquainted?" the heavyset lawman said, waiting until Lex took the other chair at the table before sitting down on the loveseat. "Ronnie, this is Ms. Walters."

The young man, who had been studying the table silently since he sat down, glanced up again as the woman stood up and offered her hand to him.

"Ronnie?" She gave him a firm handshake, treating him like an adult. *Wow, she's got beautiful eyes,* was his only coherent thought, before he blushed and swallowed.

Lex looked into the young man's light brown eyes, which conveyed sadness and more than a little fear. *Poor kid looks scared to death,* she thought sadly. *I wonder if it's me, or the circumstances?*

"You're the lady from the house, aren't you?" His eyes widened, as he scooted away in his chair. "D... don't b... b... be mad at m... m... me – Matt made me g... g... go!" He covered his head with his arms, and began crying softly.

Guess that answers that question, doesn't it? Lex stepped away from the table, a hurt look on her face. She glanced over at the sergeant, who shook his head sadly.

Roland stepped over to the table, placing his hand lightly on the boy's back. "Shh... it's okay, son. She's not here to hurt you." He looked up at the rancher, a helpless look on his lined face.

Lex sat down across from the sniffling young man. "Ronnie, look at me," she commanded in a low voice. Waiting until he complied, she looked directly into his tear-filled eyes and continued, "yeah, that was my house you were in – but I'm not mad at you, okay?" She gave him a kind smile. "I don't blame you for anything your brother did, do you understand?" Pausing to let her words soak in, she added, "I know how you feel, 'cause I have an older brother, too." She watched as the boy wiped his eyes on his sleeve, and gathered his wits about him. "Do you like it here, Ronnie?"

Ronnie partially cocked his head at her, confused by the question. Looking over at the sergeant, who had resumed his place on the loveseat, he replied, "uh, well... it's not that bad. I have guys my own age to talk to, and they gave me these nice clothes." He smiled apologetically at the lawman and continued, "I miss going to school, though. We have classes here, but it's just not the same."

Lex stood up and walked over to the window. Turning around, she folded her arms across her chest and leaned against the cold glass. "What do you want out of life, Ronnie?"

The young man seriously considered her question for several minutes before speaking. "I want to finish school, then I hope to go to college." He gave her a shy smile. "No one else in my family has ever graduated from high school – I'd kinda like to be the first."

Lex stepped over to the table, sitting on the edge. "How hard are you willing to work for your goals?" She purposely sat close, so that he would have to look up at her.

"I really want to finish school – I'll work as hard as I need to." Ronnie's light eyes sparkled with a strong resolution. "I'm NOT going to be like my brother!" he exclaimed.

Barely suppressing a grin, Lex looked him straight in the eye. "You willing to come and work on the ranch for me? You'd stay in the bunkhouse with the other hands – riding the bus to school, and then working on the weekends."

"You're kidding, right?" Ronnie asked, shifting his gaze between the two adults. "I'd be working on a ranch?" Disbelief colored his tone.

"Yep... and you'll get paid for the work you do – all you have to do is keep your grades up. I'll make sure that you have clean clothes, food, and a roof over your head. What do you say?" The tall woman held his gaze.

"Really? I can go to school *and* get paid?" he marveled, a smile lighting up his youthful face.

"That's right... you sure can." Lex nodded, then stood up. "Deal?" She held out a hand.

Ronnie flinched when he saw her hand coming towards him. "Sorry." He slowly stood and returned her grip. "When do I start?" he smiled.

Sergeant Roland cleared his throat. "Well, it'll take a few days for the paperwork to go through. Think you can handle it in here until next week?" He saw the rancher nod her head in confirmation.

"Sure! I'm supposed to go and visit Matt tomorrow, anyway." He gave the lawman a mischievous grin. "Can I tell him?"

Lex laughed. "It's okay with me, Ronnie." She pulled a card out of her coat pocket. "Here's my home number, and my cell phone number. I've got to go out of town for a few days, but call me if you need anything, day or night, okay?"

"Thanks, Ms. Walters." The young man beamed up at her. "I won't let you down, I promise."

Placing a hand on his slight shoulder, Lex chuckled. "I have complete faith in you, Ronnie. And you can call me Lex since you'll be working for me."

"Yes, ma'am." He grinned at her, then turned serious. "Thank you for giving me this chance – I won't forget it." He held out his hand solemnly.

Lex returned his handshake. "You're welcome... I can always use another good hand at the ranch." She tried to downplay the reason for helping him, since she wasn't completely certain why herself.

"Well, c'mon, Ronnie, let's get you back to the Clubhouse." Sergeant Roland put a companionable arm across the young man's thin shoulders. He winked at Lex as he led the boy out.

Oh, God... what have I done? Lex sat down on the loveseat and placed her head in her hands. *What right do I have to take care of that boy? Am I doing the right thing? What if...*

Her thoughts were halted when Sergeant Roland opened the door. "You ready to get out of here, Ms. Walters?"

Lex released a heavy sigh and rolled her eyes. "Call me Lex, Sergeant." She stood up and followed him down the long hallway.

****

Amanda looked at the mantel clock for the third time in as many minutes. *Twelve-thirty,* she sighed to herself, shaking her head. The young woman had finished her packing, put her bags in the front hall, taken a shower, and played cards with her grandparents during the course of the evening. *Where on earth is she?* Amanda wondered, pacing back and forth in the darkened den. The crackling of the fire in the fireplace was the only sound in the room, except for the occasional mutterings of the blonde woman bouncing from place to place.

Jacob and Anna Leigh had gone to bed hours before, trying to get their granddaughter to do the same. When she had refused, they good-naturedly teased her about 'letting her wayward child stay out too late', and then wished her a good night. *I know she's a grown woman... I know she can take care of herself... I know there's a perfectly good explanation for her not being here with me right now,* she thought to herself, dropping her now exhausted body onto the sofa. "God, Lex... where are you?" she sighed aloud.

"Right here," a voice from behind her uttered quietly.

Amanda squealed, then vaulted over the couch, giving Lex an armful of anxious blonde. "I'm glad you're okay," she murmured into the rancher's neck, wrapping her legs around the slender waist. "I thought... when you didn't..." she sniffled.

Lex carried her mumbling bundle to the sofa and sat down. "Shh... everything's okay..." she whispered, rocking back and forth gently.

Amanda finally calmed down, then pulled away slightly to look up into Lex's shadowed face. "Sorry. Guess I'm just really tired." She gave her lover a wry smile. "And I'm a little nervous about tomorrow. I'm afraid of how my family is going to treat you."

"Don't worry about me, I'm a big girl." Lex gave her a tender smile, wiping the tears from the younger woman's face. "I'm sorry it took me so long tonight. I had a lot of paperwork to sign." Kissing Amanda lightly on the nose, she asked, "I tried calling a couple of times, but the line was busy. Is everything okay here?"

"Uh, yeah. Everything is just fine." Amanda hid her face in the older woman's chest, embarrassed by her earlier emotional outburst.

"Amanda, sweetheart?" Lex put her hand under the young woman's chin, gently forcing her to look up. "I'm really sorry that I caused you to get so upset." She gave her a loving smile. "Aren't you even curious about where I went?" she asked, knowing her friend's very inquisitive nature.

The blonde chewed her lip thoughtfully. "Well, I figured if it was any of my business, you'd tell me when you got ready to."

Uh-oh... time to soothe some ruffled feathers, I think. "It was stupid of me not to tell you earlier, but I thought that if you knew, you'd force yourself to go." Lex looked deeply into the green eyes a breath away, almost drowning in their depths. "And I knew how much you wanted to spend time with your grandparents before we left." She cupped the beautiful face in her hands. "You have me so tightly wrapped around your little finger, I can't tell you no. One look into your eyes, and I've fallen. One touch of your hand and my heart stops. I can't deny you anything, but I'd gladly forsake everything to see your smile."

Amanda opened her mouth, closed it, and then shook her head in disbelief. "You know, for being the strong, silent type," she ran her hand lovingly across Lex's jaw, "you can bring me to my knees with just a few words." She looked down, smiling at the proof of her statement. She was on her knees, straddled across the older woman's legs. She stood, pulling her tall lover up beside her. She drew Lex's head down for a tender kiss and murmured, "let's go to bed. We can talk tomorrow." She led the willing rancher down the dark hallway and up the stairs.

Chapter
10

Lex was understandably nervous as she and Amanda walked through the airport terminal. *Were they just trying to be funny when they named it a terminal? I'm feeling pretty terminal myself right now,* she thought as she followed the lithe young blonde down the crowded walkway. *God...I don't know if I can do this,* Lex felt her stomach cramp painfully, and she looked around frantically for the nearest restroom as she felt her breakfast begin to rebel.

"C'mon, Lex... we've got to go pick up our boarding passes– according to the monitor, our flight leaves in a little over an hour," Amanda tossed behind her, not looking back.

The rancher was torn between following her heart, and emptying her stomach. Another painful cramp made her gasp and almost drop to her knees, deciding for her. "Amanda," she moaned, trying to get the younger woman's attention. *Aw, hell...* Lex made a mad dash for the ladies' room, dropping the bags outside the door to the lavatory.

Amanda turned to point out something to her partner, and saw that the dark-haired woman was nowhere to be seen. "Lex?" She stopped and looked around slowly. *Now where has she disappeared to?*

An elderly man sitting on a nearby bench waved to her, beckoning the young woman over. "Miss? Are you looking for that rather tall young lady that was behind you?" he asked kindly, patting the empty spot beside him.

"Yes, the one with the dark hair... did you happen to see where she went?" Amanda sat down next to him.

"Oh yes..." He patted her hand, "Poor thing. She doesn't fly much, does she?" His clear blue eyes twinkled.

Amanda tried to control her anxiety. "No, I'm afraid she doesn't. You said you saw where she went?" She kept scanning the people milling around them, hoping to spot Lex.

Scratching his stubbled chin, he smiled. "I could tell... she looked like a fish out of water, that one did. I like to try and fig-ure out where people are from, and where they're going – why, just the other day..."

"I don't mean to sound rude, sir... but I'm a little concerned about my friend. Where..." Amanda butted in gently, feeling an unease settle over her. *She wouldn't change her mind and leave, would she?* the young woman wondered. *No, not without telling me.*

Pointing towards the ladies' room across the walkway, he chuckled, "I figured she was feeling a mite ill, 'cause she grabbed her stomach, turned about three shades of pale, and high-tailed it over there." He was about to tell the pretty young woman more, but she absently thanked him, patted his shoulder and took off across the way.

"Excuse me... sorry..." Amanda carefully battled her way through a large group of people who had just disembarked from an arriving flight. Dropping her bags next to Lex's, the small woman shouldered through several women who were standing next to the sinks, complaining about the airline food. "Lex?" she called out, trying to find out which stall held her friend.

"Over here," a weak voice muttered from the sink on the end. The tall woman was frighteningly pale, leaning up against the wall with a wet paper towel over her eyes.

Amanda's heart clenched at the sight. *I really wasn't taking her fear of flying seriously,* she berated herself, noticing how the hand holding the paper towel trembled. Standing beside the slumped form, Amanda placed a gentle hand on Lex's arm. "Oh, Lex..." she murmured.

"Sorry..." Lex whispered, taking a deep breath and removing the damp towel from her eyes. Seeing the sympathetic look on her lover's face, she forced a smile to her lips. "I didn't mean to take off on you like that."

"Are you going to be okay?" the younger woman asked, fighting the strong urge she had to pull Lex into her arms.

The rancher swallowed several times. "Yeah." She pushed away from the wall and started towards the door. "C'mon, let's go." The ladies' room was getting more and more crowded by the moment, which wasn't helping her queasiness any. *Where in the hell did all these damned people come from, anyway?*

Once they were safely out of the restroom, Lex was almost tempted to turn around and hide in one of the stalls. Two flights had just unloaded their passengers, and the roaring throng of people was almost more than she could stand. *Now I know why I hide away on a ranch,* she thought, picking up their bags, then leaning against the wall. *I can do this,* she told herself, gathering up what was left of her nerves. Feeling a light hand on her side, Lex looked down into concerned green eyes. "Lead the way, my friend – I'll be right behind you." She motioned towards the crowd with a nod of her dark head.

Amanda started to say something, then stopped. *Maybe it'll be less crowded by our gate. We can get our passes and she can sit and let her stomach settle.* She slid the strap of her carryon over her shoulder. "Okay...stick close, and give my bag a tug if you need to make another side trip." She almost reached up to caress the unusually pale cheek, but quickly reminded herself where they were.

"Gotcha." Lex smiled, giving the bag a test pull.

The younger woman politely maneuvered them through the crowd, glancing back every few steps to check on the condition of her companion. Over halfway to their destination, Amanda noticed a fine sheen of perspiration covering Lex's brow. Stopping in the middle of the concourse, she asked, "are you going to make it? We can stop for a moment, if you need to."

"No, I'm okay," Lex assured the small blonde, although her

legs were shaking from the strain. "We're almost there, anyway."

Not able to stand it any longer, Amanda took a strong grip on Lex's arm. "Lex, you don't look okay..." She looked around for a place to sit. "C'mere... let's take a little break." She pulled the rancher towards a group of chairs by the window, watching as the tall woman collapsed gracelessly onto one. "Why don't you sit here with our bags, and I'll go get our boarding passes?" Seeing that her companion was about to argue, Amanda dropped to her knees beside Lex and added, "I think my shoulder is about to fall off from dragging this darn bag around... humor me, please?"

Lex lifted her hand and unconsciously touched her lover's cheek. "You are so transparent, sweetheart." She smiled tenderly. "Okay, you win. I'll wait for you right here."

"All right..." Amanda gave the strong thigh under her hand a squeeze. "I won't be gone but just a few minutes." She smiled at Lex and then stood, hoisting her purse to her shoulder as she hurried away.

The dark-haired woman watched Amanda's compact body move through the crowd with ease, until she finally disappeared from sight. Lex closed her eyes for a moment, only to have them pop open when the plane parked next to her window started its engines. *Shit. Just what I need. C'mon, Lexington, don't be such a damned baby!* She felt her stomach clench again painfully. Lex started to stand up, but dropped back to her chair as another cramp hit her. *I am not going to throw up again,* she thought to herself angrily. Inhaling through her nose to combat her nausea, Lex wrapped her arms around her waist, bent over, and laid her head on her knees. *Maybe I should have taken a tranquilizer,* she thought as she fought to ease her rebelling stomach.

Calm... I need to stay calm... focus on something else. Breathing deeply, Lex let her thoughts drift to her gentle lover. In her mind, she pictured the sea-green eyes, the small perfect nose, and the petite, but well-built body. She imagined holding the younger woman in her arms, burying her face in the long silky reddish-blonde hair. *I can almost smell her perfume,* she marveled to herself. *This self-hypnosis stuff really works!*

"Lex?" A soft touch to the top of her head brought the

rancher out of her musings.

"Hmm?" Lex raised her head slowly, opening her eyes to focus on the green eyes that she had just been thinking of. "Oh – hi."

Amanda sat down next to the still-sweating rancher. "Honey, you're really pale." She wiped the damp hair out of Lex's eyes. "Is there anything I can do for you?" Ignoring the disgusted stare from the woman sitting two chairs away from Lex, Amanda pushed her lover down in the chair gently, twining their fingers together.

"Nah... I think I'll live," Lex quietly teased. "And you're doing more by just being here than any medication can do." She absently brought their linked hands to her lips, and kissed the small knuckles. "Thanks."

"Hrumpph! Revolting!" The middle-aged woman glared at them, gathered her collection of shopping bags and luggage, then stormed off.

Lex grinned at Amanda's sudden blush. "Heh... maybe I should pull you onto my lap and kiss you senseless," she chuckled. "That would give the old bat something to stare at."

Amanda glanced around them. The irritated woman seemed to be the only person paying any attention to them. "Lex," she gently chided her partner, "you're so bad."

Wiggling her eyebrows comically, the dark-haired woman smirked. "I thought that's what you liked about me." She widened her blue eyes innocently.

"Nut," Amanda proclaimed, then she squeezed Lex's hand. "You must be feeling better, the color is coming back to your face."

Lex sighed. "Yeah, sorry about that. I really didn't think it would be that bad." She gave Amanda a tired look. "Were you able to get our passes?"

"Yep." The younger woman pointed to a cart nearby. "And I also procured transportation for our fine luggage." She gave a gentle kick to the duffel bag she had decided to use. *I really didn't see any need to pack much – I have plenty of clothes in Los Angeles,* she grinned to herself. *Besides, Mother will have little green kittens when I show up without matching luggage – gotta take my points where I can.* "We still have to check this stuff in."

Standing up, the tall woman offered her hand to the still seated blonde. "Right, boss. Well, let's get this over with." She pulled Amanda up, then grabbed several bags and headed towards the cart.

****

Amanda grinned, quite pleased with herself. She had managed to sweet talk an older couple into exchanging seats with them, so that Lex would have easier access to the lavatory, just in case. Sneaking a sideways glance to her silent partner, the young blonde was gratified to see that Lex seemed to be doing okay, other than the death-grip she had on Amanda's hand. *Whatever works...I'd sit on her lap if I thought it would help,* she giggled softly, *Face it, Mandy – you'd sit on her lap even if it didn't help. Oh, I've got it bad, all right.*

"What's so funny?" Lex asked, turning her head to face her friend. She took a deep breath when the plane lurched slightly.

"Umm... nothing, really." Amanda gave Lex's hand a comforting squeeze. "Just thinking."

Releasing the breath she had been holding, Lex quirked an expressive eyebrow. "About what?"

She leaned over, placing her lips next to the rancher's ear, and whispered, "I was wondering if these seats would comfortably fit two... I'm seriously considering crawling into your lap and..." her last few words were spoken almost too softly to hear, and were punctuated by a soft nibble on the older woman's earlobe.

But Lex understood, and it caused her face to flush darkly. "Umm..." she cleared her throat, "I think that would certainly help me keep my mind off flying... airplanes, anyway," she chuckled. "You have a delightfully wicked mind, my love."

"You don't know the half of it," the young blonde retorted with a sexy smile.

Oh, boy... Lex felt a slight shiver of excitement travel down her spine. *I don't know what has gotten into Amanda, but I think I like it!*

"Attention, ladies and gentlemen, this is your captain speaking. We will be landing in approximately twenty minutes. It's a beautiful seventy-eight degrees in Los Angeles..." The friendly voice over the intercom interrupted their banter.

"I can't believe we're already about to land – you're the best medicine I've ever had, Amanda," Lex said over the captain's rambling voice. She pulled their linked hands up and kissed the younger woman's fingertips. "Guess now you'll have to fly with me all the time."

Amanda giggled. "Such a terrible price to pay..." She placed her free hand on her forehead, palm out. "Oh, dear me, I guess I'll just have to suffer." Giving the rancher an impish look, she continued, "like I would ever let you out of my sight long enough to take a flight alone."

Lex smiled gently at that thought. "I don't know how I ever survived anything before you." Enjoying the happy grin that crossed the blonde's face, she whispered, "I love you, Amanda." She leaned forward and kissed the younger woman tenderly.

They pulled apart slowly, each content to sit and enjoy the strong feelings coursing between them.

****

Lex had one more anxious moment as the plane touched down, but Amanda held her hand tightly and leaned close, whispering soothing words of comfort to the visibly shaken rancher.

"Focus on my voice, Lex," she murmured. "Close your eyes and breathe deeply." Amanda felt the older woman's muscles begin to relax. "That's it..." Using her free hand, Amanda caressed the arm that was holding her hand. "I'm here with you, sweetheart – we're okay. Remember when we were feeding the ducks at the park? And how that one duck thought you were the main course?" She saw a tiny smile on her partner's face. "I love you, Lex... concentrate on me..." She continued to speak in a soft voice.

Lex was so absorbed in Amanda's quiet words, she never felt the plane land or come to a stop. She opened her eyes when she heard excited voices around her, and saw people gathering their personal items together and crowding the aisles to exit the plane. Turning her head, she was captured by intense green eyes at very close range. "We're here?" she asked hoarsely, a surprised look on her face.

"Yep. And in one piece, too," Amanda grinned. "How are you doing?"

Lex paused thoughtfully. "Great." She sounded a little shocked. "My stomach doesn't even hurt anymore." She took a deep breath, and released it slowly. "Thanks for being my security blanket," she said, giving the cute blonde a heartfelt smile.

"Mmm..." Amanda winked. "Do I get the usual perks?"

"Perks?" Lex's eyebrow rose. "What kind of perks are we talking about here?"

"Well," Amanda ran a teasing finger up the dark-haired woman's arm, "normally, security blankets get to be taken everywhere..." she grinned, "snuggled... cuddled... held tightly all night..."

Lex laughed. "I think something could be arranged." She looked around the nearly empty plane. "Ready?" Standing up and stretching her arms over her head, Lex almost laughed again as Amanda took the opportunity to tickle her ribs. "Hey! Be careful what you start, Blondie."

"Blondie?!" Amanda shrieked, giving Lex a dirty look. "You really don't want to start a name calling contest with a realtor – we can be very creative... Snookums." This last part was delivered with an evil grin.

The tall woman nearly dropped the bag she had been pulling from the overhead compartment. "What?!" Letting the bag fall into her seat, Lex put her hands on her hips. "Where in the hell did *that* come from?" She leaned menacingly over the smaller woman. "Snookums?"

"Heh... how about Sugar Lips?" Amanda grinned, keeping the bag between her and the now beet-red rancher.

"Amanda..." Lex growled, picking up the bag. "I'll show you 'Sugar Lips'." She flipped the bag onto her shoulder and stepped closer to the grinning blonde.

Picking up her own bag, Amanda batted her wide green eyes at her would-be assailant. "Umm... have I told you lately how much I love you?"

Lex smiled, then stepped into the aisle to allow the younger woman to get in front of her. "I love you, too."

"Sugar Lips!" Amanda chortled, then rushed down the gangway with a growling rancher hot on her heels.

****

"Is it always this... hazy?" Lex asked, looking up at the sky. They were on the road out of the airport in a shiny red Mustang convertible.

Amanda sighed. "Actually, it's pretty nice today. You can almost breathe without choking," she joked, wrinkling her nose. Glancing at her companion, Amanda almost laughed out loud. Lex was fighting a losing battle with her hair, trying to keep it out of her eyes. "Problem?"

"I knew I should have worn my hat," the dark-haired woman muttered, wiping another strand of dark silk away from her mouth with a grimace.

Using one hand to dig through her purse, Amanda looked at the perturbed rancher. "Do you want me to put the top up?"

"No!" Lex turned to look sheepishly at her friend. "I'm really enjoying the... semi-fresh air," she smiled. They had nearly driven the poor car rental agent crazy – he had tried to talk them into a luxury car or import. Lex wanted something 'big', with lots of headroom, and Amanda wanted something 'sporty'. So they compromised on a convertible – Lex only agreed if they could drive with the top down.

"Here..." Amanda handed Lex an elastic hair tie. She had tied her own hair back before leaving the airport. "I always have a ton of these in the bottom of my purse."

Lex took the offering thankfully and quickly pulled her long hair into a ponytail. "Thanks! I was about ready to cut it all off with a rusty pocketknife."

"You'd better not! I love your hair!" Amanda twisted sideways to glare at her partner.

Lex noticed the cars stopped ahead of them. "Amanda... honey... you wanna keep your eyes on the road, please?" She pointed ahead.

Amanda turned, then slammed her foot down hard on the brake. "Rats!" She quickly glanced up into the rearview mirror, hoping no one was directly behind them. *Whew!* Looking at Lex, she bit her lip. "Sorry about that." The rancher had one hand braced against the dash, and her eyes were closed tightly.

"No problem," Lex croaked, opening her eyes, then relaxing into her seat. "There aren't any bridges on the way to your parents' house, are there?" she asked with a grin.

"None that I can think of, why?" Amanda answered, then realized what Lex was asking. "Hey! That wasn't my fault!" She waggled a warning finger at the chuckling brunette.

"Of course not... just because that bridge had been standing for as long as I could remember without mishap, then suddenly collapses the first time you drive across – I don't see any connection whatsoever." Lex crossed her arms across her chest and smirked.

Amanda snorted. "Oh yeah... I had to time it just right, too – getting that tree to hit at just the right moment... a pure stroke of genius!" She waved an arm dramatically. "But," she reached over and grabbed Lex's hand, "the best part of my plan was making you jump into the creek after me," Amanda felt her hand being squeezed, "and then getting you to take me home with you." She smiled triumphantly.

Lex laughed. "I like the way you think!" She pulled Amanda's hand up and kissed it.

Chapter
11

Amanda's family's house was nestled snugly in the hills surrounding Los Angeles, off a tree-lined road. She pulled the car
up to a large iron security gate, then pushed a code into the key-
pad next to an intercom. As the gate creaked open, Amanda
looked over at her companion, who had a thoughtful look on her
face.

"Seems kinda sad to live like that," Lex observed.

"Like what?" Amanda asked. *Had she noticed the homeless
people we passed on the street on the way out here? She didn't
say anything at the time,* she wondered to herself.

"Spending all that money for a big expensive house, then
having to lock yourself away." Lex shook her dark head. "Why?"

Navigating the rental car down the winding road that would
eventually lead up to the house, Amanda sighed. *Why indeed,* she
wondered to herself. "I guess that's the reason I spent so much
time in Somerville," she said quietly. "This place has never felt
like home, more like an expensive hotel."

Lex turned sideways in her seat, and took the smaller
woman's hand in hers. "Oh, Amanda..." She had a sad look on
her face.

"No, it's all right," Amanda reassured her, giving Lex a

quiet smile. "I had a really great childhood with my grandparents," here she really smiled, "and if I hadn't spent so much time
with them, I may have never met you."

"Well, then, maybe I should thank your parents for letting
you come to Texas," Lex drawled. Then she was struck speechless when the house came into view. Three stories high, the light-
colored brick façade had an almost marble-like quality; six marble pillars in front helped to complete that illusion. Huge trees
covered the landscaped yard, and a wide brick walkway rounded
out the picture. "Damn," Lex murmured at last.

"Yeah. Ostentatious, isn't it?" Amanda said dryly. "I still
get lost in there sometimes." She pulled up into the circular
drive, parking in front of the walk. "C'mon, let's get this
started," she sighed, climbing out of the car.

"Oh, boy." Lex walked up the brick steps next to Amanda,
who stopped at the door and rang the bell. Before she could
question the younger woman's actions, the massive oak doors
opened inward, and a slender woman in a maid's uniform stood
within.

"Miss Amanda! Welcome home!" she exclaimed, as the
young blonde stepped forward and wrapped her arms around her
in an exuberant hug.

"Beverly! You look fantastic!" Amanda gushed, taking a
step back to study the woman. "Good grief! You must have lost
fifty pounds!"

Beverly laughed at the young woman. "Fifty-four, to be
exact..." she bragged. She then turned towards the open doorway, where a tall dark-haired woman stood. "Oh my." *She's
quite tall, isn't she?*

"Oops! Sorry about that..." Amanda chuckled, then grabbed
Lex by the arm and pulled her into the gleaming marble foyer.
"Beverly, this is Lexington Walters. Lex, this is Beverly, who
actually runs the house," she teased the older woman.

Lex stepped forward and held out her hand. "It's a pleasure
to meet you, ma'am." She saw the maid look at her strangely
before accepting her hand.

*Nice girl... but I hope Mr. and Mrs. Cauble don't catch her
being this friendly with the household staff – they'll just make*

her stay here miserable. "It's really nice to meet you, Ms. Walters," Beverly smiled sincerely.

"Call me Lex," the rancher requested. "Ms. Walters sounds like a school teacher," she grinned.

"All right, Miss Lex." Beverly looked at Amanda, who gave her a resigned look. "Miss Amanda, your father is in the library. He's expecting you."

Amanda rolled her eyes. "Thanks, Beverly. What kind of mood is he in?"

The maid shook her head as she closed the front doors. "He's been upset all day... Mr. Cauble spoke to his father this morning, and has been in the library ever since."

I bet I have a pretty good idea what the argument was about, Lex thought silently. She looked up at both women, torn. "Maybe I should just bring your bags in, then go get a hotel room." Lex started for the door. "I don't want to cause any more trouble for you with your family."

Amanda grabbed the rancher's belt. "Oh, no you don't!" She yanked her back by the strip of leather. "You're not going any-where!"

Beverly smiled, then took the opportunity to leave, stepping quietly into the next room.

Lex turned around slowly, her eyes pained. "Amanda... you know I'd do anything in the world for you. I just don't want you to be forced to choose between us and your family – that's not fair to you." She moved closer to Amanda and gently cradled the younger woman's face in her hands, not really caring where they were standing.

"There would be no decision to make... I'd choose you every time." She looked down at the ground. "You'd make me face them alone?" Amanda whispered softly, putting her hands unconsciously on Lex's waist. "Are you ashamed of me... of us?" Her green eyes brightened with tears.

"Oh God, no!" Lex shook her head emphatically. "Never!" She used her thumb to wipe a fallen tear from Amanda's cheek. "I just... I was trying to... umm... aw, hell." Lex leaned down and kissed Amanda gently. "I'll stand beside you for as long as you want me." She pulled the smaller woman into a fierce embrace. "I'll never leave you, I swear." She waited until both their hearts stopped pounding, then pulled away slightly. "But would you rather see your father alone at first? I could wait outside the door for you."

Amanda inhaled, trying to pull her lover's soapy clean scent deep into her lungs. "I don't *want* to see him alone..." She looked up lovingly into concerned blue eyes. "But I guess it would be the decent thing to do, huh?"

Lex could see the fear and sadness in the younger woman's face. *God, she looks scared half to death... how can I ask?* "Amanda? Are you... afraid... of him?" She felt Amanda pull herself closer. "Are you afraid he's going to hurt you?" *If she says yes, I won't let her out of my sight for an instant!*

"No... he's never hurt me..." Amanda looked up and saw the fierce look on her lover's face. "Hey... really. He just gets a little loud sometimes – makes my ears hurt," she joked faintly. Not seeing the look fade, she patted the rancher's stomach gently. "Lex? You okay?"

"Hmm?" Lex answered, somewhat distracted. "Yeah, I'm fine." *Damn... to be that afraid of your own father. Dad and I didn't always get along, but I was never afraid,* she grimaced inwardly, remembering, *but I think he was, a time or two.* "How about you? Is there anything I can do?" she smiled warmly down at Amanda.

The small blonde kissed Lex on the chin and stepped away. "You already have." She grabbed Lex's hand and began pulling her across the foyer into an elegant hallway. "C'mon, I want to introduce you to my father."

Lex allowed herself to be led down the well-furnished hallway. *Their hall has more furniture than my entire house,* she noticed to herself. Lex also saw the ease in which Amanda moved through the expensive home, and suddenly realized just how vastly different their lifestyles were. *Stop it! Just because their house is fancier, that doesn't make them any better than you!* Her mental chastising was halted when Amanda stopped in front of a pair of closed French doors.

"Well, here we are," Amanda exhaled. She turned and looked up at the rancher. "I've changed my mind...come in with me, please?" she practically whispered.

Running a hand lightly down the younger woman's face, Lex smiled. "Sure, just give me a sign if you want me to leave; otherwise, I'm your shadow."

Amanda leaned gratefully into the touch. "Thanks." She took a deep breath and knocked on the doors.

"Enter." The deep voice commanded from inside.

Pushing one of the doors partially open, Amanda poked her head tentatively inside. "Daddy?"

"Amanda!" the voice boomed. "It's about time you arrived. Get in here!"

Starting forward, Amanda sneaked a hand behind her back and grabbed a handful of Lex's shirt, tugging hard. "Hi, Daddy." Amanda smiled at the man sitting behind the large cherry desk.

Michael Cauble was in his mid-forties, his fair reddish-brown hair showing very little gray. Light hazel eyes hidden behind expensive glasses studied the two young women carefully as they walked into the room. He made no move to stand; he merely motioned towards two chairs that had been strategically placed in front of the desk. "Have a seat."

Lex was barely able to control her anger. *The sorry bastard hasn't seen his daughter for over six months, and he treats her like a business appointment?* She waited until Amanda sat down, gave her a smile and then occupied the other chair.

Michael leaned back in his chair, steepling his fingers together in front of himself. "Did you have a good flight?" he asked, more as a matter of form than any real concern.

Amanda, sitting up stiffly in her chair with her hands clasped in her lap, nodded. "Yes sir, very smooth."

She looks like she's in the principal's office, waiting to be chewed out, Lex thought angrily. She was about to say something when Michael turned his cold gaze on her.

"You must be Lexington Walters." He gave her a smile that didn't quite reach his eyes. "You're the one who pulled my daughter from the creek." A statement, not a question.

"That's right," Lex answered, her own smile somewhat forced. She rose from her seat to offer her outstretched hand across the desk. "Nice to meet you, Mr. Cauble."

Michael stood and accepted her hand. *Damn! She's got quite a grip.* "Yes, well..." He released her hand quickly then sat down. "I suppose you're here to collect some type of reward for your efforts?" He took in the way she was dressed – clean, slightly faded jeans, worn cowboy boots, and a denim shirt – her clothes, though pressed, gave Michael the impression of a poor, but proud woman. *I'm not going to let her sink her money-hungry claws into my daughter's trust fund,* he thought ruthlessly. "How much do you want?"

Amanda started to jump up, but Lex's hand on her arm stopped her. "Actually, Mr. Cauble, I've already gotten my reward," the tall woman grinned, then got up to stand behind Amanda's chair, resting her hands casually on the back. "I met your daughter."

Amanda saw her father redden, which was usually a sign of his explosive temper on the verge of erupting. She felt a warmth begin to flow through her, knowing that Lex was purposely diverting his attention to her instead. *I shouldn't let her do this, but it feels so good to have someone stand up for me!*

Michael stood up, his ire growing as he studied the smug look on the dark-haired woman's face. "What are you trying to say?" He wanted to reach across the desk and slap that look off her face. "Amanda," he finally addressed his daughter, "leave us for a few minutes. Your friend and I have some business to discuss."

Before the young blonde could say anything, Lex placed her hands gently on her shoulders. "Mr. Cauble, there's nothing that we have to discuss that Amanda can't hear, as far as I'm concerned."

Amanda's father stepped to the front of the desk, leaning casually against one edge. "Very well... I was just trying to save you some embarrassment, Ms. Walters." He matched stares with Lex, pointedly ignoring his daughter's sputtering. "Now." He crossed his arms over his chest. "You look like you could use money." Michael held up his hand to forestall Amanda's argument. "Amanda, be quiet or I'll ask you to leave." Looking at Lex, he continued, "I hear that you work on a ranch, and from what I've read lately, you certainly can't make any money doing that these days."

Lex could feel the waves of anger rolling off Amanda through the hands she still had on the younger woman's shoulders. "Well, the recent rains haven't helped much, but we're doing okay." She smiled when she felt Amanda's hands gently covering her own.

Michael knew of his daughter's 'life choice', but having her blatantly rub his nose in it caused him to see red. "Look, let's cut to the chase, Walters. We have money, quite a bit of it. How much do I have to give you to leave my daughter alone?"

Lex stalked around the chair, stepping right up into Michael's face. "Do you think so little of your daughter that I have to be after her money?" she growled, looking him straight in the eye. "All the gold in Fort Knox couldn't replace Amanda in my heart – I love her, and no amount of money can run me off." She stepped back and quietly added, "only her word could do that." She felt a calming touch on her back. "I know I don't look like much, but you gotta believe that I would do anything for Amanda. I'll sign any damned papers you want to disclaim any access to your precious money." Lex let out a tired breath and sat down.

"Ms. Walters," Michael began, somewhat shocked that someone would speak to him that way, "you must understand my position. I love my daughter. And I would do whatever it takes to protect her from people willing to hurt her for her money."

Amanda stood up, livid. "Hello? I'm sitting right here, Father." She used a more formal name for Michael, trying to get his attention. "I'm a grown woman, and I'm more than capable of making my own choices about my life...why can't you see that?" She stood in front of her father, laying a hand on his arm. "Do you really still think of me as this young girl with absolutely no clue about what's going on?" More softly, she added, "Daddy, I know we don't see eye-to-eye very much any more, but can't you trust my judgment on something this important?" Seeing his eyes soften, she persisted, "please?" She turned slightly, looking at Lex lovingly. "Lex?"

The rancher nodded, then wearily stood. "I'll just go get our bags out of the car." She held out her hand for the keys. "See you in a bit." Lex looked at Michael. "Mr. Cauble." She nodded, then left the room quietly.

Amanda watched as Lex left the room, noticing her slow movements. *I don't think she's quite completely recovered from the past couple of weeks. Better give her a thorough 'checkup' later tonight.* She smiled at that thought.

Michael watched his daughter's face as her 'friend' left the room. *Dear lord...* "She's not just some fling you brought to toss in our faces, is she?" he asked Amanda quietly.

The small blonde turned to face her father. "No Daddy, she's not." She gave him a resigned smile. "And I can guarantee that she's not after *your* money – just ask Gramma or Grandpa Jake."

"That's what Dad told me this morning on the phone. They seem quite taken with your farmer."

"She's a *rancher,*" Amanda argued, "and she's not some dumb cowpuncher who doesn't have any feelings." Taking a deep breath, she turned and walked over to a side table, picking up a paperweight and studying it. "I know you don't approve of what I've done with my life..."

Michael walked towards her, unsure. "Amanda, it's not that. Your mother and I just think that you could do so much more than sell real estate in a backwards little town in Texas." He put a cautious hand on her shoulder. "You were always the smart one, and lord knows, you are certainly headstrong enough to accomplish whatever you put your mind to." He gently stroked her hair. "I just don't want you to waste your talents; you've got such a good head for business. I was hoping you'd come to work for me."

Amanda spun around, shocked. "What?!" She looked up into her father's face, trying to gauge whether or not he was telling the truth. "Why the sudden change? You didn't want anything to do with me after I graduated from college."

And that had hurt, Amanda remembered. She had studied every waking moment during her college years, taking more than a full load to graduate over a year early. Amanda had majored in business, foolishly thinking that her father would finally take notice of her and welcome his younger daughter into his consulting firm. But when Amanda proudly showed him her diploma,

Michael had patted her condescendingly on the shoulder and told her to take a year or two off to travel.

Her father guided her over to a chair to sit down. "To tell you the truth," he sat down on the chair next to her, "I really didn't expect you to want to work after you got out of school. Your sister only used college as a place to keep up with her friends, so I just assumed you were doing the same."

Amanda, fighting her anger, willed herself not to cry. "Is that why you thought I took such a full load of classes? So that I could party with all of my friends?" she asked, incredulous.

Her father looked away, embarrassed. "Uh, well, I really didn't notice your class load. I just assumed you were doing a lot of extracurricular activities."

"Aaah!" Amanda growled, stood up and threw her hands in the air. She paced away from the desk, too furious to even look at her father. "I can't believe this!" She spun around angrily, finally locking eyes with him. "And now you want me to come and work for you?" Stalking over and sitting down, she asked, "why now?"

****

After a short argument with Beverly and the chauffeur, Paul, Lex was finally allowed to carry their bags into the house.

"At least let Paul help you, Miss Lex. Mrs. Cauble will throw a fit if she finds out we let a guest carry her own luggage." The maid stood in front of the rancher, wringing her hands nervously.

Rolling her eyes, Lex handed Paul half of the bags. "This better?" she smiled at his look of relief.

"Thanks, Miss Lex," the short, burly man grinned.

The rancher gave him a disgusted look. "Could you please drop the 'Miss'? At least when the bosses aren't around?"

Paul looked around carefully. "Uh, sure... Lex." He gave her a shy smile.

Beverly swatted him on the shoulder. "Paul, quit flirting and show Lex," she gave the taller woman a wry smile, "where she can put Miss Amanda's things. And show her the guestroom across the hall."

Lex lifted Amanda's duffel bag to her shoulder. "Lead on, Paul," she directed the poor flustered driver. "Thanks again, Beverly." She gave the slender maid a genuine smile as she followed Paul up the large staircase.

Shaking her head as they moved down the opulent hallway, Lex mumbled, "hell, I could sleep comfortably out here," as they passed an antique settee.

Paul chuckled. "I know what you mean. My garage apartment doesn't have as much furniture as one of these hallways – but you get used to it, I guess." He stopped in front of a door. "Here's Miss Amanda's room," then pointing to the door Lex was standing next to, "and you're welcome to use that guestroom – I think Beverly likes you."

Lex set the bags down and opened the door a bit to peek inside. "Good lord!" she muttered, then turned her attention to the chauffeur. "Why do you think Beverly likes me?"

Laughing, Paul opened Amanda's door and took the bags inside, placing them next to the bed. "Well, she normally assigns one of the guestrooms down the hall, but this is the biggest one, and the sun won't wake you in the mornings."

As she looked into Amanda's room, Lex found it hard to believe that her vivacious lover had ever lived here. *It looks so... impersonal,* she thought sadly.

The large room was furnished with only the essentials – a bed, desk, dresser, and two comfortable looking chairs. The room had obviously been professionally decorated, with the flowery bright bedspread and matching curtains. If Lex didn't know any better, she would have sworn this was a room at the Hyatt. Lex shook her head and made her way across the hallway, opening the guestroom door and stepping inside.

Similarly furnished, this room had darker furniture, set off with navy blue and maroon plaid covering the bed and adorning the windows. *Damned room is almost as big as the entire upstairs at home,* Lex thought ruefully to herself. She opened a door on the near side of the bed and was pleasantly surprised to find a huge walk-in closet, complete with oak hangers. *Better than the Hyatt, I suppose,* she chuckled. Closing the door, Lex noticed another door on the other side of the bed. "Hmm... what do we have here?" she wondered as she opened a door into a nice sized bathroom, with a large platform bathtub that took up an entire corner. "Oh yeah, that'll hit the spot." She closed the door, walked over to the bed, and opened up a suitcase. *Think I'll get cleaned up... might as well try out that tub.*

****

Amanda trudged up the stairs, replaying her conversation with her father over and over in her mind. *Why now, Daddy? Why do you suddenly want me to come to work for you?* Her father had deftly skirted around that very question, until she had finally decided to give up, and go find her missing friend. *Would I be happy working for him? At one time, I would have sold my soul to do that, and isn't that what I would be doing now? Giving up my soul?* She bit her lip in thought. Amanda knew that Lex would never leave the ranch to live in Los Angeles. *It would be like trying to cage a mountain lion – she would die in 'captivity'. She needs her freedom,* Amanda thought ruefully.

Shaking her head, the young blonde opened her bedroom door. She noticed that only her bags were sitting by the bed, and she momentarily panicked. "Lex?" she called out quietly, looking around. *Mother strikes again,* she thought sadly. All of her personal possessions were gone, *probably packed away the day I called her,* and the bookcase and dresser her grandfather had built for her were missing as well.

"Are you all right, Miss Amanda?" Beverly asked from the doorway. "Is there anything I can get for you?" *I should have warned her that Mrs. Cauble had her room packed up and put into storage.*

"I guess Mother couldn't wait to get rid of me, huh?" Amanda asked ruefully, waving an arm at the bare room.

Beverly smiled. "Actually, she said that since you wouldn't be here for very long, she didn't want you to spend all of your time packing, when you should be visiting your family." She walked over and laid a gentle hand on the younger woman's arm. "If it helps, I supervised the packing, not your mother." Her eyes were sympathetic.

Amanda let out a relieved breath. *The thought of Mother*

digging through all of my personal things... ugh! "You have no idea how much that means," she smiled brightly. "Have you seen Lex? I just finished talking to my father, and I thought she'd be up here."

We put her in the guestroom across the hall," Beverly said, chuckling softly. "Paul said that Lex nearly fainted when she saw the size of the room."

"I'll bet." Amanda raised an eyebrow at the maid's familiarity with her lover. *Lex, huh? She must really like her – that's the nicest room on this floor.* "I think I'll go check up on my friend; she's had a pretty rough day." Amanda gave the older woman a hug. "Thanks for everything, Beverly. I'm really going to miss you."

"You have certainly been missed around here, dear, but I think you'll be much happier in Texas." The maid pulled away and winked. "Now, I'm going to leave you alone so you can rest up from your trip. Dinner will be in a few hours – I'll send Sophia up to get you when it's ready." Beverly smiled and left the room.

Amanda counted to ten, then peeked out into the hallway. *The coast is clear,* she thought, then stole over and quietly knocked on the door.

No answer.

The petite woman knocked again, more firmly this time.

Total silence.

Maybe she's asleep, Amanda thought as she slowly opened the door. "Lex?" she whispered, stepping softly into the room. Looking over to the bed, she saw that it was empty, except for a set of clean clothes laid out neatly at the foot.

The bathroom door was closed, but Amanda could see a small amount of light leaking out from under the door. She knocked softly, calling out to her partner. "Lex?"

Not a sound.

As she slowly opened the door, she poked her blonde head into the steamy room, glancing around. *Aw, she looks so cute...*Lex was sound asleep in the bathtub, a damp washcloth covering her eyes.

Amanda closed the door and then locked it behind her.

"Lex?" She walked towards the sleeping woman carefully, trying not to startle her.

"Mmm..." The dark-haired woman rolled her head to one side, still not awake. She slipped a little lower in the water, until it came almost to her chin.

Kneeling down next to the tub, Amanda pulled the washcloth off Lex's face. "Lex... honey?" she murmured, pushing the damp bangs away from the still woman's face. "Hey."

Sleepy blue eyes partially opened. "Hmm?" Lex moaned, then blinked. "Amanda?" She struggled to sit up a little. "Wha...damn." She pulled one hand out of the water and rubbed her face. "Sorry... must have dozed off there."

Amanda giggled. "Do you always fall asleep in the tub?" She ran her hand down Lex's face. "Who woke you before I came along?"

This earned her a sheepish grin. "That's why I normally don't take baths – it takes waaaay too much time. But Martha would usually..." her words were cut off by insistent lips. "Mmm..." Arms worked their way around her neck, and Lex lifted both of her arms out of the water and wrapped them snugly around the sturdy body next to the tub.

"Aaah... Lex..." Amanda broke the kiss long enough to breathe. "You're getting my shirt... ummm..." a warm mouth attached itself to her sensitive throat. "Lex... my shirt..." she moaned. "Aaaack!!" Amanda suddenly found herself in Lex's lap, in the tub, fully clothed. "I can't believe..." she began, until her lips were again captured by the now heavily breathing rancher. Large hands began unbuttoning her shirt, and Amanda gasped as the cool air hit her wet, bare skin. Giving up the battle (not that she had fought all that hard, she thought later), she kicked off her shoes as those roaming hands unsnapped her jeans. "Guess a bath couldn't hurt," she mumbled around the rancher's lips.

Lex chuckled, then helped Amanda slip out of the rest of her clothes, pulling her farther into the tub. "You got that right."

Chapter
12

"So, how are we supposed to dress for dinner?" Lex asked, sprawled out on the bed, still wrapped in a towel.

Amanda stepped out of the bathroom, brushing her just-dried hair. Looking at the relaxed form on the bed, she smirked. "In clothes, preferably." She was clad only in her bra and under-wear, after slipping across the hallway to grab dry clothes while wearing only a towel.

Lex suddenly appeared behind her, handing Amanda her towel and chuckling. "Smartass." She kissed the nape of the blonde's neck. "I thought I'd just go 'casual' – whaddya think?"

"I think that if you don't get dressed, we may never make it downstairs for dinner." Amanda turned around and placed a soft kiss on the taller woman's throat. "Thankfully, my parents don't insist that we dress up for dinner – it's really not that big of a deal." She gave Lex's flat belly a gentle pat. "C'mon, let's get dressed. Sophia will probably be coming for us soon."

"Who's Sophia?" Lex asked, as she rummaged through her suitcase. "Where did you put my... oh, here they are." She pulled out socks and underwear, and tossed them on the bed.

Amanda finished getting dressed and laughed. "Sophia is the maid for this floor. Beverly said she'd come for us when dinner is ready."

Lex turned around, her neatly pressed jeans pulled on, but unbuttoned. "Should I wear a tee shirt, or one of my button-downs?" She stepped over to the closet to find a suitable shirt. "Just how casual is dinner in this place? Will I have to wade through ten different types of forks before I find the right one?" She grabbed a light blue oxford shirt and held it up to her body. "How's this?"

Walking over to the nervously babbling rancher, Amanda took the shirt from her and removed it from the hanger. "It's perfect." She draped the fabric over the broad shoulders. "Don't worry so much. It's just a simple dinner. You have eaten in public before, haven't you?" she teased, trying to get the older woman to calm down.

Lex watched as the small hands buttoned her shirt for her. "Yeah, of course I have... it's just that... well, they're... I just want to make a good impression, that's all." She took a deep breath and sighed. "I don't want your family to think I'm some sort of backwoods hick that eats with her hands."

"Honey, they're not going to think that. Just because you own a ranch, that doesn't mean you have no manners. Martha raised you much better than that." Amanda wrapped her arms around Lex's waist, pulling the tall woman closer. "And if for some reason their little snooty brains think that way, no matter how wrong it is, I don't give a damn! I love you, so they'll just have to love you too!"

"Oh, yeah?" Lex countered, pulling the smaller woman into a hug.

Amanda nodded into her chest. "Damn right."

A knock at the door interrupted them. "Miss Amanda, are you there?" A soft, lightly accented Spanish voice inquired through the door.

"Come in, Sophia," Amanda answered, taking only one step away from Lex, who finished tucking in her shirt and buttoned her jeans closed.

"I'm sorry to be disturbing you, Miss Amanda, but Mrs. Cauble asked that you and your guest join them in the drawing room before dinner," the short, heavyset woman said softly.

"Thank you, Sophia. Let me introduce you. This is Lexington Walters. Lex, this is Sophia, who spent a lot of time chasing me up and down these halls when I was a child." She gave the maid a sweet smile.

Lex stepped forward and held out her hand. "Nice to meet you, Sophia. You can call me Lex."

"Umm..." The maid was somewhat at a loss, looking up into those intense blue eyes. "Thank you, Miss Lex. It's a real pleasure to meet you." She released the tall woman's hand and smiled at them both. "I'll let Mrs. Cauble know you'll be down soon." Nodding to Amanda, Sophia left the room, still smiling.

Amanda stood chuckling, staring at the quickly closed door. "You seem to have enchanted our entire household staff." She turned and looked at Lex, who was sitting on the bed pulling on her socks.

"Oh yeah. I think I'm more of an oddity – they act like they've never seen someone wearing scruffy boots before," she commented as she eased the footwear on.

"That's not it at all, honey." Amanda sat down beside her, wrapping an arm around the broad shoulders. "It's because they're not used to houseguests treating them like people," she sighed. "I don't think my mother knows anyone's name, except Beverly's – and she only knows hers because Beverly is in charge of the staff."

Lex leaned her head over until it touched Amanda's. "That's a shame. They're all really nice folks." She kissed the blonde tresses, then stood up. "Do I look okay?" The rancher held her arms out away from her body, a little nervously.

Amanda scratched her chin, apparently deep in thought. "Hmm..." She pursed her lips. "No, you don't look *okay*." Seeing the upset look on Lex's face, she laughed and continued quickly, "you look *great!*" Amanda stood up and grabbed the older woman's hand. "C'mon! Let's go face the inquisition."

****

Amanda stood outside the closed doors to the sitting room, gathering her courage. *All right, Mandy...get a grip,* she mentally chastised. Looking at her partner, she saw that Lex had a slightly lost look on her face. "Ready?" she smiled at the taller woman.

"As I'll ever be." Lex returned her smile.

Conversation stopped and all eyes in the room turned towards the door as Amanda and Lex entered.

An auburn-haired young woman, who looked like a slightly older version of Amanda, stepped towards them, a smile on her face. "Amanda! It's so good to see you again." She gave the younger woman a strong hug, then pulled away and tugged on the end of Amanda's hair. "What did you do to your hair?"

Amanda smiled as her sister backed away. "I cut it to make it easier to take care of." She unconsciously brushed the shoulder-length blonde strands away from her face. "With taking care of Grandpa and working at the office, I just didn't have time to mess with waist-long hair."

"It makes you look older," a slender blonde woman commented from a nearby chair. "Are you going to stand there all evening, or are you going to come tell me hello?" she regally questioned, lifting a hand towards them.

Amanda traded rolled eyes with her sister, then walked over to their mother, who stood up as her younger daughter approached. "Hello, Mother," Amanda greeted the aristocratic woman. "You're looking well."

Elizabeth Cauble placed her hands on Amanda's shoulders, then leaned forward to place a light kiss on the younger woman's cheek. "Thank you dear..." She pulled away and patted her hair with one hand. "I had Antoine make it a little lighter this time." She looked her younger daughter over carefully. "You're looking a little washed out, dear – have you been working too hard? Showing strange people dirty little houses all day is not something a lady should be doing." She said the words as if work were a disease.

"No...actually, I've been on vacation for the past couple of weeks, and it's been raining too much to get any sun." *Not to mention most of my 'activities' have been indoors lately,* she grinned to herself. "And I really don't want to have another argument over my job right now." Amanda turned towards the doorway, where her lover stood quietly. "Lex, come over here." She looked at her family, then took Lex's hand. "Mother, this is Lexington Walters. She's the woman I told you about over the phone. Lex, this is my mother, Elizabeth Cauble."

The rancher looked at Elizabeth, who was a couple of inches taller than Amanda. "It's a pleasure to meet you, Mrs. Cauble." She held out her hand to the older woman, who took it with slight disdain.

"Yes, I'm sure." Elizabeth removed her hand quickly, wiping it not so discreetly with a handkerchief. *So this is the cowhand who is after my daughter's inheritance. We'll just see about that.* She gave the taller woman an icy glare.

Amanda missed the look her mother bestowed upon Lex as she grabbed the rancher's arm and casually directed her over to where her sister and a tall handsome man stood. "Jeannie, Frank... this is Lex, the love of my life." She turned to see Lex's face blush slightly. "Lex, this is my sister Jeannie, and my best friend Frank Rivers, who just happens to be married to her."

Frank shook Lex's hand with enthusiasm. "So, you're this mysterious rancher that our Mandy has been raving about!" He pulled her into a hug, and whispered into her ear, "Welcome to the family, Lex... just don't let the old battle-ax get to you." Frank released the somewhat shocked rancher, who gave him a shaky smile.

"Thanks, Frank. It's really good to meet you." Lex glanced over at Amanda, and smiled. "Although Amanda hasn't told me much about her family, I'm looking forward to getting to know all of you before we leave." Seeing her partner's face looking at her questioningly, she went on, "I'm sure you have some interesting stories to tell." Then she turned towards Jeannie and held out her hand. "Nice to meet you, Jeannie."

Amanda's sister took her hand cautiously. "Lex, it seems that we owe you our thanks for saving my sister's life." She didn't really understand Amanda's lifestyle, but knew from listening to her mother's ravings that this woman was her 'girlfriend'. *Well, I'll give my little sister one thing – she certainly has great taste,* Jeannie thought to herself. *Gorgeous eyes, and she doesn't look like the money-hungry demon Mother described, either. Hmm...*

Lex gave Jeannie a slightly embarrassed smile. "I just happened to be in the right place at the right time, that's all." She was saved from any further comments by a clear voice from the doorway.

"Excuse me, but dinner is ready, Mrs. Cauble." Beverly gave Elizabeth a small curtsy.

Elizabeth held out her hand for Michael. "Very well. Shall we all continue our conversations in the dining room?" she asked the others, taking her leave of the room, escorted by her husband.

Frank gave Lex and Amanda a wink. "Guess that's our cue to follow." He waited for Jeannie to take his arm, then followed the older couple out of the sitting room.

Lex watched as the others left, then turned and bowed to Amanda with a rakish smile. "Shall we, my dear?" she teased, holding out her arm.

Amanda swatted the offered arm, then wrapped her arms around Lex tightly. "God, I love you!" she murmured into the taller woman's chest. "Think they'd miss us if we just stayed right here, like this?"

Kissing the top of the blonde head, Lex chuckled. "Uh, yeah...I'm afraid they would," she whispered, looking over Amanda's head and seeing Elizabeth's angry glare at the doorway, before the older woman turned on her heel and fled the scene. "C'mon, sweetheart. I can hear your stomach rumbling from here. Let's go impress your family with my table manners," she teased. "I promise to use my fork instead of my fingers."

Amanda laughed. "But it would be fun to see my mother's face if you did." She lifted her head up and gave the rancher a tender kiss. "Okay, let's go watch my mother hold court at the dining room table." She pulled Lex out of the sitting room and down the hall.

＊＊＊＊＊＊＊＊＊＊＊＊＊＊＊

They entered a lavish dining room, with a table large enough to easily seat twenty people. Michael Cauble sat at the head of the table, with his wife to the right of him, and his eldest daughter to the left. Frank stood next to Jeannie's chair, waiting for the other women to take their seats. There was a place setting next to Elizabeth, and another on the other side of Frank. Before Amanda could complain about the seating arrangements, Lex gently pushed her towards the chair next to her mother, while the rancher took her place next to the grinning Frank.

He pulled Lex's chair out for her, getting an upraised eyebrow in response. "Thanks, Frank," Lex mumbled, then gave a wink to her partner across the table.

"Now that we're all finally seated," Elizabeth gave the rancher an annoyed look, "you may have dinner brought in, Beverly."

Everyone was completely silent as the servers brought in the meal, waiting until they left the room to begin speaking. "So, Lex... is this the first time you've ever been to Los Angeles?" Michael was bound and determined to show how unworldly Amanda's choice in suitors was.

Setting down her fork, the rancher smiled. "Yes it is, Mr. Cauble. I don't usually take the time to travel from the ranch, but since Amanda decided that she needed to come, wild horses couldn't keep me away." She gave her lover a smile across the table.

"What exactly do you raise on your ranch?" Frank decided that the dark-haired woman could use an ally.

Lex gave him a smile. "Cattle, mostly, but I'm trying to turn it into more of a horse ranch. What is it you do, Frank?"

The big man cleared his throat. "I played professional football for a couple of years, until I blew out my knee. Now I'm in the public relations business."

"You're *that* Frank Rivers?" Lex exclaimed. "Wow! I used to curse you when the Cowboys would play the Rams. You're one of the best defensive backs I've ever seen play the game!"

"Such a barbaric game! Grown men trying to hurt each other," Elizabeth sniffed. "But I suppose you'd be interested in *that* sort of thing, wouldn't you, Ms. Walters?"

Amanda shook her head. "I don't think..."

Lex chuckled. "Nah... I enjoy watching the game, but I'd rather be out riding than sitting in front of a television, or stuck inside with a desk job."

"Most 'desk jobs' as you put it, are very good ways of making a living. At least it's steady income." The matriarch fussed with her napkin.

"I agree, Mrs. Cauble. I just can't ever see myself locked in that sort of position – but folks that do have my complete respect." The rancher noticed the red flush rising on the older woman's face, and grinned inwardly. *Not going to provoke me with something that trivial, lady!*

Michael decided to change the subject, since the only person losing control of her temper seemed to be his normally calm wife. "Amanda, have you thought any more on my offer? You could have the office right down the hall from me, and of course you'd be making over twice what you could at that puny real estate office." He enjoyed the look of shock on the rancher's face.

Amanda looked across the table to Lex, whose face had turned quite pale. "Um... I thought we were going to discuss this tomorrow?" she directed towards her father. *Oh, Lex, don't look at me that way.*

"Amanda! That would be wonderful! You've always wanted to work with your father!" Elizabeth beamed, placing a hand on her younger daughter's arm. "We could have all of your things brought out of storage in the morning." She gave the quiet woman across the table a triumphant look.

Lex felt her whole world collapse. Dropping her fork to her barely touched plate, she swallowed the lump in her throat and mumbled, "if you'd please excuse me, I need to make a few phone calls." She promptly stood up and left the room.

Michael watched the rancher leave, a satisfied smirk on his face. "Well, Amanda, I guess we should talk about your salary."

Elizabeth cut in before her younger daughter could speak. "Michael, you know we don't discuss money or politics while we are eating – it's bad for the digestion." She turned to Amanda. "We really must do something about your wardrobe, dear. I think you've spent too much time in the company of that... woman. You look like a migrant worker, or something equally distasteful."

Amanda tossed her napkin on the table in disgust. "These

are the same damned clothes I wore when I lived here!" She began to stand up, but Elizabeth's grip on her shirt stopped her.

"Watch your language, young lady!" Michael stood up angrily, his face red. "Apologize to your mother this instant!" He pushed his chair away, prepared to make his way around the table towards his younger daughter.

"Daddy, let's all calm down here." Jeannie grabbed her father's arm, pulling gently. "It's been a really long day, and we're all tired." She gave a nervous smile as Michael sat down in his chair. Looking at her sister, she asked, "Amanda? C'mon, why don't you sit down and we can finish dinner like civilized adults?"

"I'm really not that hungry. If you will all excuse me, I'm going to check on my friend." Amanda quietly pushed her chair under the table and left the room.

Michael waited until the young woman closed the door behind her before he turned towards his wife. "Dammit, Elizabeth! You just had to start on her clothes!" He looked over at his older daughter. "And I don't want to hear anything out of you!"

"Okay, sure." Jeannie shrugged her shoulders. *Poor Amanda! They're just not going to let this go.*

"Please, Michael – calm yourself. I can't help it if our daughter had begun dressing like a... a... field hand! Did you see those jeans? They were faded! And not even pressed!" she tsked.

Jeannie stifled a giggle. "I think she looks great – and I love her hair." She turned to her husband, "What do you think? Should I get mine trimmed, too?"

"Whatever makes you happy, sweetheart..." Frank grinned at his wife. "You'd look great without any hair at all." He enjoyed the look of shock on her face.

"Eeww!" Jeannie grimaced, then stuck her tongue out at her husband.

★★★★★★★★★★★★★★★★

Amanda stalked out of the dining room, closed the door behind her, and then started down the long hallway towards the sitting room. "Lex?" She peeked her head inside, finding the large room empty. *Okay... if I were an upset rancher, where would I go?* she wondered to herself. Turning around, she almost screamed out loud when she came face-to-face with Beverly.

"Goodness!" the maid exclaimed, "I'm terribly sorry to give you such a scare! Are you all right, Miss Amanda?"

The young blonde leaned up against the doorframe, releasing a heavy breath. "I'm fine. You wouldn't happened to have seen Lex in the past few minutes, would you?"

Beverly nodded. "As a matter of fact, I have. She asked me to show her how to get to the back gardens – she said she needed some fresh air." She noticed the lines of tension on the younger woman's face. "Is it true that you'll be staying? Mr. Cauble called me earlier and told me to have your things pulled from storage tomorrow – but I wanted to check with you first."

"I'm afraid that's just wishful thinking on his part, Beverly – at the rate things are going, I'm not sure if we'll even be here through tomorrow." She spared a wistful glance down the hallway. "Um...I've got a moving truck and crew scheduled to show up in the morning – would you..."

The maid patted her on the shoulder. "I'll send them over with Paul to the storage facility. He'll make sure that they get everything." She saw the sad look on Amanda's face as the young woman looked down the hall, fidgeting. "Why don't you go and check on your friend? I'll tell everyone that you retired for the evening."

A relieved smile crossed Amanda's face. "Thanks, Beverly. I owe you one." She forced herself to walk slowly down the hallway, making her way towards the side of the house.

****

Sitting on a slight hill under a large tree, Lex looked down at the massive 'garden'. A beautiful fountain, surrounded by a ten-foot hedge on three sides, soothed the rancher's frazzled nerves. Propping her chin on an upraised knee, Lex stared at the gurgling pool, mesmerized by the play of light from the sinking sun on the stream of water.

C'mon, Lexington... pull yourself together. She released a heavy sigh. *This was just the sort of thing that you were afraid of, wasn't it? That she'd come back here, and pick up where she'd left off? All of her friends are here, and her family.* She angrily brushed away a tear from her face. "Look at this place! What in the hell could I possibly have to offer her to compare with this?" she murmured quietly, closing her watering blue eyes.

"Your love," a gentle voice whispered from behind her. "Your heart." The owner of the voice, her blonde hair set aglow by the sinking sun, suddenly blocked Lex's view. "Mind some company?" Amanda asked, touching Lex's knee with her hand.

"Uh...sure." Lex shifted so that the younger woman could sit in front of her, framed by the rancher's long legs. She wiped at her eyes, disguising the motion by using the same hand to comb her dark hair out of her face. "Sorry about running out on you like that... the walls were starting to close in on me." Lex wrapped her arms around Amanda and pulled her close.

Leaning into the embrace, Amanda sighed, then bent her head to kiss one of the strong arms holding her. "Don't apologize. I'm just really sorry that my father said what he did."

"Was it true?" Lex whispered in her ear. "Are you considering staying here, and going to work for him?" Taking a deep breath, she continued, "if that's what you want, I'll support your decision. I love you, and I want you to be happy." She lay her head on the younger woman's shoulder.

Amanda tangled her fingers into the dark, thick hair spilling over her shoulder. "What about us? Do you think I could just walk away from this...from you?" She felt the body behind her take in a shaky breath.

"No! I don't think that. But I'm also not stupid enough to disregard what a great opportunity this is for you." Lex raised her head slightly, placing a kiss just below Amanda's ear. "I could... um... give you some time to get settled, then come out here – if you want." The rancher found herself torn between her heart, which was screaming, 'Don't go!', and her mind, which was saying, 'This is the best thing for Amanda.' *Oh, God, what am I going to do?*

Amanda turned around slightly, so that she could see Lex's face. "What about your ranch?" She put a hand up to cradle the older woman's tense jaw.

"I'll sell it, or hire somebody to run it. I don't care about the damned ranch." Lex closed her eyes and unconsciously leaned into Amanda's gentle touch. "She felt a fingertip brush away another tear from her face. "I do care about you... nothing else matters to me."

Fighting tears of her own, Amanda brushed the dark bangs from her lover's face. "You'd give up your ranch for me?" she choked out.

"In a heartbeat." Lex opened her eyes and frowned. "Hey... don't cry..." She lifted a shaky hand to the younger woman's face, brushing the now-falling tears away. "What's wrong?"

"No one's EVER offered to do something like that for me." Amanda looked deeply into Lex's eyes. "Oh, Lex..." she cried.

The rancher pulled Amanda closer, kissing the top of her head. "Shhh..." She began rocking the now sobbing woman. "Please don't cry, sweetheart... I love you. Do you really think I'd let you stay here alone?"

Amanda let herself calm down before continuing. "No, I know you wouldn't leave me, but you don't have to worry. I would never ask you to give something up that means so much to you."

"What are you saying?" Lex felt a jolt of fear shoot through her. "Do you... don't you... you don't want me to stay?" she finished in a quiet voice.

"No, I don't want you to stay," Amanda smiled to herself. "I would get really lonesome in Texas without you," she finished, looking into Lex's eyes. Seeing the understanding light up the older woman's features, she grinned. "The movers are going to pick up everything in storage tomorrow; do you still want to stay? We can leave whenever you get ready."

"But what about Friday? Won't your father be upset with you?" Lex almost laughed out loud, she was so happy. *She's not staying... she's going home with me!*

Amanda wrapped her arms around Lex and squeezed tight. "He's already upset, and to quote a good friend of mine, 'you're more important than some stupid dinner party'."

"Thanks, but we're already here – might as well stick it

out." Lex pulled Amanda's chin up and gave her a sweet kiss, which was eagerly returned.

After reluctantly breaking off the kiss, Amanda sighed. "You know, this is one of my favorite places. I was hoping I would find you here." She snuggled closer, tucking her head into the older woman's chest.

"Really?" Lex murmured, rubbing her cheek on the soft blonde hair. "It just seemed so peaceful... secluded. Kinda reminds me of home," she chuckled. "Without the fancy fountain, of course."

Amanda giggled. "Yeah, it would probably scare the horses half to death, not to mention the fuss Martha would probably make over it." She raised up a little and kissed the soft skin on Lex's throat. "I used to sit out here for hours – reading... dreaming..."

"What did you dream about?" Lex asked quietly, fascinated by this peek into her lover's early life.

"When I was really young, I'd dream about the usual things...who I would marry, what I was going to do when I grew up – you know, that sort of stuff." She felt the strong arms tighten around her. "For as long as I can remember, I wanted to go to work for my father. Of course, I alternated that idea with working for Gramma, or even helping Grandpa Jake – I had a hard time deciding. But mostly, I wanted to follow in my father's footsteps."

"Oh, sweetheart..." Lex murmured sadly, seeing where this conversation was headed.

"No, wait." Amanda patted Lex's stomach gently. "Anyway, I went to college and took a lot of extra classes so that I could graduate early – I wanted to make my dad proud," she sighed. "But he really didn't take me seriously – just sort of brushed me off and told me to travel for a couple of years, like my mother had. So, in my fit of rebellion, I got my realtor's license instead, and joined a small office here in Los Angeles." Seeing the sad look on Lex's face, Amanda touched her cheek gently. "And I thank God every day that it all happened that way." She leaned forward and captured the rancher's lips, allowing her passion to take over. "Because..." she punctuated her point with a smaller kiss, "you are..." another, slightly longer kiss, "my greatest dreams come true." She met Lex's lips halfway, pulling the older woman's head down, with one hand tangled in her dark hair.

Lex greeted Amanda's passion with her own, then gasped as she felt a small hand unbuttoning her shirt. "Ah... Amanda..." The insistent hand reached inside, brushing her stomach lightly. "Oh, God... we can't..." A small mouth attached itself to her throat, as the hand began moving upward. "Mmm... No! What if someone... ahh..." The warm hand found its target, squeezing gently.

"How about," a sultry voice whispered in her ear, "we continue our conversation upstairs?" Amanda nibbled on the trembling rancher's earlobe. "I want you *right now*." She pulled away a little, enjoying the flushed look on Lex's face. "C'mon..." Amanda slowly removed her hand, then re-buttoned the older woman's shirt. "I want to try out that huge bed in the guestroom." She stood up, pulling a slightly rumpled Lex to her feet.

Returning to the house, Amanda giggled when Lex stumbled as they stepped through the kitchen doorway.

"Don't laugh; it's all your fault, you know," Lex growled, her arm wrapped tightly around the shorter woman's waist.

Amanda ushered her charge through the kitchen and towards the main foyer. Just as they were reaching the large staircase, a voice stopped them.

"I've been looking for you, Amanda," Michael stated, stepping into the foyer. "I thought we had a conversation to finish." He glared at Lex, noticing the tall woman's bedraggled appearance. "Just where exactly were you?"

Not relinquishing her hold on her lover, Amanda smiled. "We were just enjoying the peace and quiet of the gardens, Daddy." Feeling Lex begin to tense, she added, "and I think we said all there was to say earlier."

Michael frowned. "I don't think so. Come into my office, and we'll try to get all of this straightened out." He turned, expecting his daughter to follow.

"I'm sorry, Daddy, but we were on our way upstairs. Maybe you and I can NOT talk some more tomorrow." She turned, pulling Lex with her. "Goodnight."

Michael knew when to back off, and he stormed towards his office. *Dismissed! Like a servant, by my own daughter, all because of that... that... woman!* "We'll just have to see about that, won't we?" he mumbled, sitting down behind his desk, and pulling his Rolodex forward. Finding the number he was searching for, Michael grabbed the phone.

"Richards Investigations," a slightly accented female voice answered.

"This is Michael Cauble. Put James on the phone," Michael ordered, not sparing time for niceties.

"Very well, Mr. Cauble – hold one moment, please." The secretary's voice was cool and professional.

Michael waited impatiently, drumming his fingers on his desk. *There should be a law against Muzak,* he thought, as tinny strains of "The Way We Were" flooded his ear.

"Richards here," a somewhat gravelly voice intoned. "Mr. Cauble? What can I do for you?"

"James, I have a rush job for you – double your usual fee if you can get it together before Friday." Michael had pulled a pencil from his desk and was now doodling aimlessly on a notepad. A stick figure wearing a cowboy hat appeared beneath his sketching pencil.

"This Friday? Must be really important." Richards sounded intrigued. "What is it?"

"I want you to dig up everything you can find on a Lexington Walters – she's a rancher right outside of Somerville, Texas..." Michael growled. "I don't care what it costs, or how many men you have to put on it. I need it quick." The stick figure now stood on a wide platform.

The investigator chuckled. "Not a problem, Mr. Cauble. I'll send out a team in the next hour, and send you a report by tomorrow morning." He had been under Michael Cauble's employ for the past several years, and knew how well the man would pay.

"Excellent. Don't send it by courier, though. Just fax it to me. I rely on your discretion, James." Michael hung up the phone, smiling. *No two-bit dirt grubber is going to get her hands on my daughter's money.* The platform in his sketch became a gallows – a noose now around the neck of the stick figure.

****

Lex allowed herself to be led up the long staircase, her thoughts elsewhere. *Why is her family so dead set against seeing her happy? Are they really that self-centered? Or is it something else? Maybe it's because of who she's with...*

"Honey? You still with me here?" Amanda questioned, closing the guestroom door behind them. "What's wrong?" She pulled Lex over to the bed, and gently sat her down. "Lex?" Amanda lightly touched her face, seeing the rancher finally shake herself and focus her gaze.

"Huh? Oh, sorry about that. Just thinking," Lex murmured, leaning into the touch. "What were you saying?" She pulled the younger woman into her lap with a heartfelt sigh.

Amanda snuggled into Lex's arms, content to let the subject drop. "Nothing. I was just a little concerned." She kissed the tanned throat under her lips. "Are you feeling okay?"

Lex chuckled. "I've never felt better. Why don't we get ready for bed?" She stood up, lifting Amanda to her feet as well. "Oh...umm..." she mumbled, feeling small hands begin to unbutton her shirt again. She reached for the rest of the buttons, intent on helping her lover with the task.

"No... please... let me," Amanda whispered, pushing the shirt over broad shoulders and onto the floor. She began unbuttoning Lex's jeans, then quickly slid them down her hips, bumping the older woman onto the bed.

"I can..." Lex started, but quieted when Amanda placed a soft hand over her mouth. She kissed the hand, which then moved to caress her face, running lightly over her upraised eyebrows.

The younger woman smiled. "Just sit back... I've been wanting to do this all evening." She leaned over and placed a tender kiss on the rancher's lips, then began removing the well-worn boots from Lex's feet, the socks quickly following them to the floor.

Sitting on the bed, Lex could only marvel at the gentle attentiveness that her lover showed. Deciding to just lie still and enjoy the ride, she chuckled when a hand tickled her bare foot.

"Hey!" She wiggled the foot slightly.

Amanda giggled. "Sorry... you've just got such cute feet... I couldn't resist." She ran another fingertip down Lex's instep, then grabbed the end of the jeans and pulled them off the long legs. "And really sexy legs..." she murmured, running her hands up the inside of the rancher's calves, amazed at how strong they were. *She's got incredible legs... it's a shame she keeps them hidden under those jeans.*

"Ah... umm... oh, God..." Lex leaned back and closed her eyes, feeling her heart begin to pound. Her eyes opened again slightly when she heard the sound of cloth rustling nearby. Enjoying a bit of voyeurism, the rancher watched as Amanda slowly removed her own clothes, unaware that she was being watched. "You are so beautiful, Amanda," she murmured, noticing that her words caused the younger woman to blush.

"Yeah, right!" Amanda chuckled, as she walked over towards the bed. "Ugh!" she grunted as she was quickly pulled down on top of Lex. "I don't think..." Her doubts were silenced by insistent lips, which claimed hers hotly. "Mmm..." She wrapped her arms around the dark-haired woman's neck, feeling strong hands pull her closer.

"Don't worry..." Lex murmured between heated kisses, "I wasn't expecting you to do any more thinking tonight." She rolled over to cover the younger woman's body with her own.

Chapter

13

Amanda stretched stiffly, noticing with a slight frown that the sun was trying to peek in the windows. She looked down lovingly at the woman who was snuggled partially on top of her, Lex's dark head resting comfortably on her chest. *How did I ever get so lucky? Everything I ever wanted in someone, and in a really good-looking package too...* Amanda gently brushed the scattered bangs from the smooth forehead. *Why can't they just see how happy I am, and leave us alone? Everything has to be connected with money, not love, as far as they're concerned.* She released a heavy sigh, letting her head sink onto her pillow again.

"Hey... what's the matter?" Lex asked in a sleep roughened voice. "You okay?" She nuzzled the soft skin under her cheek.

Glancing down into those incredibly blue eyes, Amanda smiled. "I'm great. Just thinking." She ran her fingertips across Lex's smooth cheek. "I love you so very much, you know."

"I love you, too." Lex placed a kiss on Amanda's chest, then hugged her tight. "I don't know who to thank for sending you to me, but I'm going to spend the rest of my life loving you."

A knock on the door stopped Amanda's answer. "Miss Amanda? It's me, Beverly," the maid's soft voice floated through the door.

Lex grinned, then shrugged, as Amanda gave her a questioning look. The rancher climbed out of bed, and padded into the bathroom, closing the door behind her.

"Come in, Beverly." Amanda had just enough time to put Lex's shirt on and climb into bed as the maid stepped into the room.

Beverly gave the younger woman a knowing smile. "I'm really sorry to bother you so early, but I thought you might want to know that your mother is looking for you." She looked at the clothes strewn around the room. "And I didn't want her... interrupting... anything."

Amanda blushed. "Uh, yeah... thanks a lot, Beverly." She rubbed her face with one hand. "Do you know what she wants?"

"She mentioned something about choosing your outfit for Friday." Beverly gave her a sympathetic smile.

"Too bad... I've already chosen my clothes – she'll just have to live with it." Amanda grinned, then realized that the shirt she was wearing was inside out and buttoned crookedly, which caused her to blush again.

Lex stepped out of the bathroom, with a green towel wrapped around her body. "Good morning, Beverly," she grinned at the maid, watching from the corner of her eye as Amanda blushed furiously. "Everything okay, Amanda?" she asked innocently.

"Yeah, I guess. Beverly came up to warn us that Mother's looking for me." The blonde woman ducked her head, finding the pattern on the comforter quite interesting.

Lex walked into the closet, laughing. "Must not be looking too hard...I don't see you hiding." She stepped out, jeans on, buttoning a denim shirt.

Amanda covered her head when the maid began to laugh. "Oh, God..."

"I'll just let you get ready." Beverly winked at Lex. "And I'll tell your mother that you'll be down soon, so she won't disturb you." She laughed again as another groan was heard from under the comforter. Beverly left the room, closing the door quietly behind her.

Sitting down on the edge of the bed, Lex pulled the comforter away from Amanda's head. "What's the matter, sweetheart?" She grinned as Amanda glared at her. "You're not shy,
are you?"

' WHAP!'

Amanda slammed a pillow into the smirking rancher's face,
knocking her off the bed. Silence from below worried the
younger woman, "Lex?" She leaned over the edge of the bed,
just in time for the same pillow to knock her backwards. "Hey!"
Amanda felt the bed shift as a large body leaped up, straddling
her hips. "You wouldn't..." She started, just as long fingers
began tickling her unmercifully. "Lex!" she giggled. "C'mon..,
argh!" she squirmed, trying to fight back. "Stop! I'm gonna make
a mess if you don't quit!" she got out between gales of laughter.

Lex stopped tickling Amanda, and gently pulled the younger
woman's arms up over her head. Leaning down, she gave her
lover a soft kiss. "Bathroom's all yours, sweetheart! I'll just
straighten up in here. Nice fashion trend you're setting with that
shirt, by the way." She jumped off the bed, laughing, as Amanda
growled and tossed another pillow her way.

****

Deciding to avoid an early confrontation, Amanda had asked
Beverly to have breakfast served to her and Lex on the sun porch
off the kitchen. With the windows open, it wasn't a usual meeting place for members of the family because the fresh air often
brought small insects with it. The sun was partially blocked by
the awning that ran across the back, but Lex loved it anyway.

"That was great," Lex moaned, leaning back in her chair and
giving her lover a grateful smile. She pulled her arms over her
head and stretched until her back popped several times.

Amanda reached over and scratched the rancher's stomach
lightly. "You didn't eat much dinner last night," she said regretfully. "Did you get enough breakfast?"

Lex chuckled and swatted the teasing hand away. "Stop
that." She straightened up and grabbed her coffee cup. "Oh,
yeah. I think I even out-ate you." The dark-haired woman gave

Amanda a smirk. "What's on the agenda for today?"

"How about a drive down to the beach?" Amanda pulled her napkin from her lap and placed it on the table. "Maybe a little sightseeing?" She reached over and took Lex's hand in hers. "I thought we could just get out of the house for a little while, give my parents time to calm down." *And hopefully avoid a confrontation with Mother over my clothes for the dinner.*

Pulling their linked hands up to her lips, Lex gave Amanda's knuckles a gentle kiss. "Whatever you want, sweetheart. It's your show." She smiled as the younger woman's eyes closed. "The beach sounds good. I've never seen the ocean."

Amanda opened her eyes and rubbed Lex's hand against her cheek. "Never? Well then, that's exactly what we're going to do." She stood up, pulling the older woman up with her. "C'mon... we'll go change into some shorts, then hit the beach."

Allowing herself to be pulled through the house, Lex shook her head. "Amanda, you packed my bag – all I have are some old cut-offs. Not exactly the thing to be running around in."

"Oh yeah? Why else do you think I packed them? I've got some too, and think that they'll be perfect." The determined blonde had gotten them almost to the stairway when her mother appeared out of nowhere. "Oh, hi Mother. We were just about to go to the beach – do you want to come?" Knowing how much Elizabeth hated anything that had to do with the outdoors, Amanda couldn't resist.

"No...thank you, Amanda. I'd like a word with you," she gave the rancher an icy glare, "alone, if you don't mind."

Lex looked down at her companion, who looked as if she were ready to explode. "No problem. I'll just go upstairs and get changed." She gave Amanda's hand a strong squeeze, released it, then turned and walked quietly up the stairs.

"Come, Amanda. We'll go into the drawing room – I have coffee ready." Elizabeth turned and walked across the foyer, her daughter trailing dutifully behind.

Amanda waited until they were seated before she began speaking. "Mother, I know you've never approved of what I've done with my life, or the choices I've made, but I will not sit still for your rude treatment of Lex."

"Now, wait just a minute..." Elizabeth sputtered.

"No! *You* wait." Amanda held up a hand to forestall her mother's tirade. "I resigned myself a long time ago to the fact that I was a disappointment to you and Daddy." She took a deep breath then continued, "I'm never going to be one of your snobby little society girls, like you wanted."

Elizabeth grasped the younger woman's arm. "Amanda, that's not completely true. Your father and I respect the fact that you have a mind of your own." She released her hold to pick up a dainty coffee cup and saucer. Taking a small sip, the pretentious woman put it on the table in front of them. "Where did we go wrong? Your sister seems happy." She looked her daughter in the eyes. "What did we do to make you this way?"

Amanda blinked, unsure of the question. "What exactly are you talking about, Mother? Is this about me being gay?"

"I refuse to accept that, Amanda. You were raised in a good home." She searched her daughter's face for a clue to her questions. "It's because of Frank, isn't it?"

"What?" Amanda's mouth dropped open.

Elizabeth nodded to herself, pleased with her deduction. "You and he were quite an item, and then your sister stole him right out from under your nose." She tapped her chin with an elegant nail. "I should have seen this before. This is your way at getting even with all of us for giving your sister our blessing with him, isn't it?"

Amanda jumped up, too agitated to sit still. "Oh, for crying out loud, Mother!" She paced over to the piano, then turned to face the older woman. "I told you I was gay when I was still in high school! Frank has always been just a very good friend." She strode impatiently over to stand in front of Elizabeth. "I was the one who set him up with Jeannie. He's like a brother to me!"

"Calm down, dear. Come over here and sit down." Elizabeth patted the spot next to her on the loveseat. "We'll forget about your little outburst for now." She waited until Amanda was once again seated. "Now, about this woman you've brought with you..." Elizabeth raised her hand to silence her daughter. "Just a minute... from what Michael's parents have told us, she saved your life a few weeks ago, correct?"

For the first time since they stepped into the room, Amanda smiled. "Yes, she did. Lex had no idea who I was, but she jumped into that flooded creek and pulled me to safety, getting hurt herself in the process."

"And you stayed with her at her ranch, afterwards?" Elizabeth questioned.

"Yes. The bridge was partially destroyed, so Lex offered me a place to stay until it could be repaired." Green eyes sparkled with remembrance.

Elizabeth grasped Amanda's hands with her own, leaning forward slightly. "She's quite a strong looking woman... now tell me the truth, Amanda. We can protect you here." The older woman looked around the room cautiously, then whispered, "did she force herself on you? Are you afraid of what she might do if you don't stay with her?"

Amanda couldn't help it – she laughed. "Lex? You've got to be kidding!" She pulled away from her mother, leaning into the loveseat. "Somebody should ask her that question! I practically threw myself at her."

Watching her daughter's body language, Elizabeth came to a decision. *No, I don't think she feels threatened by that woman, but...* "You threw yourself at her? Amanda! I'm..." Another idea sprouted itself in the older woman's mind. "Hero worship," she stated smugly.

"Excuse me?"

"That's it. Since you're not being forced to stay with her, that's the only logical explanation." The older woman took another sip of her coffee. "You feel... beholden... to her for saving your life and then taking care of you. So you naturally show your gratitude by staying with her."

Amanda jumped to her feet again. "That's bullshit!" she practically yelled, then stopped when she saw the look on her mother's face. "I'm sorry, Mother." She sat down again. "You're wrong. It's not fear, hero worship, or misplaced gratitude that keeps me with Lex."

"Then what..." Elizabeth began, only to be cut off by Amanda.

"It's love. Plain and simple." Amanda looked into her

mother's eyes, hoping to see understanding there. "I can't explain how it happened, or why...but I fell hopelessly, deeply in love with her almost instantly." She stood up and slowly walked to the door. "Why is it so hard for you and Daddy to understand that?" Amanda shook her head and left the room, closing the door quietly behind her.

Elizabeth Cauble sat immobile, staring at the closed door. *We'll just see what her father has to say about this... Michael always has a few tricks up his sleeves.* She smiled, although it didn't quite reach her eyes.

****

Lex stood at the bedroom window, staring at nothing as the voice through the cellular phone wound down.

"Lexie, don't you let those folks get to you, now," Martha pleaded, after hearing what Lex had reported to her so far. "You're just as good, if not better, than any of them, honey."

The rancher released a heavy sigh. "You say that, Martha...but you haven't seen this place. It's straight out of one of those silly television shows you used to watch. I keep expecting to see Joan Collins step out of a room any minute now."

Martha laughed. "Now that would be a sight!" She sobered. "How's Amanda handling all of this? Poor thing's probably as flustered as you are, I'll bet."

"She's doing a lot better than I am, I think. Although it's been one fight after another for her ever since we got here." Lex ran a hand through her hair, then leaned forward until her forehead was pressed against the cool glass of the window. "She's a hell of a lot stronger than I thought she was, that's for sure."

"I could have told you that, Lexie. That young lady may look like the sweet, quiet type, but she's got the heart of a lion," Martha stated, matter-of-factly. "You tell her I said hello, and to not take any bunk from anyone. And make sure she knows she always has a home here, no matter what."

"Yes ma'am." Lex finally smiled. "I was kind of thinking along those exact lines, myself."

Martha chuckled. "I knew I didn't raise a fool, honey. Now

you take care of yourself, and her too – we'll have a nice barbe-
cue when you girls get home."

Lex laughed. "That sounds like a wonderful idea, Martha.
I'll talk to you tomorrow."

"All right, sweetheart. Goodbye." The beloved housekeeper
hung up the phone, already happily planning the feast.

Lex had just closed the phone when the bedroom door
opened. Turning away from the window, the tall woman crossed
the room quickly when she saw the upset look on Amanda's face.
"What's the matter, love? Are you...?" Lex stopped her questioning when the young blonde wrapped her arms around her and
buried her tear-streaked face in the rancher's chest. "Hey." She
instinctively returned the embrace, running a hand through the
soft hair. "You okay?"

Amanda sniffed, then looked up into worried blue eyes.
"Yeah...just needed to connect with you for a minute." She felt a
soft kiss on the top of her head and smiled. "I love you so much,
Lex... why can't my parents understand that?"

"Your mother gave you a hard time, huh?" Lex asked, as she
guided the younger woman over to the bed to sit down. "They
just want what's best for you," she said, pulling Amanda into her
lap. "So do I."

"I don't think that's it. They want what's best for *them*.
They've never even bothered to ask me what I wanted." Amanda
raised her arms to wrap them around Lex's neck, pulling the dark
head close for a kiss. "Mmm..." She turned to face the rancher,
straddling strong thighs.

Lex chuckled when Amanda finally broke free of the
embrace. "Is that what you wanted?" She leaned down and captured the younger woman's lips again. "Better?" she teased.

"Oh yeah... much," Amanda murmured, snuggling close,
then ran one hand lightly down Lex's side, feeling the jean-clad
leg beneath her. "I thought you were going to change?"

"I was, but I decided to call Martha instead." Lex waved the
cell phone in front of Amanda's face.

The blonde swatted the phone away. "Oh yeah? How's she
doing?"

The rancher laughed. "Ornery as ever. She sends you her

love, and said for you not to let them get to you." She paused. "And... umm... she said to tell you not to forget that you have a home there," Lex finished quietly.

"I do, huh?" Amanda questioned just as quietly, looking up into Lex's face.

Lex looked down, lost in sparkling green eyes. "Yeah... you know, I've been thinking a lot about that. And I realize that we haven't known each other that long..." Lex babbled, unsure of herself. "But I was wondering if..."

Amanda could feel the rancher's heart pounding by the hand she had placed on the older woman's chest. "Lex, honey, what are you trying to say?" She tried to calm the nervous woman by gently massaging her neck and shoulder.

"Well, um... I know you value your independence, and I'm not trying to rush you, or push you into something that you're not ready for... and it's really not that far from town..." Lex continued, still flustered.

Understanding dawned on Amanda. "Wait..." She covered the rattled rancher's mouth with her hand. "Are you asking me to move in with you at the ranch?" Seeing the telltale flush on her companion's face, she smiled brightly. "You know, I was wondering how I was going to survive when I have to go back to work next week."

Lex looked at her, trying unsuccessfully to keep a silly grin from erupting on her face. "Does this mean...?"

"Think you could handle having me under foot all the time?" Amanda teased. "Ooof!" she grunted as the breath was suddenly squeezed from her.

"YES!" Lex whooped, hugging the smaller woman to her tightly. She buried her face in the soft fragrant hair. "Under foot? I should be so lucky!" she mumbled happily. "You can either redo the guest room, or just move into the master bedroom with me. I'll try to make space in my closet," she joked.

Amanda laughed. "Let's worry about it when we get home, okay? I'm just going to have the movers put everything into storage right now. We can sort through it all later." She kissed Lex on the chin.

"We've got a pretty good sized storage shed up by the bunkhouse, if you'd rather use that. I cleaned it out about three years ago... had a bunch of Dad's junk in it – I don't think anything is even in there right now." Lex pulled Amanda's face up gently, then gave her a tender kiss. "Thanks," she whispered when they broke apart.

"For what?" Amanda asked, searching the face so close to hers.

Lex cradled the younger woman's cheek with one hand. "For bringing more happiness into my life than I ever thought was possible." She captured Amanda's lips again, this time with more fervor.

Amanda returned the kiss, threading her hands through the thick dark hair, rolling onto her back and pulling the rancher over on top of her. "Mmm..." She pulled away just far enough to speak. "Why don't we wait until this afternoon to visit the beach? I can think of better things to do around here." She pulled Lex's face down towards her.

I couldn't agree more, thought Lex with a wicked chuckle. "You're the boss."

Chapter
14

The breeze blowing off the ocean was cool, but not cold, as the two women walked side by side on the nearly deserted beach. When Lex questioned Amanda about the sparse crowd, the younger woman told her it was the wrong time of the year. "Most people just spend their time in the nearby shops for right now."

"This is great," the rancher sighed, bending over and picking up a small shell, then shoving it into the pocket of her faded cutoffs like a small child.

Amanda giggled, then looped an arm through Lex's, bumping the taller woman with her hip. "Yeah, it is." She stopped and picked up another seashell. "Here, I think you missed one." She handed the treasure to her companion, who blushed slightly.

"Thanks." Lex sheepishly put it in her pocket. "Thought that maybe Martha might like them." Then she grinned at the look on the younger woman's face. "Yeah, yeah... okay. You caught me. I like 'em." She pulled Amanda into an impromptu hug. "Thanks! I'm really having a good time today."

"You haven't seen anything yet. Wait 'til we hit the shops. Now *there* are some... interesting... sights," Amanda smiled, totally charmed by the childlike glee her lover displayed at all the vistas and sounds on the beach. Lex had dragged her playfully into the surf when they first arrived, and threatened to throw the smaller woman into the ocean until she surrendered a kiss. Later, Amanda pulled the smiling rancher towards the parking lot. "C'mon, you silly thing. Let's take your little treasures to the car, and we'll have lunch, then do a little shopping."

After a light meal of corn dogs and potato chips, Amanda directed Lex towards a row of colorful shops, slinging a large, brightly decorated straw bag over one shoulder.

"What's in the bag?" Lex asked, trying to peek inside as she walked beside her friend.

Amanda pulled away with a quirky grin. "Nothing, yet. But I like to be prepared." She pushed her wide sunglasses up on her nose.

Lex laughed, and pulled her newly acquired aqua baseball cap that stated 'Life's a Beach' down a little further over her eyes. "If you say so, sweetheart." She glanced at the younger woman's legs. "You've got a really nice tan, you know that?" She grinned at Amanda's blush.

"Thanks. I used to spend a lot of time at the beach when I lived here – just to get out of the house... you know." Amanda studied her companion with a less than clinical eye. "I've never really noticed before, but... you... have a good tan, too. How did you manage that? All I've ever seen you in, besides nothing," she leered, "is jeans." Lex not only had a nice tan, but long, very muscular legs as well.

"Well, when I'm putting the colts through their paces in the summertime, I sometimes wear cutoffs so I don't pass out from the heat," Lex admitted with a grin. Then she stopped, sidetracked by several girls jumping multiple ropes. *How in the hell do they do that?* she wondered, fascinated.

Amanda wandered ahead a few yards, entranced by a man who was making colorful sand sculptures. Just as she turned to get Lex's attention, a young man grabbed at the bag on her shoulder, backhanding her across the face to make her release the purse.

Lex looked up just as the man hit Amanda. "Hey!" she yelled, grabbing one of the long jump ropes without a second thought. The rancher started running towards Amanda, who was sitting up holding her hand against her cheek. "You okay?" Lex asked, looking over her lover carefully.

"Yeah, just caught me off guard." Amanda tried to smile, but winced instead.

The rancher patted her knee. "Okay. Sit tight... I'll be right back." Then she took off, sprinting after the thief.

"Lex! Wait!" Amanda yelled, as she watched the older woman's long legs shorten the distance between herself and her quarry. A young boy dashed over to the still seated blonde, handing her a small bag filled with crushed ice. "Thank you," she smiled at the boy, who ducked his head and blushed.

As she chased the thief down the paved path, Lex fashioned a loop on one end of her confiscated rope. She never broke pace as she dodged the seemingly endless throng of people in her path. Seeing the young man look at her in fear, she grinned. "That's right, you little shit... you'd better be scared," she growled, slowly making progress in catching up to the purse-snatcher, who quickly decided on an alternate route.

Pedestrians were knocked aside as the man took off across the sand, not even realizing when his pursuer got closer. Lex was only about ten yards away when she began swinging the rope over her head in a wide loop, closing in on the man quickly.

"URK!" the thief gasped, as the makeshift lasso around his chest stopped his progress. He wheezed again as he fell hard in the sand.

Lex fell to her knees, straddling his still panting body. She tangled her hands into the front of his sweat-stained tee shirt, a dark look on her beautiful face. "You son of a bitch!" The furious rancher pulled him up slightly, then slammed him into the sand. "I ought to kill you right here, and save the state some money." Before she could do any damage, two police officers jumped from their bicycles and pulled her off the now terrified man.

"Easy there, miss," one of the cops said, holding onto Lex's shoulder as his partner handcuffed the frightened thief. "Must have been something pretty important in that bag," he commented, handing the item to the still heavily breathing rancher.

"No..." Lex, still on her knees gasped, getting her breathing under control. "It's empty." She gave the subdued man a nasty look. "The little bastard hit my friend." As if that explained everything.

The other cop grinned as his partner handed the rope to Lex. "Nice job, by the way. We're going to need to get a statement from you, though."

"Can I go and check on my friend first?" Lex asked, standing up and brushing the sand from her knees.

"Sure," cop number two agreed, leading the thief towards a nearby police car. "We'll even have someone give you a ride back, since we need to collect a statement from your friend, too." He opened the front passenger side door for Lex, then pushed the still-dazed thief into the back seat. "Johnston here," he nodded to the burly officer behind the wheel of the car, "will drop you off on his way to the station, and we'll meet you there, okay?"

"Thanks." Lex shook his hand and sat down in the car, still shocked at what she almost did. *Damn...I could have killed that guy – thank God the police showed up when they did, or I'd be the one in the back seat.*

If I have to fend off one more... kind... person, I swear I'll scream! Amanda thought to herself. Ever since Lex took off after her assailant, concerned bystanders, offering her everything from a glass of water to a dinner date, had bombarded the young woman. Some helpful soul had even brought her a folding lawn chair to sit in, as she fretted about the location of her companion. *God, Lex... why did you take off after that guy? You knew there was nothing in that damned bag,* she wondered silently, hoping that the tall woman would return soon.

When a police car pulled up into the parking lot beside where Amanda was sitting, she immediately thought the worst. *Oh, God... what's happened to her?* She fought to keep the tears at bay, when a tall form blocked the sun in front of her.

Concerned blue eyes looked right into her soul, as Lex knelt down in front of the frazzled blonde. "Amanda?" The rancher placed a warm hand on the younger woman's knee. "You okay, sweetheart?"

"Oh, God, Lex..." Amanda began to cry, as she launched herself out of the chair and into the arms of her lover. She wrapped her arms around the older woman's neck, ending up on her knees in front of Lex.

"Easy there, Amanda... shhh," the dark-haired woman murmured in her ear, rubbing her back with a comforting motion. She slowly stood up, pulling the sobbing young woman with her.

Amanda pulled back slightly, tears still running down her face. "Are you okay?" she sniffed, a small smile forming when Lex gently wiped her face with her hand.

"Yeah, I'm fine. How about you?" Lex asked, running her fingertips lightly over her jaw, where a bruise was already beginning to form. *That son of a bitch! I should have killed him when I had the chance.*

"I'm okay," Amanda assured her, then slapped her hard on the side. "Don't you EVER do that to me again!" she demanded in a shaky tone, anger and fear in her eyes.

"Ouch!" Lex jumped. "What?" She stepped away from the younger woman, whose eyes were sparkling with emotion.

"Take off after a thief like that! Dammit, Lex! That stupid bag wasn't worth risking your life for!" the blonde fumed.

Lex stepped towards Amanda cautiously. "Him? Aw, Amanda... he's just a scrawny two-bit little purse-snatcher."

She really doesn't get it. "Lex..." Amanda began patiently, "he could have been a junkie looking for quick money – and carrying a knife or gun for protection." She put her hands on the dark-haired woman's waist. "And I don't want to lose you this soon after finding you, okay?"

Understanding raced across Lex's tanned features. "Oh...I never really thought about that. I just saw him hit you, and kinda lost it." She pulled Amanda into a strong hug. "Sorry about that." She regretfully released the younger woman when a throat was cleared discreetly behind her. Lex kept her arm around Amanda's waist as she turned around and greeted the two bicycle cops. "Oh, hi, officers. Sorry, I didn't catch your names," she grinned, as the policemen shook their heads and laughed.

****

Lex studied her companion's profile with concern, as Amanda drove them towards her parent's house. "Oh, sweetheart," she said quietly, touching Amanda's face, "that is going to be one hell of a bruise."

The side of Amanda's face was already turning purple, from her cheek down across her beautiful jaw. "I guess." She turned her head to peek into the rear view mirror, then grimaced. "Well, at least there's not much swelling – the ice really helped." She gave Lex a wry smile. "I can't believe you actually roped that guy... wish I had seen that!"

The rancher rolled her eyes. "Those cops exaggerated, I think. It looked a lot more impressive than it actually was," she smirked. "Thought we'd never get away from your fan club, though." The petite blonde had been surrounded by a throng of well-wishers, which followed the two women all the way to their car, offering all types of assistance.

"Don't remind me," Amanda chuckled. "Although I think you had your own admiration society with those two policemen," she teased, then reached up and grabbed Lex's hand, giving it a firm squeeze. "The look on that one guy's face when you turned down his dinner offer was priceless."

When the taller of the two police officers had approached Lex for a date, she matter-of-factly stated, "Sorry... but I don't think my girlfriend here would approve." Which caused Amanda to giggle, and the other cop to burst out laughing. The embarrassed officer had apologized, then offered to take them both out, which they politely declined, using the excuse that they didn't have enough time before they had to leave for Texas.

"Yeah, sorry about that. I wasn't really thinking," Lex grinned. "But it was pretty funny, wasn't it?"

Amanda shook her head. "What am I going to do with you?"

Lex gave her a sexy grin. "Oh, I'm sure you can come up with something creative."

"We'll see about that, my little thief roper," the blonde giggled, as she pulled up to the familiar security box. Before she reached out to punch in the security code, Amanda leaned over and released Lex's hand, grabbing her by the back of the neck. "C'mere." She pulled the rancher's head towards her.

Lex obeyed willingly, allowing the younger woman to take control of the situation, as chills chased down her spine. "Damn, Amanda!" she wheezed as they broke off. "How in the hell do you do that?" She leaned her forehead into the blonde's bangs, her entire body trembling slightly.

Amanda took a deep, shaky breath as well. "Whoa... that sure got the old blood pumping, didn't it?" She gave Lex another, shorter kiss. "Oh yeah... whoo!" She grinned, then released Lex and punched the code into the patiently waiting gate.

"What in the hell did you do to my daughter?" Michael Cauble yelled, when he spotted Lex and Amanda walking across the main foyer, heading for the stairs. He stormed towards the women, fists clenched at his side.

"Daddy, wait!" Amanda stepped in front of Lex, holding her hand out to block her father's path.

Shoving his daughter aside, Michael pushed the tall woman up against the stairwell, his face red with rage. "You like hitting defenseless women, cow chaser?"

Amanda squeezed between the two of them, pushing her father away. "Stop it! Lex didn't do anything to me, Daddy! I was mugged at the beach."

"What?! You were mugged?" Michael backed off, but only a step, glaring at the rancher. "Where the hell were you while my daughter was being assaulted?"

Lex wisely kept her mouth shut, allowing Amanda to handle her father. The fuming rancher knew that if she said anything, it would only hurt the woman she loved – so she concentrated on controlling her breathing. *Stay calm, Lexington... let Amanda take care of him.* She took a deep breath and released it, feeling the younger woman's hand pat her gently on the arm.

"Lex was only a few steps away, and she caught the guy – then turned him over to the police," Amanda stated proudly, putting a hand behind her to make contact with the silent woman, whose anger she could almost feel as Lex put her hands on the small waist in front of her.

Michael prudently decided to let the matter drop. "Very well." He looked at their matching ragged shorts and frowned.

"Is it too much to ask that you two change for dinner? We're not having a clambake."

Amanda felt Lex stiffen behind her, the hands on her hips tightening slightly. "Is it too much for me to ask that you and Mother act civil tonight? If not, Lex and I can go out for dinner, then fly out first thing in the morning," she asked in a calm voice, halfway hoping his answer would be negative. *Please... give me a reason to get out of here...*

Damn! She's really grown up in the past year, hasn't she? Michael mused to himself, vaguely proud. *All right...I'll play her little game.* "Of course, dear. We just got off on the wrong foot, didn't we, Lex?" He reached forward and offered his hand to the dark-haired woman. "No hard feelings?"

"Sure, Mr. Cauble." Lex took his hand in a firm grasp. "No hard feelings." But she couldn't help but feel that the man was up to something. *Probably up to no good, but we'll just play it by ear for now.*

"Thanks, Daddy." Amanda gave her father a hug. "We'll be cleaned up and changed in time for dinner." She wasn't fooled either by his sudden capitulation, but decided to accept the cease-fire for now. "C'mon, Lex..." She grasped the older woman by the arm and led her up the stairs.

Once they were safely ensconced in the guestroom, Amanda locked the door and studied her quiet companion. "Are you okay?" She ran her hands searchingly over the rancher's body. "My father didn't hurt you, did he?"

"I'm fine." Lex grabbed the wandering hands, pulling them behind her back. "He just pushed me, no damage done." She felt Amanda's hands sneak into her pockets, and she raised an eyebrow in response.

"Just checking for bruises." Amanda grinned at her unrepentantly. "Maybe I should take off your clothes and double check? No sense in taking any chances."

Lex laughed. "Sure! Let's take a shower – the lights are much better in there." She pulled the younger woman towards the bathroom and closed the door behind them.

****

After a short argument, which she won, Amanda had Lex's place setting moved from next to Frank, to across the table beside her. The entire meal was spent in tense silence, only broken by the occasional attempts by Jeannie and her husband to clear the air.

"Good grief, Mandy! Daddy told us about what happened to you today. But he failed to mention that you looked like you got into a fight with Mike Tyson and lost," Jeannie teased. "So c'mon... tell us the whole story."

Amanda's explanation about the day's events further antagonized her parents, especially since she painted her companion's part in the tale so heroically. "The police officers said the look on that thief's face was really funny when Lex pulled that rope tight, and he hit the ground. They were trying to catch up on their bikes, and saw the whole thing."

Michael glared at the rancher. "Sounds rather foolish to me, chasing down a criminal when you are unarmed." He took a sip of wine. "People have been killed for less."

"I really wasn't thinking," the dark-haired woman admitted. "I saw him hit Amanda, and totally lost it. I just wanted to make sure he paid for what he had done to her," Lex added quietly.

Uh-oh... time to change the subject, I think. "So, my lovely sister..." Jeannie smiled at the young blonde. "Give me all the juicy gossip from Somerville." She purposely ignored the glare from her mother, and winked at the rancher. "Or maybe you can fill me in, Lex."

"Sure! What do you want to know?" Lex flinched slightly when Amanda poked her leg under the table.

Jeannie gave her sister an evil grin. "Got anything on my sister? She never likes to talk about herself."

Lex grinned too, then almost yelped out loud as her leg was pinched. "Ow!" She quickly cleared her throat to cover up her slip. "Excuse me." Turning her head slightly, Lex quirked an eyebrow at her lover. "Well, did Amanda tell you about her promotion? She's now the manager of the real estate office."

"Really? Oooh... Mandy – that's great!" Jeannie almost

squealed with excitement. "But what about that Neanderthal, Rick?" She looked at Lex. "He was always so rude when I would call Amanda's office. Someone needs to knock him down a peg or two, in my opinion."

The rancher almost choked on the water she was drinking. "Well," she coughed, "there's actually a really funny story about that... ow!" A sharp pain from her just-stomped foot stopped Lex in mid-sentence.

Frank, who had been silent up until now, looked at the dark-haired woman. "You okay, Lex?" His smirk let her know he knew exactly what was wrong.

"Yeah..." She glared at Amanda, who smiled innocently. "Sudden cramp, I guess." She felt a hand rub her leg in a sooth-ing manner.

"So, what's the story?" Jeannie asked, missing the glare her sibling threw at her.

Feeling the hand on her thigh tighten into a claw, the rancher decided that discretion was the better part of valor. "Seems poor Rick not only got fired, but ended up receiving a bruised jaw and got thrown into jail for disorderly conduct." The claw straight-ened out, and gave her a loving pat instead.

Amanda quickly decided to change the subject. "So, Mother... have you decided on a cruise, or a tour of Europe this year?" she inquired, knowing that Elizabeth had one real passion in her life – travel.

"I believe I'll do Paris. The last cruise was such a disap-pointment to me. People actually brought children on board!" Sounding totally disgusted, she continued, "and they let the little heathens run wild. It was absolutely disgraceful."

Lex started to say something, but closed her mouth and con-centrated on her plate instead. *No sense in giving them any more reason to make Amanda's stay here miserable,* she thought to herself.

"Do you have something you'd like to say, Lex?" Michael had seen the tall woman begin to speak, then stop. "I'm sure that we would all be interested in whatever is on your mind."

Amanda looked at her father in surprise, but didn't say any-thing.

"I really don't think you want to hear my opinion, Mr. Cauble." Lex gave Amanda's father a small smile.

Michael returned her smile. "Don't be ridiculous! Please, share with us." He waved a hand at the table.

Feeling Amanda's comforting touch on her leg, Lex gave her partner an apologetic look. "I was just going to say that those folks probably worked and saved for years to go on a cruise, so they had just as much right to be there as anyone."

"Are you saying that I *DON'T* work for my money?" Elizabeth gave the rancher a nasty look, daring her to answer.

Lex shook her head. "No, ma'am, not at all. I'm just saying that most folks don't take a real vacation every year. But when they do, they have as much right to relax and enjoy themselves as the people whose biggest concern is where they'll go, not how much it will cost."

Seeing his mother-in-law preparing herself to attack, Frank jumped into the conversation. "Have you ever been on a cruise, Lex?" he asked, cutting the older woman off before she could get started.

The tall woman smiled, a little embarrassed. "No, never really had the time. As a matter of fact, this is the first time that I've been away from the ranch in several years." She gave Amanda a meaningful look. "But I wouldn't mind going on one, someday."

"Frank and I are taking an Alaskan Cruise as a second honeymoon next spring," Jeannie shared, helpfully. "Maybe you should consider going on one too – certainly a great way to beat the summer heat," she smiled. "I didn't visit as often as Amanda did, but the Texas summers stand out as extremely wicked in my mind. I don't know how you are able to handle it."

Lex shrugged. "I guess I'm just used to it – doesn't really bother me any."

Elizabeth saw her opportunity. "I suppose it's like the migrant workers in the Valley... they don't know any better than to stay in the hot sun all day. They're quite used to it as well, I would think."

Amanda glared at her mother. "I can't believe your attitude!"

"It's okay, Amanda." Lex placed a hand on the younger woman's arm, trying to calm her down.

"No, it's not!" the furious blonde snapped, then looked into hurt blue eyes and immediately dropped her voice. "I'm getting tired of listening to my parents take potshots at you," she whispered, forgetting the other people at the table.

Lex casually slipped her hand beneath the table, and took a firm grasp of Amanda's fingers. "We'll talk about this later, okay?" She gave the smaller hand in hers a gentle squeeze. Looking up at Elizabeth, she smiled again. "And I have to agree with you, Mrs. Cauble. If a person works all day, every day in the heat, it's much easier for them to handle it." Then, with a slight twinkle in her eye, she continued, "unlike the poor folks that have to sit in an office all the time. They break out into a sweat just walking to their cars at the end of the day."

Touché, Mother, Amanda smiled inwardly. She looked over at Lex and gave her a wink. "You about finished?" she asked, noticing the half-eaten plate of food in front of her lover with a frown.

"Yeah, just not real hungry, I guess." she returned with a sheepish shrug. Lex's stomach was still in knots over what happened earlier in the day.

"You two got any plans for tonight?" Frank asked, after a not so subtle poke in the ribs from his wife.

Amanda looked at Lex, who raised an eyebrow encouragingly. "Not really... what do you have in mind?" She looked at her sister, who was smiling broadly.

"Lex, you can't come to LA without going out at least for one evening, isn't that right, Amanda?" Jeannie winked.

The rancher looked suddenly panicked. "Umm... that's really nice of you, but I didn't bring anything to wear for a night out on the town."

Frank and Jeannie both laughed. "Actually," he said, smiling, "you'll be more suitably dressed for where we're going than Jeannie or I will."

"Okay, why not?" Lex looked at Amanda. "Do you feel up to it?" The tone in her voice made it clear that Amanda could just say no.

The young blonde smiled and patted Lex on the arm. "Sure..." She touched her bruised jaw, "Looks bad, but really doesn't hurt."

Elizabeth Cauble sighed heavily, drawing everyone's attention back to her. "I guess it's too much to ask that you actually spend some time with your father and me before you leave us." She gave Amanda a pitiful look.

"Now, now..." Michael stopped her. "I'm sure Amanda will be glad to spend some quality time with us in the morning." He gave the rancher an unreadable look. "And you too, Lex. I'd really like the opportunity to get to know you a little better." He smiled, a look that sent chills down the dark-haired woman's spine.

Why do I suddenly feel like a man at the gallows being told to jump? Lex wondered. "Sure, Mr. Cauble, if you really want to." She gave Amanda's hand a firm squeeze. "But I'm sure I can find something to occupy myself if you need to spend a little time alone with Amanda."

"That won't be necessary, Lex." *If all goes well, Amanda will send your gold-digging hide back to Texas so fast it will make your head spin,* he laughed inwardly. "If my daughter is determined to spend time with you, I'd really like for us to become better acquainted."

Jeannie stood up. "Great! We'll get ready, and meet you two in the sitting room in an hour." She grabbed her husband and hurried from the room.

Amanda released Lex's hand and stood up as well. "Guess we'd better go get ready, huh?" she asked her lover with a sweet smile. "We'll see you both in the morning," she assured her parents, as Lex joined her by the door. "Goodnight."

Halfway up the stairs, Lex pulled Amanda to a stop. "Do you have any idea where we're going tonight?"

"Sure," Amanda grinned, then continued up the stairs, a growling rancher at her heels.

"AMANDA!" Lex chased after her, laughing.

Chapter

15

Lex stood away from the pool table quietly, watching as Amanda lined up her shot. She couldn't help but smile as the cute blonde's tongue slightly poked from her mouth – the perfect picture of intense concentration.

"Don't let that innocent look fool you..." Frank whispered, "she's a first class shark!" he chuckled. "The first time we played, she beat me so badly that I had to carry her books to class for a solid week! Do you know how demeaning it is for a high school senior to be enslaved by a freshman?"

"Amanda said you were her best friend..." Lex took a sip of her beer. "How long have you known each other, if you don't mind me asking?" She shook her head as Amanda sank her shot, dancing around and waving her hand in front of her sister's face. "Uh-oh..."

Frank watched, as his wife good-naturedly threatened the blonde with her cue stick. "Don't worry, Amanda can take her." He laughed out loud at the look of shock on the dark-haired woman's face. "I'm kidding! Well, not completely. Mandy *can* take her – but they don't actually fight anymore." He took a strong swallow of his third scotch and water. The tall woman surprised them all by ordering a beer, which she was still nursing. Lex told them she really didn't drink much anymore, which was okay by him and Jeannie, since the last time they were out, they got carried away and had to call a cab. "Mandy literally ran me over on my first day at her school." He shook his head in remembrance. "I had just transferred from a small school south of Sacramento, and was completely and totally awed by this huge school. I had run myself ragged trying to find my classes, and had bent down in the hallway to tie my shoe. Then this little blonde whirlwind came flying around the corner and knocked me flat on my face."

Lex laughed. "I'll bet that was a sight! But it's nice to know she's always been like that, running from place to place." She felt a hand on her arm.

"What's so funny?" Amanda asked, reaching across Lex to grab her vodka Collins.

"Frank was just telling me how you two met," Lex grinned, seeing her lover blush.

Amanda rubbed her face. "Umm... it's your shot, Lex." She gave the older woman's stomach a gentle pat, then smiled at the rolled-eyed look she received as the rancher walked towards the pool table.

"You look really happy, Mandy." The big man studied his sister-in-law closely. "I don't think I've ever seen you smile so much." He nodded towards the pool table, where his wife was trying to ruin the rancher's shot by making faces and slinging silly comments at her.

"Yeah... I'm very happy." Amanda saw what Jeannie was doing and tossed a pretzel at her. "Stop cheating!" she yelled, getting a nasty look from her sibling. Turning her attention to Frank, she smiled warmly. "She's the one, Frank."

He nodded. "I kinda figured that by the look on your face, kiddo." The burly man smiled, remembering the long talks the two of them used to have. Amanda had sworn she would find her one true love, and not settle for anything less. Frank was the only person she had shared that with – not even her sister knew the high standards she had set for a mate. He had understood, since he had fallen completely in love with her sister the moment he met her. "Even I can see she's special, Mandy. Don't ever let her go," Frank spoke quietly, his eyes suspiciously sparkling in the smoky light of the bar.

Amanda wrapped her arms around his neck, giving him a light kiss on the lips. "Thanks, Frank. I knew you'd understand."

"I guess this means I get to take Slim here home with me," Jeannie teased, wrapping an arm around Lex's waist. "No offense, Frank, but I think I got the better end of the deal." She grinned as a long arm draped casually across her shoulder.

"I've heard about some of the wild things that go on here in California," Lex drawled, raising an eyebrow as Amanda turned around and Frank placed his chin on her head, wrapping his arms around her protectively, an innocent look on his face. "You think you can handle her?" She gave the big man a smirk.

Frank appeared thoughtful. "I dunno. Since you met her, let's see... you've nearly drowned, you got your ribs broken, you were shot, and you were attacked by rustlers." He stepped suddenly, pushing the giggling blonde forward. "Gimme back my wife – PLEASE!"

Lex impulsively caught Amanda, who snuggled happily into her arms, much to Frank and Jeannie's amusement. "Fickle, ain't she?" the rancher muttered to the other couple, only to receive a slap on the belly. "What'd I say?" she complained to the blonde.

The more I'm around her, the better I like this mysterious rancher who has stolen my little sister's heart, Jeannie thought to herself. "Okay, gang...now that I whipped Slim at pool..."

"What?!" Amanda leaned back so that she could look Lex in the eye. "How could you lose? We only had to make one shot." She spun around and glared at her sister, who was now giggling. "What did you do?" Then she felt strong arms wrap themselves snugly around her.

"I didn't think she could actually do it," Lex said, laying her head on the smaller woman's shoulder. "I said she couldn't distract me into blowing my shot."

Amanda frowned. "I'll ask again. What did she do?"

Jeannie laughed. "I tried dancing around the table like a fool– didn't work. I even blew in her ear!" She saw Amanda's eyes widen, "Nothing. So, while she was bent over about to shoot, I pinched her on the butt!" At this startling confession, everyone burst out laughing.

"Damn near knocked the guy at the next table out with the cue ball, too," the rancher admitted with an embarrassed grin.

Amanda pulled the long arms around her tighter. "God, honey... I'm sorry I missed that." She felt Lex laugh. "Are you ready for our next stop?"

Lex released a heavy sigh. "Do I want to know where we're going?"

Jeannie reached over, grabbed Lex by the hand, and started dragging her towards the door. "Dancing!" she exclaimed, as Amanda and Frank followed closely behind.

****

"What in the hell is *that* supposed to be?" Lex grumbled as a young person walked by her with bright purple spiked hair and multiple face piercings, shocking the somewhat conservative rancher.

Amanda giggled, pulling Lex through the crowd of people, right behind Frank and Jeannie. "I think it was a he, but don't quote me on that."

They found a table near the crowded dance floor; the combination of loud music and a strong beat made Lex's teeth hurt. She ordered another beer and focused her attention on the dozens of people dancing. Men dancing with women, men dancing with men, and women dancing with women all seemed to be having a good time. There were even a few wildly dressed people dancing alone, to Lex's amusement.

"See anything you like?" Amanda asked, her lips close to the dark-haired woman's ear. She could tell that Lex was a little overwhelmed, observing a lot of things that she would never see in a small town. The rancher looked particularly engrossed in a young woman who was wearing white makeup with black across her eyes and lips, studs and hoops adorning her eyebrows and nose. "Maybe I should get my nose pierced," Amanda whispered, then playfully licked Lex's ear.

"Huh?" The older woman jumped, then smiled. "C'mon..."

She grabbed Amanda's hand. "Let's go join the crowd!" Lex stood and pulled the younger woman along with her, just as a slow song began. "Perfect!" she smiled, claiming a piece of the dance floor.

Amanda linked her hands behind the tall woman's neck, snuggling her face into Lex's chest. *I really like this,* she thought blissfully, as Lex pulled her even closer.

Closing her eyes happily, Lex gently swayed to the music, enjoying the feeling of holding Amanda in her arms. Her peaceful thoughts were interrupted by a strong hand on her shoulder.

"Mind if I cut in?" a short, pudgy woman with slicked down hair asked.

"No, thank you," Lex said, turning around.

"Hey!" The woman, dressed in leather pants and a leather vest, grabbed the taller woman's arm and swung Lex around to face her. "Look, cowboy, I'd like to dance with the cute blonde." She craned her neck to look the rancher in the eye. "Why don't you go feed your horse, and I'll show the lady a good time."

Amanda stepped between the two women, thinking fast. "Lex, honey..." she said loudly, patting the rancher on the stomach, "you remember what your parole officer said. The next person you hospitalize can get you sent back to prison." She almost laughed out loud at the look on the pushy woman's suddenly pale face.

Lex gave the woman an evil grin, then glanced down at her lover. "Aw... c'mon, sugar – just this once?" She took a menacing step towards Amanda's would-be suitor. "Please?"

Deciding to find someplace else to be, the leather-clad woman turned quickly and made her way through the crowd, muttering under her breath, "I've got better things to do with my time."

"Thanks, sweetheart." Lex wrapped Amanda into a hug, kissing her lightly on the forehead. "I really didn't want to ruin tonight by getting into an argument with 'Motorcycle Mama'."

Amanda chuckled. "I was tempted to just smack her one, but I was afraid she'd scream 'lawsuit'." She wrapped her arms around Lex's neck. "Don't we have a dance to finish?"

Lex kissed her lightly on the lips and rested her hands on

Amanda's waist. "Yeah." She pulled the smaller woman to her and closed her eyes peacefully, slowly rocking once again to the music.

"I thought for sure we were going to have a brawl on our hands," Frank laughed at the table later. "We saw that woman try to cut in."

Jeannie nodded. "Why didn't you just slug her, Lex?" she asked the smiling rancher. "I know I probably would have, the rude little turd."

"Nah, I really couldn't blame her any." Lex put her arm on the back of Amanda's chair. "She had great taste in women." The rancher enjoyed seeing her lover blush. "Besides, I knew Amanda would be coming home with me," Lex winked.

Mother and Father are so wrong about her, Jeannie marveled, *She's the best thing that's ever happened to Mandy.* "You guys about ready to leave? I think Frank has had about all the fun he can stand for one night." She gestured towards her husband, whose eyes were beginning to droop.

Frank stifled a yawn. "Sorry about that... guess I'm not used to all this excitement."

"I'm pretty pooped too," Amanda admitted, leaning against Lex's arm. "How about you, babe?" She turned her head and gazed into the dark-haired woman's eyes. "Ready to go home and go to bed?"

Lex quirked an eyebrow, amused. "Is that an offer from the cute blonde?" She stood up, offering her hand to Amanda. "I thought maybe I was just getting old – I can barely keep my eyes open." She pulled the younger woman to her feet.

"You? Old? Yeah, right!" Frank took Jeannie's hand, and they followed Lex and Amanda through the still raucous crowd towards the front door. "If she's old, then I'm ancient," he grumbled to his wife.

Jeannie patted him on the rear lovingly. "Whatever you say, grandpa."

****

"I haven't been out with Frank and Jeannie in a couple of years. We used to have a lot of fun together," Amanda yawned much later that evening, towel drying her hair in the bedroom. They both had decided that smelling like stale cigarette smoke from the bars was not a good way to sleep, so they had shared a quick shower before getting ready for bed.

Lex walked out of the bathroom in her boxers and sleep shirt, and returned the yawn. "Mmm..." She fell onto the bed bonelessly. "Yeah...well, it was certainly an experience, that's for sure."

Concerned, Amanda walked over and kneeled on the bed. "Are you okay, honey? I know you maybe had one beer all night long – are you getting sick on me?"

"Nah, just tired," the rancher assured her. "I'm not used to staying up quite this late, dancing and stuff," she smiled, then grabbed Amanda and pulled her on top of her. "You coming to bed anytime soon, or are you going to play with your hair all night?"

"Well, I wanted to... oooh..." Amanda gasped as a warm hand sneaked under her nightshirt, tracing a soft pattern across her back. "Umm..." Gentle lips began nipping at her throat.

Lex felt the body on top of hers relax completely, as she continued her assault on Amanda's neck. She pulled away slightly, gazing deeply into green eyes that were struggling to stay open. "C'mon, baby." Lex sat up, pulling the blonde with her, "Let's get some sleep." She maneuvered them both under the covers, not relinquishing her hold on Amanda.

"'Night, love," Amanda murmured, placing a kiss on the older woman's throat.

"Pleasant dreams, sweetheart," Lex whispered, hearing the deep, even breathing that told her Amanda was already asleep.

Chapter
16

The four late-night revelers ended up sleeping in, so they spent the latter part of the morning enjoying each other's company for breakfast.

"So, Lex..." Frank teased, "You ready to go out dancing again? We could look for your little friend... "

The dark-haired woman chuckled. "Think I'll give it a miss...I don't want to end up bailing Amanda out of jail."

"Me? I have no idea what you're talking about." Amanda tried to look innocent, but failed miserably when Lex gave her a knowing grin. "Stop that."

Choking on her coffee, Jeannie gasped, "Mandy...you know darn good and well what Lex is talking about." She wiped tears from her eyes. "You've still got a bad temper. I was hoping that staying with Gramma and Grandpa would have had a positive effect on you." She changed her focus of attention to the still smiling rancher. "Has she taken a swing at you yet, Slim?"

"No, not..." Lex shook her head, then stopped. "Well, actually..." she grinned, "just yesterday, she slapped me."

Amanda looked shocked. "I did no such..." she paused, then rolled her eyes. "Oh, for God's sake! You deserved that – scaring me half to death, chasing after that guy." She glared at Lex. "And

I'll do it again, if you ever pull another stupid stunt like that!"

"Yes, ma'am," Lex teased, then sobered. She ran gentle fingertips over the still-purple bruise on her lover's face. "How's that feel today? Looks like all of the swelling is gone, at least." The rancher barely controlled the urge to lean over and kiss the contusion.

Capturing the hand with one of her own, the blonde smiled. "Fine. Doesn't even hurt today, honest." She happily leaned into the touch.

Jeannie sighed. *They are just so cute together!* "Well, I hate to leave such wonderful company, but I promised Mother that I'd go by and check on the gallery." She tossed her napkin onto the table. "You ready, darling?" she asked Frank, who nodded.

"Sure. I've got a couple of last-minute things to pick up before the dinner tonight, anyway." The big man smiled at Amanda then stood up and pushed his chair up to the table.

Lex gave Amanda a look. "Yeah, I still gotta get something too, I guess." She missed the wink the blonde gave Frank.

"Miss Amanda, I'm terribly sorry to interrupt you, but your father has requested that you join them in the library." Beverly stepped into the dining room quietly, a subdued tone in her voice.

"Our cue to leave." Jeannie and Frank headed towards the doorway. "Good luck, guys." She waved a hand and hurried from the room.

Amanda smiled at the maid. "Thanks, Beverly. We'll be right there." As the woman began to leave, she asked, "What kind of mood is he in, or dare I even ask?"

"That's just it, Miss Amanda. He's in a really good mood – it's very strange." She shook her head and left the room quietly.

Turning to face Lex, Amanda frowned. "I don't think I like the sound of that. You sure you want to go with me?"

The rancher leaned forward, kissing the top of the younger woman's forehead. "I'm with you, sweetheart, as long as you'll have me."

"Forever sounds pretty good to me, at least to start with." The blonde captured Lex's lips with her own, sharing a kiss full of love and promise. Pulling back and releasing a heavy sigh,

Amanda forced a smile. "Let's go 'visit', then we'll go shopping, okay?"

"Right." Lex stood up, then pulled her friend into a strong hug as soon as the smaller woman got to her feet. "One for the road." She buried her face into the soft hair. "I love you, Amanda," she spoke quietly, savoring the moment. "With all my heart and soul."

Amanda felt the tall woman tremble slightly. "I love you too, Lex." She returned the embrace, kissing the collarbone that peeked through the v-neck of the shirt Lex as wearing. "And I always will."

****

"Come in and have a seat, you two." Michael motioned the young women into the library. Elizabeth was comfortably perched on the loveseat, while he stood at the bar, a set of papers in his hand.

Amanda pulled Lex over to the sofa, which was at a 90-degree angle from the loveseat, and directly across from the bar. She sat down next to the rancher, close enough to touch if she needed to. "Good morning, Mother," she said, giving the older woman a friendly smile.

"It's almost afternoon, Amanda. But I hear you had a late night last night." She gave the rancher an almost civil look. "Lex."

The dark-haired woman smiled politely and nodded. "Mrs. Cauble."

Michael interrupted. "Coffee?" He nodded to his wife. "Oh, I'm sorry, Lex..." He raised a decanter filled with an amber liquid. "I hear that whiskey is more to your liking in the mornings." He poured a glass. "I'm afraid that all I have right now is scotch, but we can send one of the servants out for some Jack Daniels, if you would prefer." Michael watched with hidden glee as his daughter's face showed confusion.

"What are you talking about, Daddy?" Amanda turned to face her lover. "Lex?"

The rancher was looking down at her feet, a resigned look on her face. Then, taking a deep breath, she looked up and locked gazes with Amanda's father. "No thank you, Mr. Cauble. I haven't drunk hard liquor in years." She turned and met her lover's eyes. "Remember I told you about Linda?" she asked softly.

Amanda frowned, thinking. "Yes... what does that..."

"After that, I got a little wild for a while, but Martha got me straightened out." Lex felt a small hand on her leg, the presence reassuring. "I'll tell you all about it later, I promise," she whispered.

"I'm not worried, love." The young blonde smiled.

Michael frowned. *Damn that Richards! This is not going as I had planned at all.* "My mistake, Lex," he conceded the point to the dark-haired woman. *Let's just see if I can shake her up a little bit more.* "So... do you have family back in Texas, Lex?"

Confused by the sudden change in topics, the rancher nodded. "Yes, I have an older brother, Hubert."

Stepping away from the bar, Michael sat down next to his wife, who was sipping from a china cup. "How about your parents?" He leaned over and poured three more cups of coffee, offering one to both Lex and Amanda.

Lex accepted the offering politely, even though the thought of ingesting anything right now made her stomach cramp. "Thank you." She acknowledged the coffee, balancing the cup and saucer on one thigh. "My mother died when I was four, and my father... travels a lot." *No lie there, but I guess I could just say he's a drifter who would rather wonder where his next meal is coming from, than have to look at his daughter.*

Elizabeth wasn't certain what her husband had in mind, but she decided to play along. "And does your brother work with you at your ranch?"

"No, ma'am. He's a CPA in town." Lex shared a smile with Amanda. "He's not much for the ranch life."

"A professional, then. You must be very proud of him." Elizabeth gave her daughter a look. *Much more suitable than a common cowhand, that's for sure.* "You only have one sibling? Must have been lonely growing up." She gave Lex a mock sympathetic look.

Lex swallowed the lump that had formed in her throat. "I

had a younger brother, but he died about nine years ago." She felt Amanda grasp her hand for support.

"I'm terribly sorry to hear that. It's always so tragic when a child dies." Michael shook his head sadly. "Especially when it can be avoided. Wait... I seem to recall a boy named Walters that was killed at the lake around that time." He looked at the rancher, an understanding look on his handsome face. "That was your brother, wasn't it?"

"Louis..." Lex nodded, trying to keep her emotions under control. *Almost ten years ago, and it still hurts as much as the day it happened... why can't I get past this?*

Michael smiled, adjusting his glasses slightly. "That's what I thought. If I recall correctly..." He knew all of the details, since he had just read them this morning. "There was a boat full of kids, and they were hit by another boat, right?" Seeing the dark-haired woman nod slightly, a pained look on her face, he continued, "absolutely horrible. The whole affair could probably have been avoided with the proper adult supervision." Seeing Lex pale, he prodded, "don't you agree, Lex?"

"That's it!" Amanda stood up. "C'mon, Lex." She pulled the silent rancher to her feet. "We've got things to do, if you'll excuse us."

Lex allowed the younger woman to lead her through the doorway, her mind a million miles away. *He's right... I should have been there,* she mentally berated herself. *If I had been driving the boat, maybe the entire accident could have been avoided.* Numbly she continued to follow Amanda, feeling a small amount of comfort in their linked hands. The cool breeze on her face brought Lex to her senses. Looking around, she found herself standing in the garden, under Amanda's favorite tree.

"C'mere, love, sit down." Amanda sat down under the tree and patted her leg. She waited patiently until the blank look faded from Lex's face, and then she held out her arms. "Please?"

Forcing a small smile to her face, the rancher sat down in front of Amanda and stretched out, allowing the smaller woman to wrap her arms around her. Lex ended up lying between Amanda's legs, her head resting against her lover's chest.

Amanda began gently running her fingers through the thick,

dark hair, feeling Lex finally begin to relax. "I'm calling the airline. We're going home on the next flight out," the blonde murmured, angry tears threatening to fall.

"No." Lex finally spoke, her voice hoarse from holding back
tears of her own.

"Yes! There's nothing here worth putting you through this –
I'm tired of defending my actions to them, and having them try
to get to me through you." Amanda absently straightened the
bangs on Lex's forehead.

Lex turned slightly, so that she could look into Amanda's
face. "Don't let them win, sweetheart...they'll never let you live
it down." She raised a hand and caressed the unbruised side of
the younger woman's jaw. "I can handle this... they just kinda
caught me off guard, that's all."

Leaning down until their noses were almost touching,
Amanda dropped a light kiss on the rancher's mouth. "Are you
sure about this? We can be home before it gets dark tonight."

Lex raised her head slightly to capture the blonde's lips for a
more prolonged contact. "Mmm..." *Home... I think I like the
sound of that,* Lex thought for a wistful moment. "Yeah, I'm
sure. We've got a dinner to sit through tonight." She gave her
lover a small smile. "But it won't hurt my feelings if you decide
that you want to leave Saturday morning."

Amanda grinned. "That's a great idea. I'll call and change
our reservations." She wrapped her arms around the reclining
woman and squeezed hard. "Have I told you lately just how
much I love you?" she whispered into the ear next to her face.

"You may have mentioned something about it a time or
two," Lex teased, rising up slightly to return the embrace. "I'm
sorry about all that stuff with your father," she said quietly. "I
guess I should have told you about that mess before you heard it
from someone else... it was just a matter of time before somebody told you."

"No, Lex. I don't expect a day-by-day account of your life
before you met me. What I don't understand is how he knew so
much about it." Amanda had pulled away enough so that she
could look Lex in the eye, angered by the poorly hidden pain she
could see there.

The rancher swallowed. "It's a small town... my little 'binge' was certainly no secret." She closed her eyes at the gentle touch on her head. "I spent over a month drunk out of my mind... got thrown out of quite a few bars, and was even picked up by the law a time or two. I imagine that everyone in town knows all about it."

Amanda continued to run her fingers through the dark hair. "You were young, and had been terribly hurt emotionally. Didn't anyone try to help you, talk to you?"

"Yeah... right," Lex scoffed, then looked up into green eyes sparkling with unshed tears. "You've got to understand, Amanda. I was young, it's true. But I was so full of anger and hatred at how unfair I thought my life was, that most folks steered clear of me." She blinked, then looked down, afraid to see the expression on the blonde's face. "I had been so nasty to her, even Martha threatened to leave me." She took a ragged breath. "I think that the fear of losing her was what finally snapped me back to reality."

"Oh, sweetheart." Amanda pulled Lex's chin up, so that she could look into her sad blue eyes. "I don't think that Martha could ever leave you...any more than I could." She gave the rancher a gentle kiss.

After returning the kiss, Lex smiled. "God, I love you." She ran a shaky hand down the younger woman's face, then chuckled. "I don't think she was actually going to leave, either. But she did toss a bucket of muddy water on me while I was passed out on the front porch one morning."

Amanda giggled. "I'll bet that went over well." She could almost picture the young rancher's face as Martha dished out her own brand of 'tough-love'. "Wish I had been there to see that."

"If you had been there, I wouldn't have been in that situation," Lex murmured. Taking a deep breath, she started to get up. "Let's go! I think we've got some shopping to do."

"You're right, I need to pick up a few things for tonight." Amanda jumped to her feet, pulling the taller woman up with her.

Lex kept her hold on Amanda's hand as they walked towards the house. "A few things..." she mumbled, feeling the hand in hers tighten. "I thought you were going to help me get something more suitable to wear." Personally, she really didn't care what she wore, but Lex was determined not to embarrass her lover with her choice of clothing.

"Actually..." Amanda grinned, as they walked through the house and up the stairs, "you're all set. I just have to find the right thing to go with what you're wearing." She pulled Lex into the guestroom. "Just let me get my purse, and we'll go." She started to step away, then found herself pulled back into the arms of a grinning rancher.

"Aren't you forgetting something?" Lex asked, pulling the blonde into a tight embrace.

Amanda unconsciously clasped her hands behind the taller woman's neck, smiling up into twinkling blue eyes. "Hmm... you're right. I need to grab the car keys, too."

"Ah... I see." Lex ran her hands lightly up the smaller woman's ribs.

Amanda giggled, squirming slightly. "Aaaack!" She tried to back away, but found herself suddenly lifted into the air, cradled in the rancher's arms like a small child. "Lex! Stop that!"

"Seems to me someone needs her memory refreshed," Lex grinned, slowly carrying her cargo towards the bed.

Kicking her feet, Amanda unsuccessfully tried to break Lex's hold. "You're going to hurt yourself, you nut!" Then she squealed when she was tossed in the air towards the bed. "Aaaah!" Amanda landed on her back in the middle of the large bed, bouncing slightly. Before she could say a word, she was covered with a long, lean body, her wrists held together above her head with one large hand. "Lex...?"

"You know..." Hot breath on her neck caused Amanda to shiver slightly. "I could do this one of two ways..." Lex murmured, bending closer and taking a small bite from Amanda's earlobe.

"W... w... what's that?" the smaller woman gasped out, trying to get her breathing under control and failing miserably.

Lex allowed her free hand to slowly trace down Amanda's trembling body. "I could just torture you until you begged..." She kissed just below the blonde's ear.

Amanda wiggled, causing Lex to straddle her waist. "Uh-huh... and... just what sort of torture... Oh, God!" She felt a warm hand sneak inside her shirt, lightly stroking her belly.

"Hmm..." The rancher pulled away a bit, so she could look into Amanda's flushed face. "Just how much 'torture' can you stand, my little impudent friend?" Lex leaned down and captured the younger woman's lips for a long moment.

Amanda accepted the kiss greedily, trying to pull her hands free so she could tangle them in Lex's hair. "Mmm... Lex..." she mumbled still squirming, but now for an entirely different reason.

Lex pulled away from Amanda's mouth, then began working her way down the slender throat. "You know," she slowly used her free hand to unbutton the bright green shirt, "I bet I can make you beg for mercy..." She began kissing the soft skin just above Amanda's bra.

"Oh... ummm..." Amanda closed her eyes, breathing heavily. "I'll never beg, you... oh, God..." She felt a warm tongue lick lightly at her chest. All thoughts of trying to play the game flew out the window.

"Won't beg, huh?" Lex placed a series of small bites on Amanda's now exposed stomach. "You sure about that?" she gently teased.

"No... you can't make me... ah, Lex..." The younger woman was panting heavily now, as Lex continued to work her way across her belly. "Aaaah!" she squealed, eyes popping open as the rancher's long fingers began tickling her ribs. She wiggled back and forth.

The older woman continued to tickle her unmercifully, grinning wildly. "Heh... say it, Amanda." Her lover was giggling almost uncontrollably now.

"Oh, God, Lex! Stop!" Amanda sputtered out between gales of laughter. "Please!"

Lex stopped, a triumphant grin on her face. "Told you I could make you beg." Then she laughed as Amanda pulled her down for a heated kiss, and the world slipped away.

Chapter
17

Shopping, Lex decided, must have been invented by some poor slob, trying to occupy his wife and keep her out of his hair; because no sane person would actually agree to go through such torture. Slouched in a highly uncomfortable chair, the rancher sighed again as her companion tried on yet another item of clothing. She was stationed directly outside the dressing room door, mumbling replies to the younger woman's questions, as she had been for the past couple of hours.

"Now, before you say anything," Amanda warned, still behind the door, "I know that this is waaaay too formal for tonight, but I just couldn't resist trying it on."

Suddenly, standing in front of Lex was a vision in aqua. The long satin gown hung by spaghetti straps, draping over Amanda's lithe figure seductively.

"Uh..." Lex gasped, swallowing several times. She tried to get words from her brain to her mouth, but her lips couldn't form any. *Wow...*

Amanda turned around and glanced at herself in the mirror, not noticing the look of complete awe on her lover's face. Looking over her shoulder, she asked, "So, what do you think?"

Lex blinked a couple of times, then finally smiled widely.

"Beautiful," she murmured. "Absolutely stunning." She stood up and walked over until she was directly behind the smaller woman. "You've got to get this, sweetheart," she whispered into Amanda's ear, looking over the petite shoulder into the mirror.

"It's too dressy for the dinner tonight – I checked with Jeannie, and she said that most of the guests will be coming in straight from the office. Mother was going to make it a formal affair, but something came up this past week and everyone is having to put in extra time," Amanda explained, enjoying the way the shimmering material brought out the color of Lex's eyes, as she peeked over her bare shoulder.

"I don't care." Lex put her hands on the blonde's shoulders, turning the smaller woman to face her. "I'll find someplace elegant to take you...but you look too beautiful in it *not* to have it." She squeezed Amanda's shoulders gently. "Please? Let me buy it for you."

Amanda looked at the price tag. *Six hundred dollars?! Oh no, I don't think so, my love.* Covering one of Lex's hands with her own, she smiled. "Honey, I really appreciate the thought, but this dress is too expensive for you to waste your money on."

Picking up the tag and peering at it, Lex shrugged. "It can't hold a candle to what you're worth to me." Giving Amanda a thoughtful look, she smiled gently. "How about if I make it a birthday present?"

"My birthday isn't for several months – not that I don't appreciate the thought." Amanda was still blushing, still not used to such bold compliments. "And I really appreciate the sentiment behind it as well." She turned towards the dressing room. "Could you come in and help me with the zipper, please?" This was asked in a voice loud enough for the circling saleswoman to hear.

"Sure." Lex followed her into the small room, latching the door shut behind them. "Turn around and I'll..." The rancher suddenly found herself the recipient of a deep, loving kiss.

Amanda pulled away with a smile. "I love you, Lexington Marie Walters... no one else has ever made me feel as loved and special as you do." She turned so that her back was facing the tall woman. "Now unzip me and we'll get out of here."

Lex grinned and did as she was asked. Running a fingertip

down the exposed smooth back, she chuckled. "We're finally through?"

"Well," Amanda pulled the dress off, slipping into her comfortable khakis, "we can always look around some more, if you want." She looked down shyly as Lex kneeled, offering her help with her shoes. "I feel a little bit like Cinderella, going from that gown back into this." She plucked at the green polo shirt adorning her body. Stepping into the loafers, she watched as Lex tied them for her. "You're going to spoil me, you know."

"All part of my plan to keep you happy, sweetheart." The rancher gently massaged a strong calf. "Besides, I enjoy it too." She stood up and allowed Amanda to exit the dressing room first, grabbing the dress on her way out. "You almost forgot something."

Amanda shook her head. "I'm not going to win this one, am I?" she asked, watching as her lover handed the dress to the now beaming saleswoman.

"Nope." Lex chuckled, then turned to the woman at the cash register. "She's gonna need shoes to match, right?"

The painfully thin woman nodded enthusiastically. "Of course! I can tell you're a woman of refined tastes, Madam." Looking at Amanda, she asked, "what size, dear?"

Amanda smiled, but stepped back a pace. "Oh, no, that's really not necessary – I'm sure I have shoes to match somewhere." She gave Lex a pleading look.

Leaning up against the counter with her arms crossed, Lex smirked. "Size?"

"Six," Amanda sighed, shaking her head.

Leaning over to the saleswoman, the rancher whispered, "I don't care what it costs, make sure they're the most comfortable shoes you can find, okay?"

Dollar signs practically lighting up her eyes, the saleswoman scurried away. "Right away, Madam."

"I'll get you for this," Amanda muttered, watching as the saleswoman returned with a shoebox under one arm.

Lex smiled. "Oh, yeah?" She handed the clerk a credit card. "You can try, but I wouldn't waste money on a fancy dress for me..." she teased, signing for the purchases.

"Thank you, Ms. Walters, for your business. I look forward to serving you again." The saleswoman smiled, handing the hanging bag to Lex.

Amanda giggled at the look on the dark-haired woman's face. "No dress, huh?" She bent down and picked up her other shopping bags. "That's too bad. I could really see you in a slinky red number," the blonde teased, as they made their way out of the shop.

"Oh, no, that would clash with my boots," Lex disagreed, helping Amanda with her bags. "Here, I'll hold these while you unlock the trunk."

"Thanks, honey." Amanda playfully piled all the bags into the taller woman's arms.

Lex juggled the packages, trying to keep from dropping any of them. "Good grief, sweetheart," she barely kept one of the packages from falling to the ground, "I don't remember seeing you buy this much stuff." She balanced a bag on her raised thigh.

"Mandy Cauble? Is that really you?" a high-pitched female voice squealed.

Amanda spun around just in time to be wrapped up in an embrace from a tall woman with dark blonde hair. "Francine?" she asked, shocked.

The woman stepped back a pace, smiling broadly. "Oh, my God! I can't believe it! You look absolutely fantastic!" She kept a firm grasp on the smaller woman's hands, as she bounced up and down excitedly. Stopping to look at the car, she commented, "I'm glad to see you finally retired that old heap you were driving."

"Ah, hell..." Lex murmured, dropping a couple of packages. Squatting down to gather them up, she didn't notice the close scrutiny by Amanda's friend.

Francine eyed the dark-haired woman with a speculative eye. "Mandy, I see you've finally got a driver, too. You knuckle under to the pressure from your mother?" She gave the smaller woman a knowing smile. "I should have known that you'd pick a nice-looking woman. But isn't she dressed a little casual?" Although she was happily married to her high school sweetheart, the tall blonde still appreciated a nice body, and the lanky form gathering up shopping bags certainly fit that bill. *Really good looking... hmm...*

Amanda released Francine's hands, going over to help Lex with the strewn-about packages. "I'm sorry, honey...let me help you get them to the car." She turned to a slack-jawed Francine. "Would you mind opening the trunk? The keys are still in it." She grabbed a couple of bags and winked at Lex. "Francine, I'd like you to meet Lex Walters, the love of my life." She dumped her packages into the trunk, unloading the rancher's arms as well. "Lex, this is Francine Cummings, a really good friend of mine since high school."

Lex held out a hand, smiling broadly. "It's nice to meet you, Francine." She almost blushed at the other woman's close perusal of her.

"My pleasure, Lex." Francine gave her a slow once over, then winked at Amanda. "Honey, if I could find someone like this, I'd dump my husband!" She saw both women turn a deep shade of red. "So, I take it you're only visiting? Something tells me Lex isn't from around here."

The small blonde laughed. "Nope, we're leaving tomorrow. What gave her away?" She stood next to the still blushing rancher, patting her on the arm.

Francine chuckled. "Well, she has the most darling accent..." she laughed out loud. "And yours seems to have picked up quite a bit, as well."

"Yeah, well. I *have* spent the last seven months in Texas," Amanda acknowledged, as she turned towards her old friend.

"Good lord! What happened to you?" Francine suddenly noticed the bruise on Amanda's jaw. "And what does the other guy look like?" she teased.

Amanda ruefully stroked the side of her face, careful of the bruise. "I got mugged at the beach yesterday. But Lex caught him, so everything's okay now."

Francine stepped between the two women, linking an arm with each of them. "C'mon, let's go have a cup of coffee and you can tell me all about it." She led them down the sidewalk, babbling the entire time.

****

"Your friend was really nice," Lex observed quite some time later, totally relaxed as she lounged on the bed in the guestroom. "Chatty as hell, but nice."

Amanda stepped out of the bathroom, clad in only a black slip and matching lace bra. "Yeah, I know. She's one of the few friends I had in high school that didn't dump me when she found out I was gay." She sighed and sat down next to the rancher.

Lex put an arm around the younger woman and pulled her close. "I'm so sorry, love." She kissed the blonde head. "I suppose in that respect, I was a lot luckier than you."

"Really? Why?" Amanda pulled away for a moment, looking into Lex's eyes.

"I didn't have to worry about what anyone thought." Lex gave her lover a small smile. "I pretty much stuck to myself, and didn't have anyone I really considered a friend." She wiped a stray tear from underneath Amanda's sparkling green eyes. "Except for Martha, and the guys at the ranch – and none of them ever judged or ridiculed me." Lex pulled the blonde woman into her lap. "I'm glad that you had Francine, and even Frank," she teased gently.

Amanda wrapped her arms around Lex and sighed. "I had a couple of friends who stuck beside me... although there were quite a few more who acted as if I had the plague. And of course, I also had Gramma and Grandpa Jake. They were the absolute best."

"I take it your folks were in the not-so-happy-to-hear-it crowd, huh?" Lex asked, feeling warm breath on her chest.

"I guess you could say that. They *still* think it's a phase I'm going through." Amanda gave a rueful chuckle. "Mother thinks that I'm gay because Jeannie married Frank, and I'm trying to get back at all of them."

Lex laughed out loud at that revelation. "You poor thing...pining away for your sister's husband." She flinched as she received a poke from a sharp finger. "Ouch! Jeannie was right!"

Amanda sat back a little. "Huh? My sister was right about

what?"

"You *are* a bully!" Lex teased, capturing Amanda's swinging hands in self-defense. "Heh." She fell onto the bed, allowing the younger woman to straddle her hips.

"And *you* are lucky that it's almost time for us to go downstairs for the dinner..." Amanda growled, leaning down to tease Lex with a near kiss. "Otherwise, I'd show you just how much of a bully I can be." She pulled away just as the dark-haired woman raised up to catch her lips. "Teach you to tease me..." She leaned down and dropped a quick kiss, then pulled away quickly with a smile.

Lex lay back on the bed and closed her eyes. "Okay, you win." She released a heavy sigh, and let go of the small hands.

The younger woman shook her head. "I win? You've got to be kidding! You never give up without a... aaaaaah!" Amanda found herself suddenly on her back, with a grinning rancher leaning over her body. "You cheated," she muttered.

"Me? Cheat?" Lex smiled down at her lover. "I can't help it if you let your guard down like that – you shouldn't be so trusting." She leaned down and gave Amanda a loving kiss. "Let's get dressed for this shindig, before your mother busts in here looking for you."

Amanda allowed Lex to help her off the bed, then headed for the closet. "I'll just get your clothes together, then." She stepped out, carrying several items on hangers. "Here you go... time to get ready."

Lex looked at the clothing, and frowned. "Are you sure about this, sweetheart? I really don't want to upset your parents any more than they already are."

"I'm perfectly sure! It will go very well with what I'm wearing – I want you to be comfortable, you know." Amanda handed her the hangers, and smiled. "Trust me. You'll look great." She went over to the shopping bags that were sitting in the corner. "Let me slip this stuff on, and you'll see what I mean." She carried two of the bags into the bathroom and closed the door.

Sighing, Lex took the clothing off the hangers and began to get dressed. *I hope she knows what she's doing.*

Chapter
18

Milling around through the large group of people, Jeannie searched for her husband, murmuring her apologies to yet another nosy business associate of her father's. "Yes, Amanda is here, Mr. Cross... she should be arriving any moment now." She quickly stepped away from the large, sweating man, who had always seemed quite enamored of her younger sister. *Like she'd ever give your creepy butt a second look,* she thought, flinching away from his hand as it came perilously close to her rear end.

"There you are, sweetheart," a warm voice whispered in her ear, as a hand lightly patted her bottom.

Spinning quickly, Jeannie almost slapped her husband. "Frank!" she growled, pushing him in the chest. "Where on earth have you been?" Forgetting her anger immediately, she eyed her husband's sturdy form appreciatively. The black denim hugged his hips and legs well, and the gray tab collar shirt fit his broad shoulders like a glove. "You look great, honey," she smiled at him. *Every day I love him more and more...I think it was love at first sight, for me.*

Jeannie had teased her little sister unmercifully about her latest 'friend'. She had yet to meet the mysterious Frank Rivers, a transfer student who was in the same grade as she, but she had heard from her friends that he was tall, broad shouldered, and extremely handsome.

She was sitting in the study one evening poring over chemistry books, trying to prepare herself for a test the next morning, when she heard her little sister's voice in the foyer.

"Frank, c'mon... just because I'm a freshman, it doesn't mean I don't know anything about history. I love the time period during World War II. Let me help you write your paper, and you can help me with my biology paper. Deal?"

A deep chuckle answered her. "Mandy, I swear, you should become a lawyer – I'll never be able to get the upper hand in an argument with you." He allowed the blonde girl to lead him through the foyer and into another room. "You win... just don't tell anyone, okay? I'd hate to have to expl..." he stopped there, as they entered a large room with bookcases lining the walls. But the room wasn't what caught his attention... the young woman propped in one corner of a large chair near the fireplace almost took his breath away.

Amanda looked up at her friend, startled by his sudden silence. "Frank? Hey... what's..." Then she noticed where his eyes were. Oh... well, isn't this interesting? she grinned to herself.

Jeannie, for her part, was caught off guard just as much as the sturdy looking young man on the other side of the room. WHEW!! THAT'S Mandy's new friend? She didn't tell me he looked like a Greek god... she felt her mouth go dry, and her heart start to pound. "Hel... hello, Mandy... I thought I heard you come in," she managed to utter. "Who's your friend?"

After Amanda made the introductions, she silently left the room, neither of them noticing her absence. It didn't take them long to realize that they had a lot in common, in particular one cute little blonde, who never let them live it down that she had brought them together.

And for that, Jeannie mused, *I will be eternally grateful,* as she caught the adoring look her handsome husband bestowed upon her.

"Thanks, baby." The big man leaned over and gave his wife a gentle kiss on the lips. "You look absolutely gorgeous yourself." Jeannie was wearing a knee-length dark green skirt complemented by a pale yellow silk top, which had already brought her mother's wrath down upon her.

"What in heaven's name are you wearing? This is a dinner, not a sock-hop. I demand that you go and change immediately!" Elizabeth had stopped her oldest daughter at the doorway to the sitting room, her voice shaking with anger. She herself was wearing a dark lavender evening gown, which to Jeannie's eyes was far too formal for a simple dinner party.

"Sorry, Mother, this is all I have. And it still looks nicer than some of the wrinkled business suits I've seen tonight." Jeannie stood firm, knowing that her mother would get over her little fit soon enough. "Now if you'll excuse me, I have to mingle." She slipped by the older woman and began greeting her father's business associates.

"I'm glad someone thinks so! Mother wasn't quite so impressed." Jeannie gave her husband a wry smile.

"Yeah, I saw the look your mother gave you." Frank pulled her to him, wrapping his arm around Jeannie's waist. "Don't let her get to you, sweetheart. You look fantastic." Seeing a movement by the door, Frank turned his head. "Whoa," he exclaimed quietly, drawing his wife's attention in the same direction.

She craned her head over the crowd. "What...?" Taking a deep breath, Jeannie smiled. "Oh, wow..."

Amanda had stepped into the room, her partner following close behind. She was wearing a black denim skirt that fell to just below her knees, and a slightly oversized dark green silk shirt, which brought out the color of her eyes. The young blonde reached behind her body and grabbed her lover's arm, pulling Lex with her into the room. Jeannie's jaw almost hit the floor when she saw the rancher. The dark-haired woman was wearing pressed black denim jeans, shiny black boots, and a royal blue satin shirt that made her sapphire eyes stand out like twin points of light.

Frank gave out a low whistle. "They make a good-looking couple, don't they?" he whispered into his wife's ear. He caught Amanda's eye and waved them over.

The two women made their way across the crowded room. "Hey, guys," Amanda greeted, smiling warmly at them. "You both look great!" she said, giving them a wink.

"Damn, Mandy! You didn't tell us that you two would be looking so good," Frank teased, watching as a blush covered Lex's face. With her boots on, the rancher was almost as tall as he was. *I do believe little Amanda picked a winner... she's certainly something else,* he marveled to himself. "Have you seen..."

"It's about time you made it downstairs – people have been asking about you for the past twenty minutes," Elizabeth Cauble snapped, stepping between her youngest daughter and Frank. Looking at Amanda's clothes, she sniffed, "are you and your sister trying to ruin this family's reputation? How much is it to ask that you dress properly for a social function?" She was about to continue when a very distinguished older gentleman stepped forward into their little group.

"Elizabeth... don't tell me these two lovely young women are your daughters?" He took Amanda's hands into his and brought one to his lips. "Amanda Cauble... I swear you look more and more like your lovely grandmother, Anna Leigh, every time I see you." He gave her a wink over her knuckles.

Amanda smiled broadly, removing her hands from his and then stepping into his arms for a hug. "Uncle John... it's so good to see you again." She pulled away and grabbed the rancher's arm. "I want you to meet my very close friend, Lexington Walters. Lex, this is John Grayson, an old friend of my grandparents."

The tall, gray-haired man held out his hand, which Lex took and gave a hearty handshake. "It's a pleasure to meet you, sir," she smiled, enjoying the look of disgust from Elizabeth. *Gee, sorry about that, Mom... seems like everyone else here likes the way that Amanda looks.*

"So you're the young lady who saved Amanda's life." He smiled back, and noticed the look of pure adoration coming from the young blonde. "I spoke to Jacob just last week on the phone, and he told me all about Mandy's latest adventures."

Lex felt a blush rise up her neck. *Damn! Word spreads around these people quicker than a brushfire.* "Just happened to be in the right place at the right time," she said, embarrassed by the attention.

The older man laughed. "And modest, too. Well, whatever you want to call it, you have our deepest appreciation, Ms. Walters."

"Please... call me Lex, Mr. Grayson," the rancher offered, seeing Amanda's face light up in response.

"Only if you'll call me John, young lady." He gave her a knowing grin. "Perhaps I'll see you at Anna Leigh's big pre-Christmas get-together this year, Lex."

Lex glanced over at Amanda, who was nodding, a huge smile on her face. "Umm... you just might, sir."

"Excellent!" he boomed, patting her on the shoulder. Looking to Amanda he said, "Mandy, I'm sure I'll see you later." He accepted another hug from the young woman, then took a gentle grip on Jeannie's arm. "C'mon, sweetheart, tell me what you've been up to lately." He walked off with her and Frank in tow.

Elizabeth glared at the retreating man's back, then stepped up into Lex's face. "Don't think that you can fool everyone here," she whispered. "My husband will find out what you're after, sooner or later." She spun around and made her way into the group of people, greeting them with insincere words.

"What did she say to you, honey?" Amanda asked, seeing the look of resigned acceptance cross her lover's face.

Lex looked down at Amanda and gave her a small smile. "Nothing important..." She looked towards the other end of the room. "Umm... looks like they're moving everyone out." She tried desperately to change the subject.

"Good, that will give us a minute to ourselves." Amanda waited until the room had cleared, then led Lex over to the loveseat. "Sit down with me for a moment, okay?"

"Are you sure? I'd hate to make your mother more angry at you right now." Lex was concerned about the matriarch's attitude. She could handle Elizabeth's wrath as long as it was directed at her, but she didn't want to subject her partner to any more of the woman's hateful outbursts.

Amanda chuckled. "It's going to take her at least ten minutes to get everyone seated like she wants... she'll never miss us." Sobering, she reached out a hand and pulled the older woman to sit down beside her. "Lex...please don't shut me out. Anything that has to do with you is important to me." Amanda pulled their linked hands to her chest, leaning down to kiss the rancher's knuckles. "I know that my mother said something completely out of line to you. Please tell me." She gave Lex a determined look. "Or I'll just ask her myself."

"No!" Lex shook her head adamantly. "I don't want you to get into another argument with her just because of me." She looked at their hands, which were now in the younger woman's lap. "She just said that your father will keep trying to find out what I want with you," Lex finished quietly. "They seem to think I'm after your money."

"Dammit!" Amanda jumped up, only being held back by the strong grip Lex still had on her hand. "I'm going in there right now and give them both a piece of my mind!"

Lex pulled her down. "Sweetheart, as much as I appreciate your defense of my honor, let me handle them, okay?" Averting another outburst from Amanda, Lex continued, "and even though I don't want to sink to their level, I've got an idea on how to answer their questions." She smiled warmly. "So don't worry, love, I'll take care of everything."

Amanda looked into Lex's eyes, then leaned forward until their foreheads were touching, and gave the rancher a tender kiss. "Okay, I'll let you handle it. But don't expect me to stand by and watch them continue to treat you badly." She gave Lex another kiss. "Because I can't do that."

"Do you think you two can control yourselves long enough to join us for dinner?" Michael Cauble's disgusted voice carried across the sitting room.

Lex stood, then calmly led Amanda across the room, not releasing the younger woman's hand. Stopping at the doorway to look down on the angry, smaller man, she gave him a cold smile. "Thank you for coming to get us, Michael." She stressed his name, daring him to say something. "I know that you usually have one of the servants do that, but I really appreciate the personal touch." Lex patted him on the shoulder with her free hand, as she and Amanda stepped past him and started towards the dining room.

"What was that all about?" Amanda whispered, as she and Lex walked down the quiet hallway.

"Just the first part of my plan, sweetheart." Lex leaned over as they were walking and kissed the blonde head. *No more Ms. Nice... time to play some hardball,* she grinned to herself. *And I'm gonna enjoy every damned minute of it, too.*

Before stepping into the dining room, Lex tried to release Amanda's hand, but the younger woman held on stubbornly. With a mental shrug, Lex decided to stir things up a little. Reaching their designated places, she gave Amanda a quick grin and pulled out the smaller woman's chair for her.

Blushing slightly, the blonde chuckled. "Thanks." Out of the corner of her eye, Amanda saw her mother narrow her eyes. *Uh-oh... I don't know what Lex is up to, but I think it's working.*

Lex traded grins with Frank, who was seated directly across from her. Looking around the table, she could tell that the only person who 'dressed' for the dinner was Elizabeth; most of the guests were wearing business suits. She gave the smirking Jeannie a wink and sat down beside her partner.

"Since we are all *finally* seated," Michael Cauble was standing at the head of the table, addressing the group, "I would like to thank all of you for attending this evening..."

As his voice droned on, the man sitting next to Lex chuckled. "He threatened us with the loss of our jobs if we didn't show up for this little function," he whispered to her. "Jeremy down there," he nodded towards a thin, nervous looking young man who kept checking his watch, "well, his wife went into the hospital late this afternoon. She's in labor with their first child." Shaking his head in disgust, he then offered his hand to the rancher. "My name's Mark Garrett – I handle all of the accounts in the Southwest."

"Lexington Walters, but you can call me Lex. I'm a friend of Amanda's," the rancher offered, giving the dark-haired man's hand a firm shake. "You say you're in charge of the Southwest? Where are you based?" she asked, curious. *Hmm... I didn't know that – I thought he only had the one office here in Los Angeles... interesting.*

"Santa Fe, New Mexico – for the moment, at least. But I've been trying to talk Mr. Cauble into moving the office to Dallas... the weather's a little milder there." Mark lowered his voice, "You'd think that since he has family in Texas, that he'd be thrilled to have an office nearby."

Lex nodded. "Have you worked for Mr. Cauble very long?" It was nice to have a friendly face at the dinner table tonight, she mused. Glancing at her partner, Lex could see that Amanda was engrossed in a conversation with her sister.

Mark nodded. "About six years. I'm hoping to open my own office someday." He gave the rancher a grim look. "I've been offered a job here in Los Angeles, but if I'm going to relocate, it will have to be someplace without smog or crime."

"I don't blame you a bit, Mark. I can't wait to get home, myself," Lex agreed, pushing her food around on her plate. "What is this stuff, anyway? Looks like it isn't quite dead, yet."

"Lex! Quit playing with your food," Amanda leaned over and whispered, as she noticed that the older woman had 'fenced off' the main course with her vegetables.

Sighing, Lex put her fork down. "I just didn't want it to get away, that's all," she muttered.

Amanda shook her head and traded looks with Jeannie. "At least try to eat some of it, honey," she murmured. "We'll raid the refrigerator later, I promise." Looking around the table, she was somewhat relieved to see that Lex wasn't the only one not eating the dinner. *I hate when Mother decides to experiment with the menu! Last time I broke out in hives. Yuck!*

"Lex," Mark studied the dark-haired woman carefully, "are you in the real estate business too?"

She almost choked on her water. "Uh... no. What made you think that I was, Mark?"

"Well, you said you were a friend of Amanda's, and you seem too 'normal' to have come from the same social circles that Mrs. Cauble usually frequents." Mark gave her a friendly smile.

"I just assumed that you had met her through the real estate office, that's all."

Lex returned his smile with a somewhat mischievous one of her own. "As a matter of fact, we did sorta meet that way. She came out to try and put my ranch on the market." Pausing to let that sink in, she then continued, "shame that I didn't know I was supposed to be selling it at the time." She winked at him.

Choking on his wine, Mark gasped for a moment before he could ask, "tenacious, isn't she?"

"Yeah, she is. But this wasn't actually her idea – her manager sent her on a wild goose chase."

"Really?" Mark looked intrigued. "So, you're a rancher? No offense, Lex, but I was under the impression that most ranches today are run by corporations – because there's not enough money in it for the average person to make any kind of profit from it." The dark-haired woman gave him an icy glare. *Oh, hell... I definitely put my foot in my mouth this time.* "No, wait!" he held up a hand to placate her rising temper. "I honestly didn't mean anything by it... I was just curious." Seeing her calm down, he added, "sorry about that, Lex. My mouth tends to overrun my mind most of the time."

"No, my fault – I'm a little sensitive on that subject right now." Feeling a gentle touch on her leg, Lex turned to face Amanda.

"What's up?" the younger woman asked, concerned.

"Nothing... Mark and I were just discussing the ranching business." She reached under the table and covered Amanda's hand with her own. "You doing okay?" Glancing around, the rancher noticed that most of the people had finished eating, or at least finished pushing the food around on their plates. "Is this all there is to their damned dinner? You had to fly all the way across the country for half-cooked," she looked down at her plate, "whatever the hell this is supposed to be, and a few insults?"

Amanda gave her a small grin. "I think that it was more of an excuse to get me home than anything else. I wouldn't be here if I hadn't already planned to come and pack my stuff up – especially with the way they've been treating you." She squeezed the hand that she held. "I'm really sorry about all of that."

"Don't worry about it. I'm just glad you didn't have to face them alone." Lex let the younger woman lean against her and just enjoyed the contact; she'd been feeling quite out of sorts since this entire evening began. *I really don't know how I survived all these years alone without her,* she thought to herself.

* CLINK, CLINK, CLINK! *

All heads turned towards the front of the table where Michael Cauble was standing, tapping his wineglass with a knife to get everyone's attention. "Ladies and gentlemen, once again I would like to thank all of you for attending our dinner this evening, and for making this another very successful quarter." He held up his glass of wine. "I'd like to propose a toast to each and every one of you for a job well done." Waiting until everyone raised his or her glasses, he took a sip, then lifted the wine into the air once again. "And I would also like to express my gratitude to my wonderful family, because without their love and support I would not be the man that I am today." He gave Elizabeth an insincere smile. "To my beautiful wife, and my two lovely daughters," he nodded to Jeannie and Amanda, "who are the greatest blessings a man can have."

Lex covered her mouth with her napkin, stifling a chuckle. *Damn! He's spreading more fertilizer than we have in the entire south pasture,* she thought ruefully. Flinching at the elbow in her ribs, she coughed. "Ahem...uh...yes?" Giving Amanda an innocent look.

"Behave." Green eyes flashed dangerously.

Finishing his little speech, Michael stepped away from the table. "If you will all excuse me, I have some unfinished business to attend to. Feel free to have coffee or brandy in the sitting room." Once he left the room, everyone at the table seemed to breathe a sigh of relief. Conversations began in earnest, as many of the guests prepared to leave for the evening.

"I'll see you in a bit, okay? I want to have a word or two with your father," Lex whispered into Amanda's ear, then kissed it discreetly. She stood up, and placed a hand on the younger woman's shoulder. "It shouldn't take but a couple of minutes. Why don't you enjoy the company for a while?"

"Okay, but if you're not out of there in ten minutes, I'm

coming in after you," Amanda smiled up at the rancher. "Remember, we've got to leave pretty early in the morning – so you've got to get into bed at a decent hour."

Lex grinned, causing the blonde to blush. "Uh-huh... I certainly plan to," she winked. "See you in a little bit, okay?" She left the room before Amanda could say anything else.

Chapter
19

Michael sat at his desk, studying over the latest fax from his private investigator. *Bank statements... now we're getting somewhere,* he smiled to himself, thinking that he had finally got his hands on the proof he had been waiting for. But before he could begin to look at the numbers, a strong knock came at the door.

Damn... "Who is it?" he snarled, angry at the interruption. *Stupid servants... when will they learn, 'not to be disturbed' means to leave me the hell alone!*

The door opened, and a dark head poked in, as Lex walked into the room. "Ah... there you are. I think we have some things that need to be cleared up." She strode over to one of the chairs in front of his desk and sat down.

"Make yourself comfortable, Walters," he snapped sarcastically, attempting to casually hide the papers he had been trying to study. "What is it that you want? I'm a very busy man, you know."

Lex smirked, then stretched long legs out in front of her, crossing her booted feet at the ankles. "I think that it's about time we came to an understanding, Michael." She enjoyed the way he flushed with anger.

"Really? And just how to you propose that we do that? Are

you planning on leaving my daughter alone?" Michael spat, tearing off his glasses and tossing them onto the desk. He felt a sudden surge of fear as the dark-haired woman jumped suddenly to her feet, then leaned forward with her hands braced on the desk.

"Let's quit playing stupid little games, Mike," she said in a low tone. "Just what in the hell is your problem with me?" Lex continued to lean forward until she was just inches away from Michael's face. "Is it because I'm a woman? Or is it the fact that I actually *work* for a living? What is it about me that bothers you so damned much?"

Michael stood up and stepped around the desk, trying to distance himself from the imposing figure. "Because you're a woman? No." He went over and poured himself a drink, gulping the amber liquid down with a single swallow. Turning to face her, he grimaced. "Unlike Elizabeth, I have resigned myself to the fact that my youngest daughter is unnatural. There's not much I can do about that. But," he pointed the empty glass in the rancher's direction, "I can try to make her see reason when it comes to dirt-poor farmers trying to sink their claws into her bank account!" He filled the glass again, then drained it quickly.

Lex leaned against the desk, arms crossed. "Dirt-poor farmer?" she laughed. "Number one – I'm a rancher. Second – I have no designs on Amanda's money." She stood up straight and walked over to Michael, standing only a step away from the shorter man. "Third – I have more than enough money of my own; I certainly have no need for yours." She got right into his face and spoke. "Last, but not least, I love her with everything that I am...nothing you can do will change that." Hands grasped in her shirt took Lex by surprise, as she felt Michael pull her closer.

****

Amanda stood at the doorway, trying to listen to the sounds within. Not hearing anything, she opened the door just in time to see her father grab Lex by the shirt and slam her into the bar. Before she could say anything, Michael had punched her lover in the face. "Stop it!" she shouted, scrambling across the room, trying to pull her livid father off Lex. "Daddy! Let her go, now!"

She tugged at his sleeve.

Michael Cauble shook his head to clear it, and then pushed the tall woman backwards again, happy to see that he was at least able to do some damage to her before his daughter interfered. "Get out of my house… you're not welcome here," he muttered, secretly hoping that the tall woman would try and retaliate. *Then maybe Amanda would see her as I do… damned arrogant piece of trash.*

"Gladly." Lex pushed by him, wiping her bloody mouth and chin with the back of her hand. She started for the door, trying to control her anger. *Narrow-minded bastard… if he wasn't Amanda's father, I would…* her thoughts ended there as she felt a small hand touch her arm.

Amanda was able to stop her before she got to the door. "Oh, honey…" She took a strong grip on the rancher's arm and led her from the office, not bothering to acknowledge her seething father's presence. "C'mon…let's go upstairs and get you cleaned up, okay?" She slowly led the quiet woman up the stairs.

Lex allowed her lover to lead her to the guestroom, not even realizing it when she was pushed down onto the bed. *That son of a bitch, he's more worried about his damned money than he is his own daughter! I should have throttled him when I had the chance! No… he is her father… I can't do that to her.* Lex's mind continued to whirl as the younger woman stepped into the bathroom, returning with a damp washcloth and placing it onto her still bleeding mouth. "Amanda?" She finally focused on the concerned green eyes in front of her.

"Yes, I'm here, love." Amanda continued to dab at the oozing cut, wincing at the swelling and light bruising that was already appearing. "Are you okay?"

The rancher took stock of her body. "Umm… yeah, I think so." She looked into the worried face standing above her. "Yeah, I'm okay. How about you?" She was still shaking from the effort it took not to strangle the older man that was still in the office. *Damn… I gotta get this under control.*

Amanda sat down on the bed, pulling Lex close to her. "I'm *fine*. Why did my father attack you like that?" She leaned against the headboard of the bed, waiting until the older woman got comfortable before continuing. "I've never seen him so angry! He's never been the violent type before." Amanda had pulled Lex into her arms, allowing the dark head to rest on her chest, as she held the washcloth to her lover's mouth with one hand.

Lex sighed, allowing the anger to slowly seep away, leaving behind a sad weariness. "I guess I pushed him a little too far. I just wanted to find out why he hated seeing us together." She relaxed as she felt a gentle stroking of her hair. *It's taking every ounce of control I have not to go in there and toss him on his ass, after that arrogant bastard called his own daughter 'unnatural',* she fumed silently.

"What did he say?" Amanda whispered gently, continuing her stroking as she felt the body that was lying partially on her own tense up again. "It's okay, love... nothing he said could change what I feel for you." She leaned over and kissed the top of the dark head. "Or what you mean to me."

Closing her eyes, Lex allowed herself to absorb the love emanating from the younger woman, as she gently moved the washcloth away from her face. "He is bound and determined that I'm after your money... guess the only way I can change his mind about that is to send him my bank statements, or something." She took a deep breath, then released it slowly. "I'm sorry about this, sweetheart. I just wish you didn't have to be a witness to that little scene."

"Honey, look at me, please." Amanda forced Lex's face upward, until their eyes met. "What would you have done if I hadn't pulled my father away?" She searched the blue eyes, trying to find a clue to what the older woman was thinking. "Would you have fought back?"

Lex shook her head. "I don't know." She saw the love and determination in the face above her, and then looked down. "God knows I wanted to...I wanted to toss him across the room for what he said about you, and for the way they've treated you." She felt the hand on her head stop moving, then tugged her close.

Amanda felt tears begin to trail down her face as she pulled the rancher closer to her, realizing just how much Lex had figured out about her home life. *They say it's the quiet ones you have to worry about the most, because they usually notice all the little things,* she thought to herself. "It doesn't matter anymore," she murmured, feeling her defenses finally shatter completely. "I don't care what they say or do! As long as we're together, it just doesn't matter." She began to cry in earnest, then felt herself being lifted and cradled in strong arms.

****

Sitting at his desk after his daughter and 'that woman' had left, Michael shook his head. *I've lost...that damned bitch has my daughter, and I'll never make the girl see reason about her.* He angrily shuffled through the papers on his desk. *Guess there's no real sense in keeping these, now...*he thought, about to throw them away. "Ah, what the hell... I paid good money to see this, might as well look at it." Letting his eyes scan the pages, he felt the color drain from his face. "No... it's not possible," he mumbled, trying to catch his breath.

"Michael, you must simply come out of this office and tell our guests goodnight." Elizabeth stood at the door, with a pained look on her face. "They've finished up all the good brandy and scotch, and are getting quite tipsy." She saw the expression on his face and stepped further into the room. "What is it?"

The pale businessman looked up at his wife. "We were wrong, Elizabeth." He looked like he was in shock.

"Wrong? What in heaven's name are you babbling about?" She walked over to the desk and stood next to him, placing her hand on his shoulder. "Quit sounding like an idiot and tell me." She accepted the papers he handed her, a puzzled look on her face.

"Read that." Michael rubbed his eyes with one hand. *Dear God... she could ruin me...*

Elizabeth looked over the papers as reality slammed her hard. "You mean to tell me that uncouth farmer actually *owns* major stock in one of your subsidiaries? How is this possible?" She felt her legs weaken, as her husband stood and guided her to the loveseat nearby.

"From what I've read, it seems that her mother was a very wealthy woman before she married... when she died, her very sizable inheritance was divided among her three children. After the youngest child died, his portion was split up between the two remaining offspring. It appears that Walters," he still choked on the name, "turned the majority of her money over to an investment broker, and he made several wise plays on the stock market. Just happens that one of the investments is in my business." Michael shook his head. "If she finds out about this and pulls her support, I could go under."

"Good lord above! I wouldn't be able to show my face again! Imagine the humiliation!" Elizabeth fretted, then glared at her husband. "What are you going to do about it?" She glanced down and noticed the bruise and scrape on his knuckle. "What happened to your hand?" Seeing the look on his face, she paled. "Oh, no... you didn't..."

Michael stood up, then paced over to the bar and poured two glasses of scotch. Silently he walked over to the loveseat and sat down, handing his wife a glass. "I'm afraid I did. The damned woman made me so angry, I didn't even think about it." He tipped the glass up and drained it. "But I have to admit it felt really good, punching that smirk off her face."

Elizabeth took a sip of her drink, then let out a heavy breath. "Damage control... that's what we need now." She glared at her husband again. "You should apologize immediately!" *I can't believe this is happening...*

"No... that would probably make her realize that something's up. We need to be subtle about all of this." He chewed his lip in concentration. "I found out from the upstairs maid that they are planning on leaving first thing in the morning – we'll just let them go, and hope to God that she doesn't realize the power she holds." He nodded to himself. "If worse comes to worst, we'll get Amanda to keep her in line – for some reason, she seems to listen to our daughter."

"Very well, but you'd better be ready to beg for forgiveness from this woman if she ever finds out." She gave him a small smile. "Because money isn't the only thing that you would lose if she destroys you, dear." Elizabeth patted her husband on the cheek, then stood and left the room, feeling his eyes on her as she closed the door.

Chapter
20

Bright, early morning sunlight beamed down on the tall figure placing bags in the trunk of the red convertible. Lex gave the last bag a gentle shove, wondering how in the hell they were able to get them in there to begin with. *I thought she sent most of her stuff with the movers – we didn't have this much stuff before, did we?*

"Everything about loaded up?" Small, strong arms circled her waist from behind. "Frank and Jeannie should be out to say goodbye in a few minutes." Amanda pulled the tall woman close, burying her face into the broad back.

Lex stood up straight, then turned slowly. "Yep... that was the last of it." She wrapped her arms around the blonde and grinned. "Although we may have to pay freight charges for all the luggage." Leaning down, she placed a tender kiss on Amanda's mouth. Her own mouth was quite sore, and the two of them sported similar bruises on their faces. *We are definitely a matched set,* Lex thought to herself as she ran a gentle fingertip along the smaller woman's jaw. "Did you run a final check for any missing underwear?" she teased, seeing her lover blush.

"How was I supposed to know that you threw them behind the chair? I swear, Sophia giggled for hours after finding them,"

Amanda grouched, remembering the note from Beverly that
stated that she needed to keep better track of her 'unmention-
ables' so she wouldn't distract the rest of the household staff.
Looking up, she saw Lex trying not to smile. "Stop that," she
commanded. "You're going to make your lip start bleeding
again." She raised a small hand and ran her thumb lightly across
the bruised lip. "Maybe you need a stitch or two."

Kissing the thumb offered to her, Lex shook her head.
"Nah... it'll be okay." She was about to prove her point when a
voice echoed across the cool, still morning.

"You two never seem to get enough, do you?" Jeannie
teased, walking through the door with Frank. "Guess it'll just be
us seeing you off... Mother is upstairs with a migraine, and
Father is on an overseas call."

Amanda stepped away from Lex, and embraced her older
sister. "It's probably for the best, anyway. Thanks for everything,
Jeannie. I really appreciate how you've accepted Lex." She felt a
twinge of sadness at leaving.

The auburn-haired woman held her sister tightly. "I'm just
glad you finally found the person you've been looking for,
Mandy." Realizing that this was probably the last time she'd see
her little sister for quite awhile, she murmured, "I know you
probably won't be coming back to this house any time soon," *If
ever,* her mind supplied, "but Frank and I have plenty of room, if
you two would like to come and visit."

"Thanks, Jeannie." Amanda pulled away a bit and glanced
over her shoulder. Seeing the rancher give a nod, she smiled.
"Next vacation you two get, why don't you come out to the ranch
with us," she asked, feeling a large welling of pride at that statement. *Our ranch... I think I really like the sound of that.*

Lex stepped up and grinned. "Yeah... we've got quite a bit
of room ourselves." Looking over the two sisters' heads, she
winked at Frank. "And I won't even make you muck out any
stalls."

The big man stepped forward and pulled Amanda into a
fierce embrace. "Take care, Mandy! We'll try to stop by and see
you two real soon, okay?"

Amanda felt her heart surge with love for her brother-in-law and dear friend. "That would be great."

"What are your plans around Christmas?" Lex asked, shaking hands with Frank. Seeing the happy look on Amanda's face, she mentally patted herself on the back. *Good one, Lexington. You just might figure all of this out yet.*

Frank looked over at his wife, who shrugged. "Well, I was planning on hiding," he winked at the rancher. "Why do you ask?"

Lex put her arm around the tall man, and escorted him over to the two smiling sisters. "Well, since it's gonna be Amanda's first Christmas out at the ranch, I thought maybe you two would like to join us... I'm hoping to have a houseful."

Amanda looked over at her partner with adoring eyes. "A houseful, huh?" She stepped away from Jeannie and nearly flew into the older woman's arms. "Anyone I know?"

"Well, let's see... you and me, Martha and Charlie, your grandparents, the Wades..." Lex glanced over at the other couple. "And of course Frank and Jeannie, if they're willing."

Jeannie laughed, then pulled her sister away from Lex. "I don't know about Frank, but I'd love to be there!" She wrapped her arms around the dark-haired woman and laughed. Feeling the strong arms pull her close, she whispered into the nearest ear, "thank you, Lex. I've never seen my sister so happy." She pulled away a bit, then kissed the blushing woman on the cheek. "Welcome to the family, Slim."

Lex sighed, then a smirk crossed her face. *Ah, what the hell.* Seeing Amanda grin too, she kissed Jeannie full on the mouth. "Thanks, sis." She almost laughed out loud at the deep flush covering the woman's face.

Frank laughed so hard, he had to hold on to Amanda to keep from falling down. "Damn, Lex, you trying to kill me?" He saw his wife begin to stalk towards him, and raised his hands ineffectually against her attack. "Honey, wait!" he chuckled, as Jeannie slapped at him.

"Sorry, Frank, but any woman who pinches my butt gets a kiss," Lex teased, allowing Amanda to snuggle close. She pulled the younger woman towards the car. "I hate to kiss and run," she winked at Jeannie, "but our plane leaves in about an hour and a

half." She allowed her lover to get into the car, still giggling.
"We'll make up an extra spot in the barn at Christmas for y'all,
okay?" Lex ducked as Amanda's sister tossed her shoe at her,
laughing.

****

Lex took a panicked breath as she boarded the plane. *C'mon,
Lexington, you can do this. It's no different than the last time,*
she berated herself, as she felt a cold chill run down her spine.
She allowed Amanda to take the seat by the window, so that she
could stretch her long legs out in the aisle of the plane. Sitting
down, she felt a small hand grasp hers and hold on tightly.

"You doing all right, love?" Amanda looked up into the
unusually pale face, her heart aching for the upset she could feel
from her partner.

"No problem." Lex gave her lover a tiny smile, then took a
deep breath as the flight attendant closed the door on the plane.
Breathe, dammit... She listened as the ventilation system pumped
air into the plane. *See? You're not gonna suffocate, so just get
over it, idiot!* the rancher mentally chastised.

Amanda pulled a strong hand towards her, until she was able
to cradle it against her chest. Kissing the knuckles, she whispered, "it's okay, Lex." She gently, but firmly, turned the older
woman's to face her. "Look at me, honey." She waited until the
rancher complied. "Listen to my voice, okay? It's just you and
me..." Amanda felt the plane begin to taxi down the runway, but
Lex was totally transfixed on her. "Have I told you about the
time that I accidentally locked Jeannie in the trunk of the limousine? Mother nearly had a cow..." She told her partner about the
tale of two young girls, playing hide and seek, and of the complete embarrassment of a well-to-do woman that had sent her
driver to meet an important artist at the airport, only to have the
artist greeted by a crying girl in the trunk of the expensive limousine.

The story took up almost half of the flight, with Amanda
embellishing it several times to make it last. When she noticed
blue eyes disappearing under heavy eyelids, she finally just
snuggled up against the tall woman and closed her eyes. Lex

smiled lovingly down upon the blonde head. *Poor thing... this week has been really rough for her. Maybe I can do something to make up for that.* She allowed her head to lean onto the blonde one next to her, and closed her eyes.

"Ma'am? The plane has landed..." The lovely young flight attendant gently jostled Lex's shoulder, trying to wake her up.

Lex opened her eyes and noticed the empty plane, and the young woman smiling down on her. "Umm... thanks." She gave the woman an embarrassed smile. "We'll be out of here in just a second."

The uniformed lady smiled. "No real hurry. I just wanted to make sure you didn't have another flight to catch." She was folding up a blanket from a nearby seat. "If you need anything, just let me know." She gave the rancher a knowing grin, then moved down the aisle.

Oh, boy... good thing Amanda slept through that! "Sweetheart?" Lex whispered gently. "Amanda, we've landed." She kissed the head that was snuggled against her, using her free hand to brush the blonde hair away from blinking eyes.

"Mmm..." Amanda leaned up and placed a kiss on Lex's mouth. As she stretched, she realized where they were. "Oh! Did you say we've landed?" she blushed. "I was having the most incredible dream." She released Lex's hand and rubbed her face.

"Obviously," Lex smirked, standing up and stretching. Her back cracked several times as she raised her arms over her head and leaned backwards. "Damn! I hate sitting for that long." She noticed her appreciative audience. "See something you like, ma'am?" Lex teased her partner.

Amanda stood up, running a hand through her disheveled blonde hair. "You could say that!" She caught the look from the flight attendant. "And I don't think I'm the only one, either." The younger woman smiled, then wrapped her arms around the rancher and squeezed. "But she'll just have to be content to enjoy you from a distance, 'cause I'm not sharing."

Lex chuckled. "Fine by me." She enveloped the smaller woman in a fierce hug. "I love you, Amanda," she whispered, as she buried her face in the fragrant blonde hair.

"I love you too, Lex." Amanda pulled away and smiled

brightly. "You ready to go home?" Then she frowned a little. "Um, would you mind too much…"

"If we went to see your grandparents first?" the rancher smiled. "I was just going to suggest that." She carefully escorted her lover down the narrow aisles. "Let them know you survived, and then we can tell them that you're going to be moving in at the ranch." As they left the plane, Lex turned towards Amanda, who was about half a step behind her. "I enjoyed your story, by the way – forgot all about the plane."

Amanda hitched her purse up on her shoulder, then took an extra step to be directly next to the taller woman. "Really? Thanks… sorry I fell asleep on you, though." She looked up into amused blue eyes. "What?"

"Don't feel bad – I fell asleep too. The flight attendant had to wake me up after the plane was already empty." Lex looked around, trying to read the signs. "Where the hell do we pick up the damned luggage?" She spotted a map of the airport and walked over to check it out. Spotting her destination, she shook her head. "You've flown quite a bit, right?" Lex asked her partner as they made their way to the baggage claim area.

"Yes, although the last time I was so worried about Grandpa Jake, I don't remember much of the flight – Jeannie and Frank had my car sent to me by truck." Amanda followed the long legged rancher, struggling to keep up. "Why do you ask? Hey, honey, you want to slow it down to at least a reasonable jog?"

Lex stopped and turned around. "I'm sorry, sweetheart. I keep forgetting that not everyone can cover as much distance as quickly as I can." She waited for a moment until the smaller woman caught her breath. "Anyway, I was just wondering: why do they seem to make you walk all the way to the other side of the damned airport to pick up your luggage? Especially since they won't let you carry much of it with you? Seems rather ridiculous to me."

Amanda laughed. "I think travelers have been asking that same question since the first commercial flight, love." She wrapped her hand around Lex's upper arm. "C'mon! We're almost there." She led the smiling woman through the milling crowds.

Chapter 21

"Mandy!! You're back early!!" Jacob exclaimed, as the two young women stepped into the kitchen. He opened his arms as the small blonde practically knocked him down. "Hey, there... easy, honey." He hugged her tightly, looking at Lex over her head. Seeing the bruise on the dark-haired woman's mouth, he frowned. "You two okay?"

Amanda stepped back slightly, looking up into her grandfather's concerned eyes. "We're fine, Grandpa." Feeling his callused hand gently trace the bruise on her face, she smiled. "It was pretty exciting, actually." She looked around the kitchen. "Where's Gramma?"

"Right here, sweetheart." Anna Leigh called from the doorway, where she had an arm wrapped around Lex. "Goodness! You two look like you've been in a fight." She led the rancher over to where Amanda and Jacob were standing. "You *are* going to tell us why you look like this, right?"

"Sure..." the young blonde rubbed her jaw. "It's really quite a good story, too." She winked at the rancher. "But do you mind if we raid the refrigerator first? I'm starving." Amanda stepped away from her grandfather, and pulled Anna Leigh into a hug. "I really missed you, Gramma."

The older woman smiled, and held her granddaughter tight.

"We missed you too, Mandy." She laughed as Amanda's stomach took that moment to growl. "Okay, I can take a hint. We'll feed you, then you get to tell us all about your trip." Looking at Lex, she smiled warmly. "And also tell us what kind of trouble you two got into."

Lex laughed. "Don't blame me. Trouble just seems to find her!" She pointed at her lover, and then started backing up as Amanda stalked towards her. "Uh, well, it's true!" She held her hands out in front of her, trying to ward off the pending attack.

"Just you wait, Slim!" Amanda teased, seeing the tall woman blush. "I'll take care of you later, when you least expect it."

Jacob laughed, as he pulled several items from the refrigerator. "You two sit down. Hope a sandwich sounds okay to you."

"Let me help you with that, Mr... um, Jacob," Lex offered, maneuvering quickly around the giggling blonde. She pulled some of the things from his large hands and placed them on the table. Looking over at Amanda, she teased, "you gonna join us, or are you going to sit there smiling all day?"

****

"And then Lex lassos the guy with a kid's jump rope!" Amanda exclaimed, waving a potato chip to emphasize her point. "The police officers said she looked just like John Wayne, or maybe even Roy Rogers!" She grinned at her partner's embarrassment. "Then she sat on him, and the two cops had to pull her off."

Anna Leigh put a hand on the rancher's arm. "Goodness, Lexington! That was a very brave thing to do! Is that how you got hurt?" She studied the quiet blue gaze, as Lex looked down at the table.

"Uh, no. He didn't touch me." She looked up at the older woman and gave her a small smile. "And it was pretty stupid, actually. I just didn't think." She glanced across the table at Amanda. "But I tend to have that problem around your granddaughter."

The blonde woman giggled, then realized what had been

said. "Hey! Wait a minute! What did I do?"

Jacob shook his head and chuckled. "Okay, so now you've explained how Mandy ended up looking like she does, but what happened to you, Lex?" He didn't miss the exchange of guilty glances between the two young women. "Oh, c'mon, it can't be that bad, can it?" Then a thought occurred to him. "Mandy, you didn't do it, did you?" He knew his granddaughter had a fiery temper, and had been known to explode quite easily when angered.

Lex shook her head. "No, sir, she didn't. Her father did." Hearing Anna Leigh's gasp of shock, she turned to face her. "It was pretty much my own fault – I kinda pushed him into it."

"That's the biggest load of bunk I've ever heard!" Jacob growled. "There's never an excuse to hit a lady!"

"I'm no lady, Jacob," Lex argued, "and I really did keep at him until he lost control."

Amanda put her hand on the older man's arm to try and calm him, but looked at Lex. "You did no such thing, Lex. You were just trying to protect me."

"Protect you?" Anna Leigh was still in shock over the revelation that her son could strike a woman. "Dear God, don't tell me he was going to hit you, too."

Lex took a deep breath. "No ma'am. I had gone into his office last night to find out why he was so hostile towards our relationship." She looked over at her lover with sad eyes. "She never said anything, but I could tell it was tearing Amanda up inside." Turning to Anna Leigh, Lex swallowed hard. "Anyway, I asked him if it was because I was a woman, and he said no, that he was pretty much used to the idea that Amanda..." Here she paused. *I really don't need to bring that part of the conversation out, do I?* "Well, that she was gay. So then, I asked if it was because I worked for a living – that kinda set him off." She gave the older couple a gentle smile. "He thinks that I'm after Amanda's money."

Jacob looked at her quizzically. "YOU? After Mandy's money?" He burst into laughter. "Oh, that's too funny!"

"Really, sweetheart!" Anna Leigh was smiling as well. "Did you enlighten him, dear?" She covered the rancher's hand with her own.

"No, ma'am, I didn't." She shrugged. "I didn't think it would do any good, because he'd just probably think that I was lying, but I did tell him that I loved Amanda, and no amount of money could change that." She touched her mouth with her free hand. "That's when he kinda lost it and hit me."

Amanda nodded. "I opened the door to the office and saw Daddy grab Lex and push her back against the bar – he hit her before I could stop him." She exchanged a tender look with the rancher. "I'm glad we decided that we were going to leave this morning, instead of tomorrow. I don't think either one of us could have handled another day there."

Jacob sighed. "I thought we raised him better than that. I really want to turn that boy over my knee." He looked at Lex. "I'm sorry about that, child. I hate the fact that you were hurt by someone from our family."

"I don't blame you or your family, Jacob." Lex looked at the older man with respect. "Amanda and I talked about it last night. Even though he's her father, you and Anna Leigh are a whole lot more of a family to her than they are." Smiling at her lover, she continued, "and speaking of families, that reminds me of something we need to tell you, right, Amanda?"

"Hmm?" The blonde asked, then her face lit up in understanding. "Oh, yeah...that's right!" She gave the older couple a brilliant smile. "Umm... well... Lex asked, and... I..." she began to stammer. "You see... it's..."

Feeling sorry for the young woman, Lex stood up and circled around the table until she was standing directly behind Amanda. She placed her hands on the blonde's shoulders, shaking her head. "What my friend here is so eloquently trying to say, is that I asked her to move into the ranch house with me, and she accepted."

Anna Leigh clapped her hands in delight. "That's wonderful, isn't it Jacob?" she smiled at her husband. "We were just discussing that very thing this morning."

"You were?" Amanda was hard pressed to keep her jaw from hitting the table. She raised her hands and covered Lex's. "It's really not that far from town, and we'll still visit with you often."

Lex laughed. "Honey, I think it's okay." She gave the older couple a happy grin. "And you know that you have an open invitation, right?"

Jacob stood up. "We'll be sure and take you up on that offer, young lady." He helped his wife stand away from the table as well. "Now we've got some errands to run... why don't you two go on upstairs and get a little rest? You both look completely worn out."

"Good idea, love. We'll see you girls for dinner tonight?" Anna Leigh asked, as her husband wrapped an arm around her.

Amanda smiled and stood up as well, letting Lex wrap long arms around her. "Wouldn't miss it." She stifled a yawn. "But I think you're right about needing a nap. We'll see you guys later, I think." She blushed as her grandfather winked at her, just as they left the room. "God... they're just too much, sometimes," she muttered.

"What was that about a nap?" a sultry voice whispered in her ear, causing chills to chase down the blonde's back.

"Nap? Who said anything about a nap?" Amanda turned around in the tall woman's arms. "I didn't say nap, did I?" She pulled the dark head down for a gentle kiss. "Umm... let's go upstairs, okay, honey?" she murmured, grabbing a strong slender hand and pulling Lex towards the stairs.

****

Dinner last night, Lex mused, *was interesting, to say the least. Jacob knows some pretty good tales on Amanda.* She chuckled as she tossed another bag into the back of the truck. *And I had no idea that she was such a hellion when she was a kid.*

"What's so funny?" Amanda asked, bringing the last bag with her, and handing it to Lex. "You're still thinking about those stories Grandpa Jake told last night, aren't you?"

"Yep... I had no idea you were such a scamp, growing up," the rancher teased. "Remind me not to let you anywhere near the cattle, unsupervised." Jacob had related a tale of a young Amanda using the neighborhood dogs as dolls for a tea party –

complete with clothes and hats.

Amanda groaned. "God! I'm going to have to find some way of getting even with him for telling that one, aren't I?" She took another step until she was wrapped up in warm arms. "Mmm."

Lex enjoyed the embrace. *I don't think I will ever get enough of this,* she sighed to herself. "C'mon... Martha's expecting us for lunch." She kissed the top of Amanda's head, and then released her.

Jacob and Anna Leigh met them at the front of the truck. "You two will be over for Jacob's birthday next weekend, right?" the older woman asked, giving Amanda a hug.

"We wouldn't miss it for anything," Lex replied, shaking Jacob's hand. She reached out to Anna Leigh, but was surprised when the older woman wrapped her arms around her and squeezed tight.

"Thank you for making our little girl so happy, Lexington," Anna Leigh whispered in the tall woman's ear. Pulling away slightly, she said in a louder voice, "welcome to our family, dear." She felt the rancher return the hug enthusiastically.

Lex held the older woman close, a lump in her throat. "You..." she had to stop and clear her throat, "both have always made me feel like part of the family. Thank you for raising such a wonderful granddaughter." She stepped back and ran a hand across her face. "Umm... yeah." Taking a deep breath, Lex smiled. "Thanks for everything!" She felt Amanda snuggle close. "Well, ah... see you next weekend, right?" The rancher knew she was quickly losing her composure. *We gotta get out of here before I start bawling like a baby.*

Amanda could feel the fine line Lex was treading, and decided it was time for a retreat. "We've got to get going. Martha is probably getting ready to call out the National Guard by now," she joked, giving her grandparents a wink.

"You two go on. We'll see you Saturday, if not sooner!" Jacob teased, as the two young women climbed into the truck. He pulled his wife to him happily. "Those two are something else, aren't they, sweetheart?"

Anna Leigh looked up into his eyes lovingly. "Yes they are, my dearest. Let's go into the house and discuss it, shall we?" She gave him an impish grin.

Jacob laughed. "Why do I have the distinct feeling that we won't be doing much talking?" He led his wife into the house, and allowed her to pull him up the stairs.

****

The drive to the ranch was unusually silent, both women deeply engrossed in their own thoughts. Lex was worried about her partner, and how she would be able to adjust to the life they were about to embark upon together. The fact that Amanda's parents disapproved didn't matter to the rancher, but she knew in her heart that the younger woman was devastated by their hateful words. Looking sideways as she drove, Lex noticed the slight smile on her companion's face. "Penny for your thoughts?" she asked quietly.

Amanda turned away from the window absently. "Think you can afford it, Slim?" she teased, reaching over and pulling Lex's hand into her lap. She noticed the concern etched on the older woman's face. "Actually, I was just thinking about how happy I am right this very moment." She watched as several emotions flitted across the strong planes of the older woman's face.

"Really?" Lex wanted to be reassured, wanted to know that Amanda was happy with her decision, happy with the opportunity to start a life with her. "I was just thinking, if you wanted, we could always build a house in town, if you don't like living on the ranch." She braced herself for the answer. *God, Amanda... I'll go anywhere, be anyone, just for the opportunity to be with you. I hope you know that.*

The blonde woman studied her lover carefully. "But you love living on the ranch." *What on earth is going through that complex mind of hers?*

"What good is the ranch without you?" Lex pulled the truck to a stop, just before they got to the old bridge. She unbuckled her seatbelt and turned sideways, so that she could give Amanda all of her attention. Pulling the younger woman's hands towards her, she smiled. "I love you, Amanda Cauble...and I want to do everything in my power to make you happy. If that means living in town, fine." She pulled the small hands to her mouth, and gave them a light kiss. "If that means pitching a tent in the middle of the woods, that's fine too."

"Lex..."

"No, wait... please. I've got to get this out now." The dark-haired woman blinked, a tear falling down her face. "I'm not real good with stuff like this, but I want you to understand what a difference you've made in my life. I love you, and I hope we can have a long and happy life together." Lex looked deeply into Amanda's green eyes, seeing a strong love reflected back to her.

Amanda gently pulled a hand free, and wiped the tear away with her thumb. "I love you too, Lex." She looked around outside, and smiled widely. "Kinda fitting that we should start our life together here." The younger woman reached over and opened her door. "C'mon... let's stretch our legs for a minute, okay?"

Lex followed her lead, and soon both women were standing on the shore of the creek, looking down at the peaceful stream of water flowing beneath the bridge. "Full circle, huh?" the rancher mumbled, feeling the compact body tucked against her side nod. She felt at peace for the first time in her life. The woman next to her made her complete, somehow.

"Full circle, love," Amanda whispered, as she lifted her head up and pulled Lex down for a loving kiss.

Coming next from
RENAISSANCE ALLIANCE

Roman Holiday

By Belle Reilly

The sequel to Darkness Before the Dawn, a continuation of the story of Captain Kate Phillips and Becky Hanson...

Orbis airlines pilot Catherine Phillips grudgingly decides to spend a layover in Rome with Rebecca Hanson, keeping a protective eye on the recovering flight attendant. The two women are soon caught up in the magical splendor of the Eternal City, seeing the sights and drawing ever-closer to one another in the process.

Available – March 2000.

Breaking Away*

By Tonya Muir

In <u>With Faltering Steps</u>, with the world of horse racing as a background, Lacey Montgomery meets Rachel Wilson while she is investigating horse trouble for her Mafia boss, Vinnie Russo. While Lacey enlists Rachel's help in getting to the bottom of the horse mystery, the mafia crony learns about life, herself and falling in love. In <u>Making Strides</u> Lacey and Rachel are just settling into their lives together and raising Rachel's daughter, Molly, when Lacey's past strikes back, throwing both women into a whirlwind of crime and fear while they try to overcome a traumatic history and ensure themselves a domestic future.

Chasing Shadows*

By C. Paradee

In <u>The Agent</u>, FBI agent Tony Viglioni is transferred to Cleveland to work on a serial murder case. Shortly after her arrival she teams up with Assistant Coroner Megan Donnovan and together they work to solve the series of mysterious killings while exploring a deepening attraction between them. Tony and Megan continue to develop their relationship in <u>Dancing With Shadows</u> amidst the everyday stresses of work and family. The challenges of everyday living soon become secondary when a very determined rogue agent decides he wants the FBI agent permanently silenced.

Tales of Emoria: Echoes Past
By Mindancer

Jame, a peace arbiter and Emoran princess, is called back home because her partner, Tigh, an infamous warrior, possesses skills and knowledge needed to defeat a mysterious enemy threatening Emoria. With the aid of the Wizard, Goodemer, Jame and Tigh lead the Emorans to victory against the evil Wizard, Misner.

Seasons: Book One
By Anne Azel

The first two of four stories about Robbie and Janet over the course of a single year. They deal with elements of Robbie's career in film and Janet's in education. They also examine the crises that can come into the average woman's life. Seasons focuses on the courage that it takes to be female and/or gay in today's society.

Mended Hearts
By Alix Stokes

Two little girls meet at a hospital and become best friends. One of them undergoes open-heart surgery. They are separated, but meet again 24 years later. By now, the older girl, Dr. Alexandra Morgan, is a brilliant Pediatric Heart Surgeon. The younger girl, Bryn O'Neill, is a warm and loving Pediatric Intensive Care nurse. When they meet, they feel an instant connection. Will Dr. Morgan's tortured past keep her from remembering their childhood friendship?

A bonus book from RAP, Inc. – 2 stories for a bit more than the price of one!

Other titles to look for in the coming months from
Renaissance Alliance

Encounter By Anne Azel
(Spring 2000)

Forest of Eyulf: Instincts of Blue By Tammy Pell
(Summer 2000)

Bar Girls By Jules Kurre
(Summer 2000)

Tiopa Ki Lakota By D. Jordan Redhawk
(Summer 2000)

Seasons: Book Two By Anne Azel
(Summer 2000)

The Chosen By Verda Foster
(Fall 2000)

Tumbleweed Fever By L. J. Maas
(Fall 2000)

Thy Brother's Reaper By Devin Centis
(Fall 2000)

Prairie Fire By L. J. Maas
(Fall 2000)

The Copper River By Crystal Loch
(Pending completion)

Carrie Carr is a true Texan,
having lived in the state for her entire life.
She enjoys sports, spoiling her niece and nephew,
and listening to Celtic music.

Carrie can be reached by email at:
cb.zeer@worldnet.att.net